LAST DAY OF SCHOOL

D1331507

www.penguin.co.uk

LAST DAY OF SCHOOL

The Alternative School Logbook 1987–1988

Jack Sheffield

bantam

TRANSWORLD PUBLISHERS
Penguin Random House, One Embassy Gardens,
8 Viaduct Gardens, London SW11 7BW
www.penguin.co.uk

Transworld is part of the Penguin Random House group of companies
whose addresses can be found at global.penguinrandomhouse.com

Penguin
Random House
UK

First published in Great Britain in 2022 by Bantam
an imprint of Transworld Publishers

A CIP catalogue record for this book
is available from the British Library.

ISBN 9781787635531

Typeset in 11/15pt Zapf Calligraphic 801 BT by Jouve (UK), Milton Keynes
Printed and bound in Great Britain by Clays Ltd, Elcograf S.p.A.

The authorized representative in the EEA is Penguin Random House Ireland,
Morrison Chambers, 32 Nassau Street, Dublin D02 YH68.

Penguin Random House is committed to a sustainable future
for our business, our readers and our planet. This book is made
from Forest Stewardship Council® certified paper.

For Sue and Mike Maddison . . .
there from the start

Contents

Acknowledgements

Sincere thanks to my editor, Imogen Nelson, for bringing this novel to publication supported by the excellent team at Penguin Random House, including Larry Finlay, Bill Scott-Kerr, Jo Williamson, Vivien Thompson, Hayley Barnes, Richenda Todd and fellow 'Old Roundhegian' Martin Myers.

Also, thanks to my industrious literary agent, Philip Patterson of Marjacq Scripts, Newcastle United supporter and Britain's leading authority on eighties Airfix Modelling Kits, for his encouragement and good humour.

I am also grateful to all those who assisted in the research for this novel – in particular: Diane Cragg (née Balchin) retired teacher, England rugby fan and voluntary charity worker, Chawton, Hampshire; Janina Bywater, retired nurse and cryptic crossword champion, Doncaster, West Yorkshire; Helen Carr, primary school teacher and literary critic, Harrogate, North Yorkshire; Linda Collard, education trainer and consultant, fruit-grower and jam-maker,

West Chiltington, West Sussex; Rob Cragg, retired electronics executive, keen golfer, travel enthusiast and lover of wine and fine food, Alton, Hampshire; Tony Greenan, Yorkshire's finest headteacher (now retired), Huddersfield, Yorkshire; Ian Haffenden, ex-Royal Pioneer Corps and custodian of Sainsbury's, Alton, Hampshire; John Kirby, ex-policeman, expert calligrapher and Sunderland supporter, County Durham; Roy Linley, Lead Architect, Strategy & Technology, Unilever Global IT Innovation (now retired) and Leeds United supporter, Leeds, Yorkshire; Dr Michael Maddison, HMI & History Inspector, diarist & supporter of Ipswich Town FC, Harrogate, North Yorkshire; Susan Maddison, retired primary school teacher, social historian and maker of excellent cakes, Harrogate, North Yorkshire; Bob Rogers, Canon Emeritus of York and Liverpool supporter, Malton, North Yorkshire; Jacqui Rogers, Deputy Registrar, allotment holder and tap dancer, Malton, North Yorkshire; John Wright, photographer, Lancashire's finest headteacher (now retired), Barrowford, Lancashire; and all the terrific staff at Waterstones Alton, including the irreplaceable Simon (now retired) and the excellent manager Kirsty. Not forgetting a special thank you to the dynamic events manager, Nikki Bloomer, and the wonderful team at Waterstones MK.

Finally, sincere thanks to my wife, Elisabeth, without whose help the *Teacher* series of novels would never have been written.

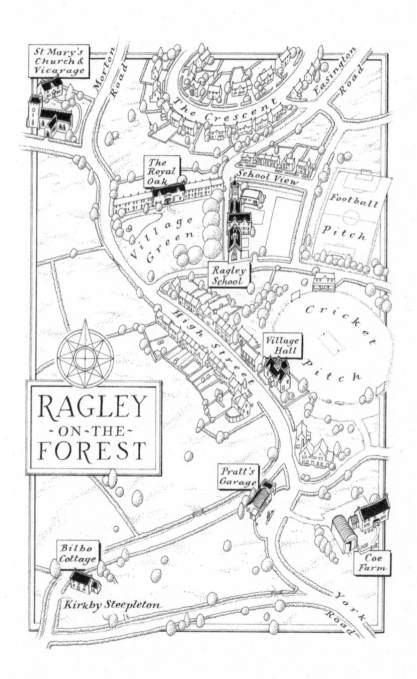

St Mary's Church & Vicarage

Morton Road

The Crescent

Easington Road

The Royal Oak

School View

Football Pitch

Village Green

Ragley School

Cricket Pitch

High Street

Village Hall

RAGLEY
-ON-THE-
FOREST

Pratt's Garage

Coe Farm

Bilbo Cottage

Kirkby Steepleton

York Road

Prologue

'I've got some news,' said Beth softly.

I looked into my wife's green eyes, gentle and loving.

'Go on then,' I said, 'tell me.'

She held me close and whispered in my ear, 'I'm expecting a baby.'

It was Saturday, 25 July 1987 and my life appeared complete. We were sitting on the village green and, in front of us, bright sunshine reflected on the high arched Victorian windows of Ragley & Morton CE Primary School where I had been headteacher for the past ten years. At that moment our world seemed perfect and the summer holiday stretched out before us.

Neither of us noticed that on the far horizon, beyond the Hambleton Hills, there were a few scattered dark clouds. We were not to know it was a portent of things to come. Our peaceful life was about to change.

Moving on was about to take on a whole new meaning.

*

That was six weeks ago and the school summer holiday was almost over. September was upon us and the academic year 1987/88 was only three days away. I was back at my desk in the school office and only the ticking of the old clock disturbed the silence as I sifted through the recent circulars from County Hall. It was the usual collection of health and safety notices, initiatives for savings on heating and responses to the government's clarion call for a National Curriculum.

However, there was one letter that caught my eye. It was from Ms Sabine Cleverley, our new Deputy Education Officer. She informed me she would visit on Monday, 7 September, the first day of term. Ms Cleverley considered herself to be a new broom and had made it clear she was a disciple of Kenneth Baker, the Secretary of State for Education. Short, squat and in her mid-forties, she was a formidable presence.

Up the Morton Road the church clock chimed the midday hour. I took a deep breath as I unlocked the bottom drawer of my desk, removed the large, leather-bound school logbook and opened it to the next clean page. Then I filled my fountain pen with black Quink ink, wrote the date and stared at the empty page.

The record of another school year was about to begin. Ten years ago, the retiring headmaster, John Pruett, had told me how to fill in the official school logbook. 'Just keep it simple,' he said. 'Whatever you do, don't say what really happens, because no one will believe you!'

So the real stories were written in my 'Alternative School Logbook'.

And this is it!

Chapter One

Silence is Golden

School reopened today for the new academic year with 130 children on roll. The Deputy Education Officer, Ms Cleverley, visited school.
Extract from the Ragley & Morton School Logbook:
Monday, 7 September 1987

'Would y'like to 'ear me whistle, sir?' asked Ted Coggins.

It was Monday, 7 September 1987, the first morning of the new school year, and I was standing by the school gate welcoming the children and parents. The ruddy-faced ten-year-old looked up at me expectantly. Son of a local farmer, Ted was famous for his ear-piercing whistle, perfected during the early mornings when he herded the cattle for milking.

'I wouldn't if I were you, Mr Sheffield,' said Mrs Pippa

Jackson, Chair of our PTA and mother of seven-year-old identical twins, Hermione and Honeysuckle. 'We saw him practising on the high street.'

'He whistled in the doorway of the butcher's shop,' said Hermione.

'And Mr Piercy ran out waving his chopper,' added Honeysuckle for dramatic effect.

Mrs Jackson blushed slightly as she ushered her girls towards the playground. 'Well, good luck for the new year,' she said.

Ted was still looking up at me expectantly.

'Perhaps later today, Ted. The school field might be the best place to hear you whistling,' I said, more in hope than expectation.

'Cor, thanks, sir,' he said and ran off towards the playground to play leapfrog with his friend, Charlie Cartwright.

I leaned my six-foot-one-inch frame against one of the stone pillars that flanked the gate and glanced up at the sign that read:

**RAGLEY & MORTON CHURCH OF
ENGLAND PRIMARY SCHOOL**
North Yorkshire County Council
Headteacher: Mr J Sheffield

I thought about how I had been happy here while the terms of a school year, autumn, spring and summer, had come and gone in the circle of life. It had been a golden summer and my thoughts drifted on a clear stream of memories. My reverie was suddenly interrupted by the formidable presence of Mrs Julie Earnshaw, a tough, no-nonsense Yorkshire lady.

'Gorra problem wi' our Dallas,' she said.

Her daughter, seven-year-old Dallas Sue-Ellen, was sucking a stick of liquorice. In her Wham! T-shirt, battered sandals and hair that had not seen a brush for weeks, she looked as though she had been dragged through a hedge backwards.

I pushed my black-framed Buddy Holly spectacles up the bridge of my nose. 'What might that be, Mrs Earnshaw?'

She considered this for a moment, took a last drag of her cigarette, pinched the glowing tip and put it in the pocket of her pinny. Then she sighed deeply. 'It's 'er feelings.'

'*Feelings?*'

'Yeah, feelings. She's gorra lot of 'em.'

'I see,' I said . . . but I didn't.

'She's allus feeling angry an' shoutin' at 'er brothers.'

'Oh dear.'

'An' she sez she keeps feeling lazy . . . jus' like 'er dad.'

'Does she?'

I looked down at Dallas as she wiped smears of snot on the back of her sleeve. 'So . . . how are you feeling this morning, Dallas?' I asked with an encouraging smile. She had swallowed the last of the liquorice.

''Ungry,' she said with a grimace. Then she glanced across at the school field where seven-year-old Tracey Higginbottom was sitting on the grass with her mother. Tracey had brought her rabbit, Fifi, to school. It was munching dandelion leaves contentedly as a crowd of children watched in fascination.

'Yer allus 'ungry,' said Mrs Earnshaw with a scowl.

Dallas gave an evil grin. 'M'dad sez we're 'avin' rabbit pie t'night,' and she ran off to join the rabbit appreciation society.

Mrs Earnshaw gave me a knowing smile. 'What can y'do wi' 'em, Mr Sheffield?'

Sometimes it's best to say nothing.

By now it was 8.30 a.m. and the church clock up the Morton Road chimed the half-hour as more of our early arrivals wandered into school.

I walked back up the cobbled drive and paused to stare up at our traditional Victorian school building with its weathered bricks and a roof of grey slate tiles. The high arched windows reflected the early-autumn sunshine and a waist-high wall of Yorkshire stone topped by iron railings bordered the playground. However, time was moving on and there were decisions to be made.

I had just passed my forty-second birthday and I was unsettled. Ten years seemed a long time to stay in one place. *Where will I be in another ten years?* I thought. *Is my professional life becoming a little too comfortable?* It was as if my constant life had become unfixed. The world had moved on and I felt I was being left behind.

For this was 1987. Margaret Thatcher was in her third term as Prime Minister; Alan Sugar was busy producing his Amstrad computers; digging the Channel Tunnel was about to commence; and Whitney Houston, George Michael and Madonna were high in the singles charts.

Meanwhile, I was still here in the school that I loved and wondering what the future held. Suddenly the slamming of a car door attracted my attention. A rusty red Mini had arrived in the car park and parked next to my Morris Minor

Traveller, and our newest member of staff, twenty-four-year-old Marcus Potts, was heaving our school computer from the boot of his car. We had bought this wonder of the modern age for £299 and during the holiday Marcus had been developing programs for the children to use.

'Morning, Marcus. Do you need a hand?'

'Morning, Jack. No, thanks. I'm fine.'

Marcus was a popular colleague. Short and stocky with black wavy hair, he loved classical music and amateur dramatics but, best of all, he was a wizard with the new computers.

When the tiny school closed in our neighbouring village of Morton their twenty-eight pupils had been transferred to Ragley. So back in January we had gained an extra class and Marcus had been appointed. There were now five classes with 130 children on roll. A temporary Portakabin classroom had been delivered to house the new class. It looked a little out of place alongside our traditional building. Although it contained a cloakroom, store cupboard and a spacious classroom, there was no running water. A sheltered walkway connected it to the main building. However, Marcus had transformed it with vibrant displays and opportunities for developing learning.

'I've prepared lots of activities, Jack,' he said with enthusiasm. 'It's amazing what you can do with sixteen kilobytes of RAM.'

I smiled in acknowledgement but I was still getting to grips with the new technology. A ram was something I associated with the local farms.

'Problem is, Jack, some of the children now have better computers of their own at home . . . ZX Spectrum, Commodore 64 . . . it's a new world.' As he hurried off to his classroom it occurred to me that he represented the new generation of teachers and sometimes it was hard to keep up.

I climbed the steps to the entrance hall and pushed open the old oak door. With a rattle of an enamel bucket Ruby the caretaker appeared.

'All done an' dusted, Mr Sheffield.' Her rosy cheeks were flushed. 'Floors mopped an' we're ready t'go.'

Ruby Dainty had a heart of gold and had been a wonderful caretaker during my time at Ragley School. When I first met her she was the downtrodden wife of the lazy, unemployed, chain-smoking Ronnie Smith. With six children whom she loved dearly, Ruby worked from dawn till dusk supporting her family while Ronnie concentrated on beer and betting slips. He had died on the last day of 1983 but then, six weeks ago and much to everyone's delight, she had married again. A childhood sweetheart, George Dainty, had returned from Spain. George had made his fortune in Alicante selling fish and chips in his shop, the Codfather. The new millionaire husband had bought a huge bungalow up the Morton Road and Ruby was adjusting to her new life of luxury.

'I'm so pleased you came back, Ruby.'

Her curly chestnut hair might now be flecked with grey but her smile was youthful. 'Ah couldn't give up f'love nor money, Mr Sheffield.'

She leaned on her mop and pushed a chamois leather into the pocket of her extra-large double-X overall. 'An' ah'd miss all t'kiddies.'

She picked up her bucket and trotted off to her caretaker's store humming 'Edelweiss' from her favourite film *The Sound of Music*.

At the far end of the entrance hall our deputy head emerged from the stock cupboard carrying an armful of sugar paper and a box of chalk. A tall, slim brunette in her early fifties, Anne Grainger was a superb teacher of our youngest children.

'Morning, Anne.'

Her usual infectious smile appeared a little strained this morning. 'Morning, Jack. I see you were in conversation with Mrs Earnshaw.'

'Yes . . . she mentioned Dallas had *feelings*.'

For a moment she looked thoughtful. 'Haven't we all,' she said quietly and hurried back to her classroom.

I didn't know what might be on her mind but it was clear something was troubling her. I would have to pick my moment. In the meantime, a busy morning was gathering pace and there was much to do.

When I walked into the school office our secretary, Vera Forbes-Kitchener, an elegant sixty-five-year-old, was concentrating on her IBM Selectric typewriter with its golf ball head. She was likely missing the time she used her old Royal Imperial with the familiar *ker-ching* of the carriage return and reflecting on the fact that some things were lost for ever.

'Good morning, Vera.'

She looked up and smiled. As always, she was immaculate in an M&S striped business suit and a cotton blouse buttoned to the neck where her Victorian brooch added a touch of class. 'Good morning, Mr Sheffield, your new registers are here.'

She always used a formal style of address when greeting the headmaster. In Vera's world there were *standards* that always needed to be kept. She glanced down at her spiral-bound notepad. 'Don't forget, Ms Cleverley is calling in. Her secretary said she would be here at twelve o'clock.' There was a hint of disapproval in Vera's voice. She did not appreciate our domineering Deputy Education Officer from County Hall.

I sighed and shook my head. 'Thanks, Vera.'

She could see the concern on my face. 'I know what you're thinking,' she said with a wry smile.

'You always do,' I said and collected my registers.

In the school hall our two other teachers were setting up for morning assembly.

Sally Pringle, a ginger-haired, freckled-faced forty-something was our art and music specialist. In her baggy flared cords, bright yellow blouse and hand-stitched purple waistcoat she always cut a lively figure.

'Morning, Jack,' she said with a grin as she set up a metal music stand, 'it's another "Kumbaya" morning.'

Sally was always a sparky presence around school and enjoyed teaching the second-year juniors who would all reach their ninth birthday during the coming academic year.

Next to her was thirty-year-old Pat Brookside, a county-standard netball player, almost six feet tall, with a blonde ponytail. 'Hi, Jack. Thought a few summer flowers would brighten up the table.' She was arranging a selection of perennials – delphiniums, dwarf lupins and hollyhocks – in a huge stoneware vase.

'Thanks, Pat. They look lovely.'

She gave me a level stare and smiled. 'My cottage garden looks a picture this year. You need to call in sometime.'

Pat taught the third-year juniors and had high hopes for this year's netball and rounders teams. At nine o'clock she volunteered to ring the bell, which would make the villagers of Ragley pause for a moment as the new school year was announced.

The ten-year-olds in my class looked up eagerly as I took the register and collected dinner money. It was time to allocate monitor jobs and this always elicited lots of interest.

The tallest boy, Rory Duckworth, nodded knowingly when he was appointed blackboard monitor. Charlie Cartwright, who had a real aptitude for mathematics, was delighted to be put in charge of the school tuck shop and Katie Parrish, a particularly bright girl, smiled when she was made library monitor. Her mother, Rebecca Parrish, had become an acquaintance during the summer holiday. A Senior Lecturer in Education at the College in York, she was also a parent governor. Meanwhile Ted Coggins, our fastest runner, was given the 'messenger' job, delivering messages from one teacher to another, and Mary Scrimshaw, a reliable time-keeper and daughter of our local pharmacist, became school bell-ringer.

After each child had been given two Manila-covered exercise books, a ruler, a Berol pen, a box of Lakeland coloured pencils, a reading record card and an *Oxford First Dictionary*, we began our first writing task. As usual, many of the children had forgotten how to write properly during the summer break but we were soon back into the routines of tables practice, sharing news and selecting reading books.

*

It was 12.25 p.m. when a smart Ford Sierra pulled up into the car park. Ms Cleverley emerged in a charcoal-grey business suit carrying a black executive briefcase and strode confidently towards the school entrance.

Vera was at her desk polishing the framed photograph of her three cats when Ms Cleverley walked in. It was common knowledge that she intended to succeed Miss Barrington-Huntley to the top job sooner rather than later. Our Deputy Education Officer was a very ambitious woman.

'Good afternoon, Ms Cleverley,' said Vera.

'I have a meeting with Mr Sheffield,' came the curt reply. Ms Sabine Cleverley cut a distinctive figure. Her jet-black hair had a severe fringe and her suit had padded shoulders à la Joan Collins in *Dynasty*.

Vera didn't approve of modern excesses. She made a point of replacing the photograph with infinite care and then opening the school diary. 'Ah yes, I have it here. Twelve o'clock.' She looked up. 'Mr Sheffield decided to have his lunch when you didn't arrive.'

Ms Cleverley frowned. 'I have a busy life. Please tell Mr Sheffield I'm here.'

Vera made no move from her seat. 'Would you care for some refreshment?'

'No, thank you. Time is short.'

Vera closed the diary and squared it away with deliberate precision to the side of her desk. Finally she stood up and gestured towards a narrow corridor full of coat pegs that linked the office to the staff-room. 'We reserved the staff-room for your meeting. Perhaps you would like to wait in there.'

Ms Cleverley nodded abruptly. 'Just inform Mr Sheffield.'

*

The hum of lunchtime conversation filled the school hall as the first sitting finished their meal. Our cook, Mrs Mapplebeck, had produced another culinary masterpiece with limited ingredients. I had just polished off a bowl of rhubarb and custard when Vera tapped me on the shoulder.

'Ms Cleverley is in the staff-room.' Her look spoke volumes.

I stood up. 'Ah, yes . . . thank you.'

Ms Cleverley had opened her briefcase and was checking her Filofax when I walked in. She didn't look up. Her long fingernails were painted with scarlet varnish and she tapped a rhythm on the coffee table.

As usual her manner was direct. There were no pleasantries. 'Have you received a copy of the authority's summary of the government's consultation document for a National Curriculum?'

'No, I haven't.'

She shook her head. 'Very well. I'll call by after school and drop one in. We shall need a comprehensive response from you by the end of the month.'

'Fine. I'll do my best.'

There was an uncanny calmness about her that exuded confidence and power. 'It's critical we raise standards quickly. We must match our competitor countries.'

'Really?'

It was clear my response fell short of expectations.

'Mr Sheffield, I do hope you understand we need a broad and balanced curriculum that sets clear objectives.'

She was beginning to talk like Kenneth Baker now.

'I believe we already do that. Our English and mathematics

schemes are held in high regard by Miss Barrington-Huntley.'

She slammed shut her Filofax and replaced it in her brief-case. 'And what about *science*, the other core subject?'

'You have only to go into Mr Potts's classroom to see how our seven-year-olds are being introduced to the physical sciences and, living here in the country, we have ample opportunities to explore the natural sciences.'

She stood up and paused by the door. '*Time* is the issue, Mr Sheffield. The majority of the school day *must* be spent on the *core* subjects. From now on a knowledge of tables will come before a walk in the woods.'

I felt like telling her we practised our tables every morning, but I remained silent. As we walked out to the car park she was still determined to drive home her agenda. 'Do keep in mind, Mr Sheffield, that it's time for schools to be *accountable* and I'll be checking on your progress.'

'Of course,' I said quietly.

'I'll be back,' she said and climbed into her car. After making a minute adjustment to her remote-control door mirrors, she turned on the four-speaker sound system and roared off.

It was good to wander back into the staff-room and a sense of normality.

'Are you OK, Jack?' asked Pat. 'Has Ms Cleverclogs given you a hard time?'

I shook my head. 'She's coming back at the end of school to drop off a summary of the new National Curriculum.'

'What's wrong with *our* curriculum?' insisted a defiant

Pat. 'We turn out literate, numerate children with a love of learning.'

'And our science and technology are second to none,' added a determined Marcus.

'Not forgetting the arts,' murmured Sally. She was eyeing up the tin of biscuits. Although she was sticking to her 'Oxford Diet' from *The Healthy Heart Diet Book*, she was getting tired of eating muesli, oatmeal and vegetable soup.

Anne looked up from her Yorkshire Purchasing Organization catalogue and the price of 2B pencils. 'It will be the end of me,' she muttered.

Vera was serving cups of tea and looked across with concern. It was unusual for our deputy head to be so subdued at the outset of the school year.

'I read a summary in the *Guardian*,' said Marcus. 'There're attainment targets for all children to reach. It's a huge document.'

'Let's hope there's still time for art and music,' said Sally, munching on a ginger biscuit.

Pat too glanced at Anne, who was sipping her tea thoughtfully. 'How're the new starters, Anne?'

'Fine, thanks.'

'Is everything OK?' asked Sally. 'You look a little down in the dumps today.'

I noticed Vera gave Sally a warning look. There was clearly something amiss.

Anne sighed deeply. 'It all blew up last night. It's been a rotten summer break and I'm glad it's finally settled.'

'What's settled?' I asked.

She put down her cup and clasped her hands. 'You might

as well all know. It will be round the village by the end of the week . . . I'm getting a divorce.'

There was a stunned silence followed by the sound of the bell for afternoon school. Back in class it was hard to concentrate. Anne was a dear friend and colleague and I hated to think of her going through such a difficult time.

At afternoon break I told her I would do her playground duty while she went into the office to share a cup of tea with Vera. I knew our secretary would be a comforting companion.

It was warm and sunny when I walked outside and, beyond the school wall, the avenue of horse chestnut trees swayed in the gentle breeze. I always found it fascinating to watch the children at play. The twins, Honeysuckle and Hermione, were winding a long skipping rope and chanting out a rhyme as two other seven-year-olds, Emily Snodgrass and Tracey Higginbottom, skipped in and out.

> *'Little fat doctor,*
> *How's your wife?*
> *Very well, thank you,*
> *That's all right.*
> *Eat a bit o' fish,*
> *An' a stick o' liquorice,*
> *O-U-T spells OUT!'*

They were full of life as another school year stretched out before them. Dallas Earnshaw was telling her classmate, Alison Gawthorpe, about her *feelings* while nine-year-old Patience Crapper was showing her friend Becky Shawcross how to do a cat's cradle with loops of string. On the field, some of the boys were playing football.

So many children . . . so many young lives.

It struck me that the one thing they had in common was that they all thought they would live for ever.

Meanwhile I was reflecting on Anne's announcement. It was well known her relationship with her husband, John, the local woodcarver, had met difficulties in recent years. Her natural zest for life had been worn down by her unimaginative partner and his compulsion for DIY projects.

I knew Vera would provide a listening ear.

At the end of school I popped my head round the office door before following the children out of school.

'Excuse me, Vera. I'm just going down to the gate to remind the children not to run across the road and check if any of the parents has a concern.' I had learned a long time ago that a couple of minutes chatting at the school gate often solved many problems.

Vera smiled and proceeded to complete her filing and tidy her desk.

A group of parents had gathered at the gate and Mrs Parrish waved when she saw her daughter skipping down the drive.

'I'm going to be in the netball team,' shouted an excited Katie.

'That's wonderful, darling,' her mother said.

Mary Scrimshaw looked up at me. 'And so am I, sir.'

'Well done, Mary. That's great news.'

The crowds built up as the children dispersed.

Suddenly Ms Cleverley appeared, carrying a Manila

folder. 'It's so busy round here I've had to park on the high street,' she grumbled. She thrust the folder into my hands. 'Anyway, here's the consultation document.'

'Would you like to come into the office?'

'No, I don't think so.' She looked around as the last of the children wandered down the drive. 'Just a quick word before I go.'

We took a few paces on to the school field where the shrubbery covered the school wall.

'Miss Barrington-Huntley is organizing a teachers' meeting and wants a few of our headteachers to debate the new curriculum. She suggested you would be ideal to lead it.'

'Yes, of course. I'm always happy to assist her. She's been a great supporter over the years.'

Ms Cleverley gave me a hard stare as if searching for a hidden meaning. 'Yes, well, I'll report back,' she said quietly.

'Fine, I'll look forward to it.'

She was determined on a parting shot. 'Mr Sheffield,' she said with a hint of menace. 'Do keep in mind this is a time for careful consideration ... not the kneejerk responses I've received from some of your colleagues. This is when we have to remain calm.'

I had learned over the years to expect the unexpected. Teaching was that sort of job. However, what happened next became an incident that would live long in the memory.

Ted Coggins suddenly appeared behind Ms Cleverley. As he put the second finger of each hand into his mouth and proceeded to take a deep breath, I realized what was coming. My warning came too late. Ted's whistle was ear-shattering.

Ms Cleverley stumbled backwards and fell into a holly bush. 'Oh, no!' she cried.

Ted was a good-hearted boy and immediately offered to help. Between us we assisted a distinctly dishevelled Ms Cleverley back to her feet.

'I'm so sorry,' I said. 'Ted didn't mean any harm.'

Ms Cleverley gave me a look that would have turned most men to stone. 'What on earth was the boy thinking? I trust the punishment will be appropriate,' and she stormed off back to her car.

'Sorry, sir,' mumbled Ted. 'Ah didn't mean t'scare that lady.'

'You just have to be more careful.'

'Y'said to come to t'school field, sir.'

'Yes, but don't creep up behind people like that.'

He gave a disconsolate nod and wandered off. At the school gate a thought occurred to him. 'Sir ... what did you think of m'whistling?'

'It's impressive, Ted. Now get off home and be careful crossing the road.'

I couldn't help but smile as I went back up the drive.

In the car park Vera was standing next to her Austin Metro and had seen it all. 'Oh dear. That will not have put her in a good mood.'

'She wasn't in one to start with.' I waved the folder. 'She gave me the notes about the new curriculum. I'll read it and then pass it to the rest of the staff.'

Vera glanced back at school. 'By the way, I've had a real heart-to-heart with Anne.'

'How is she?'

'Much better . . . relieved to share her thoughts.'

'That's good.'

Vera nodded thoughtfully. 'Anne has a lot of life in front of her and she deserves some happiness.'

'I'm glad you were there for her.'

Vera nodded. 'We've been friends for many years.'

'As we have, Vera,' I added with a smile.

She sighed and looked down at her feet. It was rare for her to address me by my first name but on this occasion it added impact. 'Jack . . . I've decided.'

'Yes?'

She took a deep breath. 'This will be my final year at Ragley. I'll retire at the end of the summer term.'

For a few brief seconds there was silence.

'I guessed it would be. I know you've spoken of it and I appreciate you telling me.' It was a poignant moment. 'You'll be missed,' I added quietly.

'Perhaps . . . but it's an opportunity for someone new . . . someone younger.'

'When do you propose to announce it to the governing body?'

'Not until next year. So it's just between us for the time being. I wanted you to have plenty of notice. I'll tell the staff at the beginning of the spring term and then I'll write to the governors.'

'As always, Vera, you're well organized.'

She looked at me thoughtfully. 'And what about you? Is the lectureship at the College still a possibility?'

I hesitated. 'Yes, but that's for another day.' Then I stood back and stared up at the school. 'As you know, I love my teaching . . . I belong here.'

'I know you do.'

She climbed into her car, placed her handbag on the passenger seat and looked up at me. 'The past is gone, Jack, and the future is unknown. Perhaps it's time for both of us to move on.' Then she put her finger to her lips and gave me a knowing look. 'But for the time being . . . silence is golden.'

I watched her drive away before setting off for home in my emerald-green Morris Minor. Bilbo Cottage was three miles away in the neighbouring village of Kirkby Steepleton and as I drove I reflected on the day. Retirement, divorce and a possible lectureship were conversations for another day. Now was the time for discretion.

As Vera had said . . . *Silence is golden.*

Chapter Two

A Different Harvest

The school choir rehearsed in preparation for Sunday's Harvest Festival in St Mary's Church. Mrs Forbes-Kitchener was absent from morning school. Mrs Grainger substituted and banked dinner money.

Extract from the Ragley & Morton School Logbook:
Friday, 18 September 1987

It was Friday morning and the school's Chair of Governors, the Revd Joseph Evans, was sitting alone at the kitchen table in the silent vicarage. He had a thin, angular figure with a sharp Roman nose and he wore a clerical collar.

Now in his sixty-third year, his solitary life often made him sad. Since his sister, Vera, the school secretary, had married Major Rupert Forbes-Kitchener in December 1982 his home had become a desolate place. Sometimes it was as if a millstone of melancholy pressed down on his gaunt frame.

The vicarage had always been tidy when Vera lived there. Now bottles and jugs for the preparation of his home-brewed wine littered the worktop while the table was covered in notes for his Harvest Festival sermon. Deep in concentration, he was reaching for a mug of camomile tea when the accident happened. He overbalanced. His chair toppled and his head hit the terracotta tiled floor.

For Joseph a very different harvest was in store.

It would change his life for ever.

In Morton Manor, Vera was also sitting at her kitchen table while checking the ingredients for a carrot cake. It was a Delia Smith recipe and she was pleased the television cook had insisted it must be prepared *exactly* as printed. After all, for Vera, *precision* was everything in home baking. She was hosting tomorrow evening's Harvest Supper, an important date in the village calendar and the prelude to the annual Harvest Festival in St Mary's Church. She had switched on the radio to the *Morning Concert* programme on BBC Radio 3 and, while she completed her shopping list, she enjoyed the soothing sound of Grieg's *Peer Gynt* Suite No. 1.

It was at that moment the telephone rang.

Three miles away in Kirkby Steepleton life in Bilbo Cottage was rather more hectic. The tiny television set on the kitchen worktop was burbling away. On *Breakfast Time* Jeremy Paxman was previewing David Steel's key speech to the Liberal Party Conference in Harrogate. I switched it off as everyone prepared to depart.

'Bye-bye, Mummy.'

'Goodbye, darling,' said Beth, 'and be a good boy at nursery.'

Our four-year-old son, John, a sturdy fair-haired boy, smiled up at her as she crouched down, wiped the residue of porridge from his face and kissed him on the cheek.

We were fortunate to have such a caring childminder as Mrs Roberts, who looked after him each school day until we returned home. John attended Temple House Nursery, a large converted manor house midway between Kirkby Steepleton and Ragley village. He had moved up to the rising-five class and had many friends. It was ideal. He loved the Lego and action games but, most of all, the mid-morning banana and glass of milk followed by a lunch of fish fingers.

It was my turn and I gave him a hug.

'Bye, Daddy,' he said and he held hands with Mrs Roberts as they walked out to her car.

'Must rush, Jack,' said Beth. 'I've got a meeting before school.' Beth was headteacher of King's Manor Primary School and it was a ten-mile drive to York. She glanced at herself in the hall mirror. With her blonde hair, high cheekbones and in a floral summer dress she looked great. She slipped on her beige Cagney & Lacey coat with fashionable padded shoulders and patted her tummy with a smile. She was four months pregnant.

My journey to school was always a joy at this time of year. Nature had blessed this quiet corner of God's own country. Beyond the hedgerows the last fields of ripe golden barley shimmered in the pale morning light while, in the far distance, a golden thread of sunshine crested the Hambleton

Hills. A tapestry of shadows flickered over the land and I wound down my window and breathed in the clean air.

On the radio Whitney Houston was singing 'Didn't We Almost Have It All' as I approached Ragley High Street. I was happy to be part of the fabric of this village and I smiled at the familiar parade of shops. Prudence Golightly was watering the hanging baskets outside her General Stores & Newsagent while, next door, Tommy Piercy, in his striped apron and straw boater, was displaying joints of local beef, pigs' trotters and his prize-winning sausages in the window of his butcher's shop.

Behind the counter of the village Pharmacy Eugene Scrimshaw was discreetly adjusting his white coat to hide his Captain Kirk uniform. His wife, Peggy, had told him in no uncertain terms that he needed to grow up and choose between a happy marriage and *Star Trek*. Eugene had replied in Klingon which went down like the Starship *Enterprise* with engine trouble.

In the doorway of his Hardware Emporium, the fastidious Timothy Pratt, known locally as 'Tidy Tim', was talking to his best friend, Walter Crapper. A consignment of bootscrapers and mop buckets had arrived and Walter was always intrigued by the way Timothy displayed his goods in neat lines on the trestle tables outside his store. Timothy, an organized soul, was equally fastidious inside: he always took pride in stocking the shelves so that the labels on all the cans were in neat alignment like guardsmen outside Buckingham Palace.

His sister, Nora Pratt, was fixing a poster on the window outside her Coffee Shop advertising the forthcoming Harvest Festival while her assistant, Dorothy Robinson, was choosing 'A Little Boogie Woogie' by Shakin' Stevens on the jukebox. Dorothy was pregnant and, after another bout of morning sickness, the music helped to put her in the mood to arrange a plate of two-day-old rock buns.

Outside her Hair Salon Diane Wigglesworth was smoking her fifth cigarette of the day and waiting for her first customer. She was wondering if, as Dorothy had done, she would one day meet the man of her dreams. The last shop on the high street was the Post Office, and village postman Ted Postlethwaite had just finished his first delivery round. As he wheeled his bicycle round the back of the shop his wife Amelia, the village postmistress, was preparing his breakfast and all was well in his world of letters, postcards and parcels.

I turned right at the village green where a large white-fronted public house, The Royal Oak, nestled in the centre of a row of terraced cottages, and pulled up at the school gate. Charlie Cartwright was throwing a stick up into the branches of a horse chestnut tree. At his feet among the detritus of leaves lay glossy brown conkers bursting out of their spiky shells.

'Be careful, Charlie,' I shouted. 'Keep away from the foot-path.' I refrained from stopping him as I recalled I had done the very same when I was ten years old.

After parking my car I walked up the entrance steps and under the tall Victorian archway on which the date 1878 was chiselled deep into the buff-coloured lintel. I failed to notice the raucous cawing of the rooks that swirled around our incongruous bell tower before they flew up the Morton Road towards the church spire.

Perhaps I should have.

*

Ruby was waiting for me outside the office door. Her face was flushed.

'There's been an accident, Mr Sheffield,' she said. The words tumbled out. 'Mrs F 'as phoned t'say Mr Evans 'as 'ad a nasty fall.'

'Oh dear! How bad is it?'

'Cut 'is 'ead. Mrs F called for an ambulance.'

'How is he now?'

'Dunno. She's at the 'ospital an' sez she'll ring soon.'

'OK, thanks, Ruby.' I could see she was shaken. 'Go into the staff-room and make yourself a cup of tea. I'll let you know when we hear anything.'

I made my way into the office and a few minutes before nine o'clock Anne and Sally walked in from the staff-room.

'Ruby told us what happened,' said Sally.

'Any news?' asked Anne.

Right on cue, the telephone rang. It was Vera.

'How's Joseph?' I asked.

'He's going to be fine.' She sounded breathless, anxiety in her voice. 'Thank goodness he managed to get to the phone. There was blood on the kitchen floor. The ambulance came within minutes. They were superb. He's sitting up now. Clearly shaken. They may keep him in overnight.'

'I'm so sorry, Vera. Everyone here sends their love. Is there anything we can do?'

It was typical of Vera to transfer at a moment's notice into work mode. 'Perhaps you could ask Anne to organize the late dinner money.'

'Of course. Anything else?'

'Not for now. I'll be in touch again later,' and the call ended.

'How is he?' asked Anne.

'Sitting up, but he's obviously had a nasty fall.'

'Poor Joseph,' said Sally.

Anne nodded. 'Thank goodness Vera found him.'

'The poor man is all alone in the vicarage,' said Sally.

'Yes,' said Anne quietly.

At morning break I was on playground duty, and I leaned against the wall under the shade of the horse chestnut trees. Anne had organized the late dinner money and everyone had rallied round in Vera's absence. Our fearsome dinner lady, Mrs Doreen Critchley, a lady with a foghorn voice and the physique of a Russian weightlifter, had volunteered to take any telephone calls while we were all teaching and our cook, Mrs Mapplebeck, was preparing school dinner. Around me was a hive of activity and, in spite of the disruption to our lives, I smiled. The shouts of children at play were the soundtrack to my professional life.

Ten miles away in York Hospital, shortly before lunch, a tall attractive lady approached Joseph's bedside.

'Hello, I'm Miss Best,' she said with an engaging smile. She had a pale oval face, a bob of ash-blonde hair and striking grey eyes. 'I'm one of the hospital volunteers.' The badge on her cream cardigan read: 'YORK HEALTH SERVICES NHS TRUST.'

'I'm very pleased to meet you,' said Joseph.

'May I call you Joseph?'

'Yes, of course.'

She sat down on the chair next to the bed. 'So, Joseph, how are you feeling now?'

'Much better, thank you. Everyone has been so kind.'

'That's good to hear. It must have been a nasty shock for you.'

'Yes, I fell backwards off my chair and the vicarage has a very unforgiving tiled floor.'

'Oh dear, that must have been dreadful.'

'It was my silly mistake. Fortunately my sister came to the rescue.'

Miss Best was curious. 'Did you say vicarage?'

'Yes. St Mary's in Ragley village. I'm the priest there.'

She smiled. 'That's wonderful. I attend St Michael le Belfrey here in York.'

'Right next door to the Minster,' said Joseph. 'The services are quite lively, so I'm told.'

She gave a wry smile, 'Actually ... a bit *too* lively on occasions.'

'Really?'

'Perhaps I'm old-fashioned.'

'Surely not.'

She clasped her long fingers as if in prayer and looked thoughtful. 'To be honest, Joseph, I go to church to find some peace in my life and for a little companionship. I find solace there each Sunday.'

'As I do,' said Joseph. He found he was enjoying conversing with this unexpected angel of mercy. 'You could always come to one of our services at St Mary's,' he said, almost surprising himself with the invitation. 'It's a lovely community.'

'Thank you. Perhaps I shall.'

Miss Best saw the lunch trolley being wheeled into the ward and stood up to leave. 'It's been a pleasure meeting you, Joseph, and I hope you'll feel better soon. I'm on duty again after lunch so I'll call by to see how you are.'

'I shall look forward to it. My sister will probably visit as well, I imagine.' His brow furrowed. 'I've caused her so much anxiety already.'

Miss Best studied his worried face. She didn't know him, of course, but she could sense that he was a gentle and caring man. She leaned forward. '"Let not your heart be troubled,"' she said quietly.

Joseph nodded. 'Thank you and, yes, I do recognize the gospel of St John.'

Miss Best smiled. 'Chapter fourteen,' she said quietly and waved as she walked away.

It was lunchtime in Ragley too when I spotted a familiar Austin Metro pulling into the car park.

We all gathered in the staff-room while Anne reversed roles and made a hot drink for Vera. Our secretary appeared composed but clearly concerned. 'He seems fine but they aren't sure if he lost consciousness so they're keeping him in overnight. Visiting is two until eight, so I'll go back after school.'

'You must go for two o'clock if you wish, Vera,' I said. 'We can manage here.'

'Yes,' said Anne. 'We're fine. I've done the dinner money. It's important he has family and friends around him.'

'That's kind of you. I'll do that. It's only two visitors at a time by the bedside,' said Vera, 'and Rupert wants to come in with me.'

There was a chorus of requests from Sally, Pat and Marcus.

'I'm sure we can all call in at intervals,' said Anne. 'We'll work it out after school.'

'Fine,' said Sally. She glanced at the clock. 'Anyway, I've got to prepare for choir practice, so I'll catch you later.'

Shortly before two o'clock Miss Best walked into Joseph's ward, pushing a trolley of books and newspapers. 'Hello again, Joseph. Can I get you anything?'

'Hello, good to see you. I'm afraid I haven't any money but my sister should be in later.'

'Why don't I leave a newspaper and you can settle up when you can?'

'That's kind of you.' He selected a *Daily Mail*. 'Will you be going to a Harvest Festival service on Sunday?'

'Yes. I thought about what you said so I may drive up to Ragley and attend St Mary's.'

'That would be lovely,' said Joseph. 'It's an eleven o'clock Communion Service.'

Miss Best looked thoughtful. 'But you may not be there of course. It will depend on the doctor's decision.'

Joseph tried not to show that he was concerned. 'Yes, but I remain hopeful.' He smiled at Miss Best. 'Strange we haven't met before. I call in frequently in my role as a part-time hospital chaplain.'

She shook her head. 'I've not been here long . . . only just retired from teaching.'

'So you were a teacher?'

'Yes, I trained at the college in Ripon. My first teaching post was in the Lake District.'

'A beautiful place,' said Joseph.

'And that's where I stayed throughout my career.'

'What brought you to York?'

'I love the city, the Minster, the history. It's a wonderful place. I live near the Museum Gardens now.'

The conversation ebbed and flowed until a bell rang.

'Oh, that's visiting time,' said Miss Best.

On the stroke of two o'clock Vera strode into the ward carrying a bag with everything Joseph might need for an overnight stay.

'I must go,' said Miss Best.

'This is my sister. Do stay to say hello.'

Vera smiled at the stranger.

'Vera, this is Miss Best, one of the volunteers. We've just had a lovely conversation.'

'Good afternoon, Miss Best.'

'Pleased to meet you and I do hope your brother recovers soon.' She turned to Joseph. 'I'll go now. Good luck, Joseph,' and she walked away.

Joseph's eyes followed her departure with interest ... and the perceptive Vera noticed.

At the beginning of afternoon school the top three classes assembled in the hall with their hymn books. Sally gathered her choir at the front, picked up her guitar and strummed the opening chords of 'All things bright and beautiful'. It sounded fine apart from Ted Coggins who wanted to sing louder than anyone else.

'Ted, could you sing a little quieter please?' said Sally.

'Yes, Miss.' Then he raised his hand.

'What is it, Ted?'

'Ah could whistle it if y'like, Miss.'

'No thank you,' said a determined Sally. 'Now ...

moving on, Open your books to "We plough the fields and scatter".'

It was just before two thirty when I called into Pat's class. She was about to conclude her lesson on famous inventors. The list on the blackboard included Louis Pasteur, Alexander Fleming and Marie Curie. Pat had told me she had discarded many of the books in our library as they only referred to *male* inventors.

'So, boys and girls, any questions?'

'Yes, Miss,' said Billy Ricketts, a lively eight-year-old with a sense of humour.

'Go on, Billy,' encouraged Pat.

'Ah were jus' wond'rin', Miss ... who invented *'omework* 'cause that's t'worst invention.'

Pat gave me a wry smile as the bell rang for afternoon break.

On Saturday evening I collected Ruby's daughter, Natasha, from Ragley to look after John while Beth and I left for the Harvest Supper.

The scent of honeysuckle was in the air as we approached the imposing Yorkshire stone building of Morton Manor and parked in a field next to a cobbled yard and a collection of outbuildings. Beyond a tall yew hedge we walked past a row of espaliered pears and beneath a walkway of metal arches that supported fragrant climbing roses and vigorous clematis. Flanking the steps that led to the grand entrance giant stone tubs of pink aubrietia and fiery red pelargoniums were in bloom.

The Major, immaculate as always in a smart three-piece

suit and regimental tie, came out to greet us. 'Good evening, Jack, and the lovely Beth. Welcome to our humble
abode.' *Understated as always*, I thought as we entered the
vast entrance hall and walked into the first reception room
where drinks were being served and Vera was the perfect
hostess, moving graciously from one guest to another.

Joyce Davenport, Vera's dear friend and the wife of our
local doctor, suddenly appeared. 'Beth, lovely to see you!
You're looking well. How many months is it now?'

'Hello, Joyce. It's four . . . and I'm fine, thanks.'

'Is Richard coming?' I asked.

'Perhaps,' she said. 'He was called out to a suspected case
of chickenpox.'

'Oh dear,' said Vera. 'Let's hope he can join us later. In the
meantime, do excuse me.' Vera had spotted Anne Grainger
standing alone and away from the rest of the party. She
hurried over concerned that Anne was simply staring at a
plate of vol-au-vents and looking distracted.

'Anne, can I get you a drink?'

She gave a start. 'Oh, it's you, Vera. Sorry, I was miles
away. That's kind. A white wine would be welcome.'

Moments later Anne was sipping thoughtfully on a glass
of Sauvignon Blanc.

'So . . . how are you?' asked Vera.

Anne gave a slight shake of her head. 'It's difficult at the
moment.'

'What have you decided?'

'Well . . . John is moving out at the end of the month.
He's renting somewhere near to his work.'

'How do you feel about that?'

'Sad but relieved. I've tried my best for many years but

he's consumed with things that have no interest for me. We never go anywhere together. Life isn't meant to be that tedious.'

Vera looked around the room. Marcus was with a group of men listening to the Major's forthright views on current politics and a certain Ken Livingstone while Sally and Pat were sitting on a sofa chatting with Joseph, his head in a bandage.

'You have friends on the staff. We're here for you.'

'Thanks, Vera. I know that. School is a blessing. At least it provides some sort of social life.'

'Do remember, Anne, I shall always be on your side.'

'I know that.' She gave Vera a perceptive look. 'And what about you? What does your future hold?'

'Nothing lasts for ever, Anne. We both know that.'

'Even marriages,' said Anne quietly. She took another sip of her wine and gave a brave smile. 'Thanks, Vera. Time to join the throng.'

'Good idea,' said Vera, 'but avoid Rupert. He's a lovely man but his views on the decline of the British Empire can become a little tiresome.'

Anne gave Vera a hug and went to join Pat and Sally.

The Harvest Supper was always a popular event and a time for everyone to catch up with village news and local gossip. A huge dining table covered in starched white cloths creaked under the weight of plates of food, including a whole salmon, a gammon joint, large slices of roast pork, new potatoes, a bowl of stewed apple, pickled beetroot, ripe tomatoes, fresh crusty bread, Wensleydale cheese and local butter. It was a welcome feast.

Eventually, after an enjoyable evening, Beth and I said

our goodbyes. As often was the case in North Yorkshire, the heavens above the Vale of York were spectacular as we drove home. The sun had dipped in the west and the sky changed from lurid red to deep purple, a firmament studded with stars.

Sunday morning dawned slowly as a pale sun rose in the eastern sky and golden autumnal light heralded a new day. The Harvest Festival beckoned and it seemed as if the whole village was on the move as we drove up Ragley High Street towards the Morton Road.

Beth was trying to remind young John to be a little quieter than usual as we walked into church and found a pew. It was good to see Joseph there, smiling bravely beneath his bandages, and sitting beside Vera.

The Revd David Wainwright had responded to Vera's telephone call and conducted the service. A trusted colleague and ecclesiastical friend since college days, David was only too happy to help.

In front of the altar was a bountiful display of local produce flanked by two sheaves of corn. Vera had brought a basket of plums and Beth had plaited a string of onions from our garden. The organist, Elsie Crapper, with the help of a dose of Valium, played 'We plough the fields and scatter' at a brisk pace. The children in the choir sang beautifully while the congregation struggled to keep up. Otherwise the service went smoothly and David touched the hearts of everyone during his sermon when he discussed poverty in Africa.

Once outside again in the sunshine, groups mingled and chatted while Miss Best thanked the priest and sought out Joseph. He had found a comfortable bench under one of the elm trees and stood up when she approached.

'Hello, Miss Best, what a nice surprise.'

She looked with concern at Joseph's bandaged head. 'Please sit down, Joseph.'

He patted the space beside him. 'Do join me.'

She regarded him with compassion. 'So . . . how are you today?'

'Much better, thank you, and pleased to be home again.'

'I'm sure you are. It really is a beautiful place and right next door to the church.'

'Yes, I'm fortunate. Did you enjoy the service?'

'It was perfect. I'm so glad I came and you were right about the congregation. I was made so welcome.'

'I do hope you'll come again.'

'Thank you, I should like that.'

Joseph looked at her intently. 'You were so kind when I was in hospital and it occurred to me that I've only ever called you Miss Best. I don't know your Christian name.'

She gave a deep sigh. 'Please don't laugh. I was named after the leader of the suffragette movement. It's Emmeline.

'But that's a beautiful name.'

'As you can imagine it was always Emmy at school but these days I tend to prefer Emmeline.'

'Then Emmeline it shall be,' said Joseph with a smile.

'Thank you. In the meantime, I presume your sister will be looking after you until you're well again?'

Joseph pursed his lips. 'Well, yes, but it's difficult. My sister is always very busy. I really don't want to be a burden to her.'

'"Cast your burden on the Lord, and he will sustain you,"' she said quietly.

Joseph gave an imperceptible nod of acknowledgement. 'Psalm fifty-five.'

Emmeline smiled. 'Well done. That's right ... and it's verse twenty-two.'

They both laughed as the first golden yellow leaves of autumn fluttered down around their feet.

After putting away the hymn books Vera sought out Beth among the crowd while I took John to play with the other children.

'How are you, Beth? We barely got the chance to speak last night.'

'Fine, thanks, and it really was a lovely event. I would have stayed to help clear up but we had to get back for John. Ruby's daughter, Natasha, was childminding for us and Jack had to drive her home.'

'I understand but I'm so pleased you could come.'

Beth scanned the crowd. 'By the way, who's that with Joseph?'

'It's Miss Best. Joseph met her in hospital. She's one of the volunteer helpers and apparently a regular church-goer. Joseph suggested she sample one of our services.'

'Good to see him looking so relaxed.'

Vera looked at her brother. He was completely at ease with his new companion as they sat together on a bench in the churchyard and chatted in the dappled sunshine.

Vera smiled. Something quite unusual had happened to Joseph.

It had turned out to be a very different harvest.

'Well, well,' she said, 'wonders never cease.'

Chapter Three

The Long, the Short and the Tall

A visiting speaker, Mr Edward Clifton, gave a talk in assembly about the forthcoming lunar eclipse. Class 1 visited Mr Short's allotment prior to the village vegetable show. Mrs Pringle organized the children's miniature garden entries.
Extract from the Ragley & Morton School Logbook:
Friday, 2 October 1987

Norbert Short, a skinny, diminutive man in his mid-fifties, pushed back his flat cap and sighed in contentment as he surveyed his allotment. *Perfect*, he thought. Big really was beautiful. He loved his world of giant vegetables. There were supersized swedes, mighty marrows and colossal cucumbers. He had spent his entire summer tending them for at least two hours every day.

Next to his shed was his greenhouse, a rickety structure of glass and timber, and he walked inside and smiled. His mammoth tomatoes were suspended in a pair of his wife's tights. He sat down on a deckchair, poured strong tea from his flask and looked out at his pride and joy. It was a pumpkin so large he had named it Big Betty after his wife but, wisely, had not shared this fact with her. Tomorrow morning his friend, Deke Ramsbottom, would be bringing his tractor to lift it from the earth.

He drank his tea, screwed the cup back on to the flask and walked outside in the autumn sunshine. The waiting was almost over. It was Friday, 2 October, and the Ragley & Morton Vegetable Show was only one day away.

When I arrived at school and walked into the school office, Vera was rolling out copies of a letter to parents advertising the Vegetable Show.

She had removed the Gestetner master sheet from the typewriter, smoothed it carefully on to the inky drum of the duplicating machine and peeled off the backing sheet. Then she began the laborious process of winding the handle to produce the copies of her letter while taking care to leave the copies to dry on the window ledge to avoid smudges.

'Good morning, Vera.'

She didn't look up. This task took all her concentration.

'Good morning, Mr Sheffield, seventeen, eighteen, nineteen.'

'I'll catch up with you later, Vera. You'll recall I'm taking my class to the allotment later today and we have a speaker in morning assembly.'

'Yes, it's in the diary, twenty-one, twenty-two.'

Vera continued to wind the handle. This year there was a

miniature garden competition for the children and she was keen to encourage as many parents as possible to support this local event; not least because her fellow members of the Ragley & Morton Women's Institute were serving cream teas.

It was 9.30 a.m. and I was checking each child's reading record folder. Ted Coggins was standing by my desk and I had signed off his next Ginn Reading 360 book when Rory Duckworth made an announcement. 'Ford Transit comin' up t'drive, Mr Sheffield.' Rory knew his cars and vans and made a point of giving me an early warning without appearing to look up from his reading book.

'Thanks, Rory.'

I looked out of the window and saw a dark blue van with the words 'Junk & Disorderly – E. Clifton of Thirkby' painted on the side in gold letters. A tall fair-haired man in his late fifties stepped out carrying a large cardboard tube.

I remembered him from his last visit when he had given an excellent talk on the reappearance of Halley's Comet. He was a dealer in antique furniture but his passion was astronomy. A confident, engaging man with a ready smile, he had a lovely way of communicating with the children and he had kept them spellbound with his stories of the universe.

'Carry on with your reading, boys and girls,' I said. 'Our visitor has arrived.'

Vera had shown him into the school hall where Pat had arranged a speaker's table and some mobile display boards. Edward Clifton, a tanned, athletic figure, wore a stylish baggy linen suit and was unpacking his tube of posters when I walked in.

'Hello again, Edward. It's really good of you to give up your time to support our work.'

'The pleasure is all mine, Jack. Good to be back and happy to help.' We shook hands and he grinned. 'Having said that . . . Mrs Pringle was very persuasive over the phone.'

'Yes. Sally remembered you from your last talk and mentioned it to our Class Two teacher, Pat Brookside. It's her class who are doing the solar system project.' I glanced up at the hall clock. 'Assembly starts at ten o'clock. If you need anything just ask in the office.'

'I'll be ready.' He looked around the hall and stared at the entrance to our reception class. 'And how's Mrs Grainger these days?'

'She's fine.'

As I returned to my classroom I wondered why he had asked.

When I took my class into the hall at ten o'clock I was pleased to see Marcus and Pat introducing themselves to Edward. Meanwhile the children were excited to see large-scale photographs of the moon and our solar system.

'Good morning, boys and girls,' said Edward. 'It's good to be back. For those of you who don't know me, my name is Edward Clifton and I've always been interested in the mystery of the stars and planets . . . ever since I was in primary school just like you.'

Immediately they were in the palm of his hand. 'I'm so pleased Class Two will be studying the lunar eclipse . . . but first, who would like to help me build our solar system?'

Dozens of hands shot into the air. Then, using a few balls from the games store, a powerful torch and a group of very willing volunteers, he described the journey of the planets around the sun and the moon's orbit.

'So, next week, the moon will pass through the earth's shadow.'

Katie Parrish raised her hand. 'It was on the news, sir, and it's called a penumbral lunar eclipse. My mum explained it.'

Edward was impressed. 'Well done. Does anyone else know the word *penumbral*?' Predictably the boys and girls in Class 2 raised their hands and Pat simply glowed with pleasure.

At the end there was a brief question-and-answer session before the bell rang for morning break. Anne collected her coffee and went outside to do her playground duty, while Sally and Pat walked across the hall to the staff-room.

'What did you think of the guy in assembly?' asked Pat.

'Great speaker,' said Sally, 'just like last time.'

Pat gave her a sceptical look. 'You know what I *really* mean.'

'Ah, well ... apart from being a dishy David Soul lookalike.'

Both Sally and Pat were fans of *Starsky & Hutch*.

'Exactly.'

'And no wedding ring.'

Pat nodded. 'I noticed.'

'He kept glancing at Anne when he was speaking.'

Pat smiled. 'I noticed that as well.'

*

Anne was drinking her coffee on the playground when Edward appeared carrying his tube of posters. She recalled their earlier conversations and his eventful life. Born in 1929 in Napier, New Zealand, as a small child he had survived the terrible earthquake of 1931.

'Hello again, Anne.'

Anne looked up into the blue eyes of this tall, attractive man and thought back to their first meeting two years ago and smiled. There had been a spark then.

'Hello, Edward. How are you?'

His weather-beaten face creased into a smile. 'Fine, thanks, business is booming. What about you?'

She paused, searching for the right words. 'A bit mixed.'

'I'm sorry to hear that.'

'By the way, another lovely assembly. You really have a gift for communicating with the children.'

'Thanks . . . that means a lot.'

The bell rang for the end of playtime. 'Sorry, Edward, I have to go.'

He nodded. 'Of course. It was good to see you again.'

Anne felt the same but said nothing.

'I've still got the shop in Thirkby if you're ever passing.'

'Thanks, Edward . . . perhaps.'

She watched him walk to the car park with that familiar long stride. Then, with conflicting thoughts, she returned to her classroom.

At lunchtime in the staff-room Sally was reading her *Daily Mirror*. 'Hey, this is interesting. A Swedish company called IKEA has just opened its first British store in Warrington. They're selling self-assembly furniture. Looks good.'

'Bit of competition for Habitat,' said Marcus.

Pat looked up. 'I've still got my mum's G Plan stuff. My cottage is full of it.'

Vera had her own views about modern furniture, particularly of the self-assembly variety, and changed the subject. 'We're serving cream teas at the show tomorrow afternoon. If anyone wants to provide a few scones they will be welcome.'

'In all modesty,' said Marcus with a grin, 'I make scones to die for.'

'I'll be there, Vera,' said Pat, 'if only to break my teeth on Marcus's creations.'

'Likewise,' said Sally, 'and there should be lots of entries for the miniature gardens.'

After an appeal by Sally for biscuit-tin lids to create a base for miniature gardens, the project had gathered momentum. Children from all classes had shown interest and during lunchtimes she had taken them out to the school field to gather leaves and twigs. With the addition of papier mâché, poster paint and plasticine plus a few pebbles and tiny mirrors for garden ponds, the results were remarkable.

Pat glanced across at Anne's empty chair. 'What about Anne?'

'I think she's in her classroom,' said Sally.

Vera nodded. 'Anne has volunteered to serve refreshments with me.'

I glanced at the clock and got up. 'That reminds me, Vera, I need to let Anne know I'm taking my class up to the allotment.'

Vera understood. In my absence Anne became acting head.

When I walked into Anne's classroom she looked pre-occupied as she stared out of the window.

'Excuse me, Anne.'

'Oh, hello, Jack. Sorry . . . miles away.'

'Just confirming I'll be taking my class to the allotment. Should be back by afternoon break.'

'Ah, yes, fine. Hope it goes well.'

As I left she had begun to put pots of wax crayons on each table along with the torn sheets from an old wallpaper samples book in preparation for the afternoon art activity.

I was completely unaware of the thoughts that were swirling around her head, trapped in her cul-de-sac of dreams. That was for another day.

The sun was shining and the locals waved friendly greetings as I led the crocodile of children down the high street. It was usual for us to do project work out of school and, at times like this, I wished Ms Cleverley could have been here to share the experience. A visit to the local allotment on the patch of spare ground behind the cricket field provided wonderful opportunities for practical maths and science activities.

Norbert Short was expecting us, leaning on the allotment fence and dressed in old blue overalls. 'Welcome t'my world, boys an' girls,' he said with a smile.

We stood alongside his plot and stared in wonder.

''Ow d'you grow 'em so big, Mr Short?' asked Mary Scrimshaw.

'Wi' m'special seeds,' said Norbert. 'Ah c'llect 'em ev'ry season. Then ah dry 'em an' plant 'em early.'

'My mam grows lettuce an' carrots,' said Charlie Cartwright. 'She sez they taste better straight from t'ground.'

'What d'yours taste like, Mr Short?' asked an expectant Ted Coggins.

For the first time a frown crossed Norbert's face. 'Ah well, it's not jus' taste that counts. Y'see, ah like t'grow 'em *big* jus' like my Big Betty over there . . . Ah mean m'pumpkin,' he corrected himself quickly.

'Why d'you call it Big Betty, Mr Short?' asked Ted.

'No reason,' said Norbert. 'Anyway, m'pumpkins usually go t'local farms t'feed cattle an' pigs.'

'What about the vegetables in your greenhouse, Mr Short?' asked Katie Parrish. 'They look lovely. Especially the tomatoes.'

Norbert beamed with pleasure. 'Would y'like t'weigh one, young miss?'

'Yes please.'

Norbert had an old timber potting table outside his greenhouse and, from his shed, he brought out an ancient set of weighing scales and imperial weights. Then he went back in the greenhouse and carefully removed a tomato from the pendulous pair of tights. He handed it to Katie who put it on the scales and added weights until the pans balanced.

'Three pounds,' said Katie. 'That's over a kilogram.'

'Well done, Katie,' I said.

Norbert shook his head. 'Don't know 'bout foreign weighin', Mr Sheffield, but that's norra bad t'mato.'

'Why d'you keep them in a pair of tights, Mr Short?' asked Mary Scrimshaw.

'Keeps 'em from dropping.'

'My mother has tights like that,' added Mary, 'but not as big.'

Norbert nodded disconsolately and considered that the sight of his wife in a pair of tights was something to behold.

The children had brought clipboards and they settled down to draw the various vegetables and write about them. I noticed Ted had written, 'Mr Short has a pair of tights and a pumpkin called Big Betty.'

Back in school it was a busy end to the day with the children completing their drawings and converting imperial weights to metric. It had been a successful visit and the children were in good spirits as they collected their miniature gardens from Sally and set off home.

The younger ones were looking forward to watching *Scooby-Doo* on ITV or *SuperTed and the Stolen Rocket Ship* on BBC 1 while another episode of *Grange Hill* awaited the older ones. According to Katie Parrish, Banksy Banks was worried about his CPVE course. I guessed she must have talked to her mother about the Certificate of Pre-Vocational Education that had been introduced a couple of years ago. I was impressed that children's television included these topical issues. It occurred to me I ought to watch it one day but I was never home in time.

On Saturday morning the distant hills were shrouded in mist and the trees were ghostly sentinels above the scattered souls of fallen leaves, amber and gold. Wild fruits filled the hedgerows and in my garden a goldfinch pecked at the wild seeds. The season was changing and a cool breeze blew the spirals of woodsmoke above the rooftops.

It was mid-morning when Beth strapped John into the back seat of her car and we set off for Ragley. As we parked on the high street Derek 'Deke' Ramsbottom drove by on his tractor and trailer to collect Norbert's giant pumpkin. Known in the local pubs as 'the Singing Cowboy', Deke was a popular village character. The sheriff's badge on his waistcoat glinted in the morning sunshine and he waved his Stetson hat.

Beth picked up a shopping bag and we walked under the sign that read:

GENERAL STORES & NEWSAGENT
'A cornucopia of delights'
Proprietor – Prudence Anastasia Golightly

It was John's favourite shop. There were large jars of sweets including liquorice allsorts, sherbet dips, penny lollies, giant humbugs, dolly mixtures, aniseed balls, chocolate butter dainties, jelly babies, liquorice torpedoes and extra-strong mints. It was also the home of a certain teddy bear.

Jeremy Bear was sitting on his usual shelf beside a tin of loose-leaf Lyons Tea and beneath two ancient and peeling advertisements for Hudson's Soap and Carter's Little Liver Pills. Prudence, a single woman in her late sixties, made all his clothes with loving care. Today he was wearing a yellow jumper, cord trousers and a white apron on which the name Jeremy had been stitched in royal-blue cotton. Back in 1940, the love of Prudence's life, Jeremy, a young fighter pilot, had been killed in the Battle of Britain and his memory lived on in the guise of Ragley's favourite teddy bear.

The bell above the door rang as we walked in.

Prudence smiled when she saw John. 'My word, aren't you growing up fast!' she said.

'I'm four,' said John confidently. He looked up. 'Hello, Jeremy.'

Such was Jeremy's status that no one considered it strange to have a conversation with a teddy bear, particularly as Prudence always answered on his behalf. 'Jeremy says as you're his friend would you like a barley sugar?'

'Yes, please,' said John.

'What a polite boy,' said Prudence.

Beth was delighted. Her constant reminders to say please and thank you were paying off.

Prudence handed over the sweet and John smiled up at his furry friend. 'Thank you, Jeremy,' he said.

The formalities over, we progressed with the shopping while John played with Trio, Prudence's three-legged cat.

On the high street, two farmers' wives, Margery Ackroyd and Betty Buttle, were deep in conversation. Margery in particular was well known as a local gossipmonger.

The richest woman in the village, Mrs Petula Dudley-Palmer, and her two teenage daughters, had just driven past in her Rolls-Royce.

'Guess what, Betty?' said Margery. ''Er daughters are still goin' t'that posh school in York. They learn Latin an' Greek. Dead languages, waste o' time.'

'Mebbe not,' said Betty. 'Ah went to a Greek island once. It were Kos, ah think. We drank this aniseed stuff in a bar an' ah got off wi' a fit lad called Andros or summat. Didn't know a word 'e said but 'e were proper 'andsome.'

'An' y'finished up wi' your 'Arry.'

'Ah know,' said Betty sadly. ''E never were one f'romance.'

They each puffed on their cigarettes and considered their respective love lives.

'I'm not one t'gossip,' said Margery, 'but you'll never guess what ah saw when ah were walkin' pas' school.'

Betty was interested. 'Go on then.'

'Remember that big 'unky good-lookin' feller what 'as that antique shop in Thirkby?'

'Ah do. Looks like that film star.'

'Well, 'e were only chattin' wi' Mrs Grainger on t'school yard yesterday. All lovey-dovey they were.'

'Mebbe he's tryin' t'get 'is feet under t'table now 'er 'usband's moved out.'

'Bit sudden, don't y'think?'

'Dunno, but 'e can sell me a brass bedstead any day.'

They shared a conspiratorial smile and walked on with secret thoughts of a night of passion with a tall blond stranger.

After loading up the car, Beth and I decided to call into Nora's Coffee Shop.

Nora Pratt was behind the counter arranging a selection of Eccles cakes. A friendly soul, she was proud to be the leading light of the Ragley Amateur Dramatic Society.

''Ello, Mr an' Mrs Sheffield. Your John's gwowin' up fast.'

The letter R had always eluded Nora.

'Hello, Nora,' said Beth. 'How are you?'

'Weally good, thank you. What's it t'be?'

'Two coffees, an orange juice and three sausage rolls, please,' said Beth.

'Wight away,' said Nora and hurried off to the coffee machine.

We found a table in the window. Across the street, outside the village hall, Deke Robinson and Norbert Short were unloading a huge pumpkin from Deke's trailer.

Beth looked surprised. 'That's enormous!'

I spoke softly. 'Apparently he calls it Big Betty after his wife.'

Beth shook her head, glanced down at John and didn't pursue the conversation.

Nora arrived with our order. She removed the obligatory ash tray and gave the tabletop a cursory wipe. 'Two fwothy coffees, one owange juice and thwee sausage wolls.'

At one o'clock the villagers of Ragley headed towards the village hall. Outside on the lawn a large marquee had been erected by the local Scouts, supervised by Major Rupert Forbes-Kitchener, and entries had been displayed on trestle tables.

George Hardisty, President of the Ragley & Morton Gardening Club and a previous champion gardener, was to be the judge. George had been the school groundsman at Ragley School when I had arrived back in 1977. He was a true 'man of the soil' and well respected. According to the Major, who would be assisting in the prize-giving, what George didn't know about vegetables wasn't worth knowing. As Ruby often said, "E knows 'is onions, does Mr 'Ardisty.' So we knew the judging would be in safe hands.

Eight-year-old Sam Whittaker and his friend Billy Ricketts had been in the woods collecting mushrooms in an old shoebox. They walked into the village hall where Dr Richard Davenport was helping his wife, Joyce, set up the Baby Burco boiler.

'Hello, boys,' said Joyce, 'what have you got there?'

'Mushrooms, Mrs Davenport, we've been c'llectin' 'em.'

'There's loads in t'woods,' added Billy.

'We thought we might win a prize,' said Sam.

''Cause t'red ones look good,' said Billy.

'I'm so sorry, boys, but we can't enter them,' said Joyce with a look of concern.

Sam considered this for a moment but he was an optimistic boy and he had missed his lunch. 'Well, can we eat 'em instead?'

'Me an' Sam could eat 'em all,' said the ever-confident Billy.

There was a pause and a smile from our friendly local doctor before his cryptic reply.

'Well, of course, you can eat them all ... but some of them you will eat only once.'

The two boys looked perplexed.

'Come on, Richard,' said Joyce, 'don't be so abstruse. Are you going to explain or shall I?'

Richard crouched down. 'Listen carefully, boys. Eating wild mushrooms can be very dangerous and you must *never* do so. The ones with white gills and those with a red cap are poisonous.'

'Flippin' 'eck,' said Sam.

Joyce took control and removed the box from the boys. 'Richard, you can deal with the mushrooms and I'll treat the boys to tea and chocolate cake.'

'Cor, thanks, Mrs Davenport,' said Billy.

'But first of all, boys,' said Joyce, 'you must wash your hands.'

Sam and Billy looked at their filthy hands and shrugged.

It seemed a fair trade-off and they followed Joyce into the kitchen.

While we all enjoyed tea and scones in the marquee George Hardisty was completing his judging. He was too long in the tooth to be fooled by some of the obvious cheating that went on from one or two miscreants. This included onions filled with putty and carrots covered in floor polish to disguise the fact that they were rotten.

Thankfully, the rest of the hundred or more competitors presented their best efforts in an honest manner. Occasionally George would taste some of the vegetables. He recognized the sweet, distinctive taste of produce fresh from the ground. Some, however, did not come up to expectations and were destined to go to local farmers for animal feed or to be made into chutney.

Vera smiled at Anne. 'Thanks for your help. It's gone well.'

'Well, all the scones were appreciated,' said Anne.

'Even the ones made by Marcus,' added Vera pointedly. In her opinion the dough had been overmixed and it was clear he had begun with cold ingredients.

'At least he tried,' said Anne.

'You're right. Perhaps I was lacking a little Christian spirit.'

Villagers were drifting off to hear the results of the judging and the ladies of the Women's Institute had begun to clear away the cups and plates.

Anne took off her apron. 'I'll get off now, Vera, if you don't mind. Lots to do. It was good to be here today . . . took my mind away from everything that's going on.'

'Have you spoken to John again?'

'He's resigned to it now and settled in his new cottage. No doubt busying himself with his DIY.'

'Yes, it did consume his life somewhat,' said Vera. 'And what about you? Are you ready to move on?'

'I'm trying,' she said quietly.

Vera watched Anne as she walked away and prayed she would soon find some peace in her life.

Anne was deep in thought as she wandered slowly up the high street and towards the Easington Road. When she reached the village green she saw a familiar blue van. At one of the wooden tables on the forecourt outside The Royal Oak was a tall, fair-haired man sipping a glass of orange juice. She returned his wave.

It was Edward Clifton.

At the end of the show Major Rupert Forbes-Kitchener approached the microphone. 'Thank you to the ladies of the Women's Institute for their delicious refreshments and we are grateful to Mr Hardisty for acting as judge. Let's show our appreciation.' There was a round of applause.

'The results can be seen in the hall and congratulations to everyone who has taken part. So thank you all for support-ing this event. Finally, there's a special award for the children's miniature gardens and this will be presented by Mrs Davenport.'

Joyce smiled and walked to the microphone. 'Well done, boys and girls. Your creations were most impressive. It was difficult to choose a winner but the prize of a book token, kindly donated by the Major, goes to Rosie Spittlehouse for her Yorkshire Dales garden complete with sheep and dry-stone walls.'

Thunderous applause greeted the little nine-year-old girl who held her mother's hand as she received her gift.

After the formalities we all trooped into the hall.

Norbert Short was disappointed to receive a mere Certificate of Merit for his giant pumpkin.

George Hardisty was a sensitive soul and sought out Norbert, who was staring forlornly at his pumpkin. 'Well done, Norbert. Y'cucumber is one o' t'best ah've seen.'

'Thanks, George. Ah'm jus' a bit sad 'bout Big Betty.'

'Big Betty?'

'Ah named it after m'wife.'

'You're brave,' said George, shaking his head.

'Ah've watched 'er grow day by day.'

George nodded, assuming Norbert was talking about his pumpkin. 'We're looking for quality. Size isn't everything an' Big Betty 'as a soggy bottom.'

'Ah know,' said Norbert sadly.

Betty Short, a large lady with a double chin and wearing a voluminous floral kaftan, was looking at the results of the judging and the gold, silver and bronze postcards propped in front of the prize-winners. Norbert had won a first prize for his two-foot-long cucumber and a second prize for his incredibly tall leek. The card in front of his giant pumpkin read: 'Unplaced. Magnificent size but sadly a soggy bottom.'

Norbert went to stand next to his wife and she gave him a glare. Her husband's obsession with large vegetables was not shared.

''Ello, Mr Short.'

It was Ted Coggins and Charlie Cartwright.

''Ello, boys,' said Norbert.

'We 'ad a good time at yer 'llotment,' said Charlie.

'An' we're sorry 'bout Big Betty 'avin' a soggy bottom.'

'What did y'say?' demanded Betty.

'Ah sed sorry 'bout Mr Short's pumpkin,' said Charlie.

'It were a big un,' added Ted graciously.

Betty stared down at the two boys. 'But why did y'call it that name?'

Charlie was an honest boy, 'Cos that's what Mr Short called it.'

'An' ah drew a picture o' Big Betty in m'book,' added Ted for good measure.

Betty turned to Norbert. ''OME, NOW!' Her face had changed from pink to crimson.

The boys looked puzzled as Betty frogmarched Norbert back up the high street while beating him around the head with his prize-winning cucumber.

Edward Clifton drank the rest of his orange juice and stood up.

'This is unexpected,' said Anne.

'I didn't want to disturb you in the marquee. I know what village gossip is like. It's the same in Thirkby.'

'It's lovely to see you,' said Anne, 'but why are you here?'

'Someone who knows you called into my shop this morning and mentioned you and John were parting.'

'Yes, we are. In fact, he's already moved out.'

'I'm so sorry, Anne. It must be very stressful.'

'At times it is.'

He looked around. There were a few mothers playing

with young children on the green; otherwise it was quiet. 'It was simply to say I'm here if you need a friend – or perhaps a coffee or a drink sometime. You've got my number.'

'That's kind of you, Edward.'

'I'll get back to the shop now. My assistant will be ready for a break.'

He drove away and Anne paused outside school under the shade of the avenue of horse chestnut trees. She stared down at the scattered leaves at her feet and thought about the life that had gone.

Chapter Four

The Calm after the Storm

A meeting of the school governors took place at 7.00 p.m. Priscilla, Lady de Coercy, was welcomed as the new governor representing Morton village.
Extract from the Ragley & Morton School Logbook:
Thursday, 15 October 1987

'I'll be late tonight. It's the governors' meeting so I'll pick up something to eat in the pub.'

Beth grinned. 'OK. Hope it goes well.'

We were in the hallway and John had already left with Mrs Roberts. I gave Beth a hug. 'How are you feeling?'

The half-term break was still a couple of weeks away and she had been working at a furious pace. Like me, she had been responding to the request from County Hall for proposals that matched the demands of the new National Curriculum and we had both been burning the midnight oil.

She gave me a tired smile. 'I'm fine,' she said. Then she stretched up and kissed me and I caught a hint of Rive Gauche by Yves Saint Laurent, her favourite perfume. I watched her as she walked out to her car. In her double-breasted long grey trenchcoat with button-down epaulettes and padded 'power' shoulders she was the epitome of the modern eighties woman.

On my drive to school I sensed a change in the weather. Once again it was the time of the dying of the light, an autumn of misty memories. Brittle leaves were scattered across the road and the smoke from a hundred chimney pots settled like a shroud over the rooftops of Ragley village. As I drove past the village hall, the ancient weathervane turned on its axis towards the east. There was a keening sound from the taut telephone wires above my head and by the time I reached the school gate a breeze had sprung up and the branches of the horse chestnut trees shivered.

Ruby the caretaker was wearing a new winter coat and sweeping leaves from the entrance steps.

'Weather's on t'turn, Mr Sheffield.'

'Looks like it, Ruby.'

'That safety man were in proper early checkin' fire distinguishers. 'E looked 'appy enough. Gave Mrs F a form.'

'OK, thanks. How's the family?' As soon as I asked I realized this could be a long answer as Ruby worshipped her six children.

She leaned on her broom. "Ad a letter from my Andy. 'E sez 'e's doin' well.' Thirty-six-year-old Sergeant Andy Smith was stationed in Northern Ireland.

'That's good.'

'Our Racquel says Krystal's lovin' school.'

Ruby's eldest daughter Racquel lived in York and was the proud mother of five-year-old Krystal Carrington Ruby Entwhistle. Ruby's granddaughter was her pride and joy.

'An' our Duggie's gorranother girlfriend.'

Duggie Smith, an undertaker's assistant and known locally as 'Deadly', seemed to have a new girlfriend every week.

'Oh yes?'

'Marlene, a new girl from that tattoo parlour in York.'

I knew the shop on Gillygate and recalled the sign in the window that read: 'Tattoos While U Wait'.

She shook her head, clearly disapproving. 'Daft as a brush is our Duggie. Thinks 'e's God's gift t'women.'

I couldn't think why. 'And how's the rest of the girls?'

'Sharon's 'appy wi' Rodney an' 'elps 'im wi' 'is milk round.'

Twenty-seven-year-old Sharon had moved in with local milkman, Rodney Morgetroyd, he of the Duran Duran hairstyle.

'An' our Natasha's still in love wi' Julian, o' course.'

Twenty-five-year-old Natasha helped out at Diane's hairdresser's as well as assisting her mother as a part-time caretaker. These days she appeared to be joined at the hip with PC Julian Pike, our lovestruck local bobby.

'And how's Hazel?'

Ruby's youngest was now in her fourth year at Easington Comprehensive School.

'Doin' really well. Loves 'er cooking lessons an' art an' readin'.'

'That's good to hear.'

'Ah love 'em all, Mr Sheffield.'

'I know you do . . . and now you've got your George.'

She looked up at me and smiled. 'Ah'm blessed.'

'So you are, Ruby . . . so you are.'

She picked up her broom and wandered off, cheeks rosy, headscarf tied in a double knot and singing to herself.

Vera was busy when I walked into the office.

'Good morning, Mr Sheffield.' She was at her desk checking the minutes for the governors' meeting. 'I've typed up the agenda and you'll recall we're welcoming Lady de Coercy as the new Morton governor.' There was a hint of disapproval in Vera's voice. She was not a fan of the flirtatious Priscilla de Coercy. 'I've informed the office she will be replacing Mr Coe.'

'Thank you, Vera.'

Stanley Coe, local farmer and habitual bully, had been a thorn in my side over many years but was now residing at Her Majesty's pleasure in prison after being found guilty of fraud and many underhand dealings. Our distinguished newcomer had been recommended by her husband, Percy, Lord de Coercy, and was generally regarded as one of the North Yorkshire county set.

At morning break Marcus was trying to persuade Sally that Operation Deepscan, the one-million-pound project to find the legendary Loch Ness monster, was money well spent.

'But they didn't find it!' exclaimed Sally. 'Think of what you could do with a million pounds.'

Suddenly the staff-room was full of opinions on how to spend a million.

'Lord de Coercy spent that on his estate on the north side of Morton,' said Vera as she boiled milk in a pan.

'More money than sense,' muttered Sally.

'He was the one that suggested his wife should become a school governor,' said a disgruntled Vera. 'She was the only candidate so she'll be at the meeting tonight.'

'What's she like?' asked Marcus.

There was a long silence. Vera's Christian values prevented her giving a true opinion. 'I'm sure we'll find out,' was her cryptic reply.

At lunchtime Lady de Coercy was reclining in her spacious lounge and smoking a King Size Benson & Hedges while sipping a gin and tonic and watching the one o'clock news. She was a lady of leisure. Having been born with the proverbial silver spoon in her mouth, Priscilla had been the one with the Silver Cross pram and a nanny who made beds with hospital corners. There had been some failures in the early days. Ballet lessons lasted only two weeks after the teacher had explained her dancing resembled a giraffe with piles, while an unfortunate nasal condition ended her singing lessons. However, following her heady days as an attractive socialite, her marriage to Percival confirmed her status as the posh neighbour with a perfect hairdo whatever the weather. She was about to switch off the TV when Michael Fish, the BBC weatherman, appeared with his cardboard clouds to stick on his map of the British Isles. He seemed in a chirpy mood, throwing in the occasional ad-lib.

'Earlier on today apparently,' he said with a confident smile, 'a woman rang the BBC and said she heard that there was a hurricane on the way. Well, if you're watching, don't worry, there isn't.'

'Silly woman,' muttered Priscilla, 'this is England not Jamaica.'

Her husband, seventy-year-old Lord de Coercy, popped his head round the door. 'Prissy-dear, Rupert rang to remind you of the governors' meeting tonight.'

'Oh, thank you, darling.'

He hobbled back to his study leaning heavily on his walking stick.

Priscilla switched off the television, picked up her copy of *Cosmopolitan* and continued to read an article titled 'Sex Life and the Older Woman'.

At lunchtime I was sitting at the same table as three seven-year-olds, Suzi-Quatro Ricketts, Alfie Spraggon and Emily Snodgrass. They had devoured their liver and onions, carrots and mashed potatoes and were about to do justice to their generous portions of cornflake tart and runny custard.

The conversation ebbed and flowed.

'My big sister does yoga,' said Alfie.

'That's nowt,' said Suzi-Quatro, 'my brother can do *Karachi*.'

Emily shook her head, 'Y'mean *karate*. Seen it on our telly.'

Suzi-Quatro frowned. 'So . . . what's yoga?'

Alfie considered this carefully. 'Well . . . it's like *slow* karate.'

Good try, I thought.

Ten-year-old Jeremy Urquhart, a studious, freckle-faced boy, was always quiet and needed occasional prompting.

'How are you, Jeremy? When Mrs Pringle was in our classroom she noticed what a good reader you are.'

'Thank you, sir. I like reading.'

'And how's your brother.'

Jeremy's teenage brother attended Easington Comprehensive.

'In trouble, sir.'

'Really?' I was surprised. The Urquhart boys had impeccable manners.

'Yes, sir. He tries to get detention most days.'

'Does he? Why is that?'

'Because he says the school is so noisy he likes to be alone so he can read a book.'

I was thinking I needed to have a quiet word with Mrs Urquhart when there was laughter from the table next to me. Suzi-Quatro's eight-year-old brother Billy was holding forth.

'WHAT DID Y'SAY, BILLY RICKETTS?' boomed Mrs Critchley. When Mrs Critchley called you by your full name you knew you were in trouble. However, Billy always had a ready answer for our fierce dinner lady.

'Don't know, Miss. Ah wasn't list'nin' to m'self.'

Mrs Critchley was rarely flummoxed but there was a pause before she replied.

'Think yerself clever, do you?'

'Yes, Miss.'

'When ah were your age if ah spoke like that ah'd be knocked into t'middle o' nex' week.'

'Did y'like Wednesdays, Miss?'

Mrs Critchley smiled. It was a rare occurrence but there was something about the pugnacious tousle-haired boy that reminded her of the young Doreen at Ragley School back in 1947 when John Pruett had recently taken over as headmaster.

'EAT YER PUDDIN',' she yelled and walked away.

Billy proceeded to slurp his runny custard and wondered if he would ever have the last word.

Sheila Bradshaw was behind the bar when I walked into The Royal Oak that evening, before the governors' meeting. As usual, with her prodigious bosom and three buttons undone on her crimson blouse, little was left to the imagination.

'What's it t'be, Mr Sheffield?'

I glanced up at the chalkboard. The special was rabbit pie, which suggested Pete the Poacher had paid a recent visit. I didn't fancy that.

'Any chance of chicken in a basket and a few chips?'

She shouted down the bar, 'Don, chicken in a basket f'Mr Sheffield.'

Her husband was a huge man who used to wrestle professionally under the name 'the Silent Strangler'. So there was never much bother that he couldn't handle.

'And a half of Chestnut, please.'

''Ow's Mrs Sheffield?'

'Fine, thanks. She's working up to Christmas, then taking time off in the spring.'

'Meks sense.' Sheila passed over the drink and turned to serve Deke Ramsbottom.

There were raised voices coming from the far end of the tap room.

Two of Deke's sons, Shane and Clint, were exchanging heated words. 'Empty y'pockets,' said Shane. 'Ah know yer at it again.'

His brother Clint was reluctant. Shane, a skinhead in a Sex Pistols T-shirt, raised his fist. The letters H-A-R-D were tattooed on the knuckles of his right hand. Conversely, Clint was wearing a baggy, slouch-shouldered red leather jacket with puffy sleeves, black leather pants and sunglasses.

Sheila reached up to remove Deke's tankard from the shelf above the bar while Deke nodded towards his sons. "E's norra bad lad is our Clint,' said Deke quietly in Sheila's ear. ''E can't 'elp bein' a big girl's blouse.'

Sheila merely shook her head as she pulled Deke's pint of Tetley's bitter. She knew that in the world of Ragley's singing cowboy this was as close as he would get to accepting Clint's sexuality.

'So what's goin' on?' asked Sheila as she pulled a pint.

'Waccy baccy,' said Deke.

Clint had reluctantly removed two joints and an Ecstasy tablet from his pockets.

At 6.45 p.m. Priscilla was sitting at her dressing table. She selected the 30-ml bottle of Giorgio Beverly Hills Extraordinary Perfume, a snip at £105, and sprayed it liberally on her throat and wrists.

'Do you want a lift?' asked Percy.

Priscilla shook her head. 'I'll take the Jag.' She blew her husband a kiss and selected a necklace. After that she fussed with her hair. It wasn't as she would like it and her personal hairdresser had gone to visit her sick mother in Staines.

It was seven o'clock and in the school hall we had pushed a few dining tables together ready for the meeting. The Revd Joseph Evans was in the chair and Vera, as secretary, was beside him. Everyone was present and Priscilla was the last to take her seat opposite Albert Jenkins, our learned local authority governor. Rebecca Parrish, parent-governor, was next to me while Anne Grainger, our teacher-governor, was making notes.

'Priscilla, my dear,' said Rupert with his usual bonhomie. 'How's Percy?'

'Curled up with his *Horse & Hound* and a malt whisky.'

Rupert smiled. 'No change there then.'

Vera frowned and nudged Joseph to start the meeting.

'Good evening, everybody, and I'll begin with a welcome to our new school governor, Lady de Coercy, who is representing Morton village. Now, if you refer to the agenda you will see the first item is the new curriculum and I'll ask Mr Sheffield to start proceedings.'

I explained that the Education Secretary, Kenneth Baker, had introduced proposals for a nationwide National Curriculum last December and we were all trying to come to terms with the implications. We had been told it would include attainment targets so teachers, parents and pupils all knew what should have been achieved in every subject as each academic year went by.

'And about time too,' muttered Lady de Coercy.

There were sharp looks from Anne and Vera.

I pressed on regardless. 'Last week I represented the school at a meeting for North Yorkshire headteachers to discuss the implications.' There were a few nods of acknowledgement. 'So I'm hoping the new proposals won't affect the great strides we've made in reading, mathematics, the natural sciences and new technology.'

'Really?' said Lady de Coercy.

'Do you wish to add something?' asked a bemused Joseph.

'Not yet,' was the curt reply.

Joseph was beginning to look concerned. 'Well, let's move on to item two and our secretary has some information.'

Vera explained our numbers on roll were likely to increase owing to the building within our catchment area and, in particular, the new executive homes on the York Road. From then on the meeting progressed smoothly. Anne described the additions to our reading scheme, Albert thanked the school for all their efforts to support village fundraising and Rebecca outlined the forthcoming fund-raising events.

Over an hour had passed when we reached Any Other Business. This was usually when Joseph closed the meeting and we dispersed.

'I have a few issues,' announced Lady de Coercy.

'Yes?' said Joseph.

She gave me a hard stare. 'Your children drop their aitches.'

It was Anne who recovered first. 'Perhaps it's worth pointing out that I receive these children as rising fives. Prior to that they have listened to the spoken word of their parents and peer group during their early years. When you get to know our school a little better you will be aware we do our best to promote a love of learning and so much more. However, there will always be a limit to our impact on the speech habits of children.'

'Thank you, Mrs Grainger,' said Joseph. 'So, if there's nothing else . . .'

'I haven't finished,' said Lady de Coercy abruptly. 'The *behaviour* of the children in the village is appalling. They sing mindless songs in the high street.'

Rebecca Parrish spoke up. 'Mrs de Coercy. I'll respond if I may?'

Priscilla glared at her. 'It's *Lady* de Coercy, if you don't mind!'

'Well, in view of my PhD, I'm actually *Doctor* Parrish but in these meetings we tend to dispense with such formalities.'

Priscilla stared in astonishment at this confident, articulate woman.

'As I was about to say,' continued Rebecca, 'my daughter, Katie, attends this school and I should like to thank all the staff for everything they do. I visit many schools in my role as a Lecturer in Education at the College in York and it is always a delight to see the good behaviour here.'

Lady de Coercy was not used to being contradicted and was keen to have the last word. 'Sadly, there's something much worse than all of this.'

We all stared at her.

'And what might that be?' asked Vera pointedly.

'Children lack *decorum* these days.'

'Such as?' I asked.

'*Eating* in the street.'

There was a stunned silence.

'Well,' said Joseph, glancing up at the faded Roman numerals on the hall clock, 'it's eight thirty so if there's nothing else I'll close the meeting. Minutes will be distributed in the usual way and I look forward to our next meeting. We'll conclude with a short prayer.' He glanced across at me. 'Perhaps Mr Sheffield would be kind enough to recite the school prayer.'

I wasn't expecting this. It was usual for Joseph to conclude our meetings with a short prayer. Everyone bowed their head except for Lady de Coercy.

'Dear Lord,
This is our school, let peace dwell here,
Let the room be full of contentment, let love abide here,
Love of one another, love of life itself,
And love of God.
Amen.'

The irony of a room *full of contentment* was not lost on everyone. There were mumbled Amens and hurried conversations as we collected our coats, turned off the lights and walked out. Lady de Coercy led the way and roared off in her Jaguar XJ6.

We said our farewells and I locked up the school and walked to the car park. Rebecca Parrish was leaning against her steel-grey Volvo 245. Rebecca was a single parent now. Her husband, a university professor, had had an affair with one of his young female students and their marriage had ended in acrimonious circumstances.

'An interesting meeting, Jack.'

I smiled. 'Yes, you could say that.'

'You've certainly got a challenge there.'

'Thanks for speaking up. It really helped.'

'Always a pleasure.'

Behind the ragged clouds a broken crescent moon hung in the sky while a silver avenue of stark moonlight filtered between the trees and lit up her long blonde hair.

'I've been meaning to ask. How's the master's coming along?'

I was in my second year of my higher degree course at the University in York. 'Fine, thanks, it's just tough fitting in all the reading and the assignments plus being a full-time teacher.'

'So, where are you up to now?'

'It's the usual weekly modules and then a dissertation in my final year.'

'What's the subject?'

'"Leadership in the Primary School". My tutor has suggested I visit Hamburg to interview German headteachers and compare their roles with my own. He's got contacts there.'

'Sounds fascinating.' She leaned towards me and laid her hand on my arm. 'Jack . . . the College would support you with your degree if you decided to apply for a post.'

I was surprised at the offer. 'I'm still not sure.' This was true – I hadn't been able to decide what to do about my future.

'Why is that?'

'I love this school.' I realized this had become my default response. I knew it merely delayed a final decision, yet I felt I needed more thinking time.

She gave me a steady stare and nodded. 'That's obvious and I have to thank you for all you're doing for Katie. She's lucky to have you in her final primary year.'

'That's kind of you.'

'I mean it, Jack, but you need to think of the future. With your experience you would fit in well in our Education Department.' She gave my arm a gentle squeeze. 'I could make sure of that.'

As she drove away I thought about her words as a sudden sharp gust of wind sprang up and a barn owl, like a ghost of the night, flew past the bell tower.

On Friday morning the rain was lashing down and high winds rattled the roof tiles. The BBC news was dominated by a great storm that had swept across southern Britain during the early hours. Frank Bough was saying it was the worst in 250 years with winds over a hundred miles an hour. Hundreds of buildings had been damaged and trees uprooted. In Kent, six of the seven famous oaks planted on the north side of the Vine cricket ground to commemorate the coronation of King Edward VII had been blown down. There were dreadful images of devastation.

Meanwhile, in Morton Manor a different stormy encounter was on Vera's mind. 'Rupert, you must have a word with Percy and persuade him to find something else for Priscilla to do with her time.'

'Yes, dear, I understand. Let me give it some thought,' and he hurried out to his study.

Vera switched on BBC Radio 3 and immersed herself in Beethoven's Symphony No. 2 in D major. 'Dreadful woman,' she muttered while she spread her home-made marmalade over a slice of toast.

At lunchtime Marcus, our resident scientist, was in the staff-room explaining the extraordinary weather. 'You see . . . cold air collided with warm air over the Bay of Biscay and this created an area of low pressure. Then the sharp temperature contrast between the two air masses caused a rapid ascent resulting in very low pressure at the surface.'

'What's that in plain English, Marcus?' asked Sally as she munched a garibaldi biscuit.

'I thought that was plain English,' retorted Marcus.

At the end of school I walked down to the school gate.

'G'night, sir,' said Mary Scrimshaw.

'So what are you doing over the weekend, Mary?'

'M'mam's makin' me a costume.'

'A costume?'

'Yes, sir, for 'Allowe'en.'

'But that's not for two weeks.'

'Ah know, sir, but we allus get sorted early an' we're all gettin' dressed up.'

'Oh yes . . . and what are you dressing up as?'

'Ah'm goin' as that brown dog in *Scooby-Doo* but ah don't know 'is name.'

She hurried off while I realized I needed to become more familiar with children's cartoons.

Meanwhile, parents were waiting to collect their children and Mrs Ricketts was there to greet Suzi-Quatro. ''Ello luv. 'Ave you 'ad a good day?'

'No, Mam.'

'Why not?'

'Our Billy said 'e wouldn't teach me 'ow t'spit like 'im.'

Mrs Ricketts looked across at me. 'Kids, eh?' She crouched down. 'Come 'ere, luv. Would y'like a hug?'

Suzi-Quatro considered this for a moment. 'Ah'd rather 'ave a Curly Wurly.'

Mrs Ricketts laughed. 'She knows 'ow many beans mek five does my Suzi.'

I wasn't entirely sure her class teacher, Marcus, would have agreed but I let it pass, smiled and waved.

Nine-year-old Rosie Spittlehouse had stayed late to collect her recorder practice music from Sally. Her mother wandered over to me.

'We're goin' t'Stratford for 'alf-term, Mr Sheffield. Ah'm looking forward to it.'

'Stratford! That's wonderful. What will you be seeing?'

She looked puzzled. 'Seein'? Well, jus' m'sister.'

'Oh, I understand. I thought you might be going to a Shakespeare play.'

'Shakespeare? No, m'sister's more into *Coronation Street*.'

It struck me that there are different sorts of culture.

A smiling Rosie appeared and they hurried off down the high street.

Lord de Coercy had given Priscilla a bag of her favourite chocolate caramels to soften the blow of having to visit the local hairdresser and mix with the hoi polloi.

She popped one in her mouth as she set off for Diane's Hair Salon on Ragley High Street. When she stepped inside she realized she would have to wait and frowned. Twenty-year-old Anita Cuthbertson was having a Toyah Willcox, a pink creation that resembled an electrocuted flamingo.

Meanwhile Diane was aware she was very much the second choice in the pecking order of Lady Muck's hairdressers but she treated her politely and offered her a cigarette and the new copy of *Woman's Realm* that she had bought that morning. There was a front cover picture of Sarah Ferguson with the headline 'She never wanted to be famous'.

'Beautiful girl,' said Priscilla, puffing clouds of smoke. 'Not entirely sure about the breeding.'

Diane wasn't sure whether she was referring to a person or a horse. 'So, what's it t'be?'

Priscilla ignored the fact she had not been addressed as 'm'lady'. She sighed deeply at the shortcomings of the proletariat. 'I want something elegant, my dear, that doesn't blow around in the wind. Sadly, my personal hairdresser has gone to visit her sick mother. Most inconsiderate.'

Diane collected a large canister of hair lacquer from the cupboard, stubbed out her cigarette and got to work.

During lunch break Anne Grainger had hurried out of school to buy some thin string from Timothy Pratt's Hardware Emporium for the afternoon curve-stitching lesson. She was deep in thought as she turned left, walked past Nora's Coffee Shop and paused outside Diane's Hair Salon.

Edward Clifton had telephoned her last night to see if she wanted to go to the cinema on Saturday evening to see *Every Time We Say Goodbye* with Tom Hanks as a World War Two pilot. She remembered that in the *Easington Herald & Pioneer* it had been described as a love story between two people from different backgrounds and she smiled at the thought.

She had to make a decision but she wasn't sure what to do. Either way, her hair had been neglected recently and she considered calling into the salon and making an appointment for tomorrow morning. It was at that moment that Lady de Coercy emerged, a silk headscarf covering her heavily lacquered hair. She was oblivious to Anne who was just out of her eyeline as she stepped out on to the forecourt and rummaged in her handbag. With a satisfied smile she took out her bag of chocolate caramels, popped one in her mouth and, greedily, selected another.

'Good afternoon, Priscilla,' said Anne.

Priscilla stood transfixed. She had never read William Shakespeare's *Hamlet* and would not have understood his phrase 'hoist with his own petard' but the meaning was there for all to see.

Poetic justice, thought Anne as the ironic reversal had played out before her.

Priscilla tried guiltily to replace the bag of sweets in her handbag but in her haste they scattered all over the fore-court and bounced on to the pavement.

'Well, well,' said Anne. 'Eating in the street.'

'It was only a sweet,' spluttered Priscilla, almost choking.

'As you were saying last night . . . no *decorum.*'

Lady de Coercy dashed to her Jaguar, jumped in and drove away.

Anne smiled. It had been a long time since she had felt as calm as this. *Everything comes to she who waits,* she thought.

With a spring in her step she returned to school eager to share her news.

Chapter Five

Better Late Than Never

Ms Brookside and Mrs Pringle met with the headteacher to discuss arrangements for Christmas productions. The school boiler was checked and confirmed to be in working order.
Extract from the Ragley & Morton School Logbook:
Wednesday, 18 November 1987

'Ah can't be late, Ruby,' said George Dainty. 'It's important.'

'Ah'll mek y'some san'wiches,' said Ruby.

George smiled. 'There's food on t'train so ah'm fine.'

'Well then, 'ave y'got ever'thing?'

He patted his pockets. 'Train tickets, wallet, notebook, pen, Underground map.'

''Anky?'

'Yes, luv.' He pulled out a large handkerchief – crisp, white and recently ironed – and waved it like a magician. It had his name embroidered on the corner, a labour of love by Ruby. In truth it embarrassed George as it reminded him of the days his mother sewed his name in his shirt, shorts and socks when he attended Ragley School after the war.

'An' don't f'get t'telephone afore y'set off t'come 'ome, so ah know yer all right.'

'Yes, luv. Train gets in late. Prob'bly won't be 'ome 'til after eleven. Y'don't 'ave t'wait up.'

She smiled. 'OK, luv.'

He gave her a kiss, hurried out to his car and set off for York railway station.

It was Wednesday, 18 November; there were important meetings in store and a day he would never forget.

In the quiet village of Kirkby Steepleton a frozen cloak of mist hung heavy over the land as Beth set off for school in her VW Golf CD Diesel. On this bitter morning the first harsh frost heralded the coming of winter. She had put on her warmest coat over a smart maternity dress and I noticed she appeared a little more tired than usual after working on a new maths scheme until late in the evening.

Then it was my turn and when I walked out my breath steamed. The smell of wood smoke was in the air as I scraped the ice from my windscreen and breathed on my key before inserting it into the lock. When I drove away, a robin, perched on the garden fence, stared at me with unblinking eyes as it practised a song of whispers. A slow dawn had greeted the new day as I drove under the torn rags of cirrus clouds on the back road to Ragley village.

I needed fuel and pulled up next to the single pump on the forecourt of Victor Pratt's garage. Our local car mechanic was the elder brother of Timothy and Nora and always seemed to be covered in grease and oil, even at the start of a working day.

'Mornin', Mr Sheffield, what's it t'be?'

I handed over a ten-pound note. 'Good morning, Victor. Five gallons please.'

He unscrewed the petrol cap and began to fill the tank. 'Ow's tha fettlin'?'

'I'm fine, thank you.' I paused for a moment before responding in kind. Victor was well known for having every ailment known to mankind plus a few that hadn't been discovered yet. 'And how are you?'

'Ah'm proper nauserated this morning.'

'I'm sorry to hear that.'

'Ah'll probably go t'see Doctor Davenport.'

'Yes, I'm sure he will help.'

He nodded sagely. 'Yurra early bird this mornin', Mr Sheffield.'

'Yes, Victor. Lots to do.'

'Jus' like George Dainty. 'E were in at t'crack o' dawn. Off t'London, 'e said. Bus'ness meetin', by all accounts. Driving 'is new Vaux'all Cavalier. Gorra posh sunroof. Waste o' time if y'ask me.'

Victor loved to grumble. He replaced the filler cap and wandered back inside with his familiar shambling gait and returned with my change. After wiping his greasy hands on his filthy overalls he stared at the coins in his hand. 'One poun' fifty,' he mumbled. There was a forlorn look on his face. 'Ah've started f'gettin' things these days,' he said sadly. 'Mebbe it's that Old Times' Disease.'

I guessed he meant Alzheimer's. 'We all forget things

from time to time, Victor. Don't worry but maybe mention it to Doctor Davenport to be on the safe side.'

He was shaking his head as I drove away.

Ragley High Street was already busy with early-morning shoppers attracted by the smell of freshly baked bread in the General Stores. Sixteen-year-old Heathcliffe Earnshaw was delivering the last of his morning papers before returning his canvas bag to Prudence Golightly, and Rodney Morgetroyd gave me a wave as he drove by on his milk float. As I approached the school gate I saw that hoar frost coated the fleur-de-lis on top of the railings and the cobbled drive was studded with ice crystals.

I parked my car, collected my old leather satchel and walked across the playground. Ruby was putting some crusts and bacon rinds on the bird table. 'Mornin', Mr Sheffield,' she shouted.

'Morning, Ruby. How are you?'

As always she didn't appear to feel the cold but I knew her arthritic fingers were beginning to cause her discomfort.

'Fair t'middlin' an' our Natasha will be in soon so we can check that old boiler.'

'How's it going with PC Pike?'

'Like love's young dream.'

I smiled. 'Victor said your George is going to London today.'

Ruby was full of pride. 'Off t'meet 'is business mates. Summat t'do wi' vestments.'

I guessed George Dainty hadn't gone to the capital to

discuss a priest's robes and was more inclined to invest some of his fortune. 'When will he be back?'

'Late t'night but ah'll wait up for 'im.'

'Give him my regards, Ruby,' and I hurried into school.

A five-minute walk away up the Easington Road, Anne Grainger was later than usual. She was in the kitchen of her mock-Tudor home slicing banana on top of her Weetabix. On the radio Rick Astley was singing his latest record, 'Whenever You Need Somebody' and Anne was swaying her hips in time to the rhythm.

There was the hint of a secret smile on her face.

At morning break I pulled on my old college scarf and duffel coat and went out for morning playground duty. The last of the leaves were falling and gathered in swirling eddies at my feet. Around me children were playing games, seemingly oblivious to the cold and, as always, their imagination knew no bounds.

I spotted Billy Ricketts pinning nine-year-old Tyler Longbottom up against the wall.

'What's going on, boys?' I shouted.

Tyler gave me a big smile. 'We're jus' playin', sir. I'm a baddy and Billy's RoboCop.'

'RoboCop?'

They broke off their game and looked at me as if I'd been born yesterday.

'E's a super 'ero, sir,' said Billy.

"Alf man an' 'alf robot,' added Tyler.

I shook my head. 'I know about Superman and Batman but not RoboCop.'

'It's a new film, sir,' said Tyler. 'RoboCop's got bionic powers.'

As the bell went for the end of playtime I called in to Marcus's classroom. He was preparing a science lesson using glass prisms.

'Have you heard of RoboCop?' I asked.

'Yes, Jack. He's an action hero, part man, part machine, played by Peter Weller.' He didn't look up, intent on bending light into a spectrum.

'Thanks,' I said and wandered off, impressed at his instant recall.

Perhaps it's a generation thing, I thought.

Miss Emmeline Best walked across the gravel courtyard of the vicarage feeling distinctly nervous. It was almost with an air of foreboding that, after tapping the door knocker, she looked up at the high elms where a parliament of rooks stared down with eyes of black glass. When Joseph opened the door, immediately all her concerns vanished.

'Emmeline, what a lovely surprise,' said Joseph with a beatific smile.

'Hello, Joseph. I do hope you don't mind me calling unannounced. I'm on my way to Easington market and was passing.' She held up a brown paper bag. 'I've been baking bread. It's one of my hobbies.'

'How wonderful. Do come in.'

'Are you sure?'

'Of course. Your company is always welcome. In fact, you can help me with the sermon I'm preparing.'

She stepped into the entrance hall. Joseph took the bread and placed it on the hall table. 'Let me take your coat.'

'Thank you, Joseph. What's the theme of the sermon?'

Joseph smiled. 'Something close to your heart.'

'Really?'

He picked up the paper bag. 'If you have time we could have tea and toast in the kitchen?'

'That would be lovely . . . So, you were saying about your sermon.'

'Ah, yes. It's *wisdom*.'

Emmeline paused at the kitchen door deep in thought. 'Then you must include Proverbs, chapter four, verse seven.'

Joseph began to fill the kettle. 'Remind me.'

Emmeline put a magnificent crusty loaf on the bread board. '"Wisdom is the principal thing."'

Joseph looked at her in admiration. 'What a remarkable woman you are.'

Emmeline's cheeks flushed. Then she looked around. 'Now . . . where's the toaster?'

'Good question,' he said, suddenly bemused, and they both laughed.

George Dainty's day had also begun well. He had enjoyed a sausage sandwich and a mug of tea on the train before arriving on time in King's Cross. Then he took the Underground on the Piccadilly line to Covent Garden where he met his cousin, Arnold Lumley, for a business lunch. Son of a Wharfedale farmer, Arnold had travelled south after university to become a financial consultant in the City. The two men had been friends since boyhood.

'These are tricky times, George. By the end of the week after the Wall Street crash the FT Index in London has lost twenty-two per cent of its value.'

'So what do you suggest?' said George.

'Caution . . . but I do have a few ideas.'

Arnold believed he could double George's investment of ten thousand pounds over the coming years. 'There's a huge number of major building projects going on in London. We need to consider those and I've lined up a meeting for later today.'

'Thanks, Arnie,' said George.

'But before that I was thinking of a fish and chips lunch. I know just the place. Not a patch on yours but not bad for down south.'

George looked delighted. 'Wi' mushy peas?'

Arnie grinned. 'But of course, George.'

After putting out the tables and chairs for school dinner Ruby walked down the drive and across the village green. It seemed strange not to turn right towards her old tiny council house on School View. She remembered those days vividly, bringing up six children and working all hours that God sent.

She thought back to her time with her first husband, Ronnie. Gone now but never forgotten. Always unemployed and always with an excuse not to work. She reached the bench under the shade of the weeping willow by the duck pond and ran her fingers over the brass plaque. It read:

In memory of
RONALD GLADSTONE SMITH
1931–1983
'Abide With Me'

She sighed and walked on. Life was different now. Now

there was always food on the table and a cosy fireside on a cold night. Her children were safe and moving on with their lives. As she set off again up the Morton Road she thought of George.

At lunchtime, following a warming school dinner of stew and dumplings, a feast on a cold day, we met up in the staff-room. A sombre conversation ensued as we reflected on recent events. Ten days had passed since the Poppy Day Massacre and the IRA bomb at the war memorial at Enniskillen in Ulster.

'The Queen and Mrs Thatcher have led the condemnation,' said Vera, her voice grave.

Anne sighed. 'Life is so precious.'

'Terrible times,' murmured Pat. 'The news is so depressing these days.'

'Last month we had Black Monday, now this,' said Sally. 'What a world we live in.'

Wall Street had led the world's stock markets into a massive downward spiral wiping millions from share prices.

'It said in the papers that it was *computers* that dictated the decline,' said Pat.

Marcus shook his head. 'Not computers . . . it was *people*.'

There were nods of agreement except from Vera, who thought computers could never be as efficient as her filing system. 'We need some good news for a change,' she said.

In London George and Arnold had completed their business and were strolling around Covent Garden market where George bought a Buckingham Palace key ring for Ruby.

Arnold glanced at his wristwatch. 'I've arranged for you to meet my stockbroker friend in Leicester Square at four o'clock.'

George nodded. 'M'train back t'York doesn't leave 'til eight so we've got plenty o' time.'

As darkness fell they wandered down Long Acre and reminisced about childhood memories and shared family holidays at Saltburn-by-the-Sea.

At the end of school I caught up with Pat and Sally for a preliminary meeting to discuss our Christmas productions for parents. Pat said she would work on an adaptation of *A Christmas Carol* with an original script written by the children while Sally said she would look out some appropriate music and songs.

I said I would talk to Anne about an infant Nativity and check with Marcus about ideas for his class. It was around five o'clock when we closed the meeting and Sally smiled at Pat. 'Girls' night out coming up.'

'Can't wait,' said Pat.

I was curious. 'What's this?'

Sally grinned. 'It's my favourite man.'

'And mine,' said Pat, almost swooning.

'Please, tell all. I've no idea what you're talking about.'

'Patrick Swayze,' they said in unison.

'We're off to the cinema tonight,' said Pat.

'It's *Dirty Dancing*,' explained Sally.

'Ah, now I understand.' The film had been the surprise hit of the year. I'd seen a photo of him and Jennifer Grey in the *Herald* and 'The Time Of My Life' had been on the radio this morning. 'So . . . enjoy your evening.'

'We shall,' said Sally and they both hurried to collect their coats before sharing a couple of hours with the sexy Houston hunk and his rippling muscles.

It was just before 7.30 p.m. when George arrived at King's Cross and made his way to the escalator that would take him to the main station. Ahead of him were hundreds of commuters hurrying to get home.

The terrible night of drama began when he heard a scream. A fire had suddenly sprung up under a wooden escalator and pandemonium broke out. Passengers fled in terror and a crowd rushed back towards him. George was bundled back towards the platform. There were yells of 'FIRE, FIRE!' and within minutes the air was filled with dense black smoke.

Around him a huge crush of frightened people was trying to escape and the acrid smell of fear filled the nightmare of the moment. Within his scrambled thoughts an image of Ruby shone through. Somehow he had to survive, if only for her. This was not a day to die.

Over the roar of the flames, George could hear the desperate cries of the trapped commuters. Amidst the chaos he was pushed up against a wall. Trapped, he could barely breathe. It was just when he was losing all hope that a young woman fell at his feet. Her head hit the floor. She lay still and there was blood in her hair.

There was no one else. Just him at the centre of the bedlam of panic. George had always thought of others above himself. This was his moment. He knelt beside her, took out his handkerchief and held it against her head. His eyes were stinging in the dense smoke and it was almost impossible to breathe. With what little strength he had left he lifted the girl and followed the crowd back towards the platform.

It felt like a lifetime but it was only minutes. George, the short, overweight Yorkshireman, the fish and chips millionaire, the gentle soul from Ragley village, became a giant in adversity. He fought for his life and the lives of others.

It was almost nine o'clock and Vera was watching television in the beautifully furnished living room in Morton Manor. She had enjoyed the acerbic wit of Anne Robinson during *Points of View* and now it was time for the BBC news.

She gripped her hands as if in prayer when the opening report came on. It concerned an emergency in London at King's Cross Station. The newsreader said, 'There has been a serious fire and fatalities have been reported.'

Vera thought back to her conversation with Ruby earlier in the day. Her friend had mentioned that George had gone to London and, for some reason, she had a bad feeling. On impulse she picked up the telephone.

'Hello, Ruby. It's Vera here. How are you?'

There was a pause. 'Oh, hello, Mrs F. Ah'm frettin'. My George should 'ave rung but 'e 'asn't. It's not like 'im an' on t'news it sed there's been a fire in London.'

'I see,' said Vera cautiously. 'I'm sure he will be fine. I could call round if you would like some company.'

'That's kind. Duggie an' Natasha are both out and 'Azel's readin' in bed.'

'I'll see you in a few minutes.'

*

On the soot-blackened streets outside King's Cross the emergency services leaped into action. Survivors were being helped out of the darkness, into the flashing lights, back from the mouth of hell.

George had never appreciated fresh air as much in his life. A fireman had directed him to safety. He was on the pavement now. The young girl he had helped had been taken away in an ambulance still clutching his handkerchief. He looked at his watch. His train home had left long ago and he knew Ruby would be worried. From his wallet he took out his BT Phonecard. There were twenty units on it and he walked to the nearest telephone box.

It was seven o'clock on Thursday morning when the phone rang in Bilbo Cottage. 'Jack, it's Vera here. Sorry to ring so early but I just wanted to let you know that Ruby's husband got caught up in last night's King's Cross fire. He's home and he's safe.'

'Oh dear. I heard about the fire on the news. What happened?'

'He was in the Underground station on his way to catch the train when the fire started. It was a dreadful experience. You will have heard there were fatalities so it's fortunate he managed to get home in the early hours.'

'And how is Ruby?'

'Shocked but very relieved. I called in to see her last night and stayed until George finally returned. It must have been a terrible ordeal for him.'

'I'm so pleased he's safe but sad for all those families who have suffered loss. In the meantime, you must be tired. Please take some time off if you wish.'

'No, I'm fine, but Natasha said she will come in this morning instead of Ruby.'

'Thanks for the call, Vera.'

I drove to Ragley under a leaden sky. On the radio T'Pau's 'China In Your Hand', number one for the second week in a row, was playing.

I pulled up on the high street and called in at the General Stores for a morning paper. The bell above the door rang as I walked in. Scott Higginbottom and Billy Ricketts were at the counter staring at the array of sweets. It was a tough choice. They had a penny each and a serious decision had to be made. It was down to sherbet dips, liquorice laces or gobstoppers. Finally it was the size of the huge gobstoppers that swayed their decision.

'A red and green gobstopper please, Miss Golightly,' said Scott.

'A yellow and blue one for me, please,' added Billy.

Prudence glanced up at Jeremy Bear. 'Aren't these polite boys, Jeremy? Do you think they deserve a barley sugar for having good manners?'

Billy was quick off the mark. 'He nodded, Miss Golightly.'

Prudence glanced up at me and raised her eyebrows. 'Yes, Billy, I think he did. Here's a sweet for each of you.'

'Thanks, Jeremy,' said the boys as they ran out.

'Good morning, Prudence.' I put twenty-two pence on the counter and picked up a *Daily Mail*.

The headline read: 'Thirty-five die after fire brings terror to hundreds of King's Cross commuters. INFERNO IN THE TUBE.'

'Good morning, Mr Sheffield. Terrible business.'

'It was on the news this morning. Very sad.'

'You will have heard about Mr Dainty. It's already all around the village.'

'Yes, Vera called me this morning.'

The bell rang again: Betty Buttle and Margery Ackroyd were calling in to buy cigarettes.

'Please could I have a packet of Hobnobs for the staff-room?'

She handed them over and I paid. 'I'll catch you later, Prudence,' I said and set off again for school.

Natasha Smith was sprinkling salt on the frozen steps when I arrived and I realized that Ruby's daughter was taking on many of Ruby's duties.

'Morning, Natasha, how are you?'

''Ello, Mr Sheffield. Up all night wi' m'mam.'

'I heard from Mrs Forbes-Kitchener.'

'She were brilliant. Stayed 'til t'early hours.'

'How's George?'

'Jus' coughin' a bit but guess what? Turns out 'e's a 'ero. 'Elped some young lass what were injured. 'E gave 'er 'is 'anky 'cause she 'ad a cut 'ead. 'Anky 'ad 'is name on an' this girl's dad, some posh bloke, were on t'news. My Julio 'eard it an' got in touch.'

'Julio?'

She blushed. 'Sorry ... m'boyfriend, PC Pike. That's what ah call 'im.'

'Are you going back home soon?'

'When ah've checked toilets ah will.'

'Well then, please tell your mother to rest today and not to worry about school.'

'OK, Mr Sheffield, ah know what t'do.'

'Thanks, Natasha. I really appreciate your help.'

She nodded. 'My mam taught me well.'

'I can see that.'

'An' ah've checked t'boiler an' it's fine.'

As I walked into the entrance hall it occurred to me the school was in good hands.

Vera was sorting the morning mail when I came into the office. She looked weary.

'Good morning, Vera. How are you? You must be very tired.'

'I'm fine. Simply relieved that George is safe. I called in to see Ruby last night and stayed with her until he finally got home. When I heard last night's television news I had a dreadful feeling something was wrong and decided to offer to sit with her. I'm so glad I did although her family soon rallied round. Julian Pike was there as well. A lovely young man.'

'I heard from Natasha that PC Pike followed up something on the news and it turns out George is something of a hero.'

'So I heard. I'm not surprised. Mr Dainty is a very special man.'

It was before school on Friday morning when Ruby burst into the school office clutching two copies of the *Easington Herald & Pioneer*.

'Good morning, Ruby,' said Vera.

'Mornin', Mrs F. You'll never guess. Mr Merry called in yesterday t'see my George.'

Montague Merry was the features editor for our local paper.

''E 'ad 'is photo tekken. Ah med 'im wear 'is bes' suit.'

'I see you've brought *two* copies, Ruby.'

'Ah bought loads. One each for all m'family. These are for t'staff-room an' you, Mrs F.'

'Oh, Ruby. That's wonderful,' said Vera. 'Thank you so much.'

'I'll be back in a minute,' I said and hurried out to tell Sally, Pat and Marcus to come to the staff-room.

Soon we were all gathered round.

'Ah'm as proud as proud can be,' said a smiling Ruby.

Under a photograph of George it read:

HANDKERCHIEF HERO

George Dainty, 54, of Ragley, was declared a hero after he helped save a London schoolgirl during the King's Cross fire.

Seventeen-year-old Kirsty Trevellan, only daughter of Detective Chief Inspector James Trevellan, received head injuries but was discharged from hospital on Thursday lunchtime. Eyewitness reports confirmed George helped the girl to safety and used his handkerchief to stem the flow of blood.

George's name had been stitched on the handkerchief by his wife, Ruby, caretaker at Ragley & Morton CE Primary School, and George was tracked down after the handkerchief was featured on the national news.

When asked how he felt on arriving back in the village he said, 'Better late than never.'

George is now safe and well and resting at his home.

Ruby rummaged in the pocket of her pinny. 'An' 'e bought me a posh key ring.' She held it up. 'Only just 'anded it over! 'E'd f'gotten all 'bout it.'

'Better late than never,' said Vera with a smile and she stood up and gave her friend a hug. There were tears in her eyes.

Chapter Six

A Whisper of Hope

Mrs Pringle organized music for the Nativity play.
Extract from the Ragley & Morton School Logbook:
Tuesday, 1 December 1987

Beneath a restless sky the moon-shadows had disappeared and a bleak day was dawning. Winter had come early. Frost dusted the branches of the trees and a first light snowfall covered the rock-hard earth. The land was in an iron grip and the back road to Ragley was a sheet of blue ice. It was a difficult drive and, as a village school headteacher, I was reminded that every day is different. It would be another day of a hundred conversations and a thousand details.

However, even though some don't start well, once in a while there are special days that end with a whisper of hope. Tuesday, 1 December, was such a day.

*

It was still dark as Vera prepared to leave Morton Manor. Over breakfast she had enjoyed the soothing sounds of 'Winter' from Vivaldi's *Four Seasons* on Radio 3 while checking the rest of the ingredients for Delia Smith's Classic Christmas Cake. Vera wanted to prepare some-thing special for the end of term to share with the staff and she had already soaked the dried fruit overnight in brandy.

As she jotted down a reminder to pick up some black treacle and cinnamon from the General Stores, the violins soaring on the radio came as a relief. Rupert had been in a bad mood when he left early to visit his daughter's riding stables. Last night Anastasia had announced she had left her current boyfriend, a regular occurrence these days. Also one of her horses was lame. Meanwhile his estate manager, a taciturn and dour Scot, had given a month's notice in order to return to the Isle of Lewis in the Outer Hebrides. 'It never rains but it pours,' the Major had mut-tered as he left and he wasn't referring to the Scottish climate.

When Vera walked out to her car she found the air was clear and cold while ribbons of freezing mist swathed the tall elms like Christmas garlands. Suddenly there was a clatter as the local bin men appeared from the back of the manor house carrying refuse to their wagon.

Dave Robinson and his cousin Malcolm Robinson were lifelong friends. They were an incongruous duo. Dave, at six feet four inches, was a foot taller than his diminutive cousin. In consequence, they were known in the village as Big Dave and Little Malcolm.

'Good morning, David, good morning, Malcolm,' said

Vera as she crunched across the gravel forecourt. 'You've started early.'

'G'morning, Mrs F,' said Big Dave. 'Yes, Malc 'as t'tek Dorothy t'see Doctor Davenport this afternoon.'

Little Malcolm was looking decidedly stressed. 'It's a check-up, Mrs F. Dorothy's reight worried.'

'I can understand that but she is a fit and healthy young woman and I'm sure everything will be fine.'

Malcolm's wife, Dorothy, was pregnant again having lost their first child to a miscarriage in dreadful circumstances last New Year's Eve.

'Thanks. Ah 'ope so,' said a subdued Malcolm.

'David, how is your Nellie? I trust she is fine.'

Big Dave's wife was also pregnant and Vera recalled that special day last July when the bin men of Ragley and Morton announced their happy news.

'Yes thanks, Mrs F.' He stopped and put down the bin he was carrying. 'So me an' Malc will both be dads in t'New Year,' he added proudly.

'That's wonderful.' She gave Little Malcolm an encouraging smile. 'I do hope your appointment goes well.'

They watched her drive away.

'Nice lady,' said Big Dave.

'Yer reight there, Dave,' said Little Malcolm with a sigh.

Big Dave studied his friend for a moment. It was important to keep him busy. 'C'mon, Malc. Get yer arse in gear an' let's shift some bins.'

When I arrived at school I called into Sally's classroom to confirm arrangements for rehearsals for Anne's Nativity play. She was sitting at her desk looking pensive while looking at last month's pay slip. She had received £1,086 gross and £753.14 net.

'Morning, Jack,' she murmured.

'Morning . . . What's wrong?'

'Bad news. Colin's lost his job. They're making cutbacks.' Her husband was an assistant finance manager in the architects' department in York. She waved her salary slip. 'So now I'm the sole breadwinner.'

'I'm so sorry. Why not mention it to Vera? She's got lots of contacts.'

Sally gave a wistful smile. 'OK, Jack.' She picked up her copy of *Carol, Gaily Carol*. 'Anyway must get on, the birth of Jesus won't wait,' and she headed for Anne's classroom to confirm the order of songs and carols for the forthcoming Nativity.

At morning break two six-year-olds, Zach Eccles and Walter Popple, were comparing their recently knitted balaclavas outside the boiler-house doors. Their mothers had used up their spare wool to produce multicoloured creations that resembled Doctor Who's scarf. They were feeling slightly uncomfortable as it was obvious to them that they were different to the other boys.

It was then that Suzi-Quatro Ricketts ran past and stopped suddenly. 'What y'got on yer 'eads?' she asked.

'Balaclavas,' said Zach proudly.

She grinned. 'Well, y'look daft,' and ran off.

'Daft?' queried Zach. 'What's she mean?'

Little Walter shook his head. 'Dunno.'

Zach's eyes lit up. 'Mebbe that's 'ow girls talk if they like you.'

Walter looked puzzled. He had warm ears but cold thoughts. Girls were different. He simply didn't understand them.

At lunchtime we were in the staff-room helping Anne prepare for her Nativity rehearsal. The coffee table was a sea of paper crowns and tea-towel headdresses.

'So, any plans for next weekend, Marcus?' said Pat as she picked up a tin of peas, a box of Kellogg's Frosties and an empty jar of Nescafé and wrapped gifts for the Three Kings in crêpe paper.

'I'm going to Harrogate on Sunday to visit the Toy & Train Collectors' Fair.'

'Should be fun,' said Pat with a hint of irony.

'Don't knock it,' said Sally. 'Colin still creeps up to the loft to play with his Hornby train set.'

'I was hoping Fiona would be coming up this weekend but she's got a lot on at present.'

Fiona was his dynamic girlfriend. They had been fellow students together at Cambridge University and she lived life to the full. Even so, he was looking forward to discussing the merits of a Class A3 Flying Scotsman locomotive with other model-train enthusiasts.

'What about you, Anne?' asked Pat as she tied a bright red ribbon around the tin of peas.

'Nothing special. Bit of housework probably.'

This of course wasn't quite true. Edward Clifton had asked her to join him for a meal and she had said yes. The only thing was that the restaurant was in a hotel on the coast near Whitby and it was a long return journey.

*

At afternoon break Walter Popple and Zach Eccles returned to their usual spot outside the boiler-house doors to discuss whether Fireman Sam would ever leave Pontypandy, his fictional Welsh village, and come to live in Ragley. Their balaclavas added a splash of colour to the gloomy day.

Then Suzi-Quatro wandered over and pointed to their multicoloured headgear again. 'So what d'you call 'em?'

'Balaclavas,' said Zack grumpily. 'Ah told yer this mornin'.'

'Where did y'get 'em?'

'Our mams knitted 'em,' said Walter.

'Ah bet they're nice an' warm,' said Suzi-Quatro wistfully.

Zach stared at this spiky-haired intruder and had an idea. 'Suzi . . . would y'like to 'ave a go wi' my balaclava?'

'Go on then,' said Suzi-Quatro.

Zach whipped it off his head and passed it over.

'Cor, thanks, Zach.' She pulled it on and ran off whooping and skipping around the playground.

'Told yer,' said Zach with a grin.

'What?' asked a bemused Walter.

'That's what girls do.'

''Ow d'yer mean?' asked Walter.

'She likes me,' said Zach and leaned back against the boiler-house doors with cold ears and a warm heart.

Darkness was falling as I walked down the cobbled drive at the end of the school day. At the gate Rebecca Parrish was deep in conversation with her daughter and her friend, Mary Scrimshaw.

'Please can I go to Mary's house to watch television?' asked Katie.

'My mum says it's OK,' said a smiling Mary.

'Are you sure that's what your mum said?' asked Rebecca.

Mary was an honest girl. 'Yes, Mrs Parrish, an' it's *Record Breakers* tonight at four thirty-five.'

'*Record Breakers*?' queried Rebecca.

'Yes,' said Katie with enthusiasm. 'Roy Castle's going to Farnham in Surrey to make the world's longest paper chain.'

Rebecca grinned, 'Really?' She glanced at me and raised her eyebrows. 'Well, you mustn't miss that. OK, I'll come to Mary's house and collect you later.'

We watched the two girls set off for the village Pharmacy.

Rebecca looked thoughtful. 'Jack, I was wondering if we could have a word. Something cropped up at college today.'

'Yes, of course. Do you want to come into school?'

There was a pause. 'No, not in school.' She glanced at her watch. 'I think I'll wait in the Coffee Shop before calling at Mary's house. Maybe you could join me.'

I was curious. 'I'll tidy my classroom and catch you up.'

'Thanks, Jack. See you later.'

I wondered what she had on her mind.

When I walked into the Coffee Shop I saw that Rebecca had found a table in the far corner. Two girls I had taught back in 1980, sixteen-year-old Katy Ollerenshaw and her friend, seventeen-year-old Cathy Cathcart, were at a table near the counter.

'Hello, sir,' they both chorused.

'Hello, girls. How are you?'

'Fine thanks, sir,' said Katy with a smile. 'We're still problem-solving.'

I guessed they weren't talking about our SMP mathematics scheme. Katy had been on the blue box of workcards, the highest level, before she had moved on to Easington Comprehensive School.

'Well, good luck.'

From the look of them they had definitely progressed in different ways. Cathy had adopted the post-punk gothic look with her black clothing, dark eye shadow, black nail varnish, spiky bracelet and Doc Marten boots. She was a huge fan of the Cult rock band. In contrast, Katy, a keen A-level student, was wearing an Aran sweater, blue jeans and a duffel coat. She had recently bought a Rick Astley record, 'Never Gonna Give You Up', and had played it countless times after completing her homework.

I waved to Rebecca, mimed two coffees and she nodded.

Meanwhile Katy went straight to the heart of the problem. 'So I'm guessing it's Wayne Ramsbottom again.'

Wayne was Deke's youngest son, now a nineteen-year-old bricklayer. I remembered teaching him to read when I first arrived at Ragley.

''E dunt seem int'rested any more,' said Cathy forlornly.

'Why's that?'

'Been chattin' up other girls.'

'I thought that might be the case,' said Katy, 'so I've brought this to cheer you up.' She had spent fifty pence on a copy of the popular *Just Seventeen* magazine.

'Oooh, thanks, Katy.' There was a picture of Rick Astley on the cover above the line 'A Secret Romantic'. 'I wish I could be famous like 'im.'

Katy gave her friend a determined stare. 'No you don't . . . just be you.'

As I collected the coffees from the counter I was aware that much had happened in their lives since those days at Ragley School when they had played netball, tidied the library and cleaned paintbrushes.

I sat down opposite Rebecca and she smiled. 'Thanks, Jack.'

'I'm intrigued.'

She sipped her coffee and I could see she was thinking how to begin.

'Well . . . there was a meeting after lunch today for the Education Department. Jim Fairbank was leading it and at the end he asked me to stay on for a quick word. There's a vacancy for a Senior Lecturer with a responsibility for placing students in local schools for teaching practice.'

'Yes?'

She leaned forward. 'Jack . . . he wants *you* and asked my opinion. I said you would be perfect.'

'I see. Thanks for the support.'

'So, what do you think?'

'Not sure.' I looked down at my coffee. My mind was suddenly full of confusion. 'I enjoy my teaching.'

'You would still be *teaching*, Jack.'

'And I love my school.'

There was a long pause. 'I know that but this is a good opportunity. Do you really want to stay in a small village school for the rest of your career?'

'Possibly.'

She shook her head. 'Think about it. You would have an improved salary and a good chance of promotion.'

'Yes, I've considered that.'

'And you've got the skill-set and the experience we need.' She looked around the Coffee Shop. There was a hubbub of conversation and the clatter of crockery. No one was within earshot. She leaned even closer. 'We have a vibrant team at the College and you would fit in well.'

'I'm still busy with my master's degree.'

'We could help you with that. There would be study time built into your timetable. I would make sure of that. Also every new colleague has a mentor to help them through their first year. We call them buddy tutors.' She gave me a level stare. 'I would be yours.'

'When do you need to know?'

'Soon, Jack ... soon.' She glanced at her watch and smiled. 'Well, Roy Castle should have finished his paper chain by now. I had better collect Katie.' She stood up. 'Thanks for the coffee. Do think about it and we'll talk again.'

As I drove home Bill Medley and Jennifer Warnes were singing 'The Time Of My Life'.

I wondered if it was.

In The Royal Oak Big Dave and Little Malcolm were celebrating.

'Three pints an' a Babycham, please, Sheila,' said Little Malcolm, 'an' one for yerself.'

'Thanks, Malc,' said Sheila. 'Don't mind if ah do.' She hitched up her skintight black leather miniskirt and began pulling the first pint. 'You're in early.'

'We all fancied a swift one afore we go 'ome. We're celebratin'.'

'Why's that?'

'My Dorothy's 'ad 'er check-up wi' Doctor Davenport. 'E sed baby's fine an' Dorothy is perfec'.'

'Fit as a butcher's dog,' added Big Dave for good measure. For the giant bin man this was the ultimate praise.

'Ah'm pleased for you, Malc,' said Sheila. 'Ah'll bring 'em over.'

Dorothy and Nellie were deep in conversation. Like their husbands they were a contrasting pair. Dorothy was a slim, five-foot-eleven-inch peroxide blonde whereas Nellie was short and stocky with a mass of wavy brown hair. The two couples were sitting at a table in the tap room closest to the television set. The adverts were on as Big Dave and Little Malcolm sat down.

Dorothy glanced up at the screen. 'She meks lovely gravy.'

It was Lynda Bellingham advertising OXO.

'Yer reight there, luv . . . jus' like yours,' said an adoring Little Malcolm.

It was quickly followed by a sexy clip of an attractive young woman in a silk negligee eating a Cadbury's Flake in a seductive manner. Nellie gave Big Dave a hard stare when his attention turned to the screen.

''Ere come the drinks,' said Nellie, looking forward to her first pint of Tetley's. Her limit these days was two pints. Now she was six months pregnant she had decided to cut down.

It was as Sheila was tottering over on her six-inch heels that the only piece of classical music they all recognized – namely Johann Sebastian Bach's 'Air on the G String', a jazz rendition played by Jacques Loussier – drifted from the television. 'Happiness is a cigar called Hamlet' ran the slogan.

Big Dave had an inspiration. 'That's what me an' Malc need. A couple o' cigars as well please, Sheila.'

'What about us?' demanded Nellie.

'Y'can 'ave a puff o' mine,' said Big Dave magnanimously.

'Not f'me, thanks,' said Dorothy, sipping her Babycham.

'Mek it three please, Sheila,' said Nellie.

Big Dave knew when he was beaten. You didn't argue with the York Ladies Darts Champion, who also had a right hook like Henry Cooper.

Just after I arrived home the phone rang. It was an elated Sally.

'Thanks for the tip, Jack. You'll never guess.'

'Why? What's happened?'

'Vera asked Colin to call into Morton Manor to have a chat with the Major and he's offered him the job of estate manager. Starts after Christmas.'

'That's wonderful.'

'He said Colin was ideal for the job: reliable, hard-working and a good administrator.'

'Well, we must celebrate.'

'We already have, Jack,' and there was laughter down the phone.

Later, while Beth was putting John to bed, I washed up the plates after our meal. Out of the leaded-pane windows the world was cold, still and silent. A bright moon shone down and the stars, like far-off fireflies, twinkled in the vast jet-black firmament. It was a night when the breath of uncertainty froze my thoughts. Suddenly a shooting star split the sky with a spear of white light and I smiled. There was a decision to be made and I needed Beth's approval.

When she came back downstairs I put a few extra logs on the fire and poured two glasses of red wine. It was time to relax . . . and talk.

'So, what do you think?' I asked.

Beth sipped her wine. 'Is it what you want?'

'Yes ... and no. It's clearly a good opportunity but it would be hard to leave Ragley.'

'When do you need to let them know?'

'Soon.'

'The money would be welcome but I know it's not just about that.'

Throughout our life together my restless soul had found peace in her presence and this was such a time.

'This impacts on us both, particularly with the new baby coming.'

She placed a hand on her bump and smiled. 'We're fine. I'll have maternity leave and we're lucky having Mrs Roberts looking after John. Before we know it he'll be starting school and we'll move on like we've always done. So ... what's it to be?'

I considered her words. With the passing years, the tapestry of our life together had moved on.

'OK,' I said uncertainly. 'I'll think about it.'

Resolutions were also being played out in Ragley village. Cathy and Katy were sitting in Cathy's bedroom listening to Billy Idol's 'Mony, Mony' on Cathy's transistor radio. She had taken her friend's advice and when Wayne had called into the Coffee Shop she had told him she wasn't interested. Wayne had decided to buy her a bunch of flowers in order to win her round again.

'Psychology,' said Katy, tapping her forehead. 'It's all down to knowing how they tick.'

Cathy smiled. It was good to have a friend like Katy.

Meanwhile, on Ragley's council estate, Zach Eccles had been sent to bed early by his mother for losing his balaclava. His insistence that it was only a loan to Suzi-Quatro and he would get it back on Monday fell on deaf ears. However, he smiled as he settled down in bed because he had taken his first step to understanding women.

Little Malcolm knew he would never understand women but he did know that he loved Dorothy. The day hadn't begun well but the news from Doctor Davenport had put their minds at rest. As they snuggled up on the sofa watching *Some Mothers Do 'Ave 'Em* with Michael Crawford and the long-suffering Michele Dotrice, Malcolm was looking forward to being a dad.

Also, Marcus was thrilled. Fiona had telephoned to say she could come for the weekend after all. However, it was clear she wasn't keen on spending her Sunday travelling to Harrogate for the Toy & Train Collectors' Fair. Marcus had agreed immediately. After all, there was more to life than staring at model trains going round a track.

In the kitchen of Morton Manor Vera was stirring her cake mix when Rupert walked in.

'You're looking like the cat that got the cream,' said Vera. 'It's presumably gone well.'

'Yes, my dear, it's been a good day.' He gave her a kiss on the cheek. 'All's well that ends well.'

Vera put down her spoon. 'So, what's happened?'

'I have an excellent replacement estate manager, my daughter has a new boyfriend and her horse isn't quite as bad as she feared.'

'That's wonderful.'

He eyed the mixture in the bowl and sniffed in appreciation. 'That smells good.'

Vera smiled and took a clean spoon from the drawer. 'Here, try some.'

He leaned forward and scraped out a generous portion. After tasting it he gave a smile of pure bliss.

'So . . . what do you think?' asked Vera.

'My dear, it's like a spoonful of Christmas.'

Perfect, thought Vera. She loved days that ended well.

Chapter Seven

A Family for Christmas

School closed today for the Christmas holiday and will reopen on Monday, 4 January 1988. Ms Cleverley visited school. The children enjoyed a games afternoon.
Extract from the Ragley & Morton School Logbook:
Friday, 18 December 1987

In the kitchen of Bilbo Cottage I switched off BBC 1's *Breakfast Time*. After five years of early mornings Frank Bough was saying farewell to the viewers but I was thinking of a different farewell. It was Friday, 18 December, the end of the autumn term and Beth's final day before maternity leave.

John was enjoying his piping hot porridge with its swirl of golden syrup. Beth kissed his forehead. 'Love you,' she said quietly.

I followed her into the hallway. 'Good luck today.'

111

'Thanks.' She pulled back her blonde hair and fastened it quickly with a bobble. 'Busy day ahead.' Then with a deep sigh she put on her warmest coat like a cloak of sadness, looked down at her bulge and gave up trying to fasten the buttons. When she stared in the mirror her cheeks were flushed and her eyes looked weary. 'I wish I wasn't so tired.' She looked up at me and kissed me on the cheek. 'I'll be late tonight. The governors and staff are putting on tea and cakes at the end of school.'

I gave her a hug. 'Yes, we've got the same but then you can put your feet up.'

Her ankles had swollen and I knew she was in discomfort. She wrapped a scarf around her neck and walked out to her car. Snow had fallen like winter confetti, a scattering over the frozen land. The weather matched her mood. It was a bleak morning.

'Hope it goes well,' I called after her.

As she drove away the village still lay under its mantle of darkness. I stood there as cold seeped into my bones and watched her tail lights disappear into the distance. By the time Mrs Roberts arrived I had dressed John so he looked like Nanook of the North.

'Party today, Daddy,' he said.

'And games,' I added and put some of his favourite Lego in a carrier bag.

He seemed happy enough and excited by the snow as they drove away.

Then it was my turn.

By the time I reached Ragley the Pet Shop Boys were singing 'Always On My Mind' and I thought of Beth and our time together. There had been many highs and lows that had brought us to this point in our lives, a journey of fire and ice. As I drove into school I was aware of another journey. It was at the centre of my professional life; namely, my teaching. For the past decade I had been the custodian of this village school and I loved my job. It would be hard to leave and, even now, there were hints of doubt. I still felt unsure.

When I walked across the playground I was surrounded by excited children.

'Soon be Christmas, Mr Sheffield,' shouted an excited Ted Coggins.

'And we're getting presents,' said the Jackson twins in unison.

'I've asked Santa for a Barbie doll,' said Hermione.

'And I've asked for a Sindy,' added Honeysuckle.

'I like My Little Pony,' said Emily Snodgrass, 'and I've written to Santa at the North Pole. My mummy put it in an envelope and she's posting it today.'

Scott Higginbottom and Billy Ricketts were not to be out-done. 'Sir, guess what? Me an' Billy are gettin' some ThunderCats toys.'

'An' we're gonna share 'em,' declared Billy with a holier-than-thou expression.

'Well done, Billy,' I said. 'Sharing is good.'

'Ah'm gettin' Transformers, sir,' said a ruddy-faced Sam Whittaker.

Nine-year-old Becky Shawcross was looking thoughtful.

'Have you written to Santa, Becky?'

'Yes, sir,' said Becky quietly. 'I like Sylvanian Families but Mummy says they cost a lot of money an' Santa 'asn't got enough pennies.'

The little girl's threadbare coat told its own story. 'I'm sure Santa will find something nice for you, Becky.'

''Ope so, sir,' and she wandered off disconsolately to play with Patience Crapper.

Only one child remained, staring up at me. It was the quiet, introverted Jeremy Urquhart, one of our best readers.

'And what about you, Jeremy?'

'I'm lucky, sir. My mum knows I love Lego and she says Father Christmas will deliver a Legoland set.'

'That's wonderful, Jeremy. When I was your age I enjoyed making models.'

He smiled. 'Best of all, sir, I love building bridges.'

A different sort of bridge building was on Ruby's mind at that moment. She was scattering salt on the entrance steps. 'Mornin', Mr Sheffield. Bit parky.'

'It certainly is and how are you?'

'Ah'm fine but ah've fallen out wi' my Duggie.' She shook her head. ''E didn't come 'ome las' night.'

'What's he up to?'

'Spends all 'is time canoodlin' wi' that Marlene.'

His previous girlfriends were history. Sonia from the shoe shop had come and gone and Tina from the mattress factory was a distant memory.

'I'm sure he's fine, Ruby, and he's not a teenager any more.'

'Yer right there, 'e goes 'is own way. Ah've no affluence on 'im any more.'

She looked sad as she put the lid on her jar of salt and I

followed her into school. I knew family was important to Ruby, particularly at Christmas.

When I tapped on the office door and walked in it occurred to me that this would be Vera's last Christmas as our school secretary, another stepping stone towards the end of an era. She had placed a magnificent Christmas cake on top of the filing cabinet and was about to cover it with her favourite Flowers of the Fields tea towel.

'That looks wonderful, Vera.'

'A little treat for the end of school,' she said with a smile.

I understood its significance. 'It's a lovely gesture. Everyone will appreciate it.'

She stood up and closed the door. 'Jack ... I've loved working here.' She spoke in hushed tones. 'And Christmas is such a special time.'

'I know ... so let's enjoy it.'

'I was looking around the office before you came in.' She gestured towards the framed school photographs that filled one of the walls, recent ones in colour, the earlier ones in black and white. 'The story of my life is here. Families come and go.' Her voice was soft. 'So many faces, so many children ... so many memories.'

'I feel the same.'

She glanced out of the window. Lazy flakes of snow drifted from a pewter-grey sky. 'The children will enjoy this weather. I've loved watching them at play.'

I saw Becky Shawcross leaning against the boiler-house doors. She was staring down at her scuffed shoes.

Vera looked keenly in her direction. 'We need to keep an

eye on that little girl. The home circumstances have changed dramatically. Mr Shawcross has gone off with another woman and left Mrs Shawcross almost destitute, struggling to pay the rent by all accounts. For the past week I've arranged for Becky to receive free dinners.'

'Thanks, Vera.' The playground conversation about Christmas presents and a Sylvanian Families set came vividly back to my mind.

She glanced up at the clock. 'Anyway, must get on.'

I nodded and opened the door. 'Good to talk.'

'Always,' she said and draped the tea towel over her cake.

At morning break, when I walked into the staff-room, a different family was being discussed: namely, the Royal Family. Vera, our ardent royalist, was serving coffee while trying to rescue the reputation of Princess Anne.

'I'm sure there's nothing in it at all,' she said.

However, Sally was on a roll. She had brought in last weekend's *News of the World*. It was her husband Colin's thirty-five-pence-worth of Sunday-morning recreation.

The headline read: 'ANNE AND ANTHONY'S 3 NIGHTS IN PARIS. Actor's dash to Princess.'

'I don't think you can deny there's been some hanky-panky going on,' said Sally while scanning the article. 'It says here: "Princess Anne and her TV heart-throb friend Anthony Andrews were fuming last night – after their secret hotel-hopping antics in Paris were revealed."'

'It's been in the news again this week,' said Marcus. 'Apparently he was filming fifteen miles away while Anne was attending an international horse-riding conference.'

'Well, I do admit . . . they both love horses,' added Vera grudgingly.

'Let's have a look,' said Pat and Sally passed over the paper. Pat shook her head and smiled. 'The reporter certainly uses colourful language. It says, "The hunky star booked into a massive £750-per-night suite at the Plaza Athena Hotel – just round the corner from Princess Anne."'

'So *not* in the same hotel,' said Vera defiantly.

'I wonder what his wife thinks,' said Marcus. 'She's the Simpsons store heiress.'

'I should imagine not a lot,' said Pat. 'According to this they . . . and I quote: "staged an astonishing cover-up so they would not be spotted together during their week in the romantic city".'

'I still think it's a lot of hot air,' said Vera.

'Which is exactly what we need at the moment,' I said with an encouraging smile. Everyone looked at me in surprise. I held up a plastic bag of balloons. 'Can I have some volunteers to blow these up for the party?'

Royal liaisons were quickly forgotten as Marcus challenged Sally to a balloon-blowing contest.

It was a few minutes before the lunchtime bell when Rory Duckworth announced, 'Ford Sierra coming up t'drive, sir.'

'Thanks, Rory.' I put to one side my list of afternoon games and stood up. 'OK, everyone. Finish off your Christmas cards, put them away safely and then line up for dinner.'

I knew Mrs Mapplebeck had prepared her annual treat, a Christmas dinner with all the trimmings, so I hoped our Deputy Education Officer's visit would be brief.

The look on Vera's face when I entered the office said it all. 'Ms Cleverley is waiting for you in the staff-room. I'll let the rest of the staff know.'

Sabine Cleverley had a face like thunder when I walked in.

'I've just passed two parents in the entrance hall. Apparently they were delivering games for some kind of activities afternoon. Pictionary and Jenga, to be precise.'

'Good afternoon,' I said simply.

'Well, have you nothing to say?'

'Well, I suppose I'm a fan of Pictionary but not so keen on Jenga.'

'Being obtuse doesn't suit you, Mr Sheffield.'

'I agree.'

She stared up at me while looking like a bulldog that had swallowed a wasp. 'So has this school finished work for the day?'

'We have a tradition here at Christmas time – on the final afternoon, we play games. The children dance, sing, enjoy a party tea and interact with children from other classes. It's a valuable social experience for everyone concerned. There has never been a complaint from parents and I'm unclear why you might have a concern with it.'

'My *concern*, as you put it, is that there is a time for work and a time for play.'

'Then we are in agreement, Ms Cleverley. Now, would you care to stay for lunch? The kitchen staff began work an hour earlier than usual to prepare a Christmas dinner, a special treat but particularly so for some of our disadvantaged children.'

'No, I won't stay. I have work to do.'

'Was there a particular reason for your visit?'

'I don't need a reason, I'm the Deputy Education Officer for North Yorkshire.'

'It's just that Miss Barrington-Huntley always used to let us know if she intended to call in.'

'I prefer to call in *unannounced*,' she replied with emphasis. 'So you need to get used to it.'

No, I don't, I thought . . . *no, I don't.*

She snapped shut her Filofax and left quickly. It didn't seem appropriate to wish her a Merry Christmas.

When I walked back into the office, Vera was looking out of the window and I stood beside her.

'The door was open,' said Vera. 'I heard every word.'

'That's the future,' I said quietly.

'Thankfully, not for me,' said Vera with gravitas. She looked up at me with a wry smile. 'So . . . not a good meeting.'

'On the contrary, Vera. It helped me to confirm an important decision.'

She gave me a knowing look. 'Go and enjoy your Christmas dinner.'

After a superb Christmas feast the hall was cleared and the children gathered with their teddy bears, dolls and toys.

It was fun to watch them at play and I wished Ms Cleverley could have seen some of the inventive decision-making with the construction kits and the extended vocabulary used to describe the benefits of a hotel on Mayfair in one of the games of Monopoly.

However, it was perhaps just as well the Happy Families card game involving Billy Ricketts wasn't shared. There was a dispute regarding the ownership of Mr Bun the Baker.

'I'm not cheatin', sir,' declared Billy, 'jus' 'elpin' m'self t'win.'

I saw that Pat had joined in a game of Twister with some of the equally long-legged members of her netball team while Sally was teaching the Jackson twins some chords on her guitar.

Meanwhile Marcus was working with a group of seven-year-olds and using boxes, batteries, bulbs and wires to build a robot with flashing eyes.

The afternoon ended as it always did with children collecting a simple gift from the Christmas tree: namely, a packet of sweets provided by Ruby, followed by Sally leading us all in a selection of carols. At the end parents drifted into school to collect the younger children and they left carrying a balloon and a Christmas card.

The older ones hurried out into the darkness.

'Goodnight, sir, and a Happy Christmas,' said Katie Parrish.

'We're going t'watch *Grange 'Ill* at Katie's,' said Mary Scrimshaw.

The two girls were now firm friends.

'Yes,' said Katie thoughtfully. 'Zammo and Jackie have a big decision to make.'

Not the only ones, I thought.

It was a lively group that gathered in the school hall after the children had left and one of the few occasions the teaching staff could meet up with the school governors and support staff in a relaxed, informal way. Refreshments had been prepared and displayed on a collection of dining tables while chairs were clustered in groups.

Rupert was serving hot drinks from a Baby Burco boiler while Vera was cutting generous slices of her Christmas cake and placing each piece on an individual white doily. Sally and Marcus were the first to taste a sample.

'Wonderful cake,' said Sally.

'It's my Delia recipe,' said Vera. 'I use it every year.'

'Beautifully moist,' said an appreciative Marcus.

'That's because I turn the fruit cake upside down every few days, prick the surface and then feed it with a liberal sprinkling of brandy. Then last night I covered it with marzipan and icing.'

'Well, it's magnificent,' said Sally while considering whether it would be polite to take a second slice.

'I would love the recipe, please, Vera,' said Marcus. 'I'm seeing Fiona's parents over Christmas and it would make a perfect gift.'

Vera recognized young love when it stared her in the face. 'It's not too late if you start tomorrow. Why not call into the manor? I've got all the ingredients.'

'Thank you, Vera,' said Marcus, delighted. 'What would we do without you?'

Vera merely responded with an enigmatic smile.

Meanwhile the kitchen staff looked different. We were all so used to seeing Mrs Critchley and Mrs Mapplebeck wearing their kitchen uniforms that it was strange to see them in smart dresses and with their hair no longer hidden under a cap.

'Hello, ladies, thank you for coming,' I said.

'Allus a pleasure, Mr Sheffield,' said the dominant Doreen. 'Good t'feel appreciated.'

'A lovely time of the year,' said Mrs Mapplebeck.

'Wonderful meal today,' I said. 'I don't know how you do it on such a tight budget.'

'Careful planning,' said Mrs Mapplebeck. 'Doreen came in early to prepare the stuffing balls.'

'They were my favourite, along with the gravy.'

'Ah did t'gravy an' all,' said Doreen without a hint of modesty. 'It were perfec'.'

I smiled and nodded. It was always best to agree with this formidable woman who also worked part-time on local farms castrating pigs.

Vera was in conversation with our road-crossing patrol officer, Lillian Figgins. 'Lollipop Lil', as she was known, had arrived wearing a fur coat and a string of pearls.

'Ah gave them pews a proper clean up t'day, Mrs F. Ah wanted it t'look nice f'Christmas.'

'Thank you, Lillian,' said Vera. 'When I called into the church I noticed a delightful fragrance of lavender.'

'It's m'new polish.'

Lillian was in charge of the group of cleaners at St Mary's. They were affectionately known as 'the Holy Dusters'.

'Well, it's certainly working,' said Vera gratefully.

On the other side of the hall Rupert and Albert Jenkins were enjoying a cup of instant chocolate and a slice of Christmas cake. 'Special times, Rupert,' Albert said, surveying the happy throng.

'Just a thought, Albert,' said Rupert quietly. 'We need a new governor now Priscilla has flown the nest.'

'I'm not surprised,' said Albert. 'She didn't fit in.'

'Yes, I heard about her being caught out eating sweets on the high street after complaining about the children doing the same. I'm not surprised she resigned.'

'So whom had you in mind?' asked Albert.

'I was thinking of George Dainty.'

'He would be ideal.'

'I was wondering if you might have a quiet word. Test the waters, so to speak,' said Rupert.

Albert nodded. 'A pleasure.'

'Thank you, Albert.'

'Just thinking . . . you're a lucky man having Vera for a wife.'

'I love her to bits,' said Rupert with a faraway look.

'It shows,' said Albert with a grin. 'A great lady. I do hope she will stay on for a few more years.'

Rupert paused before replying. 'There's life in the old bird yet.' Then he added hastily, 'I know she loves her job.'

'Therein lies the problem, Rupert.'

'Pardon?'

Albert was a great reader and Shakespeare's *A Midsummer Night's Dream* was one of his favourites. ' "The course of true love never did run smooth." '

Rupert thought that if Albert was any sharper he would cut himself.

On Saturday morning Beth and I decided to go our separate ways to do some Christmas shopping. She took John into York while I set off for Ragley. My first visit was to Piercy's Butcher's to confirm the collection arrangements for our turkey, bacon and sausages.

Mrs Dudley-Palmer was at the counter when I walked in. 'Thank you, Mr Piercy, so I'll be back on Christmas Eve for the whole order. Anyway, must rush, I'm making vol-au-vents this afternoon.'

She gave me a smile and the bell above the door jingled as she hurried out.

Old Tommy shook his head in despair. 'Vol-au-vents? What next? That weren't in my mother's cookbook. Ah were brought up on beef drippin' an' Yorkshire puddin' wi' pigs' trotters f'Sunday dinner. Proper food. No foreign muck in our 'ouse.'

'Good morning, Tommy. Here's my Christmas list.'

He scanned it quickly. 'No bother. Come early on Christmas Eve. It'll be busy again.'

When I walked out I saw Ruby who was emerging from the General Stores with a heavy shopping bag.

'Ah'm tekkin' a few bits round t'Maggie Shawcross. Since 'er 'usband left she's strugglin'.'

'That's kind, Ruby.'

'Well, Christmas is all about family an' she needs a bit o' support.'

I watched this good-hearted lady set off for the council estate, a part of Ragley village she knew so well, and reflected on her words.

I decided to call into the Coffee Shop for some mid-morning refreshment. Slade's 1973 Christmas hit, 'Merry Xmas Everybody', was on the jukebox when I walked in. Nora Pratt was serving mince pies at knockdown prices, presumably because the pastry had the consistency of concrete. I decided to play safe. 'A coffee and a crumpet, please, Nora.'

Nora smiled. ''Ello, Mr Sheffield. My Tywone is helping me out t'day. Dowothy's gone off t'do some Chwistmas shoppin'.'

Nora's boyfriend, Tyrone Crabtree, looked up shyly from behind a box of mince pies. It was well known that Tyrone had purchased thirty-two volumes of *Encyclopaedia Britannica* and he was now up to the letter D. His dream was to become a television quiz champion but currently, if the answers didn't begin with one of the first four letters of the alphabet, he was struggling.

'A cwumpet f'Mr Sheffield, please Tywone.'

A group of teenagers were close by staring at this week's *Just Seventeen* magazine. On the front cover it read: 'WET, WET, WET want to get serious.' *About what?* I wondered. It also advertised a free giant double-sided poster of Michael Jackson and Phillip Schofield, which struck me as an incongruous duo.

Albert Jenkins gave me a wave from the far corner table. Our local authority governor had more serious issues on his mind. He was deep in discussion with his friend, Stanley Hooper, Chairman of the Ragley Shed Society. President Ronald Reagan and Mikhail Gorbachev had signed an agreement to dismantle their arsenals of nuclear missiles.

'A first major step towards world peace,' said Albert in sombre tones.

Stanley nodded. 'At least Cowboy Ronnie is gettin' a few things right.'

I needed to buy a gift for Beth so I drank my coffee swiftly and then set off to Easington where the spacious cobbled square was a perfect place for a Christmas market. I parked in one of the side streets alongside Grimsby Gerry's mobile refreshment caravan. Stalls had been set up around the tall

Christmas tree with its coloured lights and I could hear the Pogues' 'Fairytale Of New York' on the tannoy system while the shoppers were singing along.

I bought a bag of roasted chestnuts and leaned against the picket fence that surrounded Santa's Grotto. Outside, the members of the Ragley Handbell Society were playing 'Rudolph The Red-Nosed Reindeer' slightly out of tune. It was enough to set my teeth on edge so I went to Shady Stevo's stall where a bargain was guaranteed.

Stevo was a heavily built, swarthy man with a long, jet-black ponytail attached to his flat cap. 'C'mon, ladies,' he was shouting, 'top-o'-the-range London fashion 'andbags, two poun' each or two f'three quid.'

Margery Ackroyd and Betty Buttle were the first to raise their hands. 'We'll 'ave two.'

'Sold to the two beauty queens on t'front row.'

'Yes but what year?' muttered Doreen Critchley from the back of the crowd.

'Now then, who fancies a real bargain?' shouted Stevo. 'In them posh shops that southerners go to, this would set y'back a fortune. It's a pendant on a chain, twenty-four-carat gold. Ah'm not askin' a fiver, ah'm not askin' a pound.' The anticipation was growing. 'It's classy. It's quality. Who wants one f'fifty pence?'

I noticed Mrs Shawcross looking in her purse. There was concern written all over her face. She glanced across to where her daughter, Becky, was standing with her friend Patience Crapper. The two girls were engrossed watching Larry Crump, the town crier, in his three-cornered hat and ceremonial frock coat. He was doing his best to be heard while ringing his bell and chanting, 'Oyez! Oyez! Oyez!'

Mrs Shawcross raised her hand along with a group of teenagers. I saw her pay her fifty pence, put the pendant in her pocket and walk away.

It was then that Stevo really caught my attention. He held up a shiny box. 'Now summat for a classy lady. It's a Braun Silencio electronic hairdryer, top o' the range. In Hoxford Street this would set y'back sixteen pound ninety-five. Who wants one for a tenner?'

On impulse I raised my hand.

'Sold t'Buddy 'Olly,' and there was laughter from the crowd.

It was when I went to collect it from his assistant, a young girl in a leather jacket, that I spotted a box with the label 'Sylvanian Families'. A group of tiny well-dressed bunnies stared back at me. 'How much?' I asked the girl quietly.

She was clearly a chip off the old block. 'Fiver,' she said and held out her hand. It seemed reasonable. I took a five-pound note from my wallet. 'Can you put it in a bag please?'

'No problem, Buddy,' she retorted with a grin.

When I walked away Stevo was holding up a Polaroid OneStep 600 camera and I saw our bin men, Big Dave and Little Malcolm, looking interested.

'We could tek pictures of our kids,' said Big Dave.

Little Malcolm nodded. 'Yer reight there, Dave.'

Stevo recognized the Ragley bin men. 'It teks *cheapest* instant pictures . . . twenty poun' in York.' He delivered the final *coup de grâce*. 'Y'can 'ave two for a tenner.'

I drove to Ragley, parked outside school and walked round to the council estate. At number 31 School View I tapped on the door. Mrs Shawcross was surprised to see me.

''Ello, Mr Sheffield. What's up? Is it my Becky? She's wi'
Patience playin' at 'er 'ouse.'

'I'm sorry to bother you, Mrs Shawcross. It was you I
wanted to see. I thought you might like this.' I opened the
bag to reveal the Sylvanian Families box.

She sighed. 'That's kind, Mr Sheffield. You'll know by
now times are 'ard.'

'I'm aware of that.'

'But it feels awkward. Ah can't accept charity.'

'The thing is, Mrs Shawcross, this will be going in the
New Year school jumble sale. I remembered Becky men-
tioning she would like some for Christmas.'

'Ah see. Well, in that case ah'll 'ave t'give y'something
back for 'em.'

'There's no need but maybe you could bring something
you don't need to put in the jumble.'

The penny dropped. For a moment I thought she was
going to burst into tears. 'Thank you, Mr Sheffield. Ah'm all
t'family she's got now. She'll love these. Ah'll put 'em somewhere safe 'til Christmas morning.'

I left her clutching the parcel.

That night, I was still awake at midnight and as I lay in bed
the happenings of the day flickered through my mind.
Ruby had summed it up well. 'Christmas is all about family,' she had said.

Next to me Beth was asleep and I knew that without
her my life would be diminished. It had begun with
attraction and progressed towards an infatuation. She
was my partner, my wife, my soulmate. Together we had
become a family in which I had learned the meaning of

unconditional love. Her hair stretched across the pillow like fragrant tendrils and her gentle breathing was soft as a lover's sigh.

I watched her as she slept and she filled my waking thoughts.

I was a lucky man.

I had a family for Christmas.

Chapter Eight

The Beginning of the End

School closed for the Christmas holiday and reopens on Monday, 4 January 1988.
Extract from the Ragley & Morton School Logbook:
Thursday, 31 December 1987

There was love and there was impossible love. For Anne Grainger on this bitterly cold morning it felt like the latter. It was Thursday, 31 December, and she was driving through a desolate monochrome snowscape to Morton Manor. Vera had invited her for coffee and she needed a listening ear. Her dear friend and confidante was the perfect choice.

Her relationship with Edward Clifton had blossomed but she was cautious about complicating her life. Their first kiss had the sweetness of wild honey and, at that moment, she'd felt as if she could stretch up and bend the sky to her will. Such was the power of this man and for Anne it was intoxicating.

Life had changed since meeting him again and another Christmas had come and gone. Edward's present had been a tape cassette of love songs. The first track was Art Garfunkel singing 'I Believe (When I Fall In Love It Will Be Forever)' and she was playing it again as she drove up the Morton Road. The gift was in contrast to the previous Christmas of 1986 when John, her DIY-mad husband, had given her a set of screwdrivers that he thought would come in useful in the kitchen. She had bought him a Black & Decker Orbital Sander which seemed to symbolize the gradual wearing down of their relationship.

As she drove towards the manor's grand entrance, she saw Vera standing in the doorway, a welcoming smile on her face. She parked and stepped out on to the gravelled forecourt. Above her the dormant trees shivered in the bitter wind and a diamond frost coated the hedgerows. Lazy swirling flakes of snow drifted down from a wolf-grey sky and covered the bone-hard land.

Vera waved in greeting. 'Come in out of the cold. The kettle's on and I've made some fruit scones. Best of all, Rupert's out for the day so we can talk.'

'Perfect,' said Anne.

'Thanks, Jack, it's been a great holiday,' said John Henderson.

Beth's parents, John and Diane, had driven up from their home in Hampshire and arrived on Boxing Day to spend a few days with us in Bilbo Cottage. They lived in Little Chawton, an idyllic village in Jane Austen country with its knapped flint-faced walls and a cast-iron water pump on the village green.

'We've enjoyed having you. Thanks for all the gifts.'

'Always a pleasure.' John was a sixty-four-year-old, weather-beaten athletic man with a keen interest in steam engines at their local Watercress Line. He glanced at his wristwatch. 'I'll start loading the car.'

As usual John and Diane had risen early and their grandson had enjoyed all the attention. Diane, a slim, assertive woman, pushed a strand of soft blonde hair behind her ear and smiled. She was sitting at the kitchen table with young John who was dipping toast soldiers into his runny boiled egg. 'Well done,' she said. 'You'll grow tall and strong like your granddad.'

And perhaps me as well, I thought.

Diane was simply a more mature version of Beth with her high cheekbones, clear skin and green eyes. There used to be tension between us but that had passed. Her younger daughter, the dynamic Laura, had once vied for my attention and had been rebuffed. However, that was long gone and Laura was making a name for herself in Australia in the fashion industry. Diane had mentioned Laura's latest boyfriend had a yacht, which tended to put my ageing Morris Minor Traveller into perspective.

On our last visit to their cottage close to Jane Austen's house, I had wondered if Diane had ever compared Beth and Laura with the fictional sisters in *Sense and Sensibility*: the cool, sensible Elinor and the passionate, idealistic Marianne. Her daughters were an equally contrasting pair.

'Beth, you must be tired,' said Diane. 'Come and sit down.'

Beth's cheeks were flushed as she busied herself at the sink. 'I'm fine, Mother, but thanks anyway.' Both women shared a determined streak.

I picked up a suitcase and walked out to John Henderson's Land Rover. He nodded towards the garden. 'Looking better now, Jack.'

The previous day had been cold, clear and sunny and we had worked side by side pruning and tidying. He had cut back the blackberry canes that were now bleached of colour and life. 'Good to cut out the old,' he said. 'Gives them a fresh start.'

'Talking of fresh starts, there's some news that Beth suggested I share with you before you leave.'

He closed the boot of the car. 'Sounds interesting.'

'Just that there might be something new for me. I'm considering leaving my headship and moving on.'

'Really? I thought you loved that school.'

'I do, but there's a chance of a teaching post at the College in York.'

'Is that what you want?'

'I wasn't sure at first but schools are changing these days with the new curriculum coming in. It's the end of teaching as I've known it.'

'I see.' He leaned back against the car. 'I thought John might have gone to your school. He would have been happy there.'

I nodded. 'We've discussed that but the new post is a good opportunity and a better salary. In any case, Beth was talking about taking John to her school. We'll know more as the year progresses.'

'Well, whatever's best.' He glanced back at the kitchen

window. 'Does Diane know? It's been wall-to-wall baby talk these past few days.'

'I think they're discussing it now. Either way we'll let you know.'

He smiled. 'New beginnings, Jack. Let's see what next year brings.'

In Morton Manor there was a roaring fire in the main drawing room and Vera and Anne were sitting in comfortable chairs by the hearth.

'Delicious,' said Anne. 'You make wonderful scones and I'm guessing the jam is home-made as well.'

'Yes, all mine,' said Vera. 'I find it very satisfying.' She gave her friend a knowing look. 'Takes my mind off the worries of the world.'

Anne sipped her coffee thoughtfully.

'So,' said Vera purposefully. 'I'm guessing it's Edward.'

Anne put down her cup and stared at the burning logs in the fireplace. 'Yes, it is.'

'I thought it might be.'

Anne sighed deeply. 'It's just that sometimes I feel I've lived my life on the wrong side of the track.'

'I know the feeling. We all go through that experience.'

'Every day I feel sad.'

'Why? Because of John?'

'Partly. He's moved on as well. There's a new woman in his life. A secretary . . . a divorcee where he works.'

'Yes, I heard.'

'Really?'

Vera gave a wry smile. 'The church cleaners don't miss much.'

Anne shook her head in mock disbelief. 'That's what comes from living in a village. I should have guessed. Edward has been discreet and thoughtful and I'm trying to be cautious.' She stared into the flickering flames as memories flooded back. 'I'm no longer that teenage girl who arrived at Ragley School on teaching practice all those years ago.'

Vera nodded. 'I knew then you would make a wonderful teacher.'

'I've loved my work, Vera. You know that.' She sat back, put down her china cup and clasped her hands. 'But in recent years it's the only thing that's kept me sane. Some days I've felt there's no end to the darkness.'

Vera studied the face of her friend and understood the conflict. 'There's nothing wrong about feeling this way. The tide is turning for you.'

Anne looked thoughtful. 'Maybe but I don't want to make a mistake again.'

Vera stood up and put another log on the fire. 'Perhaps it's time to turn your face to the sun.'

Meanwhile, in her bedroom above the Coffee Shop, Nora Pratt stood in front of the full-length mirror and sighed. It was her big day. She was reprising her role of Cinderella in the Ragley Annual Pantomime but there was a problem. Her Alpine leather corset wouldn't fit.

With a feeling of sadness she realized it was the beginning of the end. Her waistline had gradually expanded over the years. Since the age of fourteen she had worn this symbol of theatrical stardom with pride. The days of being the leading light at the annual village pantomime were over. It was time to pass it on to the next generation.

Back in the early fifties the slim, eager Nora had been given her big chance by Doris Clutterbuck, the principal actor of the Ragley Amateur Dramatic Society. In those days Doris was a powerful figure in the Ragley community. On the high street was an ornate sign that read: 'DORIS CLUTTERBUCK'S TEA ROOMS' and Doris was keen it catered for discerning customers. The sign on the door had read:

HORNIMAN'S DISTINCTIVE TEA
Rich and fragrant
The blend for the connoisseur

However, it was then, the year Nora turned fourteen, that Doris had realized even the most expensive undergarment could not hold back her expanding waistline. A life of cream teas had taken its toll. So it was with fitting ceremony that Doris passed on to Nora the treasured Alpine corset. Although it was loose on the slender, petite Nora, a few lengths of baling twine had managed to tighten the garment. That year the pantomime had been *Cinderella* and it was an evening Nora would never forget.

She had been given the part of Fairy Nuff, assistant to the Fairy Godmother, and felt wonderful when she stood in the spotlight in her frilly dress and the Alpine corset. Doris had given her her first speaking part and Nora delivered her lines almost perfectly: 'Faiwy Godmother! Faiwy Godmother! Here comes Cindewella.'

Nora also had a sweet voice and Doris had asked her to sing the opening number, the Judy Garland classic from the 1939 film *The Wizard of Oz*.

'Somewhere over the wainbow . . .' sang Nora and the audience had applauded. Ragley folk were always appreciative when one of their own was trying their best.

In later years Nora had taken over the Tea Rooms and transformed them into her Coffee Shop, a popular venue for all ages and a sanctuary for the village gossipmongers. On this cold December morning there was a poster in the window. It read:

The Ragley Amateur Dramatic Society
Presents their Annual Pantomime
'Cinderella'
Starring Nora Pratt
31 December 7.00 p.m.
In the Village Hall
Admission 50p

The two teenage friends, Katy Ollerenshaw and Cathy Cathcart, were staring at the poster. 'Y'look excited,' said Cathy.

'It's my first big part,' said Katy. 'It was good of Nora to give me a chance.' Katy was playing Prince Charming opposite Nora's Cinderella. The fact there was an age difference of over thirty years was all part of the fun of a village pantomime.

'Me an' Wayne are comin'. 'E bought *both* tickets.'

'Must be love,' said Katy.

Cathy dug her in the ribs. 'Cheeky!'

'I'm a bit nervous about my solo.'

'You'll be fine. Ah've 'eard y'practisin'. It's better than t'record.'

Katy was singing the Ben E. King classic 'Stand By Me'.

'Let's meet up this afternoon before the dress rehearsal.'

'OK,' said Cathy. 'Back here at two o'clock,' and she hurried off to the General Stores to buy a loaf of bread.

Katy stared wistfully one more time at the poster and wandered off to Piercy's Butcher's shop to collect her mother's order.

Heathcliffe Earnshaw and his girlfriend, Maureen Hartley, or Little Mo as she was known to her friends, were on their way to the Old Shed in Twenty Acre Field. It was a popular meeting place for teenage courtship.

They walked hand in hand, their feet crunching over the frozen grass. They were looking forward to their weekly kiss and cuddle.

Little Mo was a sensible, caring, hard-working girl who was excelling at school. She was the youngest of five sisters from a stable family. Her father, John Hartley, worked tirelessly following the early death of his wife and had made sure his girls grew up to be a credit to their late mother. He was aware of the courtship between Little Mo and the spiky-haired paperboy but knew Heathcliffe would never harm his bright and effervescent daughter.

As they approached the entrance to the shed they noticed a sweet smell in the air. Clint Ramsbottom was sitting on a wooden box and smoking a roll-up cigarette. He looked up, startled, but immediately relaxed when he realized who it was.

''Ello, what you two doin' 'ere?'

'Ah could ask t'same,' responded Heathcliffe, annoyed that someone had invaded his space.

'We're just out walking,' said Little Mo.

'So what's that yer smokin'?' asked Heathcliffe.

'Nowt special,' said Clint. 'Jus' wacky baccy.'

'Cannabis,' said Little Mo. 'I recognize the smell. There's a girl in my class that smokes it.'

Clint shrugged. 'Yeah, it's cannabis. So what?'

Little Mo shook her head. 'Our teacher said there's over two million people smoking cannabis and it can lead on to other drugs. She says it's dangerous.'

'Don't think so,' said Clint. 'Meks m'feel relaxed.'

'Yer gonna be in trouble,' said Heathcliffe. 'Yer brother Wayne is my mate an' 'e sez Shane will beat t'shit out o' you if 'e catches you playin' wi' drugs.'

'Dunt do me no 'arm,' said Clint.

'Mo's right,' insisted Heathcliffe. 'It's been in all t'papers. Ah know 'cause ah deliver 'em.'

'We did all this at school with Miss Beckett,' said Little Mo. 'She said there's over four hundred thousand snorting cocaine.'

Clint pinched the tip of his cigarette and sat back looking concerned. After meeting up with Vinnie Smart, the local dealer, in his pocket he had a couple more joints, a packet of Ecstasy tablets and two wraps of cocaine. 'Ah didn't know there were that many.'

'Heroin's the problem,' said Little Mo, shaking her head.

''Ow come?' asked a puzzled Clint.

'There's a quarter of a million addicts now.' Little Mo was clearly a disciple of Miss Beckett.

'So 'ave y'got some?' asked Heathcliffe.

'What?'

'Y'know what . . . 'eroin.'

'No . . . not on me.'

139

Little Mo crouched down and stared at the local farm-hand. 'I like your eyeliner. Where d'you get it?'

'Thanks, Mo. It's Ultra-Matte from Boots.'

'I wish I could get mine like that. It's really subtle.'

Heathcliffe shook his head, wondering how the conversation had moved on to ladies' cosmetics.

'Ah 'ave t'be careful. Our Shane calls me names if ah'm wearin' too much make-up.'

Little Mo sat down on an upturned beer crate and shuffled closer. 'Clint ... you shouldn't have to worry about people who don't understand.'

'That's kind, Mo,' said Clint. He stared up at the rafters. 'So what's all this 'bout 'eroin you've been learnin'?'

'It's really dangerous.'

''Ow come?'

'It affects the brain.' She watched Clint feel in the pocket of his overalls.

'You've got some, haven't you?'

Clint frowned. 'Ah will 'ave when ah meet up wi' Vinnie. 'E says you get a *rush*. It sounded good.'

Heathcliffe looked alarmed. 'Vinnie? Y'mean that Vinnie Smart?'

Clint nodded.

'Yer brother won't be pleased,' said Heathcliffe. ''E'll knock seven bells out o' 'im.'

Little Mo was determined to get back on track. 'Clint, listen ... after the *rush*, as you call it, heroin enters the brain and you feel sick.'

'Vinnie never said nowt 'bout that.'

'It's true. That's what happens. It can slow your breathing. Miss Beckett said it can lead to a coma and brain damage.'

Clint gave a deep sigh. He looked at this persuasive teen-ager in a new light. She might only be the size of two-penny-worth o' copper but she certainly packed a punch. 'So what shall ah do?'

'Don't use it, Clint,' said Little Mo. 'You mustn't. Say *no* to Vinnie.'

'E'll kill me. Y'don't mess wi' 'im.'

'Then tell your Shane,' said Heathcliffe. ''E'll sort Vinnie. Then you'll 'ave no more bother.'

But Clint was between a rock and a hard place. 'Our Shane talks wi' 'is fists.'

'It makes sense, Clint,' said Little Mo. 'It needs to stop now. Don't wait. We'll help if you like.'

There were tears in Clint's eyes. He was confused after leading a life that was misunderstood. 'Thank you,' he said quietly.

At two o'clock Katy Ollerenshaw walked into Nora's Coffee Shop. George Michael's 'Faith' was on the jukebox and Nora was behind the counter.

'Jus' come wound to t'back room, Katy. Ah've got summat for you.'

Katy was puzzled but followed Nora into a kitchen with shelves full of jars, boxes and tins. There was a battered suitcase on the table.

'A lady called Dowis gave me this a long time ago. It's weally special. It's fo' you now, Katy. Go on . . . open it.'

Katy lifted the lid slowly and stared in awe. It was the Alpine leather corset.

*

The Ragley pantomime was over and in The Royal Oak the cast of *Cinderella* had gathered after one of the most successful productions in living memory. Nora was being fêted by friends and family and everyone agreed Katy Ollerenshaw was destined for a career on the stage.

However, all was not sweetness and light in the tap room where Vinnie Smart, the chain-smoking skinhead, was talking to Clint Ramsbottom. Don the barman looked across at Sheila, who was pulling a pint for Deke Ramsbottom. 'Ah see that Vinnie's in again. Ah've 'eard 'e might be up t'no good.'

'Ah'm not s'prised,' said Sheila. "E's thick as chips an' twice as daft. Ah remember 'is mum marrying 'is dad. At t'weddin' she should 'ave jus' tekken t'ring an' not t'usband.'

'Yer right there, luv,' said Don.

Deke sipped the froth from the top of his pint. "E's a bit like my Clint is that Vinnie. Never 'ad a girlfriend. Couldn't even pull a Christmas cracker.'

It was then that Shane arrived. He had that 'if looks could kill' demeanour as he walked past the bar to the table where Vinnie was getting into a heated argument with Clint.

'Ah want a word,' he said and sat down next to his brother.

Sheila glanced up at her hulk of a husband. 'We don't want no trouble. Keep yer eyes open.'

Vinnie soon got the message. When you're facing a psychopath with a serious personality disorder it's best to do as you're told. In seconds he was sweating like a pig and giving a good impression of a nodding dog. He took a roll of pound notes from his anorak pocket and placed it on the table. Then he stood up and made for the exit as quickly as possible.

'That didn't las' long,' said Don.

Deke seemed relaxed. 'Whatever it were ah think our Shane's sorted it.'

Shane removed the rubber band from the roll of notes and slipped one of them to Clint. 'Mine's a pint,' he said. 'One for y'self an' one for our dad.'

'Thanks, Shane,' said a relieved Clint.

Shane glowered at his kid brother. 'That's an end to it. Fresh start t'morrow.'

Bilbo Cottage was quiet. Christmas was over and Beth and I were watching television in front of the fire. It was good to relax while we drank tea and shared a box of Cadbury's Milk Tray, a gift from my mother along with a Durabeam Work Torch and a bottle of aftershave called Hallmark, apparently for 'men with distinction'. My Glaswegian mother and her sister May had decided to enjoy a Hogmanay north of the border with their Scottish clan.

For the first time in many years Beth and I had not attended the Ragley pantomime. We decided it was too late for young John and, after we had tucked him up in bed, we settled down to watch *Watership Down*. It was an animated adaptation of the bestselling novel by Richard Adams in which a young buck named Fiver had a frightening vision of the future. It made me reflect on *our* future, not least my master's degree. There was still a long way to go but the possibility of support from the College in York was appealing.

It was late when we switched over to watch one of Beth's

favourites, the comedy classic *To the Manor Born* with Penelope Keith and Peter Bowles. Then, as midnight approached, we sat there holding hands while the final minutes of 1987 ticked away.

Beth leaned her head against my shoulder. 'So ... an eventful year coming up.'

I squeezed her hand. 'In more ways than one.'

'By my reckoning I've probably got seven or eight weeks to go.'

'I'm glad we extended the cottage. The extra space has made all the difference and there's more room for two children.'

Beth nodded. 'My mum said she would come up to help out when the time comes.'

'Perfect,' I said with a grin. 'It will be good to have someone here doing all the cooking and cleaning.' She gave me a dig in the ribs as the chimes of Big Ben announced the first day of 1988. I kissed her gently. 'Love you.'

'And you, Jack. Happy New Year.'

In Morton Manor Vera and Rupert were also watching television. In the highlights of the year was a review of those who had passed on and wouldn't see 1988. They included Andy Warhol, Liberace, Danny Kaye, Fred Astaire and Rudolf Hess.

'Very sad,' said Vera.

'Yes, dear,' agreed Rupert ... although his sympathies didn't extend to Rudolf Hess.

As she sipped her hot chocolate Vera wondered about Anne and what the New Year might bring for her friend.

*

It was midnight and the bells of St Bartholomew's Church in Thirkby market town were ringing. In his comfortable terraced house in the high street Edward Clifton was in bed. He felt warm, comfortable and relaxed. The old year had passed and a new one was beginning. Late-night revellers from The Cock & Bottle pub across the road were singing 'Auld Lang Syne' and a few rockets created colourful patterns in the night sky.

Predictably, as a dealer in antiques, he owned a huge four-poster bed, a relic from a local manor house. It was a very grand piece of furniture of which he was immensely proud. However, tonight was different. It was the first time he had shared it.

He stared up at the silk canopy. 'So, what do you think?'

'Wonderful,' murmured Anne Grainger.

He smiled and nuzzled her neck. 'I meant the bed.'

'Stop teasing. That's wonderful as well.' She felt blissfully happy.

'I'm so glad you stayed.' He held her naked body closer.

'So am I.'

He whispered in her ear, 'It's a wonderful way to welcome 1988.'

'I was thinking the same.'

It was the early hours before they finally fell asleep in each other's arms.

Chapter Nine

Lost in the Dark

School reopened today for the Spring Term. We had full attendance with 134 children on roll.
Extract from the Ragley & Morton School Logbook:
Monday, 4 January 1988

I awoke to a world of silence. Out of my bedroom window snowflakes fell like frozen tears, each one a perfect hexagon, briefly an individual before joining the white shroud that covered the land. It was a day when the cold was brutal and winter held the land in an iron fist. It was also one of the worst days of my professional career. When a child goes missing fears multiply with each passing hour. Monday, 4 January, was such a day . . . the day that eleven-year-old Amy Bell was lost in the dark.

The first day of the spring term appeared to begin well. It was 8.00 a.m. when I drove over the frozen cobbles of the school drive and parked next to Vera's Austin Metro. Our secretary took pride in being at her desk before anyone else.

Ruby was filling the bird table with crusts of bread and a handful of seeds. ''Appy New Year, Mr Sheffield,' she shouted as I stepped out of my car.

'And to you, Ruby.'

'Ah've cleared t'steps,' she said, nodding towards the school entrance.

'Thanks, Ruby. How are you?'

'Usual,' she said with a smile. 'M'fingers ache a bit in cold weather these days but my George bought me some posh gloves.' She held up a gloved hand. 'An' 'e gave me a furry 'at f'Christmas. 'E sez ah look like that Gobby-Choff, 'im what runs Russia.'

'Looks good, Ruby.' She could have got a part as an extra in *Doctor Zhivago*.

She nodded towards the school gate. 'Latchkeys are 'ere.'

We called the children whose parents' work meant they had to come in early and finish late 'latchkeys'. These children always carried a key so they could return to an empty house at the end of a school day.

A rusty twenty-year-old Ford Cortina that had definitely seen better days pulled up outside school. Mrs Longbottom emerged from the passenger seat along with her nine-year-old son, Tyler, and six-year-old Zach Eccles. 'Mornin', Mr Sheffield,' she shouted. 'Me an' Freda are on t'early shift this week. Are we OK droppin' 'em off now? Then Zach can come back to our 'ouse wi' Tyler at t'end o' school.' Mrs Longbottom and Mrs Eccles worked at the local shirt factory.

'That's fine, Mrs Longbottom. They can sit in the library if you like.'

'Mornin', sir,' shouted Tyler. 'Can we play on t'field?'

Mrs Longbottom gave him a clip round the ear. 'Say *please.*'

Undeterred, Tyler smiled up at me. 'Please, sir.'

Virgin snow covered the school field. The thrill of making the first footprints was still a vivid memory from when I was a boy. 'Go on, then. What about you, Zach?'

Little Zach concentrated. He had seen what happened if you didn't say please. 'Please can ah go as well, sir, please?'

I looked at this little boy in his baggy shorts, chapped knees red with the cold but completely oblivious to the bitter weather. 'OK, Zach, but don't go out of school again. Stay with Tyler.'

They ran off to roll the first giant snowball.

'Thanks, Mr Sheffield,' shouted Mrs Longbottom, 'an' 'Appy New Year.'

A mile away in one of the terraced houses up the Easington Road life was busy.

'Hurry up, birthday girl,' shouted Mary Bell.

'OK, Mum,' replied Amy as she rummaged in the cupboard under the stairs. 'Just looking for my wellies.'

'They're behind the wash basket.'

Mary was a thirty-five-year-old single mother and had learned the hard way to be organized in her life. Today was no exception. It was Amy's eleventh birthday. She checked the chocolate cake she had baked the previous evening and replaced the lid on the tin. In the cutlery drawer there were eleven small candles next to a box of matches plus a bag of balloons. All was prepared for her daughter's party that evening.

In the hallway she looked with pride at her tall, leggy daughter, her long brown hair in a neat French plait. Amy pulled on her new red padded coat along with a matching scarf and bobble hat while Mary checked her own appearance in the mirror. She looked immaculate in her light blue nurse's uniform including a starched white apron, black lace-up shoes, a navy-blue belt and her silver General Nursing Council badge. Mary was a staff nurse at the District Hospital in York and another busy day was in store.

It took a few attempts to start up her frozen two-door Opel Manta but Mary had allowed time for this. As usual, she pulled up further down the road to collect two more of the latchkey children, Jemima Poole and Siobhan Sharp.

'Happy birthday, Amy,' they chorused as they clambered in.

Jemima's brother, Jimmy, waved as he hurried past. Their dog, Scargill, a lively Yorkshire terrier, was enjoying his morning walk and barked loudly in greeting. Mary Bell was pleased she was safe in the driver's seat. Scargill had a reputation for biting your ankles if you got too close.

'Mrs Bell,' said a breathless Siobhan, 'please can you drop us off at the shop?'

'We want to buy something,' added the freckle-faced Jemima with a conspiratorial smile towards Mary's rear-view mirror.

It was a change to Mary's routine. The norm was to stop outside the school and watch the girls walk through the gate. She made a quick decision, turned left into the high street and pulled up outside the General Stores.

It was a decision that had unforeseen consequences.

*

Vera was at her desk when I walked into the office. 'Happy New Year, Mr Sheffield.'

'Happy New Year, Vera. It's a cold one.'

'Minus five according to Rupert.'

I glanced out of the window. Tyler and Zach had been joined by other early arrivals and were playing happily in the snow. 'The children don't seem to notice.'

'It's the same every year,' reflected Vera. She looked up at me and smiled, 'Generations come and go. I've watched them all grow up.' She glanced down at her numbers on the roll register. 'By the way, we've got two birthdays today. Patience Crapper and Amy Bell.' She wrote their names on her spiral-bound pad, tore off the sheet and passed it to me.

'Thanks Vera. We'll sing "Happy Birthday" in assembly.'

Pat and Sally were in the school hall setting up morning assembly when Anne walked past carrying the new box of safety scissors she had ordered before Christmas.

'Morning, Anne,' said Pat.

'Happy New Year,' said Sally. 'You're looking pleased with yourself.'

Anne smiled. 'I suppose I am.' She was wearing a new outfit: a white blouse, knitted sweater and a smart tweed skirt. Her hair had blonde highlights.

'Like the new look,' said Pat.

Sally knew her friend well. 'Come on. Tell all,' and they followed her into her classroom. Anne shut the door.

'I saw you in York market during the holiday,' said Sally. 'Then that gorgeous man suddenly appeared and I decided not to barge in.'

There was silence for a moment as Anne put down the

box of scissors and leaned back against her teacher's desk. A flurry of snowflakes tapped against the window pane. 'Yes, we've spent some time together.'

'And . . .?' said Sally, eager to hear more.

Anne smiled. 'It's early days.'

'You look happy,' said the phlegmatic Pat.

Sally grinned. 'It's good to see you looking relaxed.'

Anne realized how she valued their friendship. Their words were like a salve to the soul, a calmness over troubled waters.

'I'm in a better place,' she said simply.

Marcus was in the school library when I walked back to my classroom. He was deep in conversation with Charlie Cartwright and Ted Coggins.

'Good morning,' I said. 'What have you got there?'

Marcus raised his eyebrows. 'Slight problem here, Mr Sheffield. Charlie and Ted have decided they don't want to be farmers when they grow up.'

'That's right, sir,' said a determined Gary.

'Gary got this f'Chris'mas, sir,' said Ted. He held up a *Roy of the Rovers* annual.

'We want t'play f'Melchester Rovers, sir,' said Gary.

'Well, perhaps you could do both,' I said. 'Start off with Ragley Rovers while working on the farm.'

Marcus shook his head. 'That's not the main problem.'

'Oh . . . so what is?'

'We both want t'be striker, sir,' said Gary.

'Jus' like Roy,' said Ted. He held up the page showing the blond sharpshooter in the red and yellow strip with the number nine on his back.

'Ah, I see.' I gave Marcus a knowing look. 'Well, I'm sure Mr Potts will help you decide.'

'Thanks, Mr Sheffield,' said Marcus with a hint of irony, 'and a Happy New Year to you too.'

Jemima, Siobhan and Amy were outside the General Stores on the high street. 'You wait here, Amy,' said Jemima.

Siobhan nodded. 'We need to see Miss Golightly. It's a secret.'

'OK,' said Amy, intrigued but patient.

The bell above the door rang as the two girls walked into the shop.

'Good morning, girls,' said Prudence.

'Good morning, Miss Golightly,' said Jemima.

'And a Happy New Year, Jeremy,' said Siobhan. The girls looked up at Jeremy Bear, resplendent in his new Christmas outfit of cream shirt, brown cords and green waistcoat.

Prudence smiled. She loved it when children were polite. 'Jeremy says the jammy doughnuts you ordered for your party are in the back room.'

'Thank you, Jeremy,' said Jemima.

'He says it's a pleasure, girls.'

'They're Amy's favourite,' said Siobhan.

'I guess Jeremy prefers honey to jam,' said Jemima.

'Yes, he does,' said Prudence with utter conviction.

'So, we'll call in after school if that's all right,' said Siobhan.

'That's fine. I'll put them in a nice box ready for you to collect,' and she hurried off.

*

Across the road, sixteen-year-old Dean Skinner stubbed out a cigarette, rummaged in the pockets of his leather jacket and spat on the pavement in disgust. Then he stared at Amy Bell in the shop doorway. A skinny, scruffy youth in torn jeans and battered Doc Martens, Dean already had a criminal record after starting a fire last November in what was then our new Portakabin classroom. Playing truant from Easington Comprehensive School was a way of life for him. As usual he was looking for trouble. He had also smoked his last cigarette.

He crossed the road and pushed past Amy.

'Hey! Watch what you're doing,' she said.

'Piss off!' muttered Dean as he hurried into the shop. He ignored the two girls, saw that the shop owner wasn't in sight and ran around the counter. After grabbing two packs of Benson & Hedges he ran out and collided with Amy.

Dorothy Robinson, now in her sixth month of pregnancy, was looking out of her bedroom window and saw her husband's refuse wagon appear at the far end of the high street. She stared down at her dressing table and smiled. Dorothy had taken advantage of the January sales in the village Pharmacy and made a difficult choice regarding lipsticks. Was it to be Scarletti at £1.80 or should she splash out on Mary Quant's Red Scorcher at £3.25?

You're only young once, she had thought and, after checking the contents of her purse, she went for the Scorcher.

The pharmacist, Eugene Scrimshaw, had approved. As usual he was wearing his Captain Kirk uniform under his white coat. 'Good choice,' he said. 'Ah think that's what Uhura wears.'

'Who?'

''Er in *Star Trek*,' said Eugene. 'She's my chief communications officer on t'Starship *Enterprise*.' As the years went by Eugene was beginning to believe he actually was Captain Kirk.

'Well . . . my Malcolm will love it,' said a slightly puzzled Dorothy.

Cosmetics were not uppermost on the mind of Little Malcolm.

'Back on t'bins again, Dave,' he muttered as he picked up his first bin of 1988.

'Cheer up, Malc,' said Big Dave. 'Fresh air an' freedom.'

'Yer reight there, Dave,' said Malcolm without conviction. The strong odour of the remains of a fish supper filled his nostrils as he carried the bin from Diane's Hair Salon towards their wagon. Ragley's intrepid bin men had made an early start and were looking forward to calling into Nora's Coffee Shop for a warm pork pie and a mug of sweet tea, otherwise known as *second breakfast*.

'Hey, Dave, summat's up!' shouted Little Malcolm. 'Come on quick. It's that Mrs Skinner's son,' and he set off skidding across the pavement with Big Dave close behind.

Further down the street a youth with long dark hair had burst out of the General Stores and bumped into a young girl. He slipped on the icy forecourt and fell flat on his face. The packs of cigarettes spilled from his grasp and tumbled into the drifting snow. He turned to the terrified Amy. 'Stupid bitch!' he shouted. He jumped up and raised his fist. Then he saw the two burly bin men bearing down on him and ran off down the high street as if the hounds of hell were chasing him.

'We'll never catch 'im now,' panted Big Dave. 'Go see if that little lass is OK.'

Jemima and Siobhan had run out of the shop, closely followed by Prudence.

'Oh no,' said Prudence. 'How are you, my dear?'

The colour had returned to Amy's cheeks as she stood up. 'What a horrible boy.'

Big Dave looked concerned. 'D'yer need t'sit down, luv?'

'Yer've 'ad a nasty shock,' said Little Malcolm.

'I'm fine, thank you.' She brushed the snow from her coat. 'I ought to get off to school with my friends.'

Jemima glanced up at the two bin men. 'We'll look after her, Mr Robinson.'

'Thanks for stopping,' said Siobhan.

'What d'you think, Miss Golightly?' asked Big Dave.

'Well, she seems to be recovered. I saw the whole thing and she didn't bang her head.' Prudence studied Amy thoughtfully. 'Perhaps it would be for the best to go to school and tell Mr Sheffield what has happened.'

''E's a proper tearaway is that Dean Skinner,' said Little Malcolm. 'Allus causin' trouble.'

'You're quite right, Malcolm,' said Prudence. 'I've caught him shoplifting before now. I'll tell PC Pike. He'll know what to do.'

Amy looked fully recovered. 'Thanks for helping, everybody.'

'Wait a moment,' said Prudence. 'I think a nice sweet barley sugar is called for,' and she hurried back into the shop and reappeared with a bag of sweets. Everyone took one including Big Dave, who crunched his immediately.

'Oh dear,' said Prudence, who believed barley sugar should be savoured, not shattered. They all laughed as the tension disappeared. Big Dave and Little Malcolm wandered back to their refuse wagon and the girls walked back up the high street towards school. Meanwhile Prudence picked up the packets of cigarettes, wiped them on her pinny and shook her head. 'What's the world coming to?' she muttered.

It took a while for Vera to make contact with Mary Bell at the hospital. She was busy doing her morning rounds when the message to ring school finally reached her.

'I'll come right away if you wish,' said Mary.

'That's up to you, Mrs Bell,' said Vera, 'but there's no need. It's really just to let you know what's happened. Amy's suffered no injuries and I've spoken to Miss Golightly who saw the whole incident. She said it was a shock more than anything.'

'That's a relief,' said Mary, 'but I'm here if needed.'

'And we sang "Happy Birthday" to her at the end of morning assembly.'

'That's thoughtful. Many thanks.'

'Also, Miss Golightly has informed the police and PC Pike will be visiting the boy's home.'

'That's good to hear.' Vera heard a buzzing noise. 'Ah, I've been paged again. Thanks for letting me know.'

Marcus brought his *Guardian* newspaper into the staffroom at morning break. 'How about this,' he announced.

'Mrs Thatcher has now been in office for over three thousand days, overtaking Asquith as the longest-serving Prime Minister.'

'A wonderful achievement,' said Vera as she prepared our mugs of coffee.

'Oh dear,' muttered Sally.

Marcus pressed on. 'And, according to Sir John Nott, she thinks all men are feeble and *gentlemen* are even more feeble.'

Vera smiled. It was something she had believed for years.

'Ah well,' said Sally, 'occasionally Mrs Milk-Snatcher gets something right.'

Vera made no comment. Her political heroine needed no defence and, after all, why spoil the pleasure of a new pack of Brontë biscuits and a warming mug of coffee?

At the end of school Amy, Jemima and Siobhan looked excited as they collected their coats from the cloakroom. 'Are you going straight to the party?' I asked.

'No, sir. We're going to Jemima's first,' said Amy.

'It's *Jackanory* on telly, sir,' said Jemima. 'Rik Mayall's reading *George's Marvellous Medicine*.'

'We all love Roald Dahl,' said Siobhan. Like Amy, she was one of my best readers.

'Then we're putting on our party dresses,' said Jemima.

'And my mum will be picking us up when she finishes work,' said Amy.

It was good to see the enthusiasm in their young faces and I watched them walk out into the darkness with pride.

*

I was marking books at my desk when Sally popped her head round the classroom door.

'Jack, Albert Jenkins has called in for a quick word. He's in the staff-room. Vera's making a pot of tea.'

'Thanks, Sally.' It was always refreshing to catch up with our erudite school governor.

She grinned. 'And he's brought in some leftover Christmas cake.'

It was a close thing who reached the staff-room first!

Amy was standing outside the General Stores when it happened. She was waiting for Jemima and Siobhan to come out and smiling in anticipation.

'You again,' said a voice from behind her. It was Dean Skinner. He was holding a can of lager, the last of a pack of six he had stolen from the off-licence in Easington.

The smile left her face. 'Go away.'

'You got me into trouble this mornin'.' His eyes were like ice, glittering with frozen malice. He stepped closer and drank in her fear. She backed away towards the road as he raised his fist. 'So ah'll finish what ah started.'

Amy was too frightened to scream. She turned and ran. Her red woollen bobble hat fell on to the pavement. In a drunken haze he lurched across the road after her. The gate to the village hall was open and she ran through it. At the back of the hall beyond the orchard was a storage shed. It could have been a place to hide but she was too late. When she looked over her shoulder she saw he was right behind her. Suddenly she stumbled over a wooden pallet and fell heavily on the snow. He grabbed her by her coat and slapped her face.

'Not smilin' now are you, bitch,' he shouted. Then he unlatched the shed door and threw her inside. As she landed on a pile of sacks, she heard him slam the door and drag something heavy up against it.

Then all was silent. She stood up and pushed the door. It wouldn't budge. She beat it with her fists. 'Let me out!' she cried but there was no one to hear. There were no windows and there was no light. She was trapped.

We were all enjoying a cup of tea and a slice of Albert's cake when the telephone rang in Vera's office. When she returned there was concern on her face.

'What is it?'

She walked to the window and stared out into the darkness. 'Amy Bell's gone missing on the way home.'

'Missing?' said Anne, suddenly alarmed.

Everyone put down their cup. The mood changed immediately.

'It was Prudence on the phone. She said Amy had been waiting outside the shop while Jemima and Siobhan collected some party food. When they came out she'd gone.'

'Perhaps she went to Jemima's house?' I said. 'They mentioned they were going there to watch television before the party.'

Vera shook her head. 'Prudence said they checked there straight away. The girls ran home but she's not there. Mrs Poole and Mrs Sharp have come out to look.'

'We need to contact her mother,' I said.

'I'll do that,' said Vera. 'There's something else. One of the girls found Amy's woolly hat on the pavement.'

There was a moment's silence as the implication hit

home. Then Pat, Anne and Sally began fetching their coats and scarves.

'What can we do to help?' asked Marcus.

'We can join the search,' I said.

Anne reappeared. 'Jack, why don't you and I walk up the high street and maybe Pat and Marcus could drive up the Easington Road and start looking there.'

'We could do with someone to stay here by the telephone with Vera,' said Sally. 'I can do that.' Vera gave her an almost imperceptible nod of approval.

'I'll come with you, Jack,' said Albert.

'I'll contact Beth,' said Vera. 'You might be late.'

I prayed it wouldn't be *too* late.

I had always found it remarkable the speed with which news could travel around the village. Word was passed from shop to shop and house to house. Our local bobby, PC Julian Pike, had been off duty and enjoying a meal in The Royal Oak with his girlfriend, Natasha Smith. When they heard the news he grabbed his greatcoat and was out on the high street organizing the search.

Ted Postlethwaite, the postman, had found two torches and said he would go with his wife, Amelia, up Chaunt-singer Lane. Old Tommy Piercy and his grandson decided to search the cricket field. Diane Wigglesworth and her mother, along with a few of her regular customers, had set off down the high street towards Pratt's garage. Timothy Pratt had called his friend Walter Crapper and asked him to drive slowly down the back road to Kirkby Steepleton while George Dainty and Ruby were doing the same up the Morton Road. Big Dave and Little Malcolm were searching all the back yards they knew so well. Meanwhile Vera had asked Rupert and her brother, the Revd Joseph, to search the churchyard and the back of the vicarage. Then she and Sally waited by the phone.

By six o'clock there was still no sign of Amy. All the shops on the high street had remained brightly lit and Nora, Doreen and Nellie were serving free hot drinks from the Coffee Shop. A trestle table under the awning outside Pratt's Hardware Emporium appeared to become the command centre and at intervals we all gravitated towards it to share our news, including Vera and Sally who had become tired of sitting by a silent phone.

At seven o'clock PC Pike decided to call in a couple of his constable friends from the York Police to provide extra back-up. He came over to speak to us, concern on his face. 'If she's out in the open she might not survive. I'll need to mobilize more help before too long.'

'What about Dean Skinner and the incident this morning at the shop?' asked Anne.

'A bad lot,' muttered Albert.

'I've been to his house. There was no sign of him. We'll pick him up as soon as he gets home.'

'There could be a connection,' I said.

He nodded, deep in thought.

Time ticked by and we became more anxious. The temperature had dropped like a stone. When I took a deep breath the chilled air filled my lungs. The situation was getting desperate. PC Pike was providing leadership but we were like scattered souls in a crucible of confusion. The unthinkable was getting closer. In the midst of uncertainty it was as if we were waiting for the hammer blow.

As the church clock chimed eight we gathered again out-side the Coffee Shop and stared into the still darkness. And at that moment the dam burst. Mary Bell was overcome with a tidal wave of fear. Although she was an experienced nurse and had witnessed at first hand the suffering of patients, this was different. This was *her* child, her Amy.

Suddenly she began to weep. Anne and Pat took her into the Coffee Shop and tried to provide some comfort. I took Albert Jenkins to one side. He was the elder statesman, a man I had always respected, calm in a crisis. 'Albert, this is serious. Look around. We're losing hope.'

We stood side by side in a world of darkness. Above us twinkling stars appeared amidst the scudding clouds that promised more snow.

He gave me a level stare. 'Jack, Fyodor Dostoevsky once said, "To live without hope is to cease to live."'

I shook my head in despair. 'Albert, she's gone and we don't know where. One of my pupils is out there some-where . . . lost in the dark.'

He squeezed my shoulder and pointed to the heavens. 'Have faith, Jack. The darker the night the brighter the stars.'

It was years later that I recollected his words of hope on that bitterly cold night. I was in a second-hand bookshop in Oxford and a copy of the writings of Dostoevsky was on the shelf. It was when I read it that I remembered the moment our fortunes changed. It began with the barking of a dog.

Jimmy Poole had arrived with Scargill and it was PC Julian Pike who had the idea. 'Jemima, give me the bobble hat you found.'

She passed it over and he gave it to Jimmy. 'Jimmy, think carefully. Could Scargill follow her scent?'

'Yes,' said Jimmy. I was pleased that speech therapy had finally corrected the lisp that had been part of his young life. 'Scargill is t'best blood'ound in Yorkshire.' Jimmy was intensely proud of his Yorkshire terrier, who apparently could take on the guise of any breed at a moment's notice.

Jimmy had Scargill on a long lead and we followed him down the high street towards the village hall. Moments later the dog was snuffling in the frozen grass by the gate that led to the hall. I was puzzled. I knew a group had checked the village hall. Suddenly he nearly pulled Jimmy off his feet as he scampered round the back of the building. In a wooded area behind a couple of cherry trees was a small shed. There was a wooden pallet propped against the door. Big Dave was the first to react and lifted the pallet effortlessly while Little Malcolm pulled open the door. Amy's pale white face looked up at us. Julian Pike crouched down beside her. 'You're safe now,' he said quietly and put his greatcoat around her shoulders.

I'll never forget the cheering on the high street and Mary Bell's relief on being reunited with her daughter. After a warming hot chocolate in the Coffee Shop and a brief statement to PC Pike, Amy recovered quickly.

Mary held her daughter and asked quietly, 'Amy . . . did he touch you in any way?'

Amy shook her head. 'He slapped me once and pushed me into the shed. That's all.'

There was a nod of understanding between PC Pike and Mary Bell.

'What about my party, Mum?' she asked and her mother burst into tears once again. This time they were tears of joy.

*

On Tuesday morning we heard that Dean Skinner had been taken to Easington Police Station and charged with unlawful restraint. I was standing by the school gate when Amy Bell arrived hand in hand with her mother. Her friends Jemima and Siobhan were in close attendance. 'My party is tonight, sir,' said Amy. 'I'm so excited.' She ran up the drive with her friends.

I reflected on the resilience of youth and Mrs Bell gave me a knowing look. 'I thought I'd lost her, Mr Sheffield,' she said quietly.

So did I, I thought but said nothing.

A few mothers were arriving as we stood at the gate. All of them wanted to give Mary a hug. It was an emotional scene. You could see the relief in their eyes that it hadn't been *their* child.

Suddenly Jimmy Poole appeared on the village green with Scargill, out for their usual morning walk. Mrs Bell stared at the dog and smiled.

'What is it?' I asked.

'Just a thought,' she said with a mischievous grin.

'Yes?'

'Am I allowed to swear in front of my daughter's headteacher?'

I was curious. 'On this occasion, of course . . . but why?'

'Well, Mr Sheffield. When the butcher's opens I'm going to buy the biggest bloody bone in the shop.'

And she did!

Chapter Ten

Knickers in a Twist

The Revd Joseph Evans attended our impromptu staff meeting at the end of school. Mrs Forbes-Kitchener announced her decision to retire at the end of this academic year.
Extract from the Ragley & Morton School Logbook:
Monday, 18 January 1988

'We can't display this on the village hall noticeboard,' said a determined Vera. 'The Women's Institute must have *standards*.'

It was Monday, 18 January, and Joyce Davenport, president of the local WI, had called into school to speak to her long-time friend.

'But it's all arranged,' said Joyce. 'We had to find a replacement speaker at short notice. Melissa Montague was rushed into hospital with appendicitis.'

'I'm aware of that and her talk "Helping Hedgehogs"

would have been perfectly suitable but this is, well . . . rather vulgar.'

'Beggars can't be choosers, Vera, and I'm sure it will be of interest. After all, it's part of our social history.'

'But the title, Joyce . . . surely you don't approve.'

Joyce looked again at the poster. 'I find it quite catchy. It will definitely arouse interest and we've opened it to new-comers. We need some younger members.'

'Oh dear,' said Vera.

'And, unlike Miss Montague, Mrs Blenkinsopp is not requesting a fee, merely the opportunity to bring along cop-ies of her latest book. She's rather famous by all accounts.'

Vera looked aghast. 'You mean she's actually written a book on this subject!'

'Yes, Vera.' Joyce glanced at her wristwatch. 'Anyway, you will have to excuse me. Richard has a doctors' seminar in York and I promised to drive him there.' She gave Vera a hug and a kiss on the cheek. 'Please don't be upset, we've been friends for too long.'

With that she hurried out and Vera stared at the poster on her desk. It read:

Ragley & Morton WI
Wednesday, 20 January 1988
7.30 p.m.
'KNICKERS'
The History of Ladies' Undergarments
A talk by Alma Blenkinsopp
Author & Social Historian
Open to non-members (ladies only)
Including light refreshments

*

Forty-five-year-old Alma Blenkinsopp had led an interesting life.

She lived in Thirkby market town and was a keen member of the Liberating Spirit Evangelical Church, a happy-clappy place of worship. There was lots of arm waving, hallelujahs and a Cliff Richard lookalike who had learned to play three chords after receiving a Bert Weedon *Play in a Day* guitar book from his Aunty Maureen.

Brought up in the school of hard knocks in West Yorkshire, hers had been a life of derring-do and taking chances. In the sixties she had worn a Mary Quant miniskirt, read Homer's *Iliad* and sung Joan Baez protest songs. On a Ban the Bomb march in London she had met the handsome Digby Winfield, an old Etonian into stocks and shares. Sadly, he was also into gambling, drugs and chorus girls and after a tempestuous liaison she moved back to Yorkshire to become an Avon lady.

Ding-dong went each doorbell until one day the wealthy builder, Stanley Blenkinsopp, answered the door. After that it was ding-dong in the bedroom. In The Cock & Bottle pub Stanley presented her with a port and lemon and an engagement ring and they were married three months later. After Stanley died of asbestosis at the end of the seventies, Alma became a wealthy widow.

In the early eighties she wore her Greenham Common poncho with pride but was still searching for her true identity. It was when she was making decisions concerning Ovaltine or Bournvita followed by Garibaldi biscuits or custard creams that she realized life had lost its bite and had been replaced by a numbing routine. That was until one evening she was staring at her reflection in her bedroom mirror. She was wearing her new range of black lingerie when the idea came to her.

'I'll write a book,' she said.

As her mother had once said, 'Our Alma doesn't do anything by halves.'

At lunchtime in the staff-room Pat had brought in her *Food Aid Cookery Book*. 'I thought you might like this, Vera. There's a royal cookery page with Lady Diana's favourite recipes.'

'How kind. Thank you so much.'

'I know this will appeal,' said Pat. 'Lady Diana's Watercress Soup.'

'Perfect,' said Vera.

'Well, it would be if Lady Di has anything to do with it,' said Sally, our anti-royalist.

'I think she's a lovely woman,' said Marcus. 'Just a shame she married Charlie-boy.'

'I have some sympathy there,' said Anne. 'Sorry, Vera,' she added with an apologetic smile.

'Oh, look at this,' said Vera. 'Prince Charles's Sorrel Soup. It says here he grows sorrel at Highgrove.'

'Or perhaps it's his head gardener,' said Sally with a hint of irony. 'Also, I heard he missed eating plums in Balmoral last summer so he spent six thousand pounds for a case to be flown from London to Scotland.'

'I remember that,' said Marcus. 'It worked out at twenty-five pounds per plum.'

'How the other half live,' muttered Sally as she returned to her magazine and an article about Bruce Willis being voted the world's sexiest man.

Vera was used to this type of banter and sat back to read Terry Wogan's foreword to the book. It helped to take her mind off the WI poster and the announcement she had prepared for the end of school.

At four o'clock we all gathered in the staff-room. Vera and Joseph were already there and talking quietly.

'Hello, everybody,' said Joseph as we all sat down.

'This is intriguing,' said Marcus. 'We don't usually have a staff meeting on a Monday.'

Anne glanced at Vera and then at me as if she knew what was coming.

'I've prepared a pot of tea,' said Vera, 'if anyone would like a cup.'

There was a chorus of 'Yes, please'.

Vera put a large tin on the table and removed the lid. 'Also I made a cherry cake from my *Be-Ro Home Recipes* book that I thought you might enjoy,' and she placed plates, forks and serviettes beside it. 'So please help yourselves.' Anne sliced it up while Vera served us with tea.

'What a treat,' said Pat and everyone settled back in a chair while munching delicious cake and sipping our hot drinks.

'Thanks for staying behind, everybody,' I said, 'and you'll soon understand why Joseph has joined us in his role of Chair of Governors. I'm afraid this is not one of our normal meetings.' I turned to our school secretary, 'Vera has an announcement to make.'

There was a stunned silence and puzzled looks with the exception of Anne, who gave me a sad smile.

Vera clasped her hands as if in prayer and spoke quietly.

'I've discussed what I'm about to say with my husband, my brother and with Jack.'

There was a surprised look from Pat and Marcus who had never heard Vera calling me by my first name.

'As you all know, school has been a huge part of my life. I love my job dearly but all good things come to an end.' She sighed and looked across at Anne. 'Our years are finite in this life. It is up to us to use each one of them wisely.'

You could have heard a pin drop as we hung on every word. 'So it's time for someone else to take over. The truth is I'm not getting any younger and I need to spend more time with Rupert. He's a lovely man and I want to enjoy a little more of his companionship for the next stage of our lives.' She looked around at all our faces. 'The past cannot be changed ... but we can. I've written to the governors and they will put in place arrangements to appoint my successor commencing in the autumn term. So I'll be leaving in July. I wanted you all to know before my letter is delivered by Joseph to the governing body.'

She sat back while around her the response was both surprised and sincere. Anne wiped away a tear. Sally leaned across and held Vera's hand. Pat looked visibly shocked while Marcus shook his head and murmured, 'I'll miss you.'

After that it was a subdued group that chatted about life after Vera. We finished our tea and cake and drifted out into a bitterly cold night.

It was mid evening when the telephone rang at Morton Manor.

'Hello, Vera, sorry to disturb your evening. It's Emmeline here.'

'Emmeline, good to hear from you. How can I help?'

'I should like to volunteer to join your Flower Committee at St Mary's. I enjoy flower arranging and was wondering if I could help.'

Vera smiled. Regardless of her flower-arranging credentials, she considered Emmeline to be the perfect companion for her brother. 'Of course you can. Call into the manor and we can discuss it further.'

'That's most kind, Vera. Would Wednesday be convenient? I heard about the open meeting for your WI so perhaps I could catch up with you there.'

There was a moment's hesitation on Vera's part. 'Yes, that's fine. I'll see you then.'

It was Wednesday afternoon and the poster outside the village hall had caused a buzz of conversation among the women of the village. Meanwhile, in Diane's Hair Salon, Margery Ackroyd scanned the magazine photographs of film stars stuck around the frame of the big mirror.

'So, what's it t'be, Marge?' asked Diane.

'Ah'll 'ave a Michelle Pfeiffer.'

'Comin' up,' said Diane with false enthusiasm but, sadly, little confidence. 'So ... any news?' Margery, as the renowned local gossip, always had insights into the incongruous happenings in the village.

'Well, you'll never guess.'

Diane stubbed out her cigarette and picked up her tray of rollers. 'Go on.'

'It were Betty's birthday an' 'er 'Arry bought 'er a membership f'Cliff Richard's fan club.'

'That were thoughtful,' said Diane, lighting up another

cigarette and blowing the smoke towards the closed window.

'Not sure 'bout that. Ah told 'er 'e's tight wi' 'is money.'

'Who? Cliff Richard?'

'No, 'er 'Arry. Deep pockets an' short arms.'

''Ow come?'

'It's only four poun'.'

Diane stared at their reflections in the mirror. To her that sounded very generous.

'She said Cliff sends all t'profits t'charity,' said Margery in disgust. 'So ah told 'er straight: charity begins at 'ome.'

'Yer right there, Marge.' Diane had learned long ago to agree with her customers, particularly those who believed a quick trim, half a dozen rollers and a blast of hairspray could transform them into a Michelle Pfeiffer lookalike.

'She should be in *my* fan club,' insisted Margery.

'What's that then?'

'Cagney an' Lacey o' course. Only a fiver an y'get a free calendar, autographed photo an' a really int'restin' news-letter.'

'Sounds good,' said Diane, again with false enthusiasm. Her mother had taught her that the customer is always right and she had never forgotten.

Diane had done her best (although the 'Michelle Pfeiffer' was more of a 'Worzel Gummidge') and Margery was about to leave. 'So, d'you fancy that talk 'bout knickers t'night?' she asked.

'Ah'll be there,' said Diane . . . and this time with *genuine* enthusiasm.

*

It was shortly before seven o'clock when Miss Emmeline Best drove up the Morton Road while rooks strutted on the church tower. Their malevolent squawks echoed in the freezing air and they stared down with beady eyes on the huddle of figures below heading towards the bright lights of the village hall. She parked outside the vicarage, picked up a shopping bag, tapped the door knocker and shivered.

Joseph answered. 'Hello, Emmeline, come in out of the cold. It's lovely to see you.'

'Sorry, Joseph, I can't stay. I'm on my way to the village hall. There's an open evening for the WI.'

'Yes, I heard. Vera said she would call in afterwards.'

'We've arranged to have a chat about the Flower Committee. I've volunteered to join.'

Joseph beamed with delight. 'That's wonderful.'

'Anyway, I've brought you something. I know you enjoy winemaking so I thought you might like to try my beetroot wine. It's a great winter warmer.' She passed over the bottle.

'That's most kind. I didn't know you were interested in winemaking.'

'It was one of my hobbies when I lived in the Lake District.'

'Why not call in with Vera after the meeting? We can sample it together.'

'Thank you. I'll see what Vera says. Anyway, must rush. There was a queue outside the hall when I drove past.'

Joseph watched her drive away and then stared in delight at the bottle.

*

The hall was full and the excited chatter died down as Joyce Davenport stood up on the stage.

'Good evening, ladies. As president it gives me great pleasure to see so many new faces here this evening. We're keen to extend our membership, so if anyone would like to join our wonderful Women's Institute, please see our secretary, Mrs Forbes-Kitchener, before you leave.'

She turned to Alma Blenkinsopp. 'It's also my pleasant duty to welcome this evening's speaker and we thank her for stepping into the breach at such short notice.'

Everyone turned to the smart, fashionable lady sitting behind the president's table. She wore a beautifully tailored lavender linen trouser suit and a white blouse with a frilly collar and appeared confident and relaxed.

'There is no doubt the subject for tonight's talk has created great interest and, at the end, there will be an opportunity to ask questions and purchase a signed copy of Mrs Blenkinsopp's bestselling paperback *The Ups and Downs of Knickers*. We are also grateful to the social committee who have provided a light supper. So, without further ado, please join with me to welcome Mrs Alma Blenkinsopp.'

Applause rang out and Alma walked to the front of the stage.

'Good evening, ladies. Sadly, I'm a widow but after spending far too long grieving I decided to do something useful with my life.'

There were murmurs of sympathy and appreciation. Vera nodded in reserved approval. This lady knew how to get the audience on her side.

'A year ago I was in my underwear and wondering why

we wore garments that were often uncomfortable. It struck me that we might simply be trying to comply with an image of which *men* approve, and I asked myself why should I bother?'

The audience was clearly warming to her and there was a ripple of applause.

'Personally, as a member of the Women's Liberation Movement in the sixties, I burned my bra and felt emancipated. However, in later years I discovered ladies' underwear has gone through great changes through the ages. Today you only have to see Cher at an awards ceremony wearing a G-string bodysuit to realize how far we have come. Underwear has become *outerwear*.'

There was laughter and a few comments of 'Quite right'.

'Now, ladies, how about this. Panties were first worn during the Renaissance not only as a functional part of a lady's attire but also as a chastity device. They also prevented young men seeing their thighs if they fell off a horse. Then, in the nineteenth century, you may be surprised to hear that drawers were designed so that each leg was a separate garment, hence "a pair of drawers".'

Vera leaned forward, suddenly interested.

'By 1841 French drawers were viewed to be of great advantage to women and prevented many disorders. They were made of flannel, calico or cotton and reached as far down the leg as possible. In time they became known as smalls, britches, step-ins and, of course, *knickers* from the word knickerbockers.'

Vera thought, *I didn't know that.*

It was when Alma discussed the evolution of the corset and returned to the fashions of Ancient Greece and the

Romans that Vera sat up and began to take proper notice. She realized that this lady had done considerable research and was really quite knowledgeable. By the end of the talk Vera was visibly impressed.

After thunderous applause and a vote of thanks everyone was served with a cup of tea and a plate of sandwiches and cakes. Vera was surrounded by young women who wanted to become members and she understood that the evening had been a huge success. When the crowd was starting to thin out, she approached Alma.

'Excuse me, Mrs Blenkinsopp, may I have a word?'

'Of course.'

'I'm Vera, this year's secretary, and I just wanted to say that I had great reservations about the subject of your talk before I came but I really enjoyed it and learned a lot. I found the historical facts most illuminating. So thank you.'

They shook hands and Alma beamed with delight. 'That's most kind of you, Vera, and please call me Alma. I felt I needed to do something with my life that was not only purposeful but promoted women. I do admit the subject is rather risqué but it's a good vehicle for bringing us together.'

'I agree,' said Vera. 'So, congratulations.'

Emmeline offered to help clear the hall and she and Vera were among the last to leave. 'So, it's settled then,' said Vera, after hearing of Joseph's invitation to return to the vicarage and sample the beetroot wine. 'I'll see you there in a few minutes.' And they both drove off up the high street.

Soon the two of them were sitting in front of a roaring fire. However, the beetroot wine was not in sight. 'I wanted you to try this one,' said Joseph, holding up a dusty bottle. 'It's my Haw Wine Supreme.'

'Joseph bestows very modest titles on his home-made wine,' said Vera with a smile.

Undeterred, Joseph pressed on. 'You'll enjoy its unique flavour. I made it from the berries of the hawthorn. It's a delicate pink wine.'

Emmeline sipped it carefully. 'Ah, it's lovely, Joseph.'

'Actually, it isn't, Joseph,' said Vera. 'Emmeline is being polite.'

'Well, what's wrong with it?' he demanded.

'It's not clear.'

'That can't be helped. It's always like that.'

'Yes, mine was the same,' said Emmeline gently, 'but it can be corrected with the addition of a little pectin.'

'Really?' said Joseph, confused.

'Yes. I used to have lots of problems when I started out, particularly with acidity. I solved that with a potassium carbonate solution.'

'Oh, I see,' said Joseph, beginning to look deflated.

Vera was smiling at the exchange while Emmeline was on a roll. 'Also I had difficulties with my dandelion wine. The stalk contains a bitter milk that can contaminate the flavour but I discovered it can be easily remedied.'

'Can it?' Joseph looked bemused by this outpouring of information; apparently Emmeline was a winemaking aficionado.

'Perhaps it's time for a cup of tea, Joseph?' said Vera and gave her brother a determined look.

Joseph left for the kitchen looking a little downtrodden.

'Oh dear, Vera, I've upset him.'

'It's not you, Emmeline. He's a bit precious about his wine. He's a lovely man but there's something about his winemaking that changes him. I've quoted to him often, "Do nothing out of selfish ambition or vain conceit."'

Emmeline thought for a moment, 'Philippians two,' she said quietly.

Vera smiled, clearly impressed. 'Yes, verse three.'

'I was thinking,' said Emmeline, 'do you think Joseph might like a sausagemeat plait? There was a recipe in my *Woman's Own*.'

'He would love it. I try to cook for him once a week because, to be honest, he hasn't much idea.'

'Then I'll do it.'

'In the meantime, let's cheer him up,' said Vera.

'I agree,' said Emmeline. 'He looked a little deflated.'

'I wouldn't worry too much,' said Vera with a mischievous grin. 'I think he's got his knickers in a twist.'

They both burst out laughing and, in the kitchen, Joseph wondered why.

Chapter Eleven

The Conversion of Stanley Coe

*Mr Evans completed Bible studies lessons with Classes 2
and 4. Ms Cleverley visited school and discussed forthcoming initiatives for the National Curriculum with the
headteacher. Today was the coldest day of the winter with a
temperature of minus ten degrees.*
Extract from the Ragley & Morton School Logbook:
Friday, 12 February 1988

It had been a frozen dawn and trails of woodsmoke drifted
across a gunmetal sky. The bitter rhythms of winter had
scoured the land and Ragley village had woken up to some
equally chilling news. As I drove through the school gate
Ruby left her yard broom by the entrance steps and hurried
over to the car park.

'You'll never guess in a month o' Sundays, Mr Sheffield,'
she shouted.

'What's that, Ruby?'

''E's out!'

'Who's out?'

'That Stanley Coe. Large as life. My George saw 'im las' night. 'E were in T'Pig an' Ferret wi' all 'is duck-shootin' mates gettin' drunk as a lord. Mark my words, there'll be trouble.'

Stan Coe had caused problems for me ever since I had arrived at Ragley School. That is until his misdemeanours finally caught up with him and he was jailed for six months for fraud, bribery and corruption. Stan's nefarious activities were legendary. He had even tried to turn the hallowed turf of the village cricket ground into a building site. For Old Tommy Piercy this was nothing short of sacrilege.

'Thanks for letting me know, Ruby.'

This was bad news.

It was Friday, 12 February, and I had a sinking feeling.

When I walked into the office Vera was on the telephone. 'Yes, Ms Cleverley. I'll inform Mr Sheffield.' She replaced the receiver and gave me a forlorn look. 'She's calling in at the end of morning school.'

My day was getting worse. 'Oh dear.' Out of the window some of the early arrivals were playing in the snow. In spite of the record low temperature, as reported on this morning's news, they looked happy in their world of childhood. 'I guess you've heard about Stan Coe.'

Vera had begun to open the morning mail with her brass paper knife. She placed it on top of the pile and clasped her hands. 'It's all around the village. I see trouble ahead.'

'Too true,' I said quietly.

'Were you aware my brother has been visiting him in jail?'

'I had heard but don't know any details.'

'The problem is Joseph believes he's a changed man.'

'Hard to believe.'

'Exactly, Mr Sheffield,' and she returned to slicing open the envelopes. 'And, by the way, Joseph is in today.' She glanced up at the timetable. 'Bible studies with Mr Potts and then Ms Brookside.'

'Thanks, Vera,' and I set off for my classroom and a day that would live long in the annals of Ragley village.

It was 10.15 a.m. and Joseph had struggled with the lively children in Marcus's class but felt a little more at ease with the older ones in Class 2. The behaviour in Pat's class was always excellent, even with our well-meaning but often bumbling vicar. He had begun by talking about God and the power of prayer until Scott Higginbottom raised his hand. 'So where exactly is God, Mr Evans?'

Joseph gave an enigmatic smile. 'He's everywhere, Scott, and He will always listen to what you say.' He glanced at the clock. There were fifteen minutes remaining before morning break. 'In fact, let's do a writing exercise and you can ask questions of God.'

In the staff-room at morning break Vera served her brother with a much-needed mug of coffee. Joseph placed the children's exercise books on the table. As was often the case in his lessons, their responses were not what he had expected and we both took the opportunity to glance through a few of them.

181

Patience Crapper, as usual, didn't take prisoners. As her mother had told me many times, 'Y'don't mess wi' our Patience ... allus calls a spade a shovel.' The boisterous, assertive little girl had written, 'Dear God, How did you know you were God? Who told you?' Tyler Longbottom was even more forthright: 'Dear God, I'm from Leeds. Where are you from?'

Thankfully, Rosie Spittlehouse was generous in her praise. 'Dear God, Well done for creating the heaven and the earth but how did you get all the stars in the right places?' There were signs that Sam Whittaker was on his way to becoming a shop steward. 'Dear God, Mr Evans says Sunday is a day of rest so why does he have to work?' The thoughtful Becky Shawcross was delving into more philosophical matters. 'Dear God, We did a project about inventions. Did you already know about them before they were invented?' Conversely, the ever-practical Billy Ricketts was more concerned about God's career development. 'Dear God, After making the earth did you have another job?' So it went on and, not for the first time, Joseph wondered whether he should have chosen another career, perhaps as a librarian or a deep-sea diver.

I sipped my coffee and sat back in my chair. 'I heard from Ruby that Stan Coe is out of prison.'

'Sadly, yes,' said Vera with a sigh.

'Actually, he's a changed man,' said Joseph. 'Apart from his sister, Deirdre, I was the only one who visited him and I honestly believe the rage that was at the core of his being has drained away. He's definitely moved on. In fact, he told me the poison has been purged from his thoughts.'

'Noble words, Joseph,' said Vera, 'but this is Stanley Coe we're talking about. He's been a bully all his life.'

'A cheat,' said Anne with feeling.

'And a liar,' added Sally.

Joseph seemed determined. 'Well, it's been difficult for him in prison, particularly with some of the younger inmates.'

Vera and Anne looked askance at Joseph. Although it was admirable that he always sought the good in people there was a hapless naivety about him.

'I introduced him to a few Bible stories.'

'Such as . . . if you don't mind me asking?' said Vera with obvious scepticism.

'A very appropriate story that you know well. The conversion of St Paul on the road to Damascus,' said Joseph with a beatific smile, 'and he was most receptive.'

'I bet he was,' said Vera.

Joseph frowned. 'But, Vera, he was a broken man and now it's time to rebuild and renew. In fact, I decided to display true Christian values so I've invited him to the vicarage tonight for a light supper.'

Vera almost dropped her cup in horror. 'You've done what? That man must not set foot in our home.'

'I'm sorry you feel that way, Vera, and, of course, you will recall it's *my* home now.'

He walked out quietly and everyone looked at Vera in surprise. We had never witnessed such a disagreement between brother and sister before.

Vera recovered quickly. 'Apologies, everybody.'

Anne went to sit next to her. 'He probably thinks he's doing the right thing. Sadly, we all know better.'

Vera shook her head. 'The road to Damascus indeed. Whatever next? I had better check he's all right.'

The bell went for the end of morning break just as Vera set off after her brother and Ruby finished putting out the tables in the hall for our Reading Workshop. This was when parents and grandparents were invited in to hear children read, an initiative which had proved very successful. The rate of reading had improved along with a strengthening of parent–teacher relationships.

Vera had almost caught up with Joseph when he bumped into Ruby. 'Oh, sorry,' he said. 'My mind was elsewhere.'

'So were mine, Mr Evans,' said Ruby forcefully. 'Ah'm still frettin' over that Stan Coe wand'rin' round t'village as if butter wouldn't melt in 'is mouth. 'E's goin' to 'ell in a 'andcart is that one.' She shook her head. 'Pardon m'language, vicar,' and she hurried away.

Vera looked at her brother. 'So . . . not to Damascus,' she said quietly.

Joseph frowned, but did not reply before walking out to the car park.

Mrs Ogden was in the Reading Workshop when her six-year-old daughter, Kylie, came to sit next to her. The little girl put her reading book on the table. The title was *My Dog Is Happy*. However, Kylie had another animal on her mind. 'Can we get a kitten, Mam?'

'No, luv. Yer gran is allergic t'cats.'

'What does that mean, Mam?'

'They can't be in t'same 'ouse.'

Kylie frowned until there was a lightbulb moment. 'Well . . . can m'gran sleep outside?'

184

'Don't be daft,' retorted Mrs Ogden.

Little Zach Eccles walked by clutching his reading book and gave Kylie a shy smile. Kylie studied him carefully as he sat at another table. 'Ah'm gonna marry Zach,' she announced.

'Why's that, luv?'

''Cause 'e's nice-lookin' an' 'as lovely 'air.'

'That's good but looks aren't ev'rything.'

'An' when we play in the 'Ome Corner 'e likes ironin'.'

Mrs Ogden smiled. 'Ah well, that's different. Yes, y'can definitely marry 'im.'

'Anyway, teacher says you 'ave t'check m'reading, Mam.'

'Let's 'ave a look then.' She stared at the front cover of *My Dog Is Happy*. 'OK. What's t'name of t'dog?'

'Dunno.'

'Well . . . why is 'e 'appy?'

Kylie shook her head in disgust. 'Ah've only read it once!' Suddenly a thought crossed her mind. 'Mam, what would 'appen t'yer 'airbrush if it fell down t'toilet?'

'Why?'

Kylie looked relieved. 'Never mind,' she said and opened the book quickly.

Ruby had called in to the General Stores on her way home. When she came out there on the pavement in front of her was the large figure of the chain-smoking Deirdre Coe.

'Think yer top dog now, don't you?' said Deirdre scornfully. Her double chin wobbled as she took a final drag of her cigarette.

'If y'can't say owt nice, then don't say nowt at all,' said Ruby.

'Yurra right fancy pants now you've married Mr Moneybags.'

'Ah'm no such thing,' retorted Ruby.

'Anyway, my Stanley's back an 'e'll buy an' sell your George.'

'Oh no he won't,' said Ruby and set off up the high street.

Deirdre always liked the last word. 'Geroff 'ome, care-taker skivvy.'

Just before lunchtime I was checking the progress of each child in my reading record folder when Rory Duckworth made an announcement. 'It's that lady in 'er flash car again, sir.' It wasn't difficult to guess who he meant.

Ms Cleverley was sitting in the staff-room flicking through the pages of her Filofax and, once again, there was no acknowledgement when I walked in. *Some things don't change,* I thought as I sat down and waited. Finally she looked up at me. 'Mr Sheffield, just an update for you.'

'Yes?'

'We've collated all the responses to last year's National Curriculum Consultation document. I'm here because I noticed yours was one of the most comprehensive.'

'Thank you.' However, I guessed this had not been a compliment.

She gave me a piercing stare. 'I'm not entirely confident you have grasped the fact that schools must be *accountable*. Maths, English and science have to be at the core of the curriculum.'

'As they are in my school, Ms Cleverley, but often in a meaningful cross-curricular process. We believe in a curriculum that is based on first-hand experience and not the one-way pedagogy that existed in years gone by. You may have spotted the footnote to my response when I quoted the old Chinese proverb: "I hear and I forget, I see and I remember, I do and I understand."'

'Yes, it seemed irrelevant.'

'It was also heartfelt and I hoped someone out there might be listening.'

She shook her head. 'We have to equip children for the responsibilities of citizenship and the challenges of employment.'

'I agree. That's exactly what we are doing here.'

'But in many of the schools that I visit progress is uncertain and often slow.'

My hackles had begun to rise. 'Are you including this school?'

She smiled. 'It would be difficult *not* to include any of the schools in our authority.'

'That's not what I asked.'

'Let's just say the government does not find the status quo acceptable.'

I sighed and sat back. It would seem pointless to ask the question again. I found this woman infuriating.

She pressed on regardless. 'We shall also encourage *parents* to pinpoint deficiencies in the delivery of your curriculum.'

'And, hopefully, the strengths as well.'

She glanced at her wristwatch. 'Well, must press on,' and she snapped shut her Filofax. 'Suffice to say the first two working groups on maths and science are due to report in the summer of this year and the first set of orders will be published in the first half of 1989. So we'll progress this conversation later in the academic year.'

With that she was gone and I watched her car race out of

the school gate to return, presumably, to her ivory tower in County Hall.

It was when I walked out to the dining hall that life was suddenly brought back into focus. I sat down next to Tyler Longbottom. 'It'll be great nex' year, sir,' he said with a huge grin.

'Why is that, Tyler?'

'M'mam says ah'll be in your class.'

I gave him a guarded smile. 'Enjoy your dinner, Tyler.'

It was at moments like this that I was torn between continuing to work with the eager young children in my school and leaving behind the carping criticism of the desk-bound generals like Ms Cleverley.

After lunch I called into Anne's classroom. She was wearing an apron over yet another attractive new outfit and rolling out balls of plasticine for her afternoon craft lesson.

'Hello, Anne. I'm nipping out of school for a few minutes to pick up some screws for a model aeroplane that Jeremy Urquhart is making.' I smiled. 'He's very particular. They have to be *dome-headed* screws.'

'Fine, Jack.' She gave me a wry smile. 'A little bit fraught in there earlier today. It's not often Vera gets agitated but that dreadful Stanley Coe would try the patience of a saint.'

'Very true.'

'How's Beth? Hope she's getting her feet up.'

'She's enjoying her maternity leave and spending more time with John.'

'What about her school?'

'She keeps in touch each day. Fortunately there's an

excellent deputy head, a young man who is enjoying the challenge.'

She nodded. 'Like someone else I used to know.'

It struck me how much more content she appeared these days as I wrapped up warm before going out. The temperature seemed to have dropped even more and snow had begun to fall.

Outside Timothy Pratt's Hardware Emporium was a familiar dirty Land Rover. Stan Coe emerged from the shop carrying a roll of baling twine. A portly man in his early sixties, he gave me a fixed stare. 'Now then, Mr 'Eadteacher,' he said. It sounded more of a challenge than a greeting. 'Ah guess you've 'eard. Ah'm a changed man so t'vicar says.' There was a hint of sarcasm there. On the surface it appeared he was telling the truth but deep down I knew what lay beneath. It was a tissue of lies.

The years had not been kind to Stan as he festered on his pig farm on the outskirts of Ragley. His greed had consumed him and, while his sister Deirdre railed at his drunkenness, he continued to buy land and his estate had grown steadily.

'Remember this, ever'thing comes to 'e who waits . . . or so ah've been told.' There was still menace in his words as he stared at me. A web of veins formed purple tracks across his ruddy cheeks and gathered round his blackened nose. It was as if during his time in prison his mind had been corroded by the acid of hate. 'Ah listened to t'vicar. 'E told me t'Lord said there'll be a day o' reckonin'.'

'I'm sure there will, Mr Coe,' and I walked into the shop.

*

At the end of school parents were collecting the younger ones from Anne's classroom. Chantal Higginbottom had just passed her fifth birthday and had enjoyed her afternoon making plasticine animals.

Her mother helped her on with her coat and scarf. 'Ah were good at school t'day, Mam,' Chantal declared.

'That's good. Come 'ere an' ah'll give you a big 'ug.'

There was a pause while Chantal considered this option. 'Ah'd rather 'ave sixpence.'

Her mother looked at Anne and raised her eyebrows, 'Kids, eh?'

It was after six o'clock when Emmeline Best drove into the grounds of Morton Manor. She parked on the forecourt, picked up her large wicker trug and rang the doorbell.

Vera opened the door and smiled. 'Hello, Emmeline, do come in out of the cold.' She saw the basket. 'This looks exciting.'

They walked into the kitchen.

'I thought I could make a contribution ahead of the service on Sunday so I've brought some ivy, ferns and winter honeysuckle. There're also a few clay pots with snowdrops that you may wish to use.'

'That's wonderful,' said Vera. 'Thank you so much. I'll put them in church tomorrow morning. The Flower Committee will be in to arrange them if you wish to come along.'

'Yes, I'll be there and I'm keen to help. I've done some flower arranging in the past but I'll follow your lead of course.'

'I'm sure that will be fine. You'll gather the ladies are quite particular. We don't simply plonk them in a vase.' Vera had been a disciple of Constance Spry, the famous flower arranger, and her book *The Constance Spry Book of Flower Arranging* was her second Bible.

'I shall look forward to it.'

'Now, would you like a warm drink?'

'That's kind, Vera, but I need to get home and I promised Joseph I would call in and drop off a sausagemeat plait.'

Vera smiled. 'He will definitely appreciate some home cooking,' and with a peck on the cheek the two ladies said goodnight.

Joseph received Emmeline's home baking with great relish and then stood by the door of the vicarage to watch her drive away. He saw her pause at the gate. Suddenly there was the roar of a large Land Rover as it swerved across the Morton Road and skidded on the ice.

Stan Coe stank of beer and sweat after even more celebrations at The Pig & Ferret. He had enjoyed meeting up with his equally nefarious friends again, getting rolling drunk and boasting about his next conquest. In his stinking shirt and filthy oilskin coat he was certainly not dressed for a light supper at the vicarage. He had left it too late to call back into Coe Farm where his long-suffering sister had prepared two fatty pork chops for his evening meal.

He was approaching the gates of the vicarage at a crazy speed when he caught a glimpse of Emmeline's car. There was an almighty crash as his Land Rover ploughed into the side of her stationary vehicle and rammed it on to the snow-covered grass verge.

Emmeline screamed in fright.

Stan climbed out in fury. A woman he had never seen before was at the wheel. 'You stupid bitch,' he cried.

Emmeline peered through the cracked window at a vision of hell. Stan rested his meaty hands on the bonnet of her car. 'What the 'ell were y'doin'?' For a moment he stood there still as a snake, poised and ready to strike.

Joseph was running towards the scene at full pelt. 'Stop that, Stanley!' he yelled. He opened the driver's door and helped Emmeline out. 'Are you all right?'

Emmeline was shivering with fright. 'Oh, Joseph,' she said.

He put his arms around her. 'Come inside, my dear. You're safe now.'

'Women bloody drivers,' ranted Stan. 'Ought t'ban 'em all.' His speech was slurred.

'I saw it all,' said a furious Joseph. 'I shall ring the police.'

Stan climbed back into his car but it wouldn't start. Steam poured from the radiator. 'Bastard car,' he grunted, stumbled out and kicked a punctured tyre. With a stream of expletives he staggered off into the night.

The vicarage was a busy place during the next two hours. Joseph rang the police and PC Pike was on the scene minutes later. Victor Pratt was called and arranged for a breakdown wagon to remove the two cars. Meanwhile Vera responded immediately to Joseph's request for help and drove to the vicarage to care for Emmeline.

As always Vera was calmness personified and made a rapid assessment of Emmeline's condition. She decided that rest was the answer along with a cup of sweet tea and a digestive biscuit. Sadly, the kitchen was in a mess. To her dismay she found that Joseph had reverted to teabags instead of loose tea and the biscuit barrel was empty. She surveyed the scene in dismay. Those days of shiny work-tops, a spotless floor and china plates with delicate doilies were long gone.

It was decided Vera would drive Emmeline back to the manor to stay the night for an evening of peace, warmth and comfort.

Warmth was definitely in short supply for Stan Coe as he blundered blindly through the snow. He managed to stagger down Ragley High Street and lurched towards Pratt's garage. All feeling in his hands and feet had gone as the snow turned into a blizzard and stung his face, blurring his vision still further. He remembered there was a shortcut over the fence and across the field to his farm. Halfway there was an incongruous monkey puzzle tree next to a small pond. One of the icy branches slapped against his face and he screamed in pain. Then, almost in slow motion, he stumbled to one side, slipped and fell forwards towards the frozen pond. His head smashed against the fractured ice and, unconscious, his face sank beneath the surface.

Inside Coe Farm the evening was passing and Deirdre was wondering what had happened to her brother. She had enjoyed watching Les Dawson on *Blankety Blank* with special guests Alvin Stardust plus Ian and Janette from the Krankies but had begun to feel peckish. The two fatty pork chops she had prepared for Stan were now stone cold so she settled down with a gammon, chutney and pickle sandwich to watch *Dynasty* with Linda Evans and her favourite, Joan Collins. Joan's character Alexis was going to the movies and Deirdre was engrossed when she heard a loud knocking on the door.

'Who's that at this time?' she muttered. *Must be Stan, drunk again,* she thought.

It wasn't.

It was PC Pike with a female officer.

Chapter Twelve

Life and Death

Mrs Forbes-Kitchener was absent today during morning school on church duty. Miss Flint provided cover in the office.

Extract from the Ragley & Morton School Logbook:
Monday, 29 February 1988

As I drove to school early on the morning of Monday, 29 February, ragged clouds drifted across a spectral sky that promised more snow. It had been a bitter winter and, around me, the dormant trees shivered in the freezing wind. A difficult journey lay ahead. Eventually, fingertip softly, a grudging light began to spread across the distant fields and a land of grey-white snow emerged from the void.

Beth had seemed in good spirits when I left and her parents, John and Diane, had been a great help during the past week. The birth of our second child was expected sometime soon and it was on my mind as I crunched over the frozen cobbles and into the school car park. However, the juxtaposition of life and death was brought into stark relief when I walked into the school office.

Vera was dressed all in black.

It was the morning of Stanley Coe's funeral and Vera had agreed to support Joseph, who had been in a state of distress since the tragic circumstances surrounding the pig farmer's death.

'Good morning, Mr Sheffield,' she said quietly. 'I've prepared everything for the morning and Valerie has kindly said she will call in to supervise the dinner money and take telephone calls.' Valerie Flint was a loyal friend of Vera's and she had proved a valuable supply teacher in past years.

'Thank you, Vera. That's very much appreciated.' I studied her for a moment. She looked both immaculate and severe in her black overcoat and leather fur-lined boots. There was also a hint of tension in her demeanour. A brief service had been planned, to be led by Joseph in St Mary's Church, before Stanley Coe's coffin was taken to the crematorium.

'I know this is difficult for you, Vera, but I'm sure Joseph will be grateful you are there.'

'Looking back, it was a dreadful time for everybody.'

'I agree. And although I didn't like the man, I would never have wished such an ending for him.'

Stan Coe had been found by PC Pike on that fateful evening. The post-mortem stated he had drowned in the frozen pool while in a state of unconsciousness.

'Joseph has been very upset. Thankfully he has received

lots of support, particularly from Miss Best, who seemed to recover quickly from the experience. She's made of stern stuff.'

'That's good to hear.'

Vera glanced up at the clock and put on her black leather gloves. 'By the way, how is Beth this morning?'

'All well thankfully. Her parents have been a great support. So it's just wait and see.'

She picked up her wide-brimmed black hat and sighed. 'Time to go, Jack,' and she walked outside.

Ruby was sweeping the path to the car park. 'Good luck, Mrs F.'

'Thank you, Ruby.'

'Ah 'ope Mr Evans will be OK. 'E were lookin' proper peaky when ah saw 'im last.'

'I'm sure he will be fine. It was a shock to us all.'

'Ah'll be there outside church t'see our Duggie. 'E allus looks smart when 'e's carryin' a coffin.'

'How is Douglas these days?'

'Still got 'is 'ead in t'clouds. 'E were s'pposed t'be givin' me a lift t'school this mornin' but then large as life 'e announced 'e 'ad summat important t'do for t'funeral parlour. 'E never plans 'is life does Duggie, jus' like his dad wi' channel vision.'

Tunnel vision, thought Vera but, as usual, didn't correct her friend. 'Oh well, Ruby, must go,' and she hurried off to her car.

Back in my classroom I thought about Vera. I was pleased she had decided to attend the funeral for I knew it would be a difficult morning for Joseph. He and Emmeline had been the last people to see Stan alive.

Joseph had told me he had wrestled with his conscience, wishing he could have prevented Stan from wandering off into the snow in a drunken state. However, his priority at that moment had been to rescue Miss Best. It had proved a harrowing time for the gentle cleric.

Meanwhile my arch enemy, Stanley Coe, had moved on to a place beyond the blasphemy in his soul. It seemed strange we wouldn't meet again. Over the years I had had many fraught conversations with this devious man but those days were gone now. The memories, like a eulogy of bitter experience, had withered in the wind. As I stared through the window, I thought of what lay ahead: a different day, a time of farewells, a gathering of souls . . . a funeral.

Outside the funeral parlour in Easington, Duggie Smith was buffing up the chromium headlamps of a restored 1957 Austin FX3. The local funeral director, Septimus Bernard Flagstaff, was proud of his hearse. A distinctive local character, he was also president of the Ragley & Morton Stag Beetle Society.

Septimus took a large brass timepiece from the pocket of his waistcoat and gave Duggie a stare. A plump, grey-haired man in his sixties, he was a stickler for timekeeping. 'Punctuality comes afore godliness,' he declared. 'Isn't that right, Douglas?'

'Sure thing, Mr Flagstaff,' said Duggie. It was an adage he had heard a thousand times.

'Come on then. Get yer 'at on.'

They set off in their wing collars and black three-piece

suits looking like characters from a Dickensian novel. Fortunately, Duggie's Boomtown Rats hairstyle hid the half-smoked Castella cigar behind his left ear. When they climbed into the hearse Septimus frowned when he saw the coffin. He had been disappointed when Deirdre had called into the funeral parlour to make arrangements. 'This is our top o' t'range,' he had told her. 'An oak coffin wi' inlaid ma'ogany.'

Deirdre hadn't been interested. 'Jus' a pine one, please, nowt fancy.'

At Coe Farm Deirdre was in her bedroom getting dressed for the funeral. She stared into the full-length mirror at what she described to herself as her *fuller figure*. She was alone now. Stan had gone and so, long ago, had their parents. She could remember her mother saying, 'Legs like tree trunks, Deirdre. Buy long dresses t'cover 'em.' Her mother wasn't into compliments. Empathy was neither in her dictionary nor in her heart.

On the sideboard was a brochure she had ordered from the Transform Private Hospital in Wimpole Street in London. It advertised something called 'Lipolysis Suction' and claimed her figure would be transformed 'by removing problem areas of fat'. They also provided breast enlargement which she didn't need and stomach shaping which she did. The money would be there now. She was about to become a rich woman.

George and Ruby had walked to St Mary's Church to see who turned up for Stan's funeral. It had been the talk of the village and they were curious. Only a sparse group of mourners had arrived, including a few members of the pig-breeding fraternity, plus one of Stan's associates from the other end of the food chain, namely Herbert Cronk. On the side of his rusty white van it read:

PERFECT PIGS
Cronk's Crackling:
Quality Hog Roast Supplier

He was looking sad, mainly because he had lost a lucrative business deal with Stan. Behind him, a scruffy man in a faded grey suit and a filthy black tie was walking towards the church porch. He had a florid red face, a huge beer belly and, surprisingly, was looking pleased with himself.

'Who's that, Ruby?'

'Stan's little brother, Gerry. 'E's a builder in Thirkby an' another villain. 'E never shows 'is face round 'ere.' Ruby shook her head. 'Ah wouldn't trust 'im as far as ah could throw 'im.'

George put his arm around her shoulders. 'They come out of t'woodwork when it's a funeral.'

'Yer right there, luv.' She looked into the distance in eager anticipation. 'Ah can't wait t'see our Duggie in 'is black 'at.'

At morning break Miss Flint prepared coffee and opened a packet of biscuits. Pat had brought in a copy of last week's *Woman's Own*. The cover photo featured Sarah Ferguson with the headline 'FERGIE – You'll be a lovely mum'.

She passed it over to Valerie. It was well known that she, like Vera, was a diehard royalist and Pat was trying to make her feel welcome.

'Thank you, Pat,' said Valerie. 'I saw the Duchess at the Children of Courage service and I know the royal baby will have the best start in life.'

Sally looked up from her newspaper. 'Really?' she said with the merest hint of scepticism.

'Yes,' said Valerie with enthusiasm. 'It says here the baby is due to arrive in August and will be fifth in line to the throne. The favourite names are Elizabeth or George.'

'I heard her parents separated when she was thirteen,' Sally mused.

'Which is why she knows the importance of a loving and stable home,' retorted Valerie. She studied the article once again. 'This sounds wonderful. Apparently she and Prince Andrew will be moving into their one-point-five-million-pound home in Sunninghill Park near Windsor complete with swimming pool and stables.'

Pat glanced at Sally and gave her a warning glance. Sally took the hint and returned to her newspaper. In any case this was much more interesting. She had finished reading about the film star Elizabeth Taylor losing four stones on a crash diet and had moved on to 'Sex and the single woman'. It said that 80 per cent of single women had enjoyed a one-night stand with a man and that 76 per cent slept with their new partner on a first date.

Valerie looked across the coffee table at Sally. 'You look engrossed, Sally. What are you reading?'

Sally thought it best not to share these sexual revelations with their stand-in secretary, particularly since, as a single woman, she would have figured in both of these statistics. 'Oh, it's about losing weight.'

'Ah,' said Valerie, 'the key is getting into an old pair of jeans.'

Sally smiled. 'You're quite right, Valerie. Thank you,' and everyone returned to sipping coffee and eating custard creams.

Shortly before the lunchtime bell the telephone rang in the school office. Valerie Flint had proved an excellent stand-in for Vera. The dinner money had been checked and recorded, the morning mail sorted and a delivery of sugar paper signed for.

'Ragley & Morton School. Miss Flint speaking.'

'It's Mrs Henderson here with a message for Mr Sheffield.'

'Good morning, Mrs Henderson. I've replaced Mrs Forbes-Kitchener as secretary this morning and Mr Sheffield is teaching at present, so could I take a message?'

'It concerns my daughter.'

'Ah yes, Mrs Sheffield and I are acquainted. I do hope all is well. I understand the baby may be due this week.'

There was a pause. 'It's just that she's experiencing early contractions. However, my daughter insists they're false labour pains.'

'Sounds like Braxton Hicks,' said Valerie briskly. 'I understand many women experience them during the third trimester.'

Diane was impressed with the response. This was clearly a knowledgeable woman. 'Yes, that's what I've heard. So, if you could tell Mr Sheffield not to worry but my husband is taking her into the hospital now just to be on the safe side.'

'Very sensible,' said Valerie with her usual assertive confidence. 'I'll pass on your message. Thank you for calling.'

*

St Mary's Church was only sparsely populated when the coffin was carried in, accompanied by Elsie Crapper playing 'There is a green hill far away'. Emmeline had joined Vera at the back and both bowed their heads in prayer. Then it was Joseph's turn. His voice sounded strained but he remained calm.

Writing the eulogy for Stanley Coe had proved difficult but Joseph had chosen his words carefully. Here was a man who had broken most of the Commandments and was hated by the majority of the locals. Joseph kept it fairly short but sincere and included a few facts about Stan's life. Then to sum up he linked in the theme of 'Love thy neighbour'. Finally, he stood at the lectern with the giant Bible resting on the outstretched wings of a brass eagle.

He had chosen the popular reading from 1 Corinthians, chapter 13, verses 4 to 8, and spoke in a slow clear voice that echoed above the heads of the congregation.

'Love is patient and kind; love is not jealous or
boastful; it is not arrogant or rude. Love does not
insist on its own way; it is not irritable or resentful; it
does not rejoice at wrong, but endures in the right.
Love bears all things, believes all things, hopes all
things, endures all things. Love never ends.'

When the service closed Emmeline's eyes were full of admiration while Vera nodded in acknowledgement. It was a job well done.

The wake had been arranged by Deirdre and a small crowd gathered in the back room of The Pig & Ferret. The repast was a mean collection of crab-paste sandwiches and slices of pork pie. She grimaced as her little brother, Gerry, sauntered up to stand beside her. "Ello, Deirdre,' he said. 'Sad day.'

Deirdre nodded. There was no love lost between them. 'Yer looking well,' she lied. *More like death warmed up,* she thought.

'Ah'm fine. Business is boomin'.' He lit up a cigarette. 'Bad way t'go for m'brother.'

'It were God's will,' said Deirdre. She was feeling confident. She knew Coe Farm would be left to her and she intended to sell it and have a holiday before buying a small cottage in the Yorkshire Dales. 'Mind you, 'e'd 'ad a skinful.'

"E liked a pint did our Stan,' said Gerry with a smile.

He decided now was as good a time as any to deliver the hammer blow. 'You'll be needin' some place t'go now.'

"Ow d'yer mean?'

'Stan left t'farm t'me. It's in 'is will.'

'What yer on about? It's my 'ome. Stan allus said if I looked after 'im, cookin' an' cleanin' an' suchlike, 'e would leave t'farm t'me.'

Gerry tapped his nose with a nicotine-stained forefinger. 'But y'could never trust our Stan.' He gave an evil smile. 'Y'better get packin',' and he sauntered off to chat with his farming friends.

It was just after twelve o'clock when Valerie Flint appeared at my classroom door. 'Message for you, Mr Sheffield,' and she beckoned me outside into the corridor.

She spoke quietly as the children filed out and into the

hall. 'Mrs Sheffield has gone into hospital with her father. It's a precaution. There were signs of early contractions. Mrs Henderson said not to worry.'

I paused to take in the news. 'Thank you.'

Valerie could see the concern on my face. 'Why not ring Mrs Henderson for an update. It would put your mind at rest.'

'I'll do that.'

Diane seemed relaxed when I rang. 'No news, Jack. John said he would contact me if there were any developments.'

'I could arrange to leave now.'

'I don't think there's any need at the moment. You could simply drive in after school.'

It seemed sensible. 'Thanks, Diane. I'll do that but please let me know if you hear anything.'

Anne was clearing up the morning activity when I walked into her classroom to give her the news. 'Anne, Beth has been taken into hospital.'

'Oh, how is she?'

'I've been told nothing is likely to happen so I'll drive in after school.'

'That's fine, Jack.' She glanced out of the window. Snow was falling again. 'But please be careful. The weather seems to be getting worse.'

I found it hard to concentrate during afternoon school and by the time I'd read another chapter of C. S. Lewis's *The Magician's Nephew* during story time my mind was else-where. As the children collected their coats I was anxious to set off for the hospital.

'G'night, sir,' said Charlie Cartwright. 'Me an' Ted are watching *Droids* tonight. It's "The Revenge of Kybo Ren".'

'Oh, yes.' I hadn't the foggiest idea what he was talking about.

Ted sensed my confusion. 'It's the adventures of R2-D2 and C-3PO,' he said.

I was no wiser. 'Oh well, enjoy it, boys,' and I hurried to the office and collected my duffel coat and scarf. Minutes later I was driving down Ragley High Street in my Morris Minor. Fortunately Deke Ramsbottom had cleared the local roads with his snowplough. I relaxed a little, turned on my radio and smiled. Kylie Minogue was singing her debut single 'I Should Be So Lucky' so I guessed Stock, Aitken and Waterman were enjoying their latest success.

Valerie was tidying her desk in the office when the telephone rang. It was Diane Henderson and on this occasion her voice was a little more fraught.

'Oh, I'm glad you're there. Please could you tell Mr Sheffield to go immediately to the hospital? I've just been told things are beginning to happen very quickly.'

'I'm afraid you've just missed him. He left five minutes ago. So it should be fine as he's on his way.'

'That's good to know.'

'Best wishes, Mrs Henderson. I do hope all goes well.'

'Thank you, Miss Flint,' and she rang off.

Getting to the A19 proved slow but relatively safe. The main road was busy but I made steady progress. After a few miles everything changed. The weather worsened, a high wind sprang up and suddenly I was driving through a blizzard. My windscreen wipers squealed in protest, trying to clear the berms of snow.

There was only a mile to go when disaster struck. A high-sided lorry had tipped over and blocked both lanes of the carriageway. Cars backed up and everything came to a standstill. I sat there impatiently as the snow drifted against the side of my driver's door. Fifteen minutes went by and the temperature was dropping. There was no movement. Then, fifty yards away, I saw a flashing blue light and I was reassured. Somehow the police had managed to get to the scene.

Another fifteen minutes went by and, ahead of me, the queue of cars was firmly stuck in a mini snowdrift. I was becoming frantic. Somehow I had to get to the hospital. It was decision time. I climbed out of my car, wrapped my scarf around my face, stooped into the wind and staggered down the road. I skirted the stricken lorry and saw two police cars. An ambulance had arrived to take away the injured lorry driver. Meanwhile four policemen with bright torches were directing the cars on the other side of the road back to York.

I summed up the situation. The only way I would get to the hospital would be to walk. Suddenly, there was a tap on my shoulder. 'Hello, Jack. What are you doing here?' I looked up at the six-foot-four-inch hulk of a police sergeant towering above me. It was my close friend Sergeant Dan Hunter. He had been best man at my wedding back in 1982.

'Dan! This is a surprise.'

He shook his head. 'Jack, we've got a hell of a situation here. I've called for back-up but it will be an hour before we clear this lot. You had better get back in your car.' As he spoke the wind seemed to increase in intensity and the snow stung my eyes.

'But it's Beth. She's just been taken into hospital. The baby might be on its way. I'm trying to get there. I'm desperate, Dan.'

I saw a hint of a wry smile. Dan had always been a man to handle a crisis. He put his hand on my shoulder. 'Jack, give me your car keys.' I fumbled in my pocket and passed them over. 'I'll see to your car.' He beckoned to one of the officers. 'Billy, take Jack to the hospital then get straight back here. His wife's in labour.'

Billy grinned widely. 'C'mon, Jack. I've got three and they don't wait f'traffic jams.'

John Henderson was standing in a corridor looking anxious. 'Thank God, Jack, I was getting worried. Diane let me know you were on your way but that was ages ago.'

'So . . . any news?'

He smiled. 'Congratulations. You have another son. Mother and baby are doing fine. This one didn't hang about.' We shook hands.

I looked at the double swing doors of the maternity unit. 'Can I go in?'

'I'll get the nurse. Wait there.'

I sat down overcome with emotion and put my head in my hands.

'He's perfect,' I said and kissed Beth on her forehead. Her hair was awry, her cheeks were red and she looked exhausted. I held my son in my arms and tears filled my eyes. 'I'm sorry I wasn't here. There were problems on the road.'

'Don't worry, Jack. You're here now and our family is complete.'

'Really?'

'Yes.' She gave a tired smile. 'I'm not going through that again.'

I recognized the determination in her voice and moved on. 'There was an accident. I had to abandon my car in the snow. The police were sorting it out. I'm only here now because Dan Hunter was on the scene and organized a lift in for me.'

'He's a great friend.'

'He was there when I needed him most.'

Beth took our son back in her arms and kissed his cheek. 'Come to think of it, Dan is a pretty good name . . . a strong name. Goes well with Sheffield.'

'So it does.'

It was late when I finally drove home. Dan had left the keys in reception for me. I was looking forward to telling him the name of our son. It was a strange journey back to Bilbo Cottage. My thoughts drifted in the darkness. For Stanley Coe the time of tyranny was over and I reflected on the paradox of new life coming into the world to greet a day of endings.

Chapter Thirteen

Birds of a Feather

School closed today for the Easter holiday with 132 children on roll.
Extract from the Ragley & Morton School Logbook:
Friday, 25 March 1988

It was Friday, 25 March, the final day before the Easter holiday, and the season had turned. The first breath of spring hung in the air with the promise of warmth and light. Beneath the hard earth new life stirred and the first daffodils had opened their bright yellow trumpets. Beyond the school wall the sticky buds on the horse chestnut trees were coming alive and over the distant moors the raucous cries of curlews filled the air.

Daniel Jack Sheffield was now over three weeks old and drinking milk for England. John was intrigued to have a brother and enjoyed it when Dan grasped his finger or gave what he thought was a toothless smile.

After a lengthy conversation we had decided that John would go to Beth's school after the holiday. In our area children could start full-time education the term they would turn five years old and John's birthday was on 24 July. Once the decision had been made, Beth had ordered a school uniform for him. We hoped him being the son of the headteacher would not present difficulties. Only time would tell.

All this was going through my mind as I turned right into Ragley High Street. Suddenly I noticed furious activity outside Nora's Coffee Shop. Little Malcolm was helping Dorothy into their car. He had cleaned and polished their bright green 1973 Hillman Avenger – 1250cc, two-door Deluxe – in preparation for this moment. An overnight bag had been packed and nothing had been left to chance. Meanwhile Nora was standing in the doorway, gripping her pinny and praying all would go well. Dorothy was now two weeks late but things appeared to be happening quickly. Her baby could wait no longer and they roared off down the high street for the hospital in York.

I pulled up and walked over to Nora, who was waving as the car drove away.

'Good morning, Nora. Is everything all right?'

She looked tense. 'Mornin', Mr Sheffield. It's Dowothy's baby. Looks like t'day's the day.'

'I guessed that was it.' I studied her for a moment. 'What about you, Nora? Are you OK?'

She sighed deeply. 'Ah've known Dowothy a long time. She's like family t'me. Ah'm pwayin' this time it'll be all wight.'

'I'm sure it will.'

I glanced through the opened doorway. Natasha Smith was busy cleaning tables. 'I see you've got some help today.'

She nodded. 'Natasha's weally 'elpful an' my Tywone is callin' in later.' Then she paused and took a deep breath. 'Anyway, thanks, Mr Sheffield. Ah'll 'ave t'go.' As she walked slowly back into the shop the bell above the door jingled a muted refrain.

At morning break I was first into the staff-room. Vera had already prepared mugs of coffee and the sound of children playing drifted in through the window. Alison Gawthorpe and Tracey Higginbottom were winding a long skipping rope while Hermione and Honeysuckle Jackson jumped in and out. Together they chanted a familiar skipping rhyme.

> *'One man went to mow,*
> *Went to mow a meadow.*
> *One man and his dog,*
> *Stop, bottle o' pop, fish an' chips,*
> *Ol' Mother Riley an' 'er cow,*
> *Went to mow a meadow.'*

Vera was in a thoughtful mood. 'I do hope all goes well for Dorothy,' she said quietly.

'We'll know today according to Nora,' I said.

'And I'm told Nellie's is due soon.'

I smiled. 'They're never far apart, those two.'

'Birds of a feather flock together,' she recited with a smile as the staff-room suddenly filled up.

*

Big Dave Robinson was lost without Little Malcolm. His lifelong friend and workmate had telephoned to say he would be in touch when there was some news and Nellie was sitting by the phone in anticipation. She had woken this morning feeling unwell so Big Dave had set off down the high street to the village Pharmacy.

Eugene had come downstairs from the loft where he had constructed a mock-up of the control room of the Starship *Enterprise*. He turned the sign on the door from 'CLOSED' to 'OPEN'. Big Dave was his first customer.

'Now then, Dave. What's it t'be?'

'It's my Nellie. Gorra bad 'eadache.'

'Ah'll sort it,' said Eugene confidently.

'Ah think she's worryin' 'bout Dorothy.'

Eugene nodded knowingly. 'Ah'm not s'prised after what 'appened las' time.' He put a packet of aspirin on the counter.

'Thanks, Eugene,' said Dave and he rummaged in his overalls for some coins.

The till opened with a high-pitched *ding* and Eugene gave Dave his change. 'So ... when's your Nellie due? Mus' be gettin' close now.'

'Nex' week, she says.'

'Tell 'er we're thinkin' of 'er.'

'OK, thanks, Eugene.'

Peggy Scrimshaw was busy at the far side of the shop. 'All the best t'Nellie, Dave,' she called out.

'Thanks, Peggy.'

'Live long an' prosper,' called out Eugene as Big Dave left the shop. He raised his hand in a version of Mr Spock's Vulcan salute. Peggy glanced up from stacking cough medicine, shook her head sadly and wondered why on earth she had married a dedicated Trekkie.

It had been a busy day with reports to go out to parents and countless forms to complete for County Hall. Finally, at the end of school, the bell rang and the holiday beckoned. I decided to walk down to the school gate. The children were always excited at the end of a term and I wanted to make sure they made their way safely to Lollipop Lil's zebra crossing on the high street.

Mary Scrimshaw and Katie Parrish were deep in conversation as they approached me. 'We're having a sleepover at Mary's tonight, sir,' said Katie.

Both girls looked excited.

'An' we're going t'play Trivial Pursuit with my mum an' dad,' said Mary.

'That sounds great,' I said. 'Be careful crossing the road.'

'That's OK, sir. We have to wait here for my mum,' said Katie. 'She's bringing an overnight bag for me and she wanted a word with Mrs Scrimshaw.'

At that moment Rebecca Parrish appeared carrying a leather holdall. 'Hello, girls.'

'They're excited about tonight,' I said.

Rebecca smiled and turned to me. 'I'm hoping they can catch up on sleep over the weekend. I doubt they'll get much tonight.'

'I don't imagine so.'

Rebecca spoke quietly: 'Any chance of a quick chat before you go home?'

'Of course.'

'How about the Coffee Shop again after I've dropped off the girls?'

I guessed it was about the lectureship. 'Fine. I'll clear up and see you there later.'

She gave me that perceptive level stare that I was beginning to associate with this assertive, dynamic woman.

Anne had cleared her classroom quickly and was putting on her coat in the staff-room when Sally and Pat walked in.

'Quick getaway,' said Pat. 'You're in a hurry.'

'Yes, things to do,' said Anne, blushing slightly.

'Any plans for the holiday?' asked Sally.

'A few.'

Sally gave a mischievous grin. 'Do they include the blond Adonis?'

Anne visibly relaxed. 'Yes! No secrets from you two. We're going away for a short break.'

'When?' asked Pat.

Anne glanced up at the clock. 'Five o'clock.'

'Well, get a move on,' said Sally, 'and have fun.' She gave her a hug.

They stood by the window and watched Anne stride out towards the Easington Road.

'What do you think?' asked Pat.

Sally thought for a moment. 'I think she looks happy.'

When I walked into the Coffee Shop the jukebox was on full blast. Rick Astley was singing his number-one record

'Never Gonna Give You Up' and Nora was humming along behind the counter. Dave and Nellie Robinson were sitting at a table near the counter drinking large mugs of tea and Dave waved in acknowledgement. Nellie looked tired and was holding her head.

I spotted Rebecca sitting at the same table where we had met before and, once again, mimed two coffees. She smiled, stood up and slipped off her coat. Her figure-hugging dress emphasized her slim, angular frame.

'Two coffees, please, Nora.'

'Comin' up, Mr Sheffield. Tywone'll bwing 'em over.'

Tyrone clicked the machine into action as the telephone on the wall rang.

Nora picked up the receiver and I saw Nellie leap up in anticipation. 'Coffee Shop. Nowa speakin'.' There was a brief pause. 'Oh, Malcolm! Any news?'

It was then it happened. Nellie dashed towards the counter. In her haste she caught her foot in a chair and crashed to the floor. Dave rushed to her side, crouched down and cushioned her head. 'Nellie! Nellie! What yer done?'

She was holding her stomach. 'Bloody 'ell, Dave. Ah'm sorry.'

He knelt down beside her.

'It 'urts.' There was fear in her eyes. 'M'baby. Oh, please God, m'baby.'

Suddenly Rebecca was by Dave's side. 'Can I do anything?'

My mind was racing. 'Dave, we need to get her into hospital. It would be quicker to drive straight there rather than wait for an ambulance. My car is outside.'

'So is mine,' Rebecca said, 'and it's bigger and faster. We can be there in fifteen minutes.'

I looked up. 'What d'you think, Dave?'

He nodded. 'C'mon, luv. Meks sense.' He lifted his wife effortlessly.

I glanced back at Nora. 'Ring the hospital. Say we're bringing Nellie in.'

Nora glanced back at the phone where she had dropped it. It was swinging by its cord and Malcolm was no longer on the line.

At five o'clock Anne put her suitcase by the hall table. She had packed it the night before and was waiting for Edward. All he'd said was that they were going on a surprise holiday. Three nights. Just the two of them, away from prying neighbours and tittle-tattle.

They might be tramping across windswept moors – she had no idea where they were off to – so she had selected appropriate outfits of jeans, jumpers and walking shoes. However, just in case she needed to dress up, she had splashed out on a new outfit that was supposed to be the height of fashion, namely a navy jacket, a slim shirt from French Connection and a white crossover skirt from Miss Selfridge. Shoes by Ravel and earrings by Corocraft completed the ensemble. She smiled as she stared out of the kitchen window. It was good to feel special again.

Edward pulled up outside Anne's house in a shiny blue two-year-old Renault 4. She put her case on the path and locked the door.

'I'll carry that,' he shouted.

'Hey! New car,' she said. 'This really is a surprise.'

'I've just bought it. I didn't want to take you in the old Transit,' he said with a grin, putting her case in the boot. 'Climb in and see what you think.'

'Love it,' said Anne. 'This is different,' and she began sliding the passenger window backwards and forwards on its runners.

The gear lever stuck out from the dashboard and Edward slipped it into reverse. 'I bought it because it's like you.'

'Really?'

'Yes, it's quirky, friendly and endearing.'

'I don't think I've ever been compared to a car before,' she said.

They lolloped gently down the Easington Road. Edward said quietly, 'It's also got soft springs . . . like my bed.'

'I'm sure there's a message in there somewhere,' she murmured.

'Perhaps I ought to curtail this analogy,' he said.

'Maybe.'

The miles rolled by as they drove towards Harrogate and Bedale.

Anne stared ahead. 'So, come on then. No more suspense. Where are you taking me?'

'To the Yorkshire Dales, a lovely village called Masham. I booked a holiday cottage there.'

Anne sat back and thought that happiness wasn't the destination but rather the journey she was on.

In York Hospital events were moving quickly for both Dorothy and Nellie while Big Dave and Little Malcolm sat in a corridor outside the maternity unit.

'It'll be fine, Dave,' said Little Malcolm. 'Your Nellie's built like a ten-ton truck.'

Big Dave nodded. 'Yer not wrong, Malc.' He accepted the comparison in the spirit it was given. 'Y'don't mess wi' my Nellie,' he added defiantly.

Little Malcolm stared down at his boots. 'Dave . . . d'you believe in God?'

Big Dave was confused. This was different to their usual conversations about football, beer and fishing. 'Course ah do,' he said cautiously. 'Well, mebbe on Sundays.'

Little Malcolm glanced up at his friend. 'Ah prayed las' night.'

Big Dave leaned back in his chair. 'Amen t'that, Malc. Can't do no 'arm.'

Little Malcolm looked subdued. 'If this dunt work out my Dorothy won't get over it.'

Big Dave put his arm around Malcolm's shoulders. ''Ow long 'ave we been bes' mates?'

'For ever, Dave. Since we were kids. Yer allus looked after me.'

'An' 'ave ah ever let y'down?'

Malcolm clasped his hands and thought hard.

'Well?'

'Ah'm thinkin'.'

'There's no need. Ah never 'ave.'

'There were that time y'pinched all t'chocolates out o' m'Advent calendar.'

Big Dave shook his head. 'Not that. Ah mean a proper let-down. Serious stuff like now, not when we were kids. An' in any case them chocolates didn't taste nice. Ah did yer a favour.'

'So what yer sayin', Dave?'

'Ah'm saying your Dorothy will come good. Jus' y'wait an' see. Baby'll be perfec'.'

Little Malcolm held his head in his hands and stared at the floor again. 'Thanks, Dave.'

It was then a stout nurse with an expression that read *don't mess with me* came through the double doors and looked at the two bin men. 'Which one o' you is Mr Robinson?'

'I am,' said Big Dave and Little Malcolm in unison. They both jumped up with startled expressions.

The nurse shook her head. She didn't rate men and these two were definitely a sandwich short of a picnic. 'OK, who's married t'Dorothy?'

'Me!' exclaimed Little Malcolm.

'Well, yurra dad. Little boy. Six poun' twelve ounce. Mum an' baby doin' fine. Y'can 'ave a look if y'like.'

'Yes, please,' mumbled Little Malcolm but he was too shocked to move.

Big Dave hugged Little Malcolm in a grip that would have crushed most men. 'Well done, Malc. What did ah tell you?'

'Come on then,' said the nurse, not appreciating this show of male bonding, 'shape yerself.'

Little Malcolm looked as though he was about to burst into tears.

'Can ah come with 'im?' asked Dave.

'No, y'can't,' she said. 'Jus' the dad.'

'Any news 'bout my Nellie?'

The nurse smiled. The penny dropped. 'Ah ... Nellie Robinson? She's in another room. No news yet.'

Dave sat down again. 'Go on, Malc. Go see yer son.'

The nurse with the charisma bypass guided Little Malcolm through the double doors and Big Dave was left alone with his thoughts.

'Eventful times,' said Rebecca Parrish as we drove out of the hospital gates and passed the chocolate factory. Workers were streaming out, almost all of them female, and collecting their bicycles to ride home.

'Thanks for offering your car. It was the right decision to bring Nellie in, according to the doctor. All seems to be well now. She's in good hands.'

'How's your latest addition, by the way? I heard you have another son.'

'We named him Daniel. He's fine, doing all the usual stuff, feeding, sleeping.'

'I remember it well.'

'You have a fine daughter. You must be proud.'

'I am.' Then her tone changed. 'Pity her father didn't appreciate it.'

I said nothing, merely let the thought hover in the space between us. It was well known he had cheated on her. The relationship with one of his young students hadn't lasted long but the scars would endure a lifetime.

The miles slipped by as we drove back towards Ragley.

Finally she came back to the here and now. 'It was about the lectureship, Jack. Things are moving at the College. I was wondering if you had thought further about it because the closing date is April the fifteenth.'

'Yes, I saw the advert. I'm keen, as you know. It's just taking the final step that's difficult.'

'Well, you know my feelings and, although I'll be

involved in compiling the shortlist, it will be the Vice-Principal and a few of my senior colleagues who will make the final decision. Jim Fairbank, the department head, is clearly keen for someone of your experience but, as you well know, interviews are a different matter.'

'I understand and your support means a great deal.'

We pulled up on Ragley High Street behind my car. All the shops had closed. 'We never did get that coffee,' she said wistfully.

'Another time,' I said.

She leaned over and squeezed my arm. 'Let's do that.'

It was almost half past nine and Nora was sitting in the front room above the Coffee Shop. The television was on and the weatherman, John Kettley, he of the Sergeant Pepper moustache, was telling the viewers that a promising Easter was in store.

Nora couldn't settle. She had watched Terry Wogan introducing *A Song for Europe* and guessed that the handsome Scott Fitzgerald would probably win with 'Go'. During *Dynasty* Joan Collins, as Alexis, was in a party mood after visiting a house of ill repute but Nora took little notice. Finally, the telephone rang. The shrill tone made her jump.

''Ello,' she said breathlessly.

'It's Malcolm. Ah've got news. It's been a bit 'ectic 'cause of Nellie. Ah've been wi' Dave all night. 'E's been in a reight state. But ever'thing's OK now.'

'So how's Dowothy an' Nellie? What's 'appened?'

'Dorothy's fine, Nora. Gorra baby boy. Six poun' twelve ounce. 'E's a beauty, jus' like 'is mam. She's sleepin' now.'

'Oh, that's weally good. Give 'er my love. An' what about Nellie?'

'That's t'best of it. She's 'ad a boy as well. He came real quick. A big un. Nine poun' one ounce, sez Dave. 'E's over t'moon.'

'That's gweat news, Malcolm.'

'Yer reight there, Nora. Born on t'same day. Fancy that. We're dads now and they'll grow up like me an' Dave.'

Nora was almost in tears. The relief was palpable. 'Ah'm thwilled,' was all she could say.

The call ended and she sat down on the sofa and turned off the television. 'I wonder what their names will be,' she murmured to herself, closing her eyes. It had been a long day.

Nellie was sitting up in bed with her bundle of joy. ''E's like you, Dave, allus 'ungry.'

Dave was still in a daze. 'Ah'm a dad an' so is Malc,' he said dreamily.

'Well, try an' look 'appy,' said Nellie. 'You an' Malcolm 'ave been faffin' about like Pinky an' bloody Perky.'

'Sorry, luv. Nurse sez we 'ave t'geroff 'ome.'

'Well, go on then, y'great lump, an' come back t'morrow.' She stroked the little boy tenderly.

Dave leaned forward, kissed his son and then kissed Nellie's cheek. 'Ah'll sithee,' he said.

'We'll need a name for 'im,' said Nellie.

Dave took a deep breath. 'Ah were thinkin' Malcolm's a good name.'

Nellie shook her head. 'Ah guessed as much. Let's settle for Malcolm Robinson. That'll do.'

Dave smiled and nodded. 'Ah'll go c'llect Malc.'

*

Dorothy was sitting up in bed holding her son as if he was a thing of wonder. Meanwhile the tough nurse who didn't take prisoners had given Malcolm his marching orders. 'Come back t'morrow,' she said. 'Give yer wife some peace. She needs a rest.'

'What we gonna call 'im, Dorothy?'

'Ah know what you'd like t'call 'im,' she said with a tired smile.

'Dave's a good name. It's special. But what about you? What d'yer fancy?'

'David's fine wi' me but your name's special as well.'

Little Malcolm touched her hand gently and kissed her. Then he looked down at his son. 'David Robinson. Yer'll 'ave a great life. Yer mam an' dad love yer an' y'won't be a bin man when y'grow up.'

'There's nowt wrong wi' bein' a bin man,' said Dorothy firmly. 'What's important is bein' kind an' 'elpin' others, jus' like 'is dad.'

It was late when Big Dave and Little Malcolm drove back to Ragley. Malcolm was driving.

'Dave.'

'What?'

'That nurse said not t'come back 'til two'clock t'morrow.'

'She's like my Nellie, that one. Tough as old boots.'

'Yer reight there, Dave.'

'So back on t'bins in t'mornin', Malc.'

'Early start, Dave, if we're off t'see Dorothy an' Nellie.'

'An' our sons,' said Dave proudly.

The miles slipped by until Little Malcolm broke the silence. 'Ah guess it works sometimes.'

'What does?'

'Y'know . . . prayin'.'

Big Dave remembered his mother once saying that God was in his heaven and all was well in the world. He hadn't taken much notice then. Perhaps he should have. 'Mebbe so, Malc . . . mebbe so,' he said quietly.

Chapter Fourteen

Last Post

School reopened today for the summer term with 139 children on roll.
Extract from the Ragley & Morton School Logbook:
Monday, 11 April 1988

John William looked smart in his new uniform. Beth insisted on taking his photograph and he stood against the kitchen door in his red polo shirt, grey shorts and black shoes. Everything looked a little too large for him but Beth had insisted, like a hundred mothers before her, that the outfit was fine and he would grow into it.

John was clearly unconcerned and it was a novelty for him to set off with his mother instead of Mrs Roberts. We were lucky to have her looking after young Daniel and she seemed happy in her work. She had done a wonderful job with John and now it was Dan's turn to be looked after by this caring lady.

Beth smiled as she left. 'And don't forget to post your letter.'

When I walked out to my car the distant hills were gilded with a golden light and the yellow petals of forsythia shone brightly in the early-morning sunshine. The heady scent of wallflowers filled my senses while a pair of blackbirds chattered in the hedgerow. My journey to school was filled with the sights and sounds of new life. Ewes baaed protectively beside their newborn lambs and a pheasant with flapping wings and a shrieking cry suddenly shattered the tranquillity. On the grassy mounds bordering Ragley High Street daffodils and tulips waved in the gentle breeze.

It was Monday, 11 April, the first day of the summer term. The air was fresh and clear and gave a feeling of hope and optimism. However, somehow I knew life would never be the same again. Last night I had finally completed my application for the lectureship at the College. I had to post it but the thought of doing so was daunting. Some decisions in life were tougher than others and this was one of them.

When I walked into the office, Vera was at her desk reading our local paper, the *Easington Herald & Pioneer*.

'It's in,' she said, pointing to the 'Jobs & Vacancies' page, and passed it to me. I stared at the tiny print. It was the advertisement for a new secretary to begin in September.

'This will cause interest in the village,' I said.

Vera looked thoughtful. 'It already has. I was besieged by hopeful candidates in the butcher's on Saturday morning.

Then yesterday morning after church at least four members of the Flower Committee wanted to know the nature of the job.'

I looked at Vera, immaculate as ever in a summer dress and a beautiful hand-knitted cardigan. 'How are you feeling this morning?'

'*Mixed*, to be honest, Jack. A little sad but life continues to present new challenges.'

I noticed she was calling me by my first name more often these days. 'Anyway,' she said. 'I see we've a few more names for the admissions register.'

'I've just met a couple of them. Good luck.'

She smiled that familiar knowing smile. 'I wonder what first names will come my way. We've already had a Chantal and a Cheyenne. Whatever happened to Susan and Peter?'

'Changing times, Vera.'

'And we've certainly lived through a few of them.' She opened her pink admissions register to the next clean page and placed her Platignum fountain pen beside it.

I decided to walk down to the school gate and welcome some of the children. One of the new starters, Kevin Crapper, arrived holding his mother's hand.

'Mornin', Mr Sheffield. 'Ere 'e is. 'E's a star turn is our Kevin,' she said, full of pride.

'I'm sure he is,' I said, more in hope than expectation.

Mrs Crapper looked down adoringly at her four-year-old son, who was picking his nose and then licking his fingers. 'An' tell yer 'eadmaster you'll be five on Sat'day.'

'Ah'll be five on Sat'day,' repeated Kevin with a glassy-eyed stare.

The little boy was wearing scruffy shorts and a Superman T-shirt.

'Are you looking forward to school, Kevin?' I asked.

'No,' was the blunt reply.

Mrs Crapper looked furious. 'Don't say that t'Mr Sheffield. Why don't y'want t'come t'school?'

'Y'said school were a piece o' cake, Mam, but ah 'aven't 'ad no cake.'

Mrs Crapper pushed him towards the playground. 'Good luck, Mr Sheffield,' she said and wandered off.

There were raised voices as the next group arrived. It was Mrs Freda Fazackerly with eight-year-old Madonna and seven-year-old Dylan. They were arguing as they walked through the gate.

'Sorry, Mr Sheffield,' said Mrs Fazackerly. 'Our Dylan's a bit out o' sorts.' She crouched down. 'What's t'matter, Dylan?'

'It were Madonna. She called me the E-word.'

'E-word? What's that?' I asked.

'She's allus callin' me names,' grumbled Dylan.

'Yes, but what's the E-word?' demanded Mrs Fazackerly. I was curious as well.

'Idiot,' said Dylan.

She smiled at me and shook her head. 'Ah were never good at spellin' neither.' She watched them go their separate ways towards the school field. ''Ave a good day, Mr Sheffield,' she called out as she hurried away, looking distinctly relieved.

Meanwhile Mrs Spraggon arrived with four-year-old Kylie. The little girl looked a picture with pretty bows in her blonde hair, a checked pinafore dress, long white socks and new leather sandals. 'She's so excited, Mr Sheffield, and looking forward to school.'

'That's wonderful to hear.'

'She loves reading and says she wants to be a doctor when she grows up.'

'I'm so pleased.' I crouched down. 'Hello, Kylie, I'm sure you'll be happy in Mrs Grainger's class. So you want to be a doctor, do you?'

She gave her answer a lot of thought. 'I wanted to be a teacher but I can't.'

'Oh . . . and why is that?'

'Because my first name isn't *Mrs*.'

Mrs Spraggon smiled. 'Don't worry, Mr Sheffield. I'll explain before she finally gets to your class.'

As they set off up the drive I thought about her words. Another generation of children had arrived. Seven years at Ragley when they would change from tiny children with a simple concept of the world to eleven-year-olds with an understanding of the life that awaited them. It struck me that I might not be around to see children like Kylie grow up. The letter of application was in my jacket pocket and the postbox was only on the other side of the village green . . . so near but, at that moment, so far.

It was as I was preparing for morning assembly that Vera suddenly appeared. 'Mr Sheffield, message for you but I can deal with it if you wish.'

'Thanks, Vera. What is it?'

'Joyce Davenport has telephoned to ask if the WI can use the school projector for their next event.'

'That's fine. When is it needed?'

'She asked if it could be collected after school by the speaker and his wife so they can have a practice with it.'

'I could set it up in the staff-room for a quick demonstration. We could ask if they need a screen as well.'

'That will be helpful. Shall I say four fifteen?'

'Fine. By the way, what's the talk about?'

'Sewing through the ages.'

I smiled. 'Right up your street, Vera.'

'Yes, looking forward to it.'

At morning break Pat was on playground duty. She was coaching her netball team and Katie Parrish was enjoying her status as goal shooter while Mary Scrimshaw was proving to be a formidable wing attack. Pat was relaxed as she chatted with the girls and it was good to see them looking so content. Sadly, that wasn't the case when I walked into the staff-room where the diverse opinions regarding royalty were being shared once again.

'I see Charlie-boy is on *Panorama* tonight,' said Sally with a shake of her head.

Vera frowned. 'Yes, I'll be watching. It's called *Charles, Prince of Conscience.*'

Marcus looked up. 'I read that he's concerned about the lack of attention he receives for his involvement in the issues of the day.'

'What sort of issues?' asked Anne.

'Problems of the inner cities and youth unemployment,' said Marcus.

'Sounds a bit hypocritical to me,' said Sally. She was munching on the last digestive biscuit from the tin on the coffee table. 'What does he know about society's problems when he lives in a protected world of butlers, royal chefs and never being in a traffic jam?'

'Well, he does have a demanding role to play,' said Vera.

'But what exactly does he *do*?' asked Sally.

'He represents our country all around the world,' said Vera with a hint of defiance.

Sally sighed deeply. 'I'd rather he didn't.'

'Sorry, Vera,' said Marcus, 'but I have to agree. I'm not a fan of hereditary titles and because of an accident of birth he does live a life of huge privilege.'

'That's rather harsh. Prince Charles is a very bright man.'

'I'm not sure about that, Vera,' said Marcus. 'He scraped a few O-levels followed by a B and a C at A-level. Then to top it all he only got a Desmond at Cambridge.'

'Desmond?'

'Sorry, that's what we call the award of a two-two degree . . . as in Desmond Tutu, Archbishop of Cape Town.'

'Ah, I see,' said Vera, clearly not amused. 'Even so, a Cambridge degree is impressive.'

'Which is what I achieved but mine was significantly higher and I had no private tutors and was working evenings serving tables.' He paused. 'Sorry, everyone. Didn't mean to sound grumpy.' He looked sadly at our faithful school secretary. 'I saw the advertisement, Vera. It seemed so final when I read it. I shall miss you terribly. I feel as though I've only just got to know you.'

'That's kind,' said Vera gently.

'So apologies for ranting on,' said Marcus.

'"Forgive and you will be forgiven,"' said Vera with a smile. 'Luke chapter six, verse thirty-seven. Please think nothing of it.' She looked across the staff-room. 'It's good to disagree, isn't it, Sally? We've done it for years.'

Sally stood up and gave Vera a hug. 'I'll miss you too,' she said.

Vera glanced down at the empty biscuit tin. 'I almost forgot. I made some ginger snaps yesterday. They're in a tin on my filing cabinet.'

'Shall I get them for you?' asked Sally meekly.

'Yes, please,' said Vera. 'They're for everybody ... well, everybody who supports the royal family,' she added with a wry smile.

'I think the royal family are wonderful,' said Marcus leaping up. 'I'll get them.'

There was laughter tinged with sadness at the realization that Vera's days at Ragley were coming to a close.

Shortly after twelve o'clock I was enjoying my school dinner. Spam fritters, chips and peas was followed by a sweet course that was new to me. I glanced up at the muscular frame of our dinner lady as she walked by. 'This is delicious, Mrs Critchley. We've not had this before.'

'New recipe, Mr Sheffield. Irish marmalade puddin'. Jus' plain flour, shredded suet an' marmalade.'

'Do thank Mrs Mapplebeck.'

'It were *my* recipe, Mr Sheffield,' said Mrs Critchley defiantly.

'Your recipe? Well ... it's excellent and going down well with all the children.'

'Ah tried it on my Ernie first.'

'What did he think?'

''E said it were wonderful.'

233

I'm not surprised, I thought. 'He's a wise man.'

She paused for a moment and crossed her arms. Her biceps bulged as she considered her reply. 'Not sure 'bout that but 'e knows which side 'is bread's buttered.'

I guessed this was code for he always did what he was told.

At four o'clock Vera and I were in the staff-room setting up the carousel slide projector and screen when a Mini Clubman Estate pulled into the car park.

'It's Joyce,' said Vera. 'She's prompt.'

Joyce Davenport looked concerned when she tapped on the door and walked in. 'Sorry to disturb you but I'm in a fix.'

Vera glanced up at me and I took the hint. 'I'll leave you to it,' I said.

'No, please stay, Jack, and share my humiliation. To be honest you may be able to help.' Joyce took a deep breath. 'It's about next week's WI talk.'

'Yes,' said Vera calmly. 'Sewing through the ages. I have the posters ready for you.' She put a copy on the coffee table. 'I was going to put one on the village hall noticeboard on my way home.' It read:

Ragley & Morton WI
Wednesday, 20 April 1988
7.30 p.m.
'SEWING THROUGH THE AGES'
A slide show by
Edwina Crump
Including light refreshments

'Oh no! Please don't.'

Vera looked puzzled. 'Pardon?'

'That's what I thought it was but it isn't.'

'Isn't what?'

'It's not *sewing*. Mrs Crump's writing was appalling and I misread it.'

'You had better explain,' said Vera.

Joyce looked distraught. 'And they're coming now.' She glanced up at the clock. 'Mr and Mrs Crump will be here in a few minutes.'

'Joyce,' said Vera sternly. 'Please tell me what the problem is.'

'Lillian Figgins was on the phone to me saying she had bumped into Mr and Mrs Crump at a car boot sale in Thirkby. They're regulars on the car boot circuit apparently. Known as Noddy and Big Ears for some reason.'

Vera was losing her patience. 'Yes, Joyce, that's all very interesting but what is the problem?'

'Well, Lillian said Mr Crump was looking forward to giving a WI talk in Ragley.'

'*Mr* Crump?' said Vera. 'Not his wife? Are you sure? What does he know about sewing?'

'That's what I'm trying to tell you, Vera. It's not sewing. Mr Crump has just retired after a thirty-five-year career in the *sewage* business.'

'Sewage!' exclaimed Vera.

I thought Joyce was going to burst into tears. She sat down heavily in one of the chairs while Vera took a deep breath. 'So, let's get this clear, Joyce.' She picked up a poster and pointed to the title. 'It's not sewing through the ages . . . it's *sewage* through the ages.'

Joyce couldn't speak. She merely nodded.

At that moment a rusty, ageing Ford Cortina pulled up in the car park and a portly bald-headed man in a flat cap got out followed by an equally portly lady.

'We need a strategy . . . and quickly,' said Vera. 'We have to put them off.'

'I have an idea,' I said. 'How about saying you're double-booked.'

Joyce looked up with hope. 'It might work. But who are we double-booked with?'

Vera gave me an expectant look. 'How about you, Jack? A talk on education. It would be perfect.'

'I'm not sure. I'm keen to help, of course.'

'Then it's settled.' She looked at Joyce. 'Let me handle it.' There was a knock on the door. Vera pointed to the kettle. 'Joyce, make a pot of tea.'

I opened it and a smiling couple walked in.

'Good afternoon, I'm Jack Sheffield, headteacher.'

''Ow do, ah'm Noel Crump an' this is m'wife, Edwina.'

He removed his cap and I couldn't help but notice he had the most enormous pair of ears I had ever seen. They were like taxi doors.

'Pleased to meet you,' I said. 'Let me introduce you to Mrs Forbes-Kitchener, our school secretary, and Mrs Davenport, the president of the Women's Institute.'

'It's an 'onour,' said Noel, almost bowing.

'Would you like a cup of tea?' said Vera.

'That's very kind,' said Edwina, nodding profusely. It appeared she nodded every time she spoke.

'Ah see you've got t'projector, Mr Sheffield,' said Noel. 'That's very kind. Ah've got 'undreds o' slides so ah'll need a bit o' practice.'

'Please take a seat,' said Vera.

There was a rattle of crockery and a stern look from Vera as Joyce put cups and saucers on the table. Eventually the tea was poured and we settled down.

'I'm so pleased you could come,' said Joyce.

'My Noel were thrilled when y'replied t'my letter,' nodded Edwina. "E's never done a talk afore but 'e's really int'restin' once 'e gets goin'.'

There was an awkward silence.

'Would you like a biscuit?' asked Vera, opening the tin.

'Oooh, ginger, m'favourite,' said Noel.

"E loves 'is ginger biscuits does my Noel,' said Edwina with a few more nods for good measure. 'Allus 'as two wi' a cuppa.'

Noel began chomping on a biscuit. 'Ah 'ad a packet ev'ry week at t'sewage works,' he said through a mouthful of crumbs.

'So, what was it like at the sewage works, Mr Crump?' I asked. 'It sounds as though you've had an interesting life.'

'That's right,' said Noel, suddenly so animated his ears actually flapped. 'It might be jus' sewage t'you but for thirty-five years it's been my bread and butter.'

I noticed Joyce winced slightly.

'That's right,' nodded Edwina. "E started out when they jus' put sewage on t'land an' ploughed it in.'

It was not an appealing thought.

'And what was your last job?' I asked, eager to move the conversation on.

He sat up and thrust out his chest.

'Go on, luv,' said Edwina. 'You tell 'em.'

'Well,' he said proudly. 'Jus' afore ah retired ah were in charge o' sewage sludge settlement.'

'That's most interesting,' said Joyce with little conviction.

I thought I had better get to the nitty-gritty and help out in an hour of need. 'Now unfortunately, there's a problem . . . and it's my fault.'

Vera's eyes widened and Joyce sat back and sipped her tea nervously.

'I'm really sorry but there's been a mix-up with the booking. I've been asked to speak as well on that night.'

''Bout sewage?' asked Noel.

'Not exactly. The thing is, in the meantime, I thought you could have a trial run with your slides after I've shown you how to work the projector. Then maybe next month you could come into school one evening and present your talk to myself and some of the staff. It would be good before speaking to a larger audience.' I looked at Vera. 'Also, the staff would be interested, wouldn't they?'

Vera pursed her lips. 'I'm sure they would, Mr Sheffield.' She turned to Joyce. 'And Mrs Davenport would love to attend,' she added pointedly.

'Of course,' muttered Joyce.

'That's very kind, Mr Sheffield,' nodded Edwina. 'Isn't that right, Noel?'

'It is that,' said Noel, reaching for the compulsory second biscuit.

It was just before five o'clock: I had helped Mr Crump load the projector and screen into his car and a relieved Joyce had set off for home.

'Thank you, Jack,' said Vera. 'A noble gesture.'

'Looks like I've got to give a talk to a hundred ladies.'

'Don't worry. We'll put on a special spread and I really am grateful, Jack. Joyce was in a terrible state. I'm sure there will come a day when we'll smile about it.'

'I'm not sure the staff will be pleased to be invited to a slide show about sewage.'

'Perhaps you could set it up on one of Mr Baker's in-service days and call it an insight into environmental issues.'

'They know us too well to fall for that.'

'Time to go home, Jack,' said Vera with a smile. 'An unexpected end to the day and I've got a new WI poster to prepare.'

In the distance I heard the church clock chime five o'clock. It was then something came to mind. I stared across the village green to the post office and the bright red post box.

'Just remembered . . . I had a letter to post.'

'You've missed it, Jack. Last post was four thirty.'

Chapter Fifteen

Mice and Men

Mrs Grainger completed maypole-dancing rehearsals prior to Monday's May Day celebrations in the village. Mrs Pringle and Ms Brookbank collected artwork for a display in the marquee. Mr Potts arranged to collect straw bales to create seating on the village green. The Revd Evans took morning assembly on the theme of animals and pets.

Extract from the Ragley & Morton School Logbook:
Friday, 29 April 1988

'Animals?' said Vera in surprise. 'Did you say animals?'

'Yes,' said a bemused Joseph. 'What's wrong with that? An animal service is a good idea.'

'I agree . . . but not in church!'

It was 8.30 a.m. on Friday, 29 April, and a brother and sister disagreement was in full swing when I walked into the office.

'Anyway,' said Joseph defiantly, 'it's already advertised and in assembly I shall be encouraging the children to bring along their pets.'

Vera walked back to her office. 'I just hope you know what you're doing,' she muttered.

Joseph's assembly certainly captured the children's attention and a few were determined to bring their pets to church on Sunday. They were still talking about it at lunchtime, when the conversation on my dinner table was lively.

Zach Eccles was particularly excited. 'Ah'm bringin' Pinky an' Perky, sir. M'dad med a cage for 'em.'

'Pinky and Perky?'

'M'two mice, sir. They're m'bes' friends.'

'An' ah'm bringin' Fifi, sir, m'rabbit,' said Tracey Higginbottom.

'That's lovely, Tracey.'

Jemima Poole was not to be outdone. 'M'brother's bringin' Scargill. 'E's famous now after findin' Amy in that shed.'

It was about that time I began to hope Joseph had considered the possible outcome of a Yorkshire terrier in the same building as a rabbit.

On Friday evening Vera decided to use a subtle ploy and sent Emmeline to the rescue. As always, Joseph was delighted when she arrived on his doorstep.

'Hello, Joseph. Vera rang to say you might want some help with the service on Sunday.'

'Did she?' he said guardedly. 'Well, that's very kind, Emmeline. You may have gathered she's not entirely pleased.'

'You mean with the children bringing their pets into church?'

'Exactly. Secretly I think she believes there are occasions when men have no sense and for some reason women are superior.'

Emmeline gave a fixed smile and said nothing.

'Anyway, do come in. I was preparing my sermon.'

Soon they were sitting at the kitchen table and drinking tea.

Joseph showed Emmeline his notes. 'I've done some research on St Francis of course but I was looking for something else.'

Emmeline smiled. 'I've got an idea.'

'Wonderful,' said Joseph. 'What is it?' He found he was becoming hugely reliant on this remarkable woman. Meeting her had enriched his life.

'How about the Robert Burns poem "To a Mouse"? You know, the one that says "the best-laid schemes of mice and men". I recall he was ploughing a field and upturned a mouse's nest and then went on to apologize. It would add interest and is a bit quirky.'

'Excellent idea,' he said and scribbled it down.

'With that in mind, Joseph,' said Emmeline, recalling her conversation with Vera, 'and, just wondering, but will there actually *be* any mice in church?'

'Yes, two.'

'You will make sure they are secure, won't you?'

'Never fear, my dear.'

Emmeline smiled. It was a long time since she had been called *my dear*.

*

On Saturday morning I helped Beth pack her car for her two-night stay in Hampshire with her parents. John and Diane were keen to spend the May Day holiday with their new grandson and Beth seemed happy to leave me to support the forthcoming May Day activities in Ragley. They set off bright and early and it seemed strange waving them off, but I was committed to a variety of jobs on behalf of the school, the first one being helping Anne set up the maypole on the village green.

At nine o'clock I set off for Ragley High Street where I parked outside the General Stores just as Ruby was coming out.

'Mornin', Mr Sheffield.'

'Good morning, Ruby. Lovely day.'

'Let's 'ope it stays fine f'May Day. That's allus speshul.'

'It certainly is.' It was good to see her looking so relaxed and content with her life. 'I recall that once you were the May Queen.'

She gave a wistful look. 'Ah were sixteen. That's when my George wanted t'be m'boyfriend but 'e never said an' Ronnie beat 'im to it.'

'All's well that ends well, Ruby.'

'Yer right there.' Suddenly the look on her face changed. 'Speak o' t'Devil. Look who's comin',' she said as a filthy old truck trundled down the high street. 'It's Deirdre, with that Gerry Coe.'

'I wonder how she is these days. I heard Stan left the farm to his brother.'

'She were real upset but Gerry said she can stay on as 'ousekeeper. She weren't bes' pleased an' did y'notice she were lookin' daggers at us when they drove past?'

'That's sad, Ruby. Some things don't change.'

'Y'know what they say, Mr Sheffield. A leopard never changes its stripes.' She hurried away to meet up with Natasha who was now the regular Coffee Shop assistant.

In the General Stores Prudence's three-legged cat, Trio, was sleeping on a sack of potatoes when I walked in. 'Good morning, Prudence.' I glanced up. 'And good morning, Jeremy.'

'Good morning, Mr Sheffield. Jeremy says he's looking forward to the May Day holiday.'

I nodded in acknowledgement to Jeremy, resplendent this morning in his new spring outfit of white shirt, khaki shorts and sunglasses. 'Yes, I'm here to help with the maypole.'

'Takes me back,' she said wistfully.

I smiled. 'It's always a special event.'

'Anyway, what's it to be, Mr Sheffield?'

'Just a loaf of bread, please, and two pounds of potatoes.'

She shooed her cat away and selected a few potatoes from the sack. 'I'll be taking Trio to church tomorrow for the first time. The vicar said he would bless all the animals so I couldn't miss that.'

'Yes, should be interesting,' I added cautiously.

I was putting my shopping bag into my car when Dorothy and Nellie walked by pushing their identical prams and I couldn't resist having a look at their babies. David and Malcolm, all pink cheeks and kicking legs, were both sucking furiously on matching blue dummies.

'Good morning,' I said with a smile. 'How are your boys?'

'Fine thanks, Mr Sheffield, an' 'ow's young Dan?' said Nellie.

'Like yours, growing fast,' I said cheerfully. 'Love the prams by the way. Really distinctive.'

They looked as though they had been props in a *Mary Poppins* film: large, cumbersome and shiny.

'It were Malcolm what spotted 'em,' said Dorothy, 'an' 'e told Dave.'

'They were on Aussie Frank's stall in Thirkby market,' said Nellie.

'Aussie Frank? I don't know him.'

''Onest as t'day is long,' said Dorothy. 'Picks up all sorts on 'is travels.'

''E's a mate o' Deke's,' said Nellie. 'Supplies 'im wi' 'is spurs an' sheriff's badge an' Stetson 'ats. 'E can lay 'is 'ands on owt y'like, can Aussie Frank.'

'So he's an Australian, is he?'

Nellie grinned. 'No, Mr Sheffield. 'E's from 'Uddersfield.'

'Then why is he called Aussie Frank?'

''E 'as a tattoo of Skippy t'kangaroo on 'is arm,' said Nellie.

'An' 'e's a big fan o' Kylie Minogue,' added Dorothy.

'Makes sense,' I said without conviction.

'Well, give our best t'Mrs Sheffield,' said Nellie and they wandered off pushing their prams proudly.

There was lots of activity on the village green. Marcus was working with Deke's sons, arranging a large semi-circle of straw bales in preparation for Captain Fantastic's Punch and Judy Show. I was with Anne when the maypole arrived. It had been collected by Deke Ramsbottom on his tractor and trailer from one of the Major's outbuildings.

Sally and Pat had come along to help and, guided by Anne, we topped the maypole in the traditional manner with eight bell garlands. Finally, when it was erected by members of the local Scout troop, we stood back to admire it and watched the long, coloured ribbons drift in the breeze.

'Perfect,' said Anne. 'Thanks, everybody.'

The weather forecast was good and we were confident all would go well.

At the far side of the green the Major was supervising some of the young men from the Combined Cadet Force to erect a huge marquee. This is where the ladies of the Women's Institute would be serving refreshments and Vera was giving them precise instructions.

Pat, Anne and Sally decided to join Vera when Rebecca Parrish arrived at my side. 'Busy times, Jack.'

'Good to see you, Rebecca.'

'The PTA have organized a Bring and Buy stall so I'm here to collect the trestle tables later this morning to go in the marquee.' She looked me up and down and smiled. I was wearing gardening boots, patched jeans and an old rugby jersey. 'You look different without a collar and tie.'

'I guess I do.'

'How about a coffee? There's something I want to share with you.'

When we walked into Nora's Coffee Shop, on the juke-box Billy Ocean was singing 'Get Outta My Dreams, Get Into My Car'.

'My treat this time, Jack,' she said.

We sat at a corner table and Natasha Smith served us with coffee and cake.

'Thank, Rebecca. This is welcome. Where's Katie?'

'At my mother's in Malton for a long weekend. It's good for them to catch up.'

'Likewise. Beth left this morning for a couple of nights with her parents in Hampshire.'

She sipped her coffee and looked at me thoughtfully. 'I heard your application just beat the deadline.'

'I delivered it by hand eventually.'

'I thought I would let you know that word has gone round there's a particularly strong candidate. It's a woman who's already in Higher Education. Works in a prestigious college down south and is well qualified by all accounts. Her husband has a new job in North Yorkshire, hence the need to move.'

'I guessed there would be a strong shortlist.'

'It definitely will be. The Vice-Principal is very particular but I'm pleased you're going for it, Jack.'

'If it doesn't work out I'm happy here.'

There was silence as each of us was lost in our own thoughts.

Suddenly she put down her cup and gave me that familiar look. 'I'm watching Eurovision tonight. You're on your own. So am I. A light supper and a bottle of wine. How about it? Would make a change to have some company. It's been a long time.'

I hesitated. This was unexpected. I thought back to our first meeting. She was a beautiful woman with porcelain skin and long blonde hair but the lines around her eyes had hinted at stressful times in the past. However, it was only when she spoke of her husband and his betrayal that the atmosphere was suffused with acrimony. Recently she had become more relaxed, seemingly accepting her new life.

'Thanks. Can I see how today develops and give you a ring?'

She smiled and spoke quietly. 'That's another reason you could be good at this job. You think carefully before you act. You don't jump in where angels fear to tread.'

'I'm no angel, Rebecca.'

'Jack . . . neither am I.' She looked out of the window. The ladies of the WI were gathering by the marquee. 'Time to go.' She stood up. 'Ring me.'

After a busy afternoon in Ragley I returned to the eerie silence of Bilbo Cottage and was enjoying a cup of tea when the phone rang. It was Beth.

'How's it gone?' she said.

'Everything's ready. The maypole is up and Sally put a children's art display in the marquee. Looks great. Vera seems to have been baking cakes to feed the five thousand. So, a good day. What about you?'

'The children are loving the attention and, to be honest, I'm enjoying the break. I think we'll be settling down to watch the Eurovision Song Contest once the boys are in bed.' I could hear their television in the background. 'Have you eaten? There's some cold chicken in the fridge.'

'Thanks. I got an invite from Rebecca Parrish to join her for supper and watch the song contest.'

'Are you going?'

'Don't think so. It's not a party. Just the two of us. She fancied some company.'

'She could be your colleague if you get the job. Could be a useful contact. There's no harm in going. Anyway, must go, Mum's serving up her famous watercress soup.'

Shortly before seven o'clock I was in Rebecca's spacious and elegant bungalow on the Easington Road. She had prepared a speedy spaghetti bolognese while sipping a glass of Merlot. The room was warm and comfortable and full of books and prints. Rebecca wore tight jeans and a white T-shirt. Her feet were bare. We settled down on a huge sofa and she switched on the television. It was clear she wasn't entirely interested in the song contest beamed live from Dublin. The sound was turned low and became background noise to our conversation.

There was a pause when, unexpectedly, Switzerland beat the United Kingdom by just a point in the last vote to win the title. A Canadian singer, Céline Dion, was the winner with the song 'Ne partez pas sans moi'. She had a great voice. It was then Rebecca switched off the television and selected another bottle of red wine.

'Rebecca, I ought to be going. It's been a lovely evening. Thanks for the hospitality. You have a lovely home by the way.' I stood up and looked at the titles on one of the book-cases. 'We share similar tastes in fiction.' There was a shelf of hardbacks featuring Dickens, Hardy, Austen, Trollope and Tolkien.

'Reading is one of my passions,' she said and came to stand by me.

'I see you've still got many of the Penguin paperbacks . . . John Braine, Richard Adams, John Wyndham. I love all these.'

'Yes, I kept all my books and disposed of Simon's. He wasn't into fiction.' There was a cold finality to her words.

'I'm sorry you were hurt so badly.'

She gave a barely perceptible shake of her head and sighed deeply. 'I picked the wrong man, Jack, even though he gave me a beautiful daughter. In the end I had no respect for him. He was more of a mouse than a man.'

'You look happier now and you clearly enjoy your work.'

She gave a sad smile. 'Yes, that's something.'

I picked up my jacket from the back of a chair and slipped it on. 'Well, thanks again. I'll say goodnight.'

She held my hand, stretched towards me and kissed me gently on the cheek. 'Thanks for your company, Jack.' She straightened the collar of my jacket and stood back. Then she tugged the bobble from her hair and shook it free. It was as if it was an act of release. There was a pause. 'I'm hoping it's not the wine talking but I'm tempted to ask you to stay . . . but I know you would say no.'

I didn't say no.

I didn't say anything.

I merely returned the knowing smile and walked out into the darkness.

On Sunday morning Beth rang me before I set off for church and asked me how my evening with Rebecca had gone. I simply said it was relaxed and I had enjoyed both the supper and the song contest. The conversation was brief as Dan began to cry for his next feed and Beth rang off hastily. It reminded me of the reality of my life.

When I walked out to my car it was a bright sunny morning that lifted the spirits. Swallows had returned to their nests in the eaves of Bilbo Cottage, the hedgerows were teeming with new life and almond trees were in blossom. The sun was shining as I set off. My thoughts drifted and reflected on my evening with Rebecca. A bright woman and a talented educationalist, she had revealed a vulnerability that had surprised me.

It was definitely a different scene to normal when I arrived at St Mary's Church. Children carrying pets were filling the pews along with some of the regular congregation who were concerned that their regular seat was occupied by a guinea pig or, heaven forbid, a long-tailed rat.

Joseph, however, seemed at ease when he launched into his sermon. 'In Exodus, the Ten Commandments remind us to treat animals with respect and care and I know everyone here will make sure they look after their pets and they will be kind to each other.'

There was a growl from Scargill but, undeterred, Joseph carried on.

'St Francis of Assisi was born in Italy almost eight hundred years ago and he is the patron saint of animals. He was something of a wild youth but he decided to give up his wealth and work for God.' There were nods of approval from Vera and Emmeline. So far so good. 'He loved all creatures,' continued Joseph, 'and allegedly even preached to birds.'

A loud meow from Trio caused some stifled laughter but Joseph was now in full flow. 'The dove is mentioned in the Bible more often than any other bird, in fact over fifty times. We associate the dove with peace on earth and peace in our church.'

It was at that moment Zach realized Pinky and Perky were becoming agitated.

Joseph turned to his list of the animals. 'Now let us pray. Dear Lord, please deliver our pets from any pain and suffering including the mice, Pinky and Perky; Fifi the rabbit; Scargill the Yorkshire terrier; Beowulf the bull mastiff; George the guinea pig; Roland the rat; Flossie the French poodle; and Thatcher the stick insect.'

Vera looked up sharply and frowned.

'We place them in Your capable hands and ask for healing and strength. In Jesus' name. Amen.'

There was a communal Amen followed by a growl from Karl Tomkins's bull mastiff. That was the moment Pinky and Perky made their bid for freedom. Mr Eccles had failed his GCE woodwork back in the sixties and clearly needed a refresher course in making a mouse-proof cage.

'They've gone!' shouted Zach followed by a loud scream. Amelia Postlethwaite, the postmistress, jumped up quickly as Pinky and Perky sought refuge under her pew. It was then that Prudence Golightly's cat suddenly took interest as a tasty lunch scampered close by. Within seconds bedlam broke out as the larger animals sought to devour the smaller ones.

It was Emmeline who saved the day.

With remarkable reflexes, she scooped up Pinky and Perky in her shopping bag and hurried into the vestry where she put them in an empty cardboard box. She knew where Joseph kept the spare Communion wafers, selected two and dropped them in the box. Pinky and Perky were delighted with their unexpected Sunday lunch while Emmeline hoped God wouldn't mind.

*

The following day the May Day celebrations proved the best I could remember. Fortunately the weather was perfect. The new leaves of the weeping willow on the village green caressed the lush grass and the first flower stalks on the horse chestnut trees provided a promise of the summer days ahead.

Anne was delighted with the maypole dancing. The rehearsals had proved rewarding. Each girl wore a pretty headband of flowers. They skipped in and out in perfect time until the ribbons were plaited around the pole. The dance was reversed and the ribbons were unravelled followed by huge applause from the large crowd.

Don and Sheila Bradshaw had set up a bar on a trestle table and I sat down with a glass of warm beer outside the marquee. The Ragley & Morton Brass Band played 'Jerusalem' watched by a group of morris dancers who were sitting on straw bales waiting their turn. Old Tommy Piercy's hog roast was doing a roaring trade while Vera and her colleagues began serving cream teas at one end of the Women's Institute marquee.

As children settled on the bales to watch Captain Fantastic's Punch and Judy Show I walked into the Bring and Buy Sale. There were cakes, books and bric-a-brac. Rebecca was there, relaxed and smiling. 'Is there anything of interest that catches your eye, Mr Sheffield?' I recognized the whimsical mood.

'What about this?' I picked up a copy of the 1986 *Jackie Annual*. On the front it said: 'Something Special – Just For You!'

'Sorry,' she said with a smile. 'It's taken.'

'Really?'

'Yes,' she added with a mischievous grin. 'I bought it. It deals with affairs of the heart.'

'In that case I'll settle for the lemon drizzle cake.'

'A wise choice,' she said. 'As always.'

I was pleased we had spoken.

It had been an eventful few days and on Tuesday morning before I left for school there was a letter waiting for me. It was from the College in York inviting me to attend for interview for the post of Senior Lecturer in Primary Education at 9.00 a.m. on Wednesday, 18 May 1988.

Chapter Sixteen

Everything Changes

Miss Flint provided supply cover in Class 1 during the interviews for a new school secretary.
Extract from the Ragley & Morton School Logbook:
Monday, 16 May 1988

It had been a slow dawn until the first rays of sunlight appeared over the distant hills like a wire of gold. A gilded light caressed the land as I looked out of our bedroom window. It was Monday, 16 May, the beginning of an eventful week. In two days' time I would be attending for interview at the College and this afternoon a new school secretary would be appointed.

When I walked into the office Vera was studying the curriculum vitae for each of the four applicants for the post of secretary.

'Good morning, Mr Sheffield.' She passed over a typed sheet of paper. 'Based on their letters of application I do think we've got the best four candidates. I've put them at thirty-minute intervals straight after lunch.'

'Thank you, Vera. So, apart from you, I presume it's just Joseph and myself?'

'Yes. Joseph felt that's sufficient. Just the headteacher and Chair of Governors, plus myself of course, who knows the job.'

'Exactly,' I said with a smile.

'And I've spoken to Valerie. She will be here in good time to take your class.'

Valerie Flint had agreed to do supply duty.

'Thanks, Vera.' I knew it was an important day for her and she was dressed in her smartest business suit and a crisp linen blouse. 'How do you feel about meeting your eventual successor?'

'Mixed, I suppose. Even so, I'm optimistic that someone else who will love the school as I do will take up the reins.'

'Well said. I'm sure we'll find the right person.'

She sat down again at her desk and for a moment I studied that familiar profile. I pondered that even the fiercest of flames are extinguished one day and Vera's passion for Ragley School had burned brightly for many years. Generations of children had come and gone and she could recall them all.

I tried to depart on a lighter note. 'And Vera . . . do make sure you give Joseph the chance to get a word in edgeways.'

She gave me a wry smile as I hurried out.

*

At morning break I was on playground duty and it was good to see the children at play. Mary Scrimshaw and Katie Parrish came over to speak to me.

'We were just thinking, sir, that this is our last term at Ragley,' said Katie.

'I'm sure you'll enjoy Easington School,' I said. 'It's the next stage in your life. It will be exciting.'

'We've enjoyed it here, sir,' said Mary.

'That's right,' agreed Katie. 'Life is great.' She paused and a flicker of sadness crossed her face. 'I'll miss it when I'm grown up.'

I was aware she'd had a lot to deal with in her short life. 'Growing up can be fun as well,' I said. 'Loads to look forward to.'

'And we've made a joint decision, sir,' said a determined Mary.

'What's that?'

'We've decided when we grow up we don't want husbands,' declared Mary.

'Why is that?'

Katie smiled, 'Well, sir . . . we just want someone to help with the housework.'

'Ah well . . . good luck with that,' I murmured as they wandered off to play two-ball against the school wall.

At one o'clock Joseph and I were in the school office while Vera welcomed the first candidate and asked her to wait in the staff-room.

The list before me read:

Mrs Irene Blunt, 54. Thirkby
Mrs Joan Fothersgill, 36. Easington

Mrs Samantha Laycock, 42. Easington
Miss Victoria Penny, 24. Morton

I needn't have worried about Joseph getting a word in because none of us did. Mrs Blunt never stopped talking. We were given a potted life history including two failed marriages, a couple of typing qualifications and an interest in horoscopes.

'Sorry,' said Vera apologetically after the red-faced and decidedly bumptious Mrs Blunt made an exit to the car park. 'She looked good on paper.'

'Never mind,' said Joseph. 'Onwards and upwards.'

'Whatever that means,' murmured Vera as she went to the staff-room to collect Mrs Joan Fothersgill.

This was a much more rewarding experience. Mrs Fothersgill definitely impressed. She was well qualified, spoke with confidence and clearly wanted the job. Her only weakness was the fact it was twenty years since she had typed a letter.

Next in was Mrs Samantha Laycock, a short, stout lady who assumed she had already got the job. 'I have a new approach to filing,' she said, 'that will benefit the school.'

'What is that?' asked Joseph while Vera remained unusually quiet.

'I dispense with it entirely.'

Vera couldn't help but break the silence assuming she had misheard. 'Did you say dispense with it?'

'Yes, the future is *computers*, not paper.'

'So where would you put all the communications from County Hall?' I asked. 'We get lots of those every week about health and safety, holiday dates, attendance reports and so on.'

'I would tell them to move with the times,' said Mrs Laycock.

Joseph was keen to bring the interview to a close before his sister self-imploded. 'Have you any questions for us?'

'Yes, when would I start?'

'Monday the fifth of September, if successful,' I said pointedly.

Mrs Laycock looked puzzled. 'If successful?'

'Yes,' I said and stood up. 'It's been a pleasure meeting you, Mrs Laycock. We shall telephone this evening to let you know.'

'Before seven then,' she said. 'Bingo starts at half past.'

I had begun to be concerned. Vera and I had tried hard to select what appeared to be the strongest applicants and things were not looking good. However, Miss Victoria Penny provided a refreshing change. A petite and polite young lady who worked part-time in the music shop in York, she came over as honest and capable.

Her typing qualifications were excellent and she was familiar with the idiosyncrasies of a Gestetner duplicating machine. Finally, it was Vera who asked, 'What are your views on filing systems?'

I waited with bated breath.

Miss Penny looked thoughtful. 'Well, it would make sense to see what filing system is currently in place and learn how to use it. I would hope there may be a chance for some training if I was successful.'

It was three o'clock when we retired to the staff-room to make our decision. Joseph looked appealingly at his sister. There was no doubt who would have the last word.

'I was impressed with Mrs Fothersgill but I do believe Miss Penny would be the ideal choice.'

'Agreed,' I said.

'Perfect,' said Joseph and Vera smiled.

The way ahead was clear.

The following morning a delighted Miss Penny joined us for morning coffee and, when the bell went for the end of break, we left her with Vera. As we walked out Vera opened the top drawer of the filing cabinet. 'This has taken many years to perfect but it really does work well,' she said and the attentive Miss Penny hung on to every word.

At the end of school our local authority governor, Albert Jenkins, popped his head round my classroom door. 'Just called in to wish you all the best for tomorrow.'

'That's kind, Albert.'

'Are you well prepared?'

'I think so.'

'Well, Cicero put it wisely, Jack,' he said with a smile. '"Whatever you do, do it with all your might." Show your enthusiasm. A bit of *con brio* goes down a long way in an interview.'

'*Con brio?*' I pondered for a moment. 'With . . . something?'

'With *spirit*, Jack. With *vigour*.'

'I shall, Albert.'

'And Vera seems pleased with the new appointment.'

'Yes, delighted.'

He sighed. 'Remember Plato's quotation, Jack: "Everything changes and nothing remains still." '

*

After a sleepless night, Wednesday morning dawned bright and breezy. Beth gave me a hug before she left with John. 'Good luck, Jack. Do your best. Let me know as soon as you can.' Then, after Mrs Roberts had collected Dan, I was alone with my thoughts. An important day lay ahead, one that could change our lives.

I rang school to check all was well. Valerie Flint had agreed to do supply duty in my class during my absence. Vera answered immediately. 'Hope it goes well, Mr Sheffield,' she said. 'Valerie is well prepared so there are no concerns.'

'Thanks, Vera.'

'Everyone sends their best wishes.'

I sensed a hint of sadness in her voice. It was a significant week for both of us with my interview this morning and a new secretary waiting in the wings.

'I should be back by lunchtime, Vera.'

When I walked out to my car a thrush with a speckled breast was perched on my garden fence trilling a spring-time melody while above me a flock of starlings wheeled in formation towards the Vale of York. I wound down the window to breathe in the clean air. I drove past woods carpeted with bluebells and green unripe barley in Twenty Acre Field. The rich tapestry of a familiar countryside flew by until I turned south towards York and the city centre. Once again I marvelled at the Minster when it came into view and dominated the medieval skyline. York, the jewel in Yorkshire's crown, was spread out before me.

I parked on Lord Mayor's Walk. Above me the city walls, built of magnesian limestone, shimmered in the morning sunshine. They stood as a reminder of the days when

defences were needed that would repel an invader. Across
the road was my old college where I had trained as a teacher
back in the sixties. As I walked through the archway into
the red-brick quadrangle it was a view laced with memories. As a student reading English Literature I had been
introduced to the poems of T. S. Eliot. After twenty years I
felt I had come full circle to be here again.

At reception I was directed towards a spacious common
room where tea was being served. A cheerful administrator
was there to welcome me, clipboard at the ready. At the far
end of the room groups of academics were collecting mail
from labelled pigeonholes. Three of the candidates had
already arrived, two men and a woman.

The first to speak to me was a tall, slim woman with a
flawless complexion. Her long brown hair was tied back in
a ponytail and she wore a beautifully tailored dark business suit. 'Hello, I'm Candice Kelsey from West Sussex.' Her
smile was engaging and she exuded a calm confidence. 'By
process of elimination you must be Jack Sheffield. There's
four of us for the interview.'

She nodded towards two men sipping tea and engaged
in conversation. One was short, rotund and balding; the
other was bearded and smoking a pipe.

'Pleased to meet you. Yes, I'm Jack, head of a local village
school.'

'Are you familiar with the College?'

'I used to be a student here.'

'So, you'll know it well. I'm told it has a wonderful ethos.'
She was very direct. It felt almost as though my interview
had already begun.

'Yes, it has. I enjoyed my time here and the students are really well prepared prior to their probationary year.'

'That's good to hear. My college is just the same.'

'Well, I wish you luck. You're already doing the job, so that will stand you in good stead.'

She smiled as if appraising me for the first time. 'That's kind, Jack, unlike the two gentlemen over there who thought I was here to serve the hot drinks. Both are head-teachers. They discounted me immediately.'

'I'm sorry to hear that.'

'I'm used to it. Anyway, let's hope we both give a good account of ourselves and there are no regrets at the end of the day. Fortunately, I have another interview next week in Leeds.'

The lady with the clipboard reappeared. 'Could you follow me please?'

'Good luck, Jack,' said Candice.

As was the custom we were seen in alphabetical order. The portly David Bartram went in first, followed by Candice. Then it was a close thing between George Shaw and myself but the third letter made the difference. As he was summoned I wondered if his parents had a sense of humour and had given him the middle name of Bernard.

At ten thirty-five, my name was finally called and, when I walked in, my heart was beating like summer thunder. It was a déjà vu moment, an echo of time in a busy life. There had been other interviews but this could change my life. I took a deep breath as I surveyed the faces in front of me.

'Please take a seat, Mr Sheffield. Thank you for

attending. I'm Donald Fox, the Vice-Principal. We're here to appoint an additional Senior Lecturer to join our Education Faculty and I shall be inviting my colleagues to ask questions. Please feel free to ask any yourself at the end of the interview.'

There were four members on the panel. 'The panel before you comprises, to my left, Mr James Fairbank, Head of the Education Faculty, and to my right Professor Jenny McKay, Head of Humanities, and our admissions coordinator, Dr Eva Garcia. I'll ask Mr Fairbank to begin proceedings. I'm aware he knows you well.'

The slim, angular man in a sober grey suit was just as I remembered him.

'Good morning, Jack,' he said quietly. 'For the benefit of colleagues, Jack was one of my students in the sixties. Perhaps you could tell us a little about your career to date and why you have applied for this post.'

It was a gentle, reassuring beginning and Jim was clearly giving me an opportunity to relax into the interview.

'Good morning and thank you for the opportunity of this interview.' I took in all the faces, expectant and inquisitive. 'The College is a special place for me. Looking back, I realize now how fortunate I was coming here. It put me on a pathway to becoming a better teacher. When I left, I recall Mr Fairbank saying that all children have talent and it was up to me to identify it and nurture it. He also told me I should never underestimate children because they will always surprise you and he was right.'

'You have a good memory, Jack,' said Jim with a gentle smile.

'For the past ten years I've been headteacher of a local

village school and, before that, I was a deputy headteacher of a large primary school for six years in a disadvantaged area in West Yorkshire. I've had a rewarding career supporting staff and doing my best to provide effective leadership. In recent years I've spent more time supervising students on teaching practice from this college, so I'm familiar with the support procedures you offer to students. I feel ready to move on in my career, hence my application for this post.'

Jim glanced at the Vice-Principal. The overture was over. It was time to move on. Suddenly the questions came thick and fast. Professor McKay asked me about the impact of the new National Curriculum and kept coming back at me again and again to justify my beliefs in a cross-curricular approach to learning. She appeared to believe it was at odds with the new framework and frowned occasionally as she made hurried and copious notes.

Dr Garcia, an effervescent lady with long black wavy hair and perfect olive skin, was much more positive and thanked me for supporting students on teaching practice. She asked if the process could be improved in any way and I suggested earlier preliminary visits could assist all parties towards effective preparation. She scribbled notes while Jim Fairbank came in with another question. This is where it became interesting.

'Mr Sheffield, it's clear you love your present role as headteacher. So, I ask you directly ... are you making a mistake applying for a post where you are no longer in charge? In other words, to what degree are you willing to be a team player?' There was a hint of a smile on his lips.

I paused for a moment before replying. 'I believe my

leadership style has developed over the years. I'm not an enlightened despot. I listen to the views of others and support positive initiatives whenever I can. When a new and exciting enterprise is completed successfully the best feeling is when we sit down knowing we did it *together*.'

He turned to the Vice-Principal. 'Thank you. No more questions.'

It was over quickly. The only query I raised was the issue of County Hall's requirement of three months' notice and this was answered succinctly.

Lunchtime was in full flow when I arrived back at school. All the staff had been waiting anxiously for my return, including Miss Flint. Marcus had forsaken a delicious sweet course of prunes and custard to hurry into the staff-room and join the others.

'So,' said Anne, looking around, 'we're all here ... how did it go?'

'Fine, I think. A few tough questions but I feel I answered them well. They're ringing me this evening so I'll find out then.'

Vera insisted on a blow-by-blow account of every question and seemed to evaluate each of my responses with surgical precision. It felt like being interviewed all over again. Finally, we all sat down with a welcome cup of tea and returned to normality. Afternoon school beckoned and there were children to teach.

Back in Bilbo Cottage I was waiting for Beth when she arrived home from school. She had started going in for a few days each week in preparation for returning full-time after the half-term holiday. Mrs Roberts had driven off after passing over young Dan to me and I carried him out in my arms to the driveway. Beth jumped out to unstrap John from the back seat and he ran in through the open door.

She picked up Dan and gave him a hug and a kiss; then she looked up at me expectantly. 'So . . . any news?'

'Not yet.'

'How was it?'

'I answered all the questions. Lasted around half an hour. The Vice-Principal clearly rules the roost and I'm guessing it will be his final decision.'

'Who was on the panel?'

'There were four altogether—'

Beth turned towards the house. 'Did you hear the phone?'

Dan was gurgling away contentedly but that was the only sound we could hear.

'Sorry, Jack. Go on. Hearing things I guess.'

John had just found his Lego car on the hall table when the telephone rang. He picked it up immediately. John had watched his mother answer the phone many times and was excited to have a go himself.

'Hello,' he said cheerfully.

'Hello,' came the reply. 'Could I speak to Mr Sheffield please?'

There was a long pause. 'I'm John.'

The Vice-Principal realized he was speaking to a child. 'Hello, John. Is Mr Sheffield your daddy?'

'Yes.'

'Could you get him for me please?'

'No. He's busy.'

'I think he would want to talk to me.'

'Who are you?'

'My name is Mr Fox.'

'I don't like Mr Fox ... and Mummy and Daddy don't like Mr Fox.'

'Why is that?'

'He wants to eat Peter Rabbit.'

'I know, but I'm not that Mr Fox. I'm a really nice Mr Fox.'

'That's good.'

'John, can you see your daddy or mummy?'

'No.'

'Where are they?'

'Talking to my brother.'

'And where's your brother?'

'With Mummy.'

'And where's Mummy?'

'Talking to my daddy.'

'Are they in the garden?'

'Yes. Do you like Lego?'

'Yes.'

'I've got a Lego car.'

'That's good. John, could you put the phone down please and call for your mummy or daddy?'

'OK.'

John did as he was told and replaced the receiver to end the call.

'Let's get him inside,' said Beth.

I looked with concern at Dan. 'Mrs Roberts said he had just been fed.'

'He's grizzling for something,' said Beth.

'I'll take him while you get your coat off.'

I went into the kitchen and Beth looked down at John who was playing contentedly with his toy.

'Mummy, I've been talking to a man.'

'Have you?'

'Yes, on the telephone.'

'When?' There was a note of alarm in her voice.

'Just now. He likes Peter Rabbit.'

'Who does?'

'Mr Fox. He said put the phone down and I did.'

'Jack! There's been a call. Do you think it could have been the Vice-Principal? John put the phone down.'

'Oh no.'

'Jack, it's not his fault. He did as he was asked.'

'Yes, I understand but we need to ring back . . . I'm changing a nappy here.'

The phone rang again and Beth snatched it up. 'Hello.'

'Is that Mrs Sheffield? It's Donald Fox here from the College.'

'Vice-Principal. Good of you to call.'

'I've just had an enlightening conversation with your son that ranged from Lego to Beatrix Potter.'

'Yes, he can be a chatterbox.'

'Never fear. His vocabulary was very good. I'm sure you're very proud. You'll gather I'm hoping to speak with Mr Sheffield.'

'Yes, of course.' Beth turned to me. 'Jack, the Vice-Principal for you.'

I passed Dan to Beth and picked up the receiver in a cloud of Johnson's Baby Powder.

'Jack Sheffield here, Vice-Principal. Thank you for calling.'

'Mr Sheffield. I'm pleased I've caught up with you. You had an impressive interview today and after consulting with my colleagues I should like to offer you the post of Senior Lecturer.'

'Thank you. That's good news.'

'So . . . do you accept?'

Like a single shaft of hope answers tumbled into place. Everything changes but the essence of some things remains the same. I was still a teacher.

I took a deep breath. 'Yes . . . I do.'

Chapter Seventeen

Making a Life

Candidates for the headship visited school today.
Extract from the Ragley & Morton School Logbook:
Friday, 10 June 1988

It was a new dawn. A disc of golden light shimmered in the eastern sky on a day filled with birdsong and the buzzing of insects. Jill Dando was giving a news update on *Breakfast Time* as I finished my Weetabix.

'Interesting day in store, Jack,' said Beth as she brushed John's hair in the hallway. 'Headship interviews this afternoon. Hope they make the right choice.'

'I'm sure they will.'

'And a meal at the manor tonight,' she added. 'A lovely end to the week.' They both waved as they walked out to the car and I watched them drive away.

It was Friday, 10 June, and this morning I would be

meeting my successor. The four shortlisted candidates had been given the opportunity to call into school before driving up to County Hall for the afternoon interviews. Ms Cleverley had informed me it was a very strong shortlist and all were ready and primed to meet the challenge of the National Curriculum. I wondered if there was a message there. It sometimes felt as though Ms Cleverley worked in an office that was built on words. We needed support and it was not always forthcoming.

Vera had arranged for two of the candidates to visit from 9.15 a.m. to 10.15 a.m. and the other two from 10.30 a.m. to 11.30 a.m. This meant Miss Flint was coming in to cover my class. Vera had cut out the advertisement from the *Times Educational Supplement* and pinned it to the staff-room noticeboard.

It read:

Headteacher required for Ragley & Morton Church of England Primary School, North Yorkshire, to commence September 1988. Application forms from County Hall, Northallerton.

Underneath was a list of the shortlisted candidates who were due to visit.

9.15–10.15: Mr Paul Goodyear & Mrs Isobel Hutton
10.30–11.30: Ms Elizabeth Drummond & Miss Emma
    Hartley

Mr Paul Goodyear, a balding, ruddy-faced man in his forties, was the first to arrive in a rusty gold-coloured Morris

Marina. Sartorial elegance had clearly passed him by and he shambled from the car park in a crumpled suit that had seen better days.

In contrast Mrs Hutton, a woman of about forty, was wearing a smart tweed suit; she was dropped off at the school gate by her husband. He was driving a Ford Granada, reminiscent of John Thaw and Dennis Waterman screaming around corners in their Consul GT 3.0 litre version in *The Sweeney*. Fortunately, unlike our television heroes, she was unlikely to smash in the door, pin me to the ground and yell in my face, 'You're nicked!'

In fact, she was a pleasant lady and keen to know much about the school. She took a great interest in Anne's classroom, clearly impressed with the outstanding work of our experienced deputy headteacher. She stayed for the full hour, unlike Mr Goodyear who was keen to depart for County Hall. He had been a deputy headteacher in Malton for fifteen years and this was his sixth interview. I sensed he had done all this before and was becoming tired of the experience. However, he professed to know exactly what to write in a letter of application. Mrs Hutton, in contrast, made good contact with every member of staff, which went down well, particularly with Pat who discovered they shared an interest in drama.

It was when the second pair of interviewees arrived that it got interesting.

At morning break we gathered in the staff-room while keeping an eye on the expected new arrivals. The first car to pull into the car park was a Citroën 2CV – that quirky car affectionately known as the 'Tin Snail'. From it emerged a slim, five-foot-six-inch thirty-eight-year-old woman with a short bob of brown hair. She checked her wristwatch and then stared up at the school. It reminded me of the day I arrived in Ragley back in 1977. When I saw the school I knew I could be happy here. After a moment, she reached into her car, picked up a small notebook and slipped it into the jacket pocket of her two-piece business suit. She walked across the playground, smiling at the children as she did so.

Suddenly a smart, sleek Audi 100 pulled up, dwarfing the Citroën. A tall woman with long black hair got out, looking as though she had just completed a photoshoot for *Vogue* magazine.

'Wow!' said Pat. 'That's an Armani suit.'

'An expensive lady,' said Sally. 'Perhaps I should have worn a dress today instead of cords.'

The final interviewee strode confidently towards the school entrance without hesitation and I walked to meet them. 'Good morning and welcome to Ragley. I'm Jack Sheffield, the headteacher.'

'Hello, Jack,' said the taller of the two, immediately oozing confidence. 'I'm Elizabeth Drummond. My friends call me Lottie. I'm deputy head at a girls' prep school in Surrey.' We shook hands.

'And I'm Emma Hartley,' the other said with a gentle smile. 'I'm very pleased to meet you. I'm a primary-school deputy head from Skipton. The opportunity to visit is much appreciated.' She looked around at Sally's display of children's painting. 'Impressive artwork.'

'That's thanks to Mrs Pringle. You can meet her now. Let's go into the staff-room and then I'll show you around the school.' We walked in and Anne, Sally and Pat introduced themselves. It was a friendly start. 'And this is our secretary, Mrs Forbes-Kitchener.'

'Good morning, ladies, and welcome,' said Vera. 'Would you like a coffee?'

'Yes, please,' said Miss Hartley. 'That's very kind.'

'No thank you,' said Ms Drummond. 'Have you any herbal tea?'

'Not today,' said Vera.

'Just water then.'

Emma took her coffee and Anne beckoned her. Immediately they were engaged in conversation.

Ms Drummond stood by the window and Vera passed her a glass of water. She sipped it with affected elegance without wetting her glossy red lips. Children were playing happily outside and Marcus was on duty.

'Good to see the girls practising their netball,' she said. 'Fitness is so important, don't you think?' It was clearly rhetorical as she pressed on with what felt like a sermon. 'There are so many unfortunate distractions these days . . . comics, sweets, an excess of sugar. *A healthy body and a healthy mind* is my motto. Have you ladies seen *Lyn Marshall's Everyday Yoga* on the BBC? It's ideal exercise. She demonstrates a routine that stretches the entire body.'

Sally gave me a wide-eyed look and replaced the lid on the biscuit tin.

When the bell went, Anne, Sally and Pat stood up to return to their classrooms.

'Please may I look in reception first of all?' asked Miss Hartley.

'That's fine with me,' said Anne. 'Perhaps you could

show Ms Drummond around, Jack, and then we'll do a swap.'

'I'm keen to see the older children,' said Ms Drummond, 'so I can assess their progress against my class. It would make an interesting comparison. I have some particularly bright children in my school.'

'As do we,' I said simply.

When we walked through the hall I heard the sound of a telephone ringtone but it was coming from her leather shoulder bag. With practised ease she took out a large black plastic mobile phone. It was the size of a brick and had a stubby aerial sticking out of the top.

'Excuse me. I must take this,' and she walked back into the entrance hall. Her conversation was brief and I heard her say, 'I'll let you know.' There was a pause followed by: ''Bye, darling.'

I was intrigued. 'How long have you had a mobile phone?'

'A month. It was a birthday gift from my husband. He's a generous man. Little change out of two thousand pounds.'

I looked in astonishment. 'That sounds expensive.'

'But so convenient.' She held it up. 'It's a Nokia Cityman 1320. Here, have a look.'

She passed it over. The flat face was covered in numbers plus buttons with abbreviations such as CLR and SEL that made no sense to me. I was surprised by the weight. 'It seems really heavy.'

She shrugged. 'Perhaps. Only a little over one and a half kilos.' She took it back and put it in her bag. 'You should get one,' she said with a slightly condescending smile.

'Bit pricey for me.'

'Oh well. Each to his own. My husband is a top IT executive at Unilever. Works in Brussels but has just signed a
new two-year contract based in Leeds. He likes to keep me
happy.'

By the end of the visit it was clear Ms Drummond held
Miss Hartley in low esteem and didn't view her as a con-
tender. Her manner on occasions had been dismissive.

We gathered in the entrance hall. 'Well, I hope you found
the visit helpful,' I said. 'And best of luck for the interview.'

'Yes, looking forward to it,' said Ms Drummond. 'My
husband was keen for me to fill my time up here with
something useful.'

'Have you got other interviews lined up?' I asked.

She frowned. 'I'm hoping that won't be necessary.'

'What about you, Miss Hartley?' I asked.

'This is my first interview for a headship so I'm just hoping it goes well. I really love the school. The ethos is
excellent, just like mine in Skipton.'

'That's good to hear,' I said.

'If you don't mind me saying,' interjected Ms Drummond, 'it strikes me that the salary for a small school like
this is very poor for a man. I'm rather surprised you've continued in this post for so long.'

'I've been very happy here.'

'And salary isn't everything,' countered Miss Hartley.

'Well, perhaps for you it's enough to make a living,' said
Ms Drummond.

Miss Hartley gave her a penetrating stare. There was
clearly more to this young woman than met the eye: steel
behind the smile. 'I don't see it that way,' she said.

Ms Drummond shook her head. 'Really. So how *do* you see it?'

'For me it's not about *making a living* . . . it's about *making a life.*'

The office door was open and Vera came out to join me in the entrance hall. We watched them drive away. Their interviews at County Hall were only an hour away. 'So, what do you think, Vera?'

'I agree with Miss Hartley about making a life,' she said softly. 'That's exactly why we're here.'

It was afternoon break. Sally was on duty while Anne, Pat and Marcus were discussing who might be the next headteacher.

'So, any preferences?' I asked.

'Mrs Hutton or Miss Hartley for me,' said Anne. 'I would be happy with either.'

'Same for me,' said Pat. 'I wasn't keen on Mr Goodyear. Didn't seem interested.'

'The guy seemed pleasant enough when he came into my classroom,' said Marcus.

'We would have to knock him into shape,' said Pat.

'What about Ms Drummond?' I asked.

Anne looked at the others. 'Well, we were unanimous, Jack.'

'Really?'

'Yes, it was a definite *no.*'

I looked at Vera. 'You're quiet,' I said.

'Well, I won't be here of course but, whoever they appoint, I'll make sure Miss Penny knows how to run the school.'

*

278

At the end of the school day I was in the office when Vera answered the telephone. 'It's Miss Barrington-Huntley,' she said and handed me the receiver. Then she went out and closed the door.

'Hello, Miss Barrington-Huntley. Sorry to keep you waiting. I was busy with a parent. How are you?'

'Fine thank you, Jack. End of an eventful week. Congratulations on the new post.'

'Thank you. It was a difficult decision to leave Ragley.'

'I fully understand. I'm ringing to let you know I've just had a conversation with the Vice-Principal at the College and there's no problem regarding your transfer from this authority. You've given three months' notice which is fine and it would appear we've found an ideal replacement for you.'

'Are you permitted to let me know who it is?'

'Yes. It's Miss Hartley.'

'I'm delighted. She clearly loved the school and made excellent contact with the staff. I'll support in any way I can.'

'That's another reason for ringing. I spoke with her after the interview and she's keen to meet with you and get to know the school. I had planned to call in myself on the first of next month. It's a Friday. So could you put that in your diary?'

'Yes, of course. It will be good to meet up again.'

'That apart, Jack, I wanted to thank you for your contribution over the years. Ragley & Morton is a school of which we are very proud.'

'I've enjoyed my time here and have always valued your support.'

There was a pause and a hint of laughter. 'Thank you, Jack. I was just thinking that we didn't get off to a good start. When we first met in November 1977 my prize hat was burned on your bonfire.'

'Yes, I've never really lived that down.'

'On a more serious note, Jack, keep in mind that you are halfway through your career. There are important years ahead, a time to use the experience you have gained for the benefit of others, the next generation of teachers. When the National Curriculum is fully introduced, don't lose sight of your philosophy – please share it with your students. You'll no doubt find satisfaction in your new role. However, soon you will have to say goodbye to your village school and move on.'

I realized her words had gravitas and a new destiny awaited me.

'Thank you,' I said.

'So, I'll see you on the first of July at midday. Until then, enjoy your weekend and best wishes.'

At Morton Manor the sun was setting and shadows of gold and amber filtered through the branches above me. In her tranquil kitchen Vera was at peace after a wonderful meal. There had been six of us after Joseph and Emmeline had been invited to join us. Beth in particular had enjoyed putting on a smart dress and leaving the children in the care of Natasha Smith. While we chatted with the Major and Emmeline, Joseph wandered into the kitchen where Vera was preparing coffee and mints on a tray.

'A wonderful evening, Vera. Many thanks for the invitation. Emmeline has loved it.'

Vera pressed the plunger on the cafetière and considered her brother for a moment. 'Joseph, has it occurred to you that Emmeline would make the perfect partner not just for evenings such as this but for life?' Joseph blushed and Vera understood. 'For goodness' sake, do something about it before it's too late.'

'Too late?'

'Yes . . . make a decision before you lose her.'

'Lose her . . . what do you mean?'

'To someone else.'

Vera understood that love was a complex companion and at times life became a fragile friend. She picked up the tray and walked to the kitchen door. 'Sometimes you are just so *slow.*'

He stood there in a daze.

Vera served the coffee and spoke quietly to Emmeline. 'I think Joseph wants a word. He's in the kitchen.'

The Major looked up from his coffee. 'So, come on Jack. You've had time to think about it. Next month you'll be saying goodbye to your precious school. Have they made the right choice? How do you feel about Miss Hartley taking over from you?'

'Definitely the right decision.' Suddenly I remembered something.

'What is it?' asked Beth.

'It's just what she said before she left. It struck a chord.'

'What was that?'

'She said there was more to the job than making a living. It was more about *making a life.*'

'How right she is,' said Rupert.

Emmeline walked into the kitchen and sat down beside Joseph at the kitchen table. He was deep in thought. 'Vera said you wanted a word, Joseph.'

'Did she?' He clasped his hands as if in prayer. 'Actually, yes, she's right.' He leaned forward and rested his hands over hers. He took a deep breath. 'Emmeline . . . I hope you won't mind me asking but you must know how I feel about you.'

Emmeline smiled at him. She'd sensed when she first met him that he was a gentle, caring man; as the months had passed she'd come to know it was true. 'No, Joseph, I don't.'

'Oh, really? Well, you're beautiful, intelligent and kind.'

'Those are kind words.'

'So . . .'

'Yes?'

'I wonder if you would consider being my wife.' Joseph pressed on before Emmeline could respond. 'Of course I don't expect you to answer me straight away. I know you will need time to think about this. Also, I'm aware I'm no oil painting and I don't have a lot to offer you.' He paused for breath.

'Joseph . . . do you love me?'

'But of course I do! Didn't I tell you?'

Emmeline smiled. 'In that case the answer is yes.'

'Really? Are you sure?'

'Yes I am.'

'Well, we must buy you a ring . . . an engagement ring.'

'That would be lovely and we can wait a little while before we get married so that it's all planned perfectly.'

'My dear Emmeline. You've made me the happiest man in the world.'

When they walked back into the lounge Vera looked up expectantly.

She saw the look on their faces and knew that someone else was looking forward to making a life.

Chapter Eighteen

All Good Things

Pupils in Class 1 visited Easington Comprehensive School.
Extract from the Ragley & Morton School Logbook:
Thursday, 30 June 1988

It was the end of school on Thursday, 30 June, and the children in my class were excited after their second introductory visit to Easington Comprehensive School. They had spent the afternoon meeting their subject teachers along with other pupils from the catchment area. As they filed out of class I saw Jeremy Urquhart smiling and eager to speak to me. It was good to see this quiet, introverted, bespectacled boy so animated.

'What is it, Jeremy?'

'Sir . . . I made a friend.' There was a rare excitement in his voice.

I smiled. 'That's good news.'

'He's from Crayke village, sir. His name's Peter and his dad is in the RAF. I met him when we were shown the library. He loves reading and we're going to join the chess club.' The words tumbled out.

'I'm so pleased for you. Be sure to share your news with your mother.'

'I shall, sir,' and he ran off to begin his new world of friendship and fraternity, completely unaware it was a relationship that would last a lifetime.

I had just sat down at my desk to mark a few maths books when there was a tap on my classroom door. It was Rebecca Parrish. Her daughter, Katie, was in the cloakroom area with Mary Scrimshaw. 'You go to Mary's,' she said, 'and I'll collect you from there.'

'OK, Mum,' Katie replied with a smile. The two girls walked out to the playground in animated conversation about the long-haired science teacher they had met who looked like Barry Gibb from the Bee Gees.

'Excuse me, Jack, have you got a moment?'

'Of course. Come in.'

Rebecca closed the door behind her, leaned back on one of the desks and stretched out her long legs. 'Sorry to trouble you but I'm on my way home from a faculty meeting and Jim Fairbank asked me to pass on a message.'

'Good to see you, Rebecca. What's the message?'

'Actually, it's an invitation.'

I sat back in my chair. 'Sounds interesting.'

She pushed a lock of long blonde hair from her face and gave me that direct stare I had begun to know so well. 'There's been an impromptu decision to have a department soirée before we close for the summer break. I'm afraid it's tomorrow evening so sorry about the short notice. We're meeting up for a drink in York in The Black Swan. It was Jim's idea but he mentioned it could be an opportunity for you to meet your new colleagues. Staff only, I'm afraid, no partners. I'll be getting there around seven.'

'Thanks. Can I let you know? I'll need to check with Beth.'

'That's fine but try your best and if you want a lift I'll pick you up.'

I put down my pen and smiled. 'It's really happening. Suddenly the new job becomes real.'

She nodded knowingly. 'You'll find it's busy at the outset.'

'I'm looking forward to it. A new challenge. Moving on.'

'Well, give me a call when you've decided. It's sure to be a relaxed social occasion before the more formal department meetings over the summer. Jim seemed keen to go through student placements with you for the next academic year but that could be at a time of mutual convenience.'

Then she paused and looked out of the window. The playground was empty. There were no sounds outside in the corridor. All was quiet in our cocoon of space. 'There was something else that's been on my mind.'

'Yes?'

She spoke quietly. 'The other evening, Jack. I'd had a few drinks. Things were said.' She sighed deeply. 'Since Simon left it's been difficult.'

I sensed the memory of the parting from her husband still clung to her like sackcloth and ashes. The pain lingered on.

'I'm sorry, Rebecca. So what is it? Do you still miss him?'

'I miss how it used to be. Small, silly things. When we first met I would dress up to go out. Then when I walked downstairs he would say, "You look nice." That doesn't happen any more. So I'm making a new life now with Katie and my work. That's enough for now, I guess.'

I became aware of the vulnerability behind the confident professional. For a few revealing moments she had floated on a mist of thoughts above the abyss of her life. Rebecca Parrish was a complex woman.

At that moment there was a knock on the door and Vera appeared. 'Excuse me, Mr Sheffield. Miss Barrington-Huntley is on the phone for you.'

'Sorry, Rebecca. Must go.'

'Don't worry, Jack. I understand.' She gave a wry smile. 'Everyone wants a piece of you. Catch you later.'

As usual, Miss Barrington-Huntley came straight to the point. 'Jack, just confirming tomorrow. Is midday still convenient?'

'That's fine. Would you like a school lunch?'

'Sadly, no.' There was a riffle of papers. 'I'm afraid it will be a short visit. I have to be back in Northallerton by one o'clock.'

'I understand.'

'See you then. Goodbye.'

There was the buzz on the line as the call ended and I thought back to the support I had received from her over the years. Our Chief Education Officer really was a remarkable lady.

*

It was six o'clock when I arrived back at Bilbo Cottage. Beth was in the kitchen preparing a chicken salad while watching the small portable television. The tennis from Wimbledon was dominating the news. Twenty-year-old Boris Becker had defeated Pat Cash in a match that had ended with a colourful outburst from the Aussie tennis star. Apparently calling the young German an effing smart-arsed Kraut hadn't gone down too well.

Beth switched off and gave me a kiss on the cheek. 'John is playing in the garden and Dan is asleep. How was your day?'

'Fine. Let me finish this.' I began slicing a stick of celery while Beth wandered off to check on our sons.

Later, when the boys were in bed, Beth and I sat on our garden seat and sipped cool lemonade. On this balmy evening the scent of yellow Peace roses filled the air and the sky was as blue as a starling's egg.

'Something cropped up today,' I said. 'Rebecca Parrish called in after school to pass on a message.'

'Oh yes . . . what about?'

'The Education Department at the College is meeting up for a drink in York tomorrow evening. It's staff only. Sounded like a mix of business and pleasure. She mentioned Jim Fairbank wants to discuss school placements with me but because of the short notice it could keep until after the end of term.'

'You must go, Jack. It's important for you to meet up with your new colleagues.'

'Are you sure? It starts at seven so it would be a quick change after school.'

She grinned and looked me up and down. 'Not a problem. Just tidy yourself up a bit.'

I glanced down at my ageing flared polyester trousers, which had clearly seen better days. An elegant style had never been one of my strong points.

After checking up on the boys again, we relaxed and settled down to watch a debate on ITV's *This Week* programme. It questioned whether we should negotiate with hostage-takers. Over two years had passed since the journalist, John McCarthy, had been kidnapped by Islamic Jihad terrorists in Lebanon and the interview with his girlfriend was heart-breaking. It reminded us how fortunate we were to have each other.

On Friday, 1 July I awoke to a perfect morning. A pink dawn crested the horizon and Kirkby Steepleton was bathed in sunshine. In the far distance a low mist caressed the sleeping earth and I could tell another humid day was in store. As I walked out to my car, bright-winged butter-flies hovered above the buddleia bushes and cuckoo spit sparkled in the lavender leaves while the drone of bees was the sound of summer.

As I drove on to Ragley High Street early-morning shoppers were sharing news outside the General Stores while Young Tommy Piercy was loading his little white van. He had expanded his grandfather's home-delivery service while learning his trade as a butcher. A prudent and cautious young man, the sign on the back read 'NO PIES ARE LEFT IN THIS VAN OVERNIGHT'.

When I finally pulled into the school car park the sun

was warm on my back. Joseph's A40 was parked next to Vera's car and there was excited conversation in the school office when I walked in.

'That's an excellent idea, Joseph,' said Vera.

Joseph gave me a sheepish look. 'I've taken Vera's advice, Jack.'

'As I have since 1977,' I responded with a grin.

Vera took Joseph's hand. 'I'm so pleased.' She looked up at me. 'Joseph and Emmeline are going to York to buy an engagement ring.'

'That's wonderful news, Joseph.' I shook his hand. 'Congratulations. I'm delighted for you.'

'Well, Emmeline thought we had better get a move on,' he said.

Vera smiled up at her brother. 'Our hearts are restless . . .' she quoted.

Joseph thought hard. 'Ah, yes . . . St Augustine,' he said.

Vera nodded in acknowledgement. 'Job, chapter twenty-eight,' she announced.

Joseph raised his eyebrows and pursed his lips. Vera's knowledge far exceeded his. '"You have made us for yourself, O Lord,"' he said, trying to rescue the situation.

'"And our heart is restless until it rests in you,"' said Vera, completing the quotation. Then she gave Joseph a stern look. 'Now where in York do you intend to go?'

He looked confused. 'I thought I would ask Emmeline.'

Vera took a deep breath. Her brother was a lovely man but, on occasions, simply infuriating. 'Yes, Joseph,' she said, trying to be patient. 'It's important to let Emmeline make that decision but I would recommend you go into Stonegate first. You'll find Barbara Cattle's shop there. It's excellent for antique and period jewellery. Knowing Emmeline's interest in history, I think it may appeal to her.'

Joseph nodded hesitantly. 'Yes . . . thank you.'

'Failing that,' continued Vera, 'go to one of the more modern jewellers and perhaps look for a diamond solitaire ring . . . fitting for such a lovely lady and in no way ostentatious.'

I guessed Joseph and I were both thinking the same thing.

The oracle has spoken.

Joseph squeezed her arm in affection and left for the car park feeling slightly bemused following his rapid introduction to gemology.

It was morning break and Pat was on playground duty. In the staff-room Sally had abandoned her Yorkshire Purchasing Organization catalogue and the search for bristle brushes and dipped into her hessian bag. She pulled out her May issue of *Cosmopolitan* and moved on from the article '100 Reasons to Fall in Love' to one of more immediate interest: 'Why Men Go Off Sex'. She sighed deeply and munched on a second custard cream.

'Miss Hartley will be here after lunch,' I said. 'I expect she will want to visit each classroom.'

'That's fine, Jack,' said Anne. 'Looking forward to getting to know her.'

'I'm happy to look after her on arrival,' said Vera as she added the hot milk to our coffee.

'And introduce her to the wonders of your filing system,' said Marcus with a mischievous grin.

Vera merely smiled and served the drinks.

*

When the bell rang for lunchtime, I looked out of my class-room window as an imposing lady in a beautifully tailored linen suit stepped out of a bright red Austin Montego. She collected a hessian shopping bag from the passenger seat and strode purposefully across the playground. It was our Chief Education Officer and I hurried to meet her.

She was in conversation with Vera when I arrived in the entrance porch. Always an imposing figure, Miss Barrington-Huntley greeted me with a warm smile. 'Hello, Mr Sheffield. I was just thanking Mrs Forbes-Kitchener for all her loyal service over the years and trusting she will knock the new secretary into shape.'

Vera nodded knowingly. She was wondering if there was time to do the same to the new headteacher.

'Welcome to Ragley,' I said. 'Thank you for calling in.'

'The office is free, Mr Sheffield,' said Vera, gesturing towards the open door.

As we walked in from the entrance hall I saw Miss Barrington-Huntley scanning the children's artwork and writing on the display boards and nodding in appreciation. We sat facing each other across the desk and from the shop-ping bag she took out a neatly wrapped present tied with a blue bow. 'This is for you, Jack. Just a little something. Unfortunately I won't have the chance to see you before you leave at the end of the month. I'm down in London sharing thoughts about the National Curriculum.'

'Thank you. This is a surprise.' I opened the gift. It was an elegant Platignum pen in a smart blue box.

She smiled. 'I heard from your secretary that you have a hobby.'

'You mean *writing*.'

'Exactly.'

'Yes. I write short stories in my spare time. It's something I've enjoyed since I was a boy.'

'That's wonderful, Jack.'

'They're mainly for my mother.'

I could see she was intrigued. 'So . . . what do you write about?'

'School, mainly. I simply record the happy and occasionally poignant times in my professional life. The stars are the children, of course.'

She nodded. 'As they should be.'

'I enjoy it and, with respect, it's a change from responding to the paperwork from County Hall that comes in every week.'

'Ah yes.' She pursed her lips at the gentle rebuke. 'And on the increase, I'm afraid. There are days when I despair.'

I nodded in agreement. 'That apart, I wanted to say how much I've appreciated your support. There have been some difficult moments in the past but I've enjoyed my time here. I'm sure Miss Hartley will love it as well.'

She nodded. 'We're lucky to have such talented professionals in North Yorkshire and I have no doubt Miss Hartley will carry on your good work.'

'It's good of you to say but I shall miss Ragley.'

She studied me for a long moment and then spoke softly. 'Jack, as Geoffrey Chaucer once said, "All good things come to an end."' She sighed and looked at the school photographs that lined the wall. I guessed what she was thinking. So many eager faces. So many hopes and dreams. 'Nothing lasts for ever and happiness can be fleeting. You have one life and it's very precious. Make the most of every day.' She stood up. We shook hands one final time and the meeting was over.

As I watched her drive out of school I was aware that another small piece of my life as a headteacher had drifted away.

At lunchtime when I walked into the hall, Billy Ricketts, head down, ran straight into me. He was clearly in a hurry. 'Sorry, sir,' he said breathlessly.

'You shouldn't run in school, Billy. You might cause an accident.'

He nodded. 'Ah know, sir. Ah can't 'elp it sometimes.'

I crouched down and looked at this tousle-haired boy with his red cheeks and scratched knees. 'What's wrong, Billy? You look angry. Why is that?'

He sighed and shook his head. 'Dunno, sir. Ah'll ask m'mam when ah get home.'

Billy always had an answer even if at that moment the logic escaped me. I smiled. 'Go and enjoy your dinner, Billy, and take care.'

'Thank you, sir,' he said with a grin. 'It's m'favourite pudding t'day an' Mrs Critchley allus gives me a second 'elpin'.'

He quick-marched to his seat and sat down. Then he folded his arms and looked up expectantly at our dinner lady.

'What you up to, Billy Ricketts?' demanded Mrs Critchley with a look that would have stopped a clock at ten paces.

'Nowt, Miss.'

'Ah know that look. Butter wouldn't melt in yer mouth.'

'We can't afford butter, Miss. M'mam says it's too 'xpensive.'

'An' she's right,' said a determined Mrs Critchley. 'As true as eggs is eggs.'

Billy merely nodded. He wanted to say they couldn't afford eggs either but had learned a long time ago to let Mrs Critchley *always* have the last word.

I sat at a table with Marcus and some of the girls who had just passed their eighth birthdays. I smiled as the young scientist struggled with some of the questions that were coming his way in between mouthfuls of roly-poly pudding and custard.

'How can the universe have no end, Mr Potts?' asked Hermione Jackson.

'And why can't I see my eyes?' asked Honeysuckle.

Marcus was gathering his thoughts when Tracey Higginbottom added, 'Why are we born young, sir? It would be a lot simpler if we were born old.'

Marcus put down his spoon. 'Now . . . where to begin . . .'

I left him to solve the secrets of the universe and returned to my classroom to set up for afternoon school.

The children in my class had just settled to their 'Countries of the World' project work when Rory Duckworth announced, 'Little Citroën coming up t'drive, sir.'

I looked out of the window and saw Emma Hartley pull up in the car park. She stepped out and paused for a moment in front of the school, standing there in a bright summer dress, taking in the sights and sounds. She surveyed the scene before her: the old bell tower, the Victorian brickwork, the huge sports field and the Yorkshire stone entrance porch. I smiled because that was what I had done when I first arrived at Ragley School. She walked slowly up the drive towards the entrance steps where Vera was waiting.

Vera was keen to welcome our new headteacher and introduce her to some of the basic administration that kept the school working efficiently. So it was nearly one thirty when they appeared at my classroom door. I shook hands with Emma and she gave me a warm smile. 'Thank you so much for this opportunity.'

'You're very welcome. We can talk later if you wish but I'm guessing you would like to call into each classroom.'

'Yes please, starting with Mrs Grainger if I may.'

Vera led the way and soon Emma was immersed in the world of our youngest children.

It was clear that Anne and Emma immediately held each other in mutual respect. Anne was the consummate professional and the children were busy producing colour wheels with pastel crayons. It was a hive of activity.

'This is wonderful, Mrs Grainger,' said Emma.

'That's kind of you to say. I love teaching this age group.'

'I always found it the most demanding,' said Emma.

Anne smiled. She was even more convinced she would enjoy working alongside this perceptive lady.

Emma crouched down next to five-year-old Chantal Higginbottom.

'And what's your favourite colour?'

'Ice cream, Miss,' said Chantal with utter conviction.

Emma looked up at Anne and they shared a conspiratorial smile.

By afternoon break Emma had called into each classroom and I decided to do playground duty to let Pat, Sally and

Marcus continue to discuss their plans for the next academic year with their new headteacher. Vera was serving tea in the staff-room as the conversation ranged from maths schemes, sports activities, visits to the seaside and the impact of computer technology. It was as Vera passed me a mug of tea that she gave me a knowing look and nodded towards the animated group. In that moment I saw how it would be. Ragley was about to evolve. It was the changing of the guard.

At the end of school Emma called in to my classroom. The children had gone and the room was quiet. 'How did it go?' I asked.

'Wonderful. I feel so fortunate. This really is a lovely school.' She looked around my classroom, taking in the book corner, maths resources and vivid displays. 'I shall continue the good work, Jack.' I could see she meant it.

'Call in whenever you can. The staff will appreciate it.'

As I watched her drive away I recalled Miss Barrington-Huntley's words: *All good things . . .*

At the vicarage Joseph was in the kitchen pouring three glasses of his latest home-made wine. He had asked Vera to drop in to celebrate the engagement. Vera and Emmeline were in the lounge admiring Emmeline's ring.

'It's beautiful,' said Vera.

'Thank you,' said Emmeline. 'Joseph took me to Barbara Cattle's shop in York. I loved the selection of vintage rings.' She stretched out her hand. Over seventy years old, it was from the Edwardian era, an intricate lacy design with a cluster of gemstones. Vera touched the ring gently and smiled at Emmeline. She could see it meant so much to this gentle and caring woman.

She squeezed her hand. 'He's a good man, Emmeline. I'm so pleased for you.'

'"I have found the one whom my soul loves,"' recited Emmeline quietly.

Vera nodded and whispered, 'The Song of Solomon, chapter three.'

There was the clink of glasses. Both women looked with trepidation towards the kitchen.

'Here it is,' shouted Joseph from the kitchen. 'My best effort yet.'

'It's his latest creation, Vera . . . Elderflower Extreme.'

'Extreme?'

'Yes, you'll soon understand.'

'Oh dear!' said Vera.

It was six thirty when Rebecca pulled up outside Bilbo Cottage and walked towards the front door. She looked relaxed in a bright yellow halter-neck dress. Beth saw her from the kitchen window and waved.

'Come in, Rebecca. Jack is almost ready. I've told him to smarten up and put his suit on.'

Rebecca looked thoughtful. 'Not many of the men in the department wear suits these days. To be honest, they're a scruffy bunch.'

'Oh well, first impressions and all that,' said Beth with a grin.

Rebecca glanced around the kitchen. There was a half-built Lego castle on the floor. 'How are the boys?'

'Fine. Growing up fast.'

'I'm not sure how late we'll be back. My head of department is keen to meet up with Jack.'

'No problem. I'll probably settle down to watch Wimbledon.' Beth looked more closely at this tall slim woman. Her hair was perfectly coiffed and she wore the merest hint of make-up. 'Lovely dress,' Beth said.

'Thanks.' She lowered her voice. 'Actually, it's an old one from Leak & Thorp in York. They had a sale last year.'

Twenty minutes later Rebecca and I were in York and we queued in traffic on Goodramgate. She gave me a nudge, raised her eyebrows and pointed at a launderette with a big sign in the window: 'Drop Your Pants Here'. It was good to relax and be a passenger for a change and watch the tourists with their cameras and the groups of students venturing out to sample the nightlife. The narrow streets were full of people enjoying the sights of this wonderful city. I stared out of the open window as we drove past St Helen's Square. A busker was singing a selection of Tom Paxton songs and a crowd had gathered.

Finally, we parked near Whip-Ma-Whop-Ma-Gate, reputed to be York's shortest street, and walked towards Peasholme Green. We paused at the entrance to The Black Swan. A couple were staring at a street map of York and looking bemused. They wore baseball caps, matching bright red blousons and the man carried a camera with a lens so long that it should have required a government health warning. He flashed a smile reminiscent of a Colgate advert. ''Scuse me, mah friend.'

Rebecca and I were used to this. 'Yes?' she said patiently.

'Me and mah little lady here thought we would call into

York, England, to get a taste of *Ye Olde Medieval England*.'
He held up his guidebook. 'Ah mus' say it's mighty fine.'

'That's good to hear,' said Rebecca.

'We've just done Munich, Germany, and Paris, France.'
We waited for the question.

'We're lookin' for where Guy Fawkes was born.'

Rebecca gave precise directions.

We talked for a while and they were clearly puzzled by
the 'narrow sidewalks' and the 'freaky accents'. However,
on departing, they generously confided that our 'little bitty
Minster would make a fine country house'.

When we finally entered The Black Swan it was as if we
had stepped back in time; the half-timbered building dated
from the fifteenth century. We made our way out to the beer
garden. Before us was a gathering of academics relaxing
together and sharing news. I looked around me in surprise.
My new colleagues resembled a hippy convention.

Then I turned to Rebecca. 'Perhaps I shouldn't have
worn a suit.'

She gave me a sad smile. 'Just a thought, Jack.'

'What's that?'

'Maybe you've been living in the shadows for far too
long.'

Chapter Nineteen

A Fond Farewell

Miss Victoria Penny visited school to work alongside Mrs Forbes-Kitchener in the office. Miss Emma Hartley, prospective headteacher, attended morning assembly. Final year reports were sent to all parents.

Extract from the Ragley & Morton School Logbook:

Wednesday, 20 July 1988

It was Wednesday, 20 July, and I stared out of the bedroom window as a sliver of golden light crested the horizon and bathed Bilbo Cottage in the sunshine of a new day. Dawn raced across the land and caressed the distant trees. Time was passing quickly and I was in the middle of the final week of term. My eleventh and final year as a village school headteacher was drawing to a close.

In the kitchen it was the usual pattern of hectic activity before Mrs Roberts arrived to look after young Dan. I was packing my leather satchel with the pupils' report books I had completed last night. The television on the worktop was on in the background and Jeremy Paxman and Kirsty Wark were reporting that Prime Minister Margaret Thatcher was losing confidence in her Chancellor, Nigel Lawson. Beth was also losing confidence in young John's table manners as he tackled a huge bowl of Crunchy Nut cereal while spilling drops of milk down his newly washed school uniform.

A few miles away life was much more peaceful in the kitchen of Morton Manor. Vera was sitting at the kitchen table completing her list of jobs for the day while listening to a Vivaldi violin concerto on BBC Radio 3. She had organized a party that evening at the manor for all the school staff and governors plus a few friends, and she knew her plans were perfect.

On the window ledge was a recent framed photograph of Joseph and Emmeline and Vera smiled as she reflected on the events of recent weeks. They had decided to marry in the autumn and she had never seen her brother looking more content as when they had last visited. Emmeline was the perfect companion for Joseph and, when they'd left the manor together, she'd known they would have a life that would never be dull . . . it would shine.

When I climbed into my Morris Minor Traveller on this sunlit morning I realized that soon I would stop taking my familiar drive to school. It was a journey I had come to know so well and I wound down the window to enjoy the warm breeze. Honeysuckle and wild raspberries were rampant in the hedgerows and in the fields cattle had sought welcome shade under the sycamores. When I reached Ragley High Street I slowed up just as I had done all those years ago as I took in the sights of the local shops.

In the General Stores Prudence Golightly had made an early start. She had dressed Jeremy Bear in his new summer outfit. It was a striped sailor shirt with white flannel trousers and a straw boater. She gave me a friendly wave as she watered a bright tub of pelargoniums. Next door Old Tommy Piercy was on the forecourt outside his butcher's shop. He was directing the arrangement of his window display with military precision while his grandson, Young Tommy, stacked the quality assortment of sausages, lamb chops and pork pies.

Outside the village Pharmacy Eugene Scrimshaw was upset. He was wiping the window ledge with a soapy sponge and swearing under his breath in Klingon. His wife, Peggy, had refused to wash and iron his Captain Kirk uniform and, in Eugene's out-of-world alternative life, it was important to look smart in his mock-up of the Starship *Enterprise*, otherwise known as the attic.

Conversely Timothy Pratt was a happy man. His friend Walter Crapper had proposed another visit to Skegness in their Sprite Finesse touring caravan. The previous evening Tidy Tim had been sitting with Walter at the kitchen table making a model working crane out of Meccano pieces. When it was complete Timothy had prepared two mugs of Ovaltine and served them along with a plate of his sister's crunchy flapjack. When Walter made his suggestion, Timothy had said eagerly, 'Ah can prepare an itinerary.'

Walter had rested his hand tenderly on top of Timothy's. 'You're good at that.'

So it was that on this summer's day, as he arranged his new stock of garden gnomes outside his shop, Timothy thought of fresh air, freedom and friendship.

The door of Nora's Coffee Shop was open and George Michael was singing 'One More Try' on the jukebox. Outside in the morning sunshine, next to the blackboard advertising cream teas, Nora was sharing her exciting news with Dorothy and Nellie, who had parked their prams outside the shop. Last night Nora's boyfriend, Tyrone Crabtree, had got down on one knee next to the display of jammy doughnuts and proposed marriage. Nora had almost dropped a plate of rock buns at the news. She leaned forward, kissed his balding head and said, 'Oh, Tywone, let's celebwate.'

For a moment she looked wistfully at the baby boys, David and Malcolm, who were outgrowing their prams. Motherhood had passed her by but a new life of frothy coffees and custard tarts stretched out before her with the man she loved.

Outside her Hair Salon, Diane Wigglesworth was leaning against the window and smoking a cigarette. After many years of failed relationships she had finally decided to give up on men altogether. The ones she met were either seeking a cheap haircut or free sex . . . but more often both. She gave the merest hint of a nod of acknowledgement as I drove slowly by. Meanwhile, outside the Post Office, Amelia Postlethwaite gave her husband Ted a welcome hug and a kiss as he parked his bicycle after finishing his first delivery of the day. Life was bliss for this happy couple in their world of packets and postal orders.

As I turned right by the village green I spotted Sheila Bradshaw outside The Royal Oak. She was wearing a tight red leather miniskirt and a revealing crop top while supervising a delivery of beer crates. As he rolled the barrels of Chestnut Ale down the ramp to Don in the cellar, the drayman was finding it hard to concentrate. I reflected on the people I had come to know so well. It was good to see the high street coming alive as the familiar cycle of life continued in this beautiful village.

When I walked into the office our new secretary, Miss Victoria Penny, was already hard at work and Vera was explaining how to complete the register for new admissions. Miss Penny appeared keen and confident as she scribbled on a notepad. In a pretty summer dress and with her fair hair tied back in a ponytail, she looked up at me. 'Good morning, Mr Sheffield,' she said with a smile.

'Hello, Victoria. Thank you for coming in.'

'Miss Penny is a very quick learner,' said Vera with absolute conviction.

'And there's so much to learn,' added Miss Penny. 'I wanted to make an early start. Fortunately I've been given the morning off from the music shop to spend time with Mrs Forbes-Kitchener. It's proving so helpful.'

I could see why Vera thought this young lady would be the perfect choice to succeed her.

At ten o'clock Rory Duckworth looked up from his SMP workcard on the properties of isosceles triangles and announced, 'That little Citroën's back again, sir.' I had invited Emma Hartley to join us for morning assembly and also provide an opportunity for her to meet up with Victoria Penny. Vera welcomed her into the office and soon new bonds of professional friendship were being formed.

After the bell rang for morning assembly Anne played 'Morning Has Broken' on the piano and the children filed in quietly, class by class, and sat cross-legged on the wood-block floor. Joseph had arrived for his Bible stories lesson with the children in Marcus's class and to welcome our visitors. He found a chair alongside Vera and Miss Penny. However, all eyes were on Miss Emma Hartley, who sat beside me at the front of the hall.

I stood up and spoke with gravitas. 'Boys and girls. This is a very special morning. We have an important visitor in school. Her name is Miss Hartley and next term when you come back from the summer holidays she will be your new headteacher.' I turned to Emma. 'Miss Hartley . . . welcome to our school.' As I sat down again there were wide-eyed looks from the younger children and a knowing accept-ance from the older ones.

Emma Hartley stood up and spoke in a clear voice. 'Good morning, girls and boys.'

The children responded in the familiar manner. 'Good morning, Miss Hartley. Good morning, everybody.'

Emma smiled and surveyed the sea of expectant faces. 'I'm so pleased to be here today and I should like to thank Mr Sheffield for his invitation. It will be a pleasure for me to come and work in your wonderful school. I have visited every classroom and met your teachers and I shall look for-ward to working alongside them next term. I have also met the new school secretary, Miss Penny, and I'm sure we shall make a good team.' Victoria Penny lowered her head and blushed slightly.

Emma paused to look at me and then to acknowledge Vera on the other side of the hall. 'Soon I shall be coming to live in Morton village so I shall be a neighbour of Mrs Forbes-Kitchener. I am aware that you will be sad to say goodbye to your headteacher and to your secretary. They have done so much for this school and I promise them I shall work hard to keep up the high standards they have set.'

I saw Vera glance across the hall at me and knew what she was thinking. The carousel of children that came and went over the years had been the pattern of our lives. Soon it would be over and this was the beginning of a long goodbye.

Emma scanned the hall once again. 'To the older girls and boys in Mr Sheffield's class, I say good luck in your next school. To the rest of you I have an important message. I want you to look after the young ones who will be starting school next September for the first time. Will you do that for me?'

There was a chorus of yeses.

'Remember . . . our school is a family where we care for each other.'

When she sat down there was spontaneous applause.

It was shortly before lunchtime and Joseph had survived an eventful lesson with the seven-year-olds in Marcus's class. He sat down to read their responses to a lesson that seemed to drift away from the one he had planned. As usual this gentle and well-meaning man had struggled with the thought processes of young children.

The confident twins, Hermione and Honeysuckle Jackson, were adamant they really didn't need God's help as Joseph had suggested. Hermione had written, 'Dear God, don't worry about me. I always look left and right.' Her sister was equally confident. Honeysuckle had declared, 'Dear God, I always use Mrs Figgins's zebra crossing so me and my sister are fine.'

Tracey Higginbottom was unclear about God's ageing process. In her folder she had written, 'Dear Mr Evans, you said *The Lord Thy God is One* but he must have been older than that.'

Alfie Spraggon was unconvinced that Noah could have enjoyed a fish supper every night and wrote, 'Dear God, Mr Evans said the animals went in two by two but how could Noah catch fish if he only had two worms?'

Suzi-Quatro Ricketts, clearly influenced by the pecking order in her family, insisted that 'The first commandment was when Eve told Adam to eat an apple.' In the Rickettses' household her mother's word was law. However, it was the thoughtful Emily Snodgrass that made Joseph ponder. She had written, 'Dear God, my granddad died last week. He was my friend. So why do you let people die?'

He was battling with this philosophical issue when the door opened and the staff-room suddenly filled up.

By the time I walked in, the room was very crowded so I immediately volunteered to do Sally's playground duty. I wanted the new team of Emma and Victoria to have this informal opportunity to share their news with the staff. Soon the room was full of lively conversations and ideas for the future. As I walked out with my mug of coffee Vera followed me into the entrance hall. 'Jack,' she said quietly. 'I think we can be happy we're leaving the school in safe hands.'

'Yes, Vera, we are.'

Just before the lunchtime bell Emma and Victoria thanked Vera for the productive morning and decided to walk into the village to Nora's Coffee Shop. They were keen to have a chat about meeting up in the holiday after I had passed over the school keys. As they walked side by side down the school drive I wondered what the reaction would be among the locals when these two newcomers walked in.

It was Vera's half-day in the office and she was keen to return to the manor to make final preparations for the party. She was pleased that the weather was perfect for a gathering in the evening sunshine. When I walked in she had just finished a conversation on the telephone with her husband. Major Rupert Forbes-Kitchener had grown used to being told exactly what to do when Vera was organizing an event.

Vera had told him to collect a large hamper of Fat Rascals from York. Bettys Café, without the expected apostrophe, was Vera's favourite tea shop and the plump scones were one of Yorkshire's famous delicacies. Packed with citrus peels and vine fruits and decorated by hand with almonds and cherries, they were simply delicious.

She put down the telephone, tidied her desk and picked up her handbag. 'Lots to do, Mr Sheffield,' she said, back in formal mode. 'See you tonight at seven.'

'Looking forward to it. Is there anything I can do?'

'Thank you but it's all in hand.' She paused by the door.

'Before I go I thought I would remind everyone to give out their report books at the end of school.' She frowned for a moment. 'Mr Potts gets distracted sometimes and they musn't be forgotten.' She strode out purposefully closing the door behind her. It struck me that Vera was never off duty.

It was a busy afternoon and at the end of the day I gave out the children's report books in sealed envelopes for the adult in their home to sign and return.

'What's it say, sir?' asked Ted Coggins.

'The truth, Ted,' I said with a smile.

'Oh 'eck,' he muttered.

'Don't worry, you've worked hard.'

'Thanks, sir.' He paused and looked up at me expectantly. 'Did y'mention m'whistlin'?'

'No, I didn't.'

'Pity, sir, 'cause ah can now whistle t'National Anthem really loud.'

'Oh, can you?'

'Would y'like to 'ear it, sir?'

'Perhaps another time, Ted.'

'OK, sir,' and he ran off back to his life on the farm.

After tidying my desk I walked into the staff-room where Pat and Sally were discussing what to wear for the evening.

'Definitely a dress,' said Sally. 'I can't turn up in my baggy trouser suit.'

'Same here,' said Pat. 'It sounds quite a classy party.'

'I've a Laura Ashley sailor dress,' said Sally. 'It's a generous size.' She patted her tummy. 'Hides a multitude of sins.'

'You're fine,' said Pat with an encouraging smile.

'Thanks,' said Sally. 'Just wish I had a figure like yours.' She looked at me. 'What about you, Jack?'

'Beth has bought me a cream cricket blazer. I'll look like a waiter.'

'Beth has taste, Jack,' said Pat. 'You'll look perfect for a society soirée.'

I wasn't convinced.

At that moment Marcus popped his head around the door. He looked excited. 'Rushing off, Jack, if you don't mind. Picking up Fiona from the station.'

He dashed out to the car park.

'Young love,' said Sally with a grin. 'I remember it well.'

Pat put the kettle on and we sat drinking coffee and talking about the happy times we had enjoyed together over the years.

'There will be changes next term,' said Pat with a sad smile in my direction. 'Things will be different.'

Outside the door we heard the rattle of an enamel bucket and Ruby singing 'Edelweiss'.

'But some things will stay the same,' said Sally and we all laughed.

When Beth and I arrived at the manicured, peacock-strutting grounds of Morton Manor it was a perfect evening. Albert Jenkins, in a smart three-piece suit, gave me a thumbs up from the other side of the car park. I smiled and waved back. I knew what it meant. Following covert discussions with Rupert and myself, he had arranged for the delivery of a very special gift for Vera.

A wonderful scene met our eyes as we walked past the

rose garden. Men in suits and women in colourful dresses were sipping drinks and nibbling on canapés. Tables covered in snow-white cloths were filled with plates of cucumber sandwiches, Tommy Piercy's sausage rolls and a variety of sweetmeats. Soft music filled the air. Joyce Davenport had arranged for the Easington Ladies String Quartet to play a selection of Brahms and Schubert classical pieces under the shade of an elegant lattice gazebo.

There were many familiar faces. Anne Grainger and Edward Clifton were now accepted as a couple and looked relaxed as they were served with a glass of Pimm's at the drinks table. Sally Pringle and her husband Colin were deep in conversation with Dan and Jo Hunter. Jo Maddison, as she was then, had been a teacher at Ragley when I first arrived and Dan was one of my oldest friends. Marcus Potts and his partner, Fiona Beckwith, were chatting with Rebecca Parrish about the recent advances in computer technology while George Dainty was serving Ruby with a plate of vol-au-vents and a glass of home-made lemonade. So many faces . . . so many friends.

Beth tugged my hand. 'Come on, Jack. I want to congratulate Joseph and Emmeline.'

The happy couple were standing behind a trestle table serving an aperitif of Joseph's latest home-brewed wine. Thanks to Emmeline's expert guidance Joseph had finally produced a drink that was fit for human consumption. In his spidery writing he had labelled each bottle 'Strawberry Sunset Spectacular', which Emmeline thought was a little over the top. However, for the first time in living memory, guests were coming back for a refill and Joseph was thrilled.

'Hello, Beth,' said Emmeline as she poured a glass of wine. 'You must try Joseph's latest. It's his best yet.'

Beth raised her eyebrows, understanding the subliminal message. 'Cheers,' she said raising her glass, 'and I'm so pleased for you.'

'Thank you.' Emmeline looked across at Joseph, the happiness in her soul shining from her eyes.

A dozen conversations later Beth wandered off to talk to Marcus and Fiona and catch up with their news. There was talk of moving to Cambridge or even America. Rebecca Parrish came over to join me. She looked stunning in a black cocktail dress.

As she sipped her glass of Pimm's she looked me up and down. 'Nice jacket, Jack.'

'Thanks. Trying to make an effort.'

'You've succeeded. Perfect for a summer's evening.'

A gentle breeze sprang up and disturbed her long blonde hair. 'So, almost there. Just a couple of days left.'

'Yes, I've already packed a lot of my possessions.'

'Will you be sad to leave?'

'Probably. On Friday I shall be writing my last entry in the school logbook. So, yes, I guess there will be sadness. End of an era.'

'An end for me as well as school governor. With Katie moving on to secondary school I'll be relinquishing my role.'

'Well, thanks for all you've done. Your support has meant a lot.'

She pushed a stray lock of hair from her face. 'That goes both ways, Jack.'

There was a tap on my shoulder. It was Albert Jenkins. 'Excuse me, Jack, but it's time,' and he hurried off to talk to Rupert who had placed a large heavy box under one of the trestle tables.

'What is it?' asked Rebecca.

'Something special . . . for Vera,' and I made my way over to stand with Beth.

Albert Jenkins tapped a silver spoon on a crystal glass and the ringing tones caught our attention. We gathered round in a huge semicircle. Albert looked at Vera and smiled. Then he stepped forward and spoke in a clear voice.

'As the longest-standing school governor, it is my pleasure to thank Mrs Forbes-Kitchener for organizing this splendid event . . .' He paused. '. . . with a little help of course from the Major,' and there was a ripple of laughter. 'It is at times like this that we value friendship and none more so than on this special evening.

'As you all know, I love my Latin: *amicitia pulchra est*. It simply means: *friendship is beautiful*.' He looked at Vera. 'It is also a gift that Vera has bestowed upon us all. When I look around I know how much you value that friendship. Vera has touched the lives of everyone here, never complaining or asking for anything in return. Her life has been one of service. We are indeed fortunate to have such a special lady in our village.'

There was applause and cries of 'Hear, hear!'

Albert held up his hand for silence once again. 'Vera has been secretary of our local school for as long as I can remember and with that in mind it gives me great pleasure to present her with a small token of our appreciation. It is a slightly quirky gift but I know she will appreciate the thought behind it.' He turned to Rupert, who lifted the box from under the table. It was tied with a large red ribbon in a neat bow.

Vera was clearly surprised. She undid the ribbon and opened the lid. Then she peered inside and stood back in wonder. 'It can't be . . . but it is!'

Rupert stepped forward and lifted out a magnificent classic refurbished 1947 Royal Imperial typewriter.

'Simply wonderful,' said Vera, clearly almost overcome with emotion. 'It's like welcoming back an old friend.' She stretched out her long, elegant fingers and caressed the keys that she knew so well.

Then she looked up, tears in her eyes. 'Thank you, every-body. It's perfect.'

It was late when Beth and I drove home under a purple sky and a crescent moon. A million stars twinkled like fireflies in the firmament.

I looked across at Beth. 'You're quiet,' I said.

Her eyes were on the winding road. 'Just thinking.'

'About what?'

'Endings and new beginnings, I suppose,' she said quietly.

'In what way?'

'I was wondering what it will be like when our time comes?'

'For retirement?'

'Yes. It will be our turn one day.'

'That's a long way off.'

'It's just that time seems to move more swiftly the older we get.'

'Perhaps it does.'

'At least we gave Vera something very special this evening.'

'The typewriter?'

'No, Jack, much more than that . . . we gave her a fond farewell.'

Chapter Twenty

Last Day of School

School closed today for the summer holiday and will reopen on Monday, 5 September when Miss Emma Hartley will take over as headteacher replacing Mr Sheffield, who is taking up a new post as a Senior Lecturer. Mrs Forbes-Kitchener retired today as school secretary and will be replaced next term by Miss Victoria Penny. The governing body attended our annual Leavers' Assembly. Ms Cleverley, Deputy Education Officer, sent her apologies.

Extract from the Ragley & Morton School Logbook:
Friday, 22 July 1988

It was the dawn of a new day and a breathless promise had settled over the land. The distant hills shimmered in a heat haze as the sun rose in the eastern sky. It was Friday, 22 July, and my final day as headteacher of Ragley & Morton CE Primary School had arrived.

I showered, put on my best suit and ate a hasty breakfast of Frosted Flakes. It was also the end of term for Beth's school and she collected some of John's favourite toys to take with him for a games afternoon. He was excited as he looked forward to the last day of his first term in full-time education. It was his fifth birthday on Sunday and Beth's parents were driving up from Hampshire this evening to stay for a few days. They were bringing with them John's birthday gift of a smart new tricycle.

After Mrs Roberts had collected Dan I walked out with Beth and John to her car. When John was settled she gave me a hug. 'Good luck today. Hope it goes well.' She kissed me on the cheek. 'Are you OK? You look a little sad.'

I shook my head. 'I'm fine. Just thinking.'

'What about?'

I sighed. 'I suppose it's because I knew this day would arrive at some time. It brings it home that I've merely been the *custodian* of my school and now it's time to pass on the responsibility to the next in line. I've done my best and I'm moving on.' I looked into Beth's green eyes. 'So I take that back. You were right in the first place. I *am* sad.'

She squeezed my hand. 'Jack, go and enjoy the day. You've earned it. Then we can begin the next stage of our lives. There are exciting times ahead.' I knew she was trying to lessen the pain of separation and, with a heavy heart, I watched her drive away. Then it was my turn. As I drove on the back road out of Kirkby Steepleton I turned on the radio. The Communards were singing 'There's More To Love' and, as I hummed along, I agreed.

When I arrived in Ragley High Street I pulled up outside the General Stores and the bell above the door gave a familiar tinkle as I walked in. The diminutive Prudence stepped on to the raised boardwalk behind the counter. 'Good morning, Mr Sheffield. You're looking very smart today.'

'Good morning, Prudence.' I glanced up. Jeremy Bear was on his usual shelf wearing a multicoloured Hawaiian shirt, red beach shorts and a striking pair of sunglasses with bright yellow frames. 'And good morning to you, Jeremy. I like the outfit.'

'He's very excited,' said Prudence. 'Tomorrow we leave for our summer holiday and Ruby's daughter, Natalie, is looking after the shop.'

'That's wonderful news, Prudence. Where are you going?'

'We're renting a cottage on the coast in Kent. It's a lovely place.' She looked up at her dearest friend. 'I helped him pack his suitcase last night.'

The significance of the location did not escape me. It was close to where her fiancé had been killed in the Battle of Britain. However, there was some solace for Prudence that the love of her life lived on in the guise of Yorkshire's best-dressed teddy bear.

'Please could I have a cake for the staff-room, Prudence? It's for the teachers during afternoon tea.'

She smiled. 'A special treat on your final day, Mr Sheffield? I have just the thing.' She disappeared into the back room.

I scanned the front pages of the papers on the rack next to the counter. It was an eclectic assortment of news. Apparently the Labour Party was losing votes owing to its promise to pull out of the Common Market after the people had voted overwhelmingly to stay in. There was also a report on the hostage, Terry Waite, who was suffering greatly in a cellar in Beirut. In complete contrast the front page of the *Daily Mirror* informed the nation that Prince Charles wanted to dance like Michael Jackson. It wasn't an inviting image.

Prudence reappeared with a huge date and walnut cake. 'A gift, Mr Sheffield,' she said simply. 'With *our* compliments for your final day.' She glanced up at Jeremy and I thanked them both.

Vera was busy in the office when I arrived. She was printing out a note to parents on our Roneo spirit duplicator. It informed them that school would reopen on Monday, 5 September. There was also a list of holiday activities for the children including a treasure hunt, a cricket match, a painting competition and a teddy bears' picnic on the village green.

Vera stopped winding the handle. 'Good morning, Mr Sheffield,' she said, 'and looking particularly dapper this morning, if I may say so.'

'Thank you, Vera. Thought I would make an effort. We have a busy day ahead.'

'Definitely,' she said and looked down at the spiral notepad on her desk. There was a list of memos. 'I've arranged for a spare school key to be cut for Miss Hartley and confirmed with the office that Ruby's caretaker hours need amending before the start of next term. Also, Rupert and Joseph will be here shortly and Ms Cleverley rang. She won't be coming to our Leavers' Assembly.'

'Any reason?'

'She's busy, Mr Sheffield.' There was more than a hint of disdain in her voice. 'However, she did thank us for the invitation.'

At ten o'clock the hall was full for our annual Leavers' Assembly. It was the morning parents were invited into school as we said goodbye to our top juniors who would be moving on to secondary education. It was when I stood up and said, 'Good morning, everybody,' and the children replied in cheerful unison, 'Good morning, Mr Sheffield,' that I realized this was the last time I would say this at the start of our school assembly.

A day of endings had begun.

My words followed a familiar pattern. I thanked the parents for attending and told them coffee and biscuits would be served during morning break. Then Anne sat down at the piano and played 'One more step along the world I go' which the school leavers in my class sang with gusto. This was followed by Joseph talking about moving on to the next stage in our lives. He recited Proverbs, chapter 3, verse 5, and told us to trust in the Lord. 'He will guide us on the right path,' he said with utter conviction. I saw Vera nodding in agreement while many of the children looked confused.

Then it was Sally's turn to play her guitar and she accompanied her choir in a rendition of 'When I needed a neighbour'. This was followed by Anne at the piano and we all joined in the communal hymn, 'All things bright and beautiful'. Finally quiet descended as Mary Scrimshaw stood up and, much to her mother's delight on the back row, the confident girl recited the school prayer perfectly.

I knew the difficult part had arrived when I stood up again. I had a lump in my throat and I tried hard to compose myself. I began by thanking the governing body and the PTA for their continued support for the school. The funds they raised had made a huge impact on the growing number of books in our school library.

Then I moved on to the teachers. I said it had been a privilege to work with such dedicated colleagues, and especially Anne Grainger for her work as deputy head-teacher. I saw Anne, hands clasped as if in prayer, clearly suffering mixed emotions and trying hard not to cry. Sally Pringle leaned closer to hold her hand. Meanwhile Pat Brookside and Marcus Potts gave me encouraging smiles and I realized they were the future of our profession.

I turned to the ancillary staff and thanked Mrs Mapplebeck and Mrs Critchley for all their hard work in the kitchen. Suddenly I spotted Billy Ricketts stare in surprise at seeing the fearsome Mrs Critchley out of her uniform and wearing a flowery summer dress. She caught his eye and gave him a smile. It was a special moment and I recognized it as a small indication of our caring school.

Thanking Ruby, our caretaker, was harder for me. So much had happened in her life since we first met back in 1977. She was sitting next to Vera and dabbing her eyes with one of our secretary's embroidered lace handkerchiefs. I mentioned Ruby's love of the school, her long service and even the gift of sweets she gave to each child at Christmas. I told everyone we were lucky to have such a dedicated lady looking after our school building. Ruby bowed her head and rubbed her arthritic hands and I wondered how much longer she would continue her daily toil. I invited everyone to show their appreciation and the applause rang loud and long.

I waited for quiet once again. 'And now I should like to thank a very special person. Mrs Forbes-Kitchener retires today after long and dedicated service to our school and, as headteacher, I have been fortunate to work alongside her for many years. As secretary her commitment to ensuring our school runs smoothly is second to none. Mrs Forbes-Kitchener has many qualities, not least as a problem-solver, and as I look around this hall I see many teachers, parents and children who have benefitted from her guidance. For this I thank her and I know we all wish her well in her retirement.'

Once again there was spontaneous and heartfelt applause. Vera gave me a gentle smile but then leaned towards the open double doors that led from the hall to the office. There was always the chance of an important telephone call and, as far as she was concerned, she was still on duty.

I could see that the children in my class were getting excited as the time drew near for the presentation of books. It was now an established tradition for each school leaver to receive the gift of a book paid for from funds raised by the Parent–Teacher Association.

'And now, everybody, it is my pleasure to invite our parent-governor, Mrs Parrish, to read out the names of our school leavers and to ask Major Forbes-Kitchener to present the books.'

I settled down again and watched them come up one by one, the children I knew so well. I had been their headteacher since they first walked into our village school as rising fives and now they appeared all grown up. The lanky Rory Duckworth, now taller than Marcus Potts, nodded knowingly when he was handed Roald Dahl's *The Big Friendly Giant* and Katie Parrish was thrilled to receive the classic tale of *The Nutcracker*. I knew Charlie Cartwright would enjoy *The Jolly Postman* and Mary Scrimshaw was clearly intrigued when she was given *The Polar Express*. Ted Coggins, the lover of animals, grinned from ear to ear when the Major handed over *The Tiger Who Came to Tea*. So it went on . . . a carefully chosen book for each of our top juniors who walked away triumphantly as if they had won an Olympic medal.

It was then that the unexpected happened! Joseph stood up as if he was about to deliver a sermon. I glanced down at my order of service. This was not on the list. 'Ladies and gentlemen, boys and girls,' he said in a sonorous voice. Puzzled, I looked up wondering what was coming next. 'As Chair of Governors,' he said with a gentle smile in my direction, 'we couldn't let Mr Sheffield leave us without giving him a token of our appreciation that will help him recall many happy memories as headteacher of our school.'

Anne and Sally stood up and, from behind their chairs, they picked up a large album with stiff covers. They gave it to Joseph, who put it on the table before me. 'First of all,' he said, 'members of the Parent–Teacher Association got together to create a magnificent photograph album. Everyone contributed and we gathered lots of images that reminded us of the events we have shared with Mr Sheffield since his arrival back in 1977.'

'Open it, sir,' cried some of the children in my class.

On the first page was a large photograph of my class

from ten years ago when we went camping at Skythorns near Grassington. I recalled the sense of adventure when we climbed up Gordale Scar and sat on the banks of Semerwater. There were friendships formed then that would last for ever. I flipped over some of the pages, revealing memories of maypole dancing, sports days, trips to the seaside and the arrival of our Portakabin classroom.

'What a thoughtful gift,' I said. 'I shall spend many happy hours looking through it. Thank you, everybody.'

Then it was the turn of Pat Brookside and Marcus Potts to stand up with yet another large and weighty tome. They carried it out carefully and placed it on the table. 'This one contains letters from the children,' said Pat.

'There's a message from every pupil,' added Marcus. He opened it to the first page where Suzi-Quatro Ricketts had written: 'Good luck, Mr Sheffield. You are the best headteacher I have ever had.'

It occurred to me that I was the only headteacher she had ever had.

I turned the pages and glanced at the messages, precious single sentences from five-year-olds and lengthy pages of neat writing from the eleven-year-olds. It was writing from the heart, an anthology of aspiration.

I looked up at the sea of eager faces. 'Boys and girls, this is a gift I shall always treasure. Thank you so much for your messages and kind words.'

The smiles of the children almost brought tears to my eyes. I stood there lost in the moment until I was rescued by Rupert. The Major stood up and in a commanding voice said, 'Ladies and gentlemen, boys and girls, we have one more surprise for Mr Sheffield.' There was a hubbub of excited chatter among the children. This was an assembly like no other and they were loving seeing their headteacher in a state of shock or as Ruby would have said . . . *completely flummoxed!*

I saw Anne and Sally collect a large rectangular object from Anne's classroom and bring it carefully to the front of the hall. It was covered in a drape of white linen. To add to the intrigue Marcus and Pat also appeared from the other side of the hall carrying a tall artist's easel. They propped it open and Anne and Sally placed the large rectangular gift on it.

Then Rupert announced, 'This is a particularly special gift from the teachers and I invite Mr Sheffield to reveal what lies beneath.'

I felt like royalty opening a theatre as I swept back the white sheet.

The present took my breath away. It meant so much. The watercolour painting in a pinewood frame was simply beautiful. It was a view of Ragley School reminiscent of the first morning I had viewed it so long ago. A shaft of sunlight turned the ancient walls the colour of honey and, over the bell tower, a skein of geese flew in perfect formation. The leaves on the horse chestnut trees were turning yellow and gold and there were children playing in the yard. The Hambleton Hills, flecked with purple heather, loomed in the background and a neat signature in the bottom right-hand corner read 'Mary Attersthwaite 1988'.

Our talented local artist had produced yet another wonderful depiction of our school. I knew in that moment I would treasure it for ever. This was the school I loved and

I had tried to serve it to the best of my ability. Over-whelmed, I stood there almost speechless and trying to hold back the tears when the children began to clap. Sud-denly the adults joined in and the applause echoed in the Victorian rafters.

When the bell went for morning break the younger chil-dren ran out on to the playground while the pupils in my class shared their gift of a book with their parents. Anne hurried outside to do playground duty while Vera and Ruby helped the dinner ladies wheel out the Baby Burco boiler on a dining trolley and serve coffee and biscuits. It was good to see both staff and parents relaxing together and chatting in groups.

My album of photographs had attracted attention and parents gathered to look through it and recall happy times gone by and how fashions had changed. I was sipping cof-fee and looking at my painting when Rebecca Parrish came to stand by my side. There was a swish of silk and a hint of Dolce & Gabbana perfume.

'A splendid gift, Jack,' she said quietly. 'A wonderful memory for you.'

'Yes, the school will always be part of my life.'

'I'm one of many who have appreciated your work and I'm so pleased Katie came here. She has so many good friends now and is well equipped for the challenges ahead in secondary education.'

'It's been a pleasure to teach her. I'm sure she will do well.'

'It's kind of you to say, Jack.' She looked around as par-ents began to drift outside. 'You'll get next term's timetable through the post next month. When you do, give me a call and we can go through it together.'

'Thanks. I shall.'

'Perhaps over lunch,' she added with a smile and walked away.

At twelve o'clock the dinner bell rang and the children settled to a ham salad followed by a block of Wall's ice cream, a treat between two wafers. I sat on a table full of my school leavers, who related the meals they would miss most, including liver and onions, sausage and mash and Spam fritters. They agreed it was Spam fritters that headed the list and they hoped it would be on the menu at the comprehensive school.

It was when I was returning to the staff-room that I bumped into Deke Ramsbottom in the entrance hall. He was wearing his usual cowboy hat, leather waistcoat and shiny sheriff's badge.

'Hello, Deke. This is a nice surprise.'

''Ow do, Mr Sheffield. Ah've brought summat for yer las' day. My lads 'ave 'ad a whip-round in t'pub an' we've bought a barrel o' Chestnut Ale 'cause we know that's what y'fancy.'

'That's terrific, Deke. What a kind gesture.'

'It's on m'tractor. Ah could leave it at yer cottage if that suits.'

'Yes please, Deke. I'll sample it tonight.'

'We were jus' sayin' that you've done a grand job, speshully teachin' my Wayne t'read. 'E came on leaps an' bounds after that.'

He gave me a wave as he left, only to be replaced by yet

another visitor. Old Tommy Piercy arrived in his striped butcher's apron.

'Ah thought you an' your good lady might like a couple o' growlers,' he announced. He held out a brown paper bag containing two of his famous pies, known locally as *growlers*. It was now the stuff of legend that Tommy had learned how to make quality pork pies when he was an apprentice to his Uncle Randolph Piercy, a master butcher in Leeds. Tommy had learned the art of forcing a precise mixture of meat, fat and gristle into a case of cold-water pastry. The result was a superior pork pie that Tommy regarded as the finest in Yorkshire.

I realized this was no mean present. It was a gift from the culinary gods.

'This is wonderful,' I said. 'My wife will be thrilled, particularly as her parents are coming to stay.'

Tommy considered this for a moment. 'In that case I'll send Young Tommy roun' wi' two more.'

'That's kind, Tommy. They will love them, I'm sure.'

'Where are they from then, 'er mam an' dad?'

'Hampshire.'

Tommy's face was etched with concern. 'Y'mean they're southerners?'

'Yes, Tommy.'

'In that case it'll mek a change for 'em to eat summat decent.'

In Tommy's non-politically correct world southerners were in the same bracket as vegetarians. He placed the brown paper package on my desk with reverence.

'Ah'll sithee,' he said with a smile and wandered back across the high street.

*

329

When the bell went for afternoon school we decided to make the most of the perfect sunny weather and the boys and girls in my class carried out lots of our games equipment. We set up a variety of activities. Pat invited boys and girls to play rounders while I organized a cricket match. Marcus prepared a multitask obstacle race with skipping ropes and cane hurdles and Sally and Anne set up bean-bag races. Children of all ages drifted from one teacher to another. It was good to see the children so relaxed and enjoying the freedom of this diverse afternoon. For my part I looked around at my colleagues whom I had grown to know so well. It was the end of our time together and for a moment I felt as empty as the cloudless sky.

At afternoon break I decided to stay outside with the children while everyone else joined Vera in the staff-room to enjoy a cup of tea and a slice of my gift of a cake. I was leaning against the wall when Anne suddenly appeared carrying a mug of tea, black with a slice of lemon, and a slice of date and walnut cake wrapped in a tissue.

'Didn't want you to miss out, Jack.'

'Thanks, Anne.'

We stood there watching the children at play while I sipped my tea and ate my cake.

'Are you having a holiday?' she asked.

'Yes, down in Hampshire. Beth's parents said we could have their cottage for a week in August while they go to the coast.'

'You'll enjoy that. It's lovely down there. Jane Austen country.'

'Looking forward to it.'

'So, just a week?'

'Yes. There's lots of prep to do before the new term . . . meetings, timetables, school placements.'

'I guessed there would be. Probably similar here. I'm meeting Emma in a couple of weeks.'

'Vera has organized a set of keys for her. I'll pass mine on to you.'

'Thanks,' she said simply.

'Any plans for the holiday?' I asked.

She grinned. 'You'll never guess. Edward rang last night and asked if I would like to go to Paris.'

'What did you say?'

'I said yes!'

'Are you keeping this to yourself?'

'No, I'll be telling Vera at the end of school.'

'And Sally and Pat?'

'Yes . . . but only after Vera.'

Even in matters of the heart there was a pecking order.

Then she pursed her lips and stared out across the playground. 'He's a good man, Jack. I'm happy with him. My life has been humdrum for so long. He's brought some excitement.' There was colour in her cheeks and she gave a deep sigh. 'I had forgotten what it was like.'

'I'm pleased for you,' I said and we both walked back into school.

Finally the bell went for the end of school and the children filed out amidst great excitement. My desk was littered with thank-you cards and, once the girls and boys had all left, I sat down to look through them.

In the cloakroom area outside my classroom, I heard

Ruby singing 'Climb Every Mountain' from *The Sound of Music* as she finished mopping the tiled floor. She stood in the doorway and leaned on her mop. 'Ah've finished, Mr Sheffield.' Her cheeks were flushed and she pushed her greying curls away from her face. 'All t'classrooms are tidy an' me an' our Natalie will be in durin' the 'oliday t'give that 'all floor a good fettlin'.'

'Thank you, Ruby. Are you going home now?'

'Yes, ah need t'get George's tea on – egg, bacon an' chips, one of 'is favourites.'

'He's a lucky man.'

She gave that faraway look I had come to recognize. 'Nowt's too good f'my George.' True love had arrived late in life for Ruby and she treasured every moment.

'Have you and George planned a holiday?'

She smiled. 'Yes, 'e's booked a posh cottage in Whitby. Ah've seen t'pictures. All mod cons. Jus' a week but it'll be lovely.'

'Well, enjoy it, Ruby. You've earned a break.'

There was a pause while she propped her mop against the classroom door and stared down reflectively at her swollen fingers. 'Ah'm not as young as ah used t'be, Mr Sheffield. It catches up wi' yer when y'least expect it.'

'The same for all of us,' I said, 'but your Natalie is a great help.' Deep down I was hoping Ruby would pass on her responsibilities to her young, fit and capable daughter.

Ruby nodded. 'She is that, Mr Sheffield. Mrs F says she's God's gift.'

'And she's right.'

'Well, ah'd best gerroff.' She gave me a sad smile. 'It's

allus been a pleasure workin' for you an' Mrs F. Ah wish y'luck in yer new job.'

'Thank you, Ruby. I was a lucky man coming here to Ragley. We've had some good years, haven't we?'

She picked up her mop and bucket. 'Best o' my life, Mr Sheffield.'

I heard her singing again as she packed away her cleaning materials in her store cupboard. This time it was her favourite: 'Edelweiss'.

It was almost six o'clock and I was now sitting at my desk in the office. For the final time I lifted out the leather-bound school logbook and opened it to the next clean page. My first entry had been on 1 September 1977 when only eighty children had been on roll. We had grown since then in many ways.

When I looked back through my entries of the past eleven years I realized the record that would be read in the future was simply a bland, sanitized version of events. The real stories were much more interesting but would remain hidden for the time being.

I had just completed the few sentences that reflected the final day of the school year when Vera walked in. She smiled as I blotted the page, closed the logbook and locked it in the bottom drawer of the desk. Then she shook her head. 'It doesn't really tell the whole story, does it, Jack?'

I sat back and sighed. 'Very true. So many stories, Vera . . . as yet untold.'

'Perhaps you will tell them one day. It would make an interesting tale.'

'Maybe,' I said quietly.

She walked to her desk and sat down. The surface was now completely empty. Slowly she opened each drawer in turn. They contained registers, a list of telephone numbers and a metal money box for dinner money. I watched her as she closed each drawer one by one. 'What is it, Vera? You look miles away.'

She stroked the surface of her polished desk with her long, elegant fingers. 'All things pass,' she said softly. 'That's the way of it, Jack. We should be used to it by now. Time takes away the days of our lives like a thief in the night but leaves us with our memories.'

We were silent for a moment as the clock ticked and the big hand moved on to the next faded Roman numeral.

'I walked to school today,' she said. 'It was such a lovely morning.'

'Then I'll lock up and walk with you down the drive.'

Vera smiled. She knew it was my way of saying goodbye. She had cleared her desk and put the picture of her three cats in a hessian shopping bag alongside her brass paper-weight and her pencil sharpener. Meanwhile, I locked my desk and checked the windows and doors for the final time before walking out to the entrance hall and turning the key in the lock of the old oak door.

We strolled side by side down to the gate and looked up at the large metal sign. 'There will be a new name there in September,' said Vera. 'I confirmed the replacement with the office. On September the first it will say Miss Emma Hartley.'

A breeze sprang up and above us the avenue of horse chestnut trees stirred with a sibilant whisper. We both turned to look back at the school.

'It will go on, Jack. Never fear.'

'So many memories, Vera.'

She shook her head. 'Isaiah chapter forty-three, verse eighteen, Jack. The Bible tells us not to dwell on the past.'

'Easier said than done.'

'Perhaps, but we have a new life now. I can give Rupert the time he deserves and you can move on with your family and your work. There are young students out there who want to be good teachers. You can help them on that journey.'

For the last time, in a dappled light, we parted.

And in a heartbeat my last day of school was over.

Jack Sheffield grew up in the tough environment of Gipton Estate, in North-East Leeds. After a job as 'pitch boy', repairing roofs, he became a Corona Pop Man before going to St John's College, York, and training to be a teacher. In the late seventies and eighties, he was a headteacher of two schools in North Yorkshire before becoming Senior Lecturer in Primary Education at the University of Leeds. It was at this time he began to record his many amusing stories of village life as portrayed in *Teacher, Teacher!*, *Mister Teacher*, *Dear Teacher*, *Village Teacher*, *Please Sir!*, *Educating Jack*, *School's Out!*, *Silent Night*, *Star Teacher*, *Happiest Days*, *Starting Over*, *Changing Times*, *Back to School* and *School Days*.

Last Day of School is his fifteenth novel and concludes the story of life in the fictional village of Ragley-on-the-Forest.

In 2017 Jack was awarded the honorary title of Cultural Fellow of York St John University.

He lives with his wife in Hampshire.

Visit his website at www.jacksheffield.com